FAT H

Richard Francis runs the MA in Novel Writing at Manchester University, where he is Professor of Creative Writing. He has also taught American literature and has published in the fields of utopianism and contemporary poetry. He has lived in North Africa and the USA. His previous novels include *Blackpool Vanishes, Swansong, The Land Where Lost Things Go* and the highly acclaimed *Taking Apart the Poco Poco*. He lives in Stockport.

Praise for *Taking Apart the Poco Poco*:

'A comic novel with a heart and soul, the kind of book one always wants to read but can never find.' Nick Hornby, *Books of the Year, Observer*

'Richard Francis proves himself to be a superb comic chronicler of ordinary emotions and ordinary lives . . . a delight . . . Definitely a book to be devoured in one go.' *Time Out*

'*Taking Apart the Poco Poco* took an almost ostentatiously standard subject . . . and treated it with delicate intensity.' Adam Mars-Jones, *Books of the Year, Guardian*

'This is a deliciously funny book.' *Observer*

FAT HEN

*

Richard Francis

FOURTH ESTATE · *London*

First published in Great Britain in 1999 by
Fourth Estate Limited
6 Salem Road
London W2 4BU

ISBN 1-85702-938-0

Typeset by Avon Dataset Ltd, Bidford on Avon, B50 4JH.
Printed in Great Britain by Clays Ltd, St Ives plc,
Bungay, Suffolk.

For my mother
and
for Jo, William and Helen

'Thou on the land, and I on the sand,
And Jack on the gallows-tree!'

Sir Walter Scott, *Guy Mannering*

1948

Chapter One

Donald walked into the park, legs bent, arms dangling. It was blowy. He kept his teeth poking out till they went dry in the wind.

In the middle of the grass he sniffed the air, then bent down and pretended to do up his shoelaces, even though they were done up already.

Head-high the air was nothing, just blowy, then down a bit grassy, then earthy when he went head down bum up. There was a worm.

He stood up again, but kept his arms long, hands down by his knees. The worm looked like the stuff inside the cat when it got run over. And a dandelion looking what his father said, happy as Larry.

A girl came along. She looked along his look. 'What's the worm's name?' she asked.

'*I* don't know,' he said back. Her hair was like lumpy custard.

'I got a worm at my house.'

She looked a bit more. Then still looking at the worm she asked, 'Are you a ape or what?'

He put his tongue between his lips and blew like you do when you're thinking and the air going out makes your top lip bounce up and down on your tongue. He remembered apes did that as well, just blow off with their lips while they're peeling a banana, then scratch their head for a minute, then swing up the side of the cage so that they can eat their banana right up near the top where nobody can grab it off of them. They went to the zoo on a hot day and

3

you could smell the old bananas and orange peel. Mum said, 'Giving bananas to those things.'

He tried to think what he used to do with his hands and arms when he wasn't being an ape himself, but couldn't. They hung at each side but that was like an ape too, and if he scratched himself that would be like one, and if he put his finger in his ear that would be like one as well. Whatever you did with them, even nothing, came out like an ape.

'It looks just like my worm.'

'Maybe it's its brother.'

Suddenly she was off running towards the playground part of the park where the spider's web roundabout and the swings were. She was gone so fast he didn't tell her about when he ate a worm. It was crunchy in the middle where all the ground it had eaten was, and the outside part tasted like lips, only saltier.

Her legs were running so quickly they looked as if they were going a bit backwards, like wheels do in the cowboys. When she got to the playground part she was whizzing even more. If you're at the swings yourself you have to climb on and get sitting and reach down with your legs and give the ground a little push but most of your push gets lost somewhere and then after a few pushes you start swinging properly at last. But she seemed to be swinging right off. Then she jumped off at the top part of her swings and straight away she had got into the spider's web and was galloping round. You move faster when you're far away.

The wind blew so hard suddenly that it made his ear on the wind side ache. The trees along the edge of the park by the road went bent. One of those black-and-white dogs was running towards them, the sort that always run with their legs stiff and that have hair in their eyes. Suddenly its hair blew out of its eyes and stood on end as if it had had a horrible shock. Straight away it turned and ran right towards Donald. It stood and looked up at him. The hair on its head was blowing to one side now, and its tongue was hanging out of its mouth the same side so it looked as if it had been blown too. It began to bark, loudly. It was just like when your mum thought you had done something and you hadn't done it. Then the dog ran over to the playground. It stopped and barked at the spider's web. Donald could see it barking. Perhaps it thought it was the spider's web that was making the wind blow so hard.

He suddenly wished he was the dog, barking at the girl. Serve her right, he thought. She was taking no notice but galloping the spider's web round and round, winding the wind.

Donald went up so high he didn't weigh a thing. Norman went down and hit the bottom so his face went gooey. Then Donald went down himself, ordinary speed the first half then so fast he wanted to pee for a split second and then he stopped too, which squashed him tight so all his air went out. Norman rose from the seesaw seat like a grey balloon, then came back down as hard as the hammer dad whacked at the fair.

The slider had only gone halfway up and didn't bong the gong. Dad just laughed. He said it was his wound. In the war when he came back from Africa with his wound and they went to visit him in hospital he said, 'I'm as happy as Larry.' His face was yellow with a big smile.

Norman said: 'My grandpa and grandma died.'

They stopped seesawing and went level, with Norman down just a bit.

'They died in their bed,' Norman said. 'They raunged about and then they died.'

The girl who had a worm at home must have gone off when Donald wasn't looking, because she was coming back into the park now. 'That girl runs like Billy-o,' he told Norman.

Norman looked at her and then looked back. 'Their eyes popped out,' he said.

5

Donald pretended to look at the girl again, but his heart had started to beat. He pictured Norman's grandpa and ma struggling in their bed, and then all of a sudden them being dead.

'They had a heart attack,' Norman said.

Donald's heart slid and shook in his chest. He held on tight to the iron handle of the seesaw. It was cold, and had smooth dents on it.

He lay in bed. He could hear the wireless on downstairs. There was the palm tree music on it.

His grandad wasn't dead yet. He had a pocket watch. The way it slid in and out of his waistcoat pocket was so smooth it reminded you of how a sweet goes when you suck it until it's flat. They gave it him when he left work. He had left work because he was nearly dead and couldn't work any more. Like when you're too young even to go to infant school because you've only just stopped being the sort of being dead you do before you're born.

The trees bending in the wind, the girl running, the spider's web going round and round, him and Norman going up and down. The park was like the inside of grandad's watch, all the wheels and springs going round and up and down and backwards and forwards.

The wind would have the shed roof off again, likely as not. The chickens were making a hullabaloo in the garden. They'd probably decided that the wind was foxes, come to get them. What Jack wanted going to the pub on a night like this for, you'd have to be a Dutchman. Probably give him bone ache in his broken leg. He was always talking about the way the cold got in. Rose imagined his gammy leg with cracks still in, like the side wall of the house where it wanted pointing. Get the wind in there and he'd know about it. She pictured him limping along the dark streets and the thought came into her head: he could be going anywhere.

She looked into the fire. It was burning very hot tonight with the wind going past the chimney and drawing it. When he was in the desert he used to send her those little forces' mail letters which he drew pictures on so that they looked like postcards, pen drawings of palm trees and camels. Once a pond with a fishing boat lolled on its side on the beach. Probably an oasis.

The pictures were a way of using up the space. He couldn't say much because of the censorship. Then he started off with a sentence about the way the stars shone at night, or how blue the sky was in the daytime, things they wouldn't need to scrub out. She'd never thought to herself, what if he had weekend leave at one of those towns like in the Bible, and got a come-hither from some Arab girl. She'd trusted him all that time, in those far-off places. But since he'd been sent back with his injury she wasn't so sure. He kept more to himself, somehow, than he had before. Hardly surprising, when you thought about it, given what he'd been through. She'd tried to get him to talk about what happened when he got injured, but he wouldn't tell her much. Once he even wagged his finger at her, just like a schoolteacher.

So now, after a hard day's work, he nips in for a bottle of beer down the George, and she imagines him getting up to all sorts.

Dad looked up from his book. He did a little stirring action with one hand. He gave her that straight look he always gave nowadays when he was on the want, no please in it, just an order. His doleful moustache made her irritable and also want to laugh at the same time.

'I don't know whether you've gone dumb or I've gone deaf,' she told him, as she had umpteen times before. He carefully put the spoon he didn't have back on the saucer that wasn't there, and bent his head to read again.

'Camp or tea?' she asked him.

'Camp.' Didn't even stop his eyeballs flicking from one

7

word to the next. His moustache managed to look as if it was having a read as well.

'Camp?'

'Camp.'

He would. He only drank it made with milk, and she didn't have enough to give him a whole cup of it.

She went out to the back kitchen, got a bottle off the shelf, and poured some in a pan. She'd left the door ajar to carry on hearing the wireless. There was a waltz on now. She pretended she was feeling cheerful, and waltzed the pan across to the sink. Ooompa-pa ooompa-pa stick it up your jumpa-pa. Pa.

She turned the tap on. It squeaked. Everything that could squeak in this household, did. Also the tap was set just a little cockeyed. Good old dad.

What Jack said about him was he could do nearly anything, meaning he did do anything, but he only did it nearly.

She'd asked dad about the tap, it being his trade when all was said and done. He'd given it one of his slow looks. Bent down slow. Pointed his eyes at it slow. Aimed his moustache at it slow. Thought about it slow. He'd been slow on purpose, so she'd know that there was a fat unwilling wall he had to clamber over first. The trouble was he did this slow business so often that it was becoming part of his nature. It had become tangled up with growing old, and getting daft.

He had made nothing of it, as she expected. The tap was spot-on as far as he was concerned. He carried on looking at it after he'd said this, like looking a PS. Just so she'd know he hadn't been jumping to conclusions. Or in case the tap had any thoughts about going cockeyed as soon as his back was turned. But he could look as long as he liked, it was cockeyed anyway.

She'd turned away from him so she wouldn't be tempted to say something she would regret later and just as she did she had caught a glimpse of his face out of the corner of her eye and realised that he was holding his head at exactly the same angle as the tap. He had been *inspecting* it cockeyed!

She only turned the tap on slightly but the water splashed as it hit the low stone sink. She shoved the pan under quickly, high up to minimise the sound, and let in the same part water as milk. Then she carried it over to the stove, got the matches from the windowsill, lit a ring and put it on to boil. She was just turning back towards the living-room to tell dad it was on the go when there was a knock on the back door.

Donald walked across the dark bedroom. His bare feet slapped across the cold lino like a duck's feet do. He had his hands out in front of him in case anything was in the way, even though he knew nothing was. When he got to the wall near the door he put one hand up high and reached the switch straight away. There was the big lump of the whole switch, and then a little hole in the middle of it, and in the middle of the hole the actual switch part, which had a stalk and a round cold head, like a halma piece when dad played it with grandad.

He pulled it down. There was a tiny bit of time when it stayed still dark, the tiniest bit of time that you could get, the same size as a hundred-and-thousand, and then the light came on.

The noise of the wind went soft when the light was on, as if it was somebody else's wind now. He ran back to his bed and climbed into it again. Then he pulled his book out from under the pillow.

He turned to the page. There was the plane, with a puff of smoke on it. There were the men falling out. The main man fell down and down with no parachute. All the other ones had parachutes. The main man was bigger than the others. He nearly fell right out of the picture. Down below him was a forest of Christmas trees. His whole face was screaming. He had his hand out with his face behind it.

9

Then there was another picture of the trees, bigger this time, with snow at the top of each one, like the sharp part at the end of a spear. Then the man fell into one of the trees, and knocked off all the branches one by one, each one bigger than the one before, like when Aunty Eunice played the piano and pressed all the notes in turn so they went deeper and deeper.

Then he fell down the last bit. He had his arms and legs out like a gingerbread man and his mouth was still wide. He landed in a snowdrift and went right in.

Then the men who had parachutes came sailing down. They undid themselves when they landed and then they looked about to see where the main one was. They put hands over their eyes to see better in the dark, like you do in the sunshine. One of them pointed and they all looked forwards along his point so their bottoms stuck out the other way. In the next picture the main man's arm was poking out of the snow like a bent stick.

The other men ran up and began to tug the main one out of the snow with their small hands. Up he came, his face drooping as if he was asleep. Once when Donald had gone into the living-room his grandad was sitting in his armchair and his face was drooping so much that it looked as if it was going to slide right off of his head. He was making a rough noise which sounded like the noise your face might make if it was coming off. Donald thought he must be dying, and even when he woke up, and his nose and mouth and eyes all jumped back to their proper places, Donald still felt a little bit frightened, as if he'd seen something he shouldn't have seen.

The main man didn't open his eyes. His face stayed droopy. They began to carry him away.

The writing said: *fell further than any other man in history, and lived to tell the tale.* Mum had read it so often he knew it by heart. He could read himself now, but he couldn't read this bit because he knew it already.

He put the book back under the pillow and went across

the room to turn the light off again. It went much darker than before. It was like turning your eyes off, not the light. The darkness was so black it hardly let you breathe. Walking back to his bed through it was like walking through the clothes in his mum and dad's wardrobe. His bed wasn't there and wasn't there, and then it was when he didn't expect it any more, so he banged into it. He climbed on, and found the opening in the sheets, and was just sliding in when the window of his bedroom lit up.

It wasn't a car. Cars just lit up the bottom part of the curtains for a moment, and then were gone again. Whatever this was shone right up to the top.

He lay in his bed, watching the lit window. It didn't go away.

After a time he got out of bed again and crept across the room towards the window. He bent down below the sill and pulled the curtains apart just enough to get one eye in the gap. Then he put his eye there and looked.

Meanwhile, spectators of every description thronged forward to occupy their respective stations, and not without many quarrels concerning those which they were entitled to hold. Some of these were settled by the men-at-arms with brief ceremony; the shafts of their battle axes, and pummels of their swords, being readily employed as arguments to convince the more refractory. Others, which involved the rival claims of more elevated persons, were determined by the heralds, or by the two marshals of the field, William de Wyvil, and Stephen de Martival, who, armed at all points, rode up and down the lists to enforce and preserve good order.

Talk about going round the houses. Ernie had to remind himself he was by a fire, with the wind blowing up a storm outside, Rose rustling up a drink, music on the wireless, no hurry whatsoever. Not go fidgeting at it. Take it one word at a time, as it's doled out to you. There's always a lot less hurry than folks make out, that's the point. Walter Scott was writing in the days when people didn't go around

11

with ants in their pants, they had time to read a proper book. One word at a time. He told himself: not forgetting, you're supposed to be enjoying it.

He looked at the fire. It was burning hard but not throwing out a lot of heat, with the wind. It was funny that, he thought, you'd think hot would be hot, but you could have a fire burning so fast it didn't carry. It looked like somebody with bright yellow hair standing on end.

He turned back to the book but didn't start reading it just yet. He let all the words stay put. There was such a lot of them. But the combat had to be led up to, or you'd just say you what? Over before it begun, like the bride said to the groom.

He turned the page, still not reading anything, trying to picture going straight into a scene where one knight gallops up to another knight and fetches him a knock with one of those ball gadgets with spikes coming out of it. You wouldn't give tuppence which one came out on top. You have to have the background filled in, so that you know who's what, what they're wearing, which is on whose side, what lady has each one's gage, even how all the audience got themselves sat down, like in this bit. He turned back a page. This bit. No skipping. Come to think, the audience was stood, not sitting, like the crowd on the terraces at Stockport County. And giving each other a poke when they got half the chance.

It was all that young lass's fault. She sits there behind her desk, with her shoulders squared off and her hair coiled round her ears, that telephone style as they call it. Worst of all's the scent she has, mauve as her dress, like those Arabian cachous you have to buy by the ounce because that amount costs as much as other sweets do by the quarter. They're little and dry, like taking pills, with a perfume taste that reminds you of something you've never quite got hold of, like the atmosphere inside a church, maybe a minaret, makes you think of somewhere abroad, but depressing at the same time. Oh hello, Mr Bradbury, she says, how nice to see you again. Oh aye, he says. Much as to say, don't pour gravy over it for my sake, missy. Come here for a book? she says. Oh dear, he replies, blinking a bit, as if he thought it was somewhere else. I wanted my shoes soled, matter of fact. He aggravated himself saying it, having soled his own shoes since he was a boy, and made them from scratch for years, not just his, the family's.

'There's a new Agatha Christie come in.'

'I've got something else in mind.'

'Suit yourself, Mr B.' She looks at her fingernails, just as if she was going to file them. She's always calling people Mr B and Mrs C, to show how well she knows her customers, and cut them down to size. Then she blows on the tips of her fingers as if she wants to puff the filings into the air, almost as bad as pretending to blow cigarette smoke at your face. She knows how to mix it without moving her bottom from the stool.

'I will, thank you, young lady.'

He went over to the shelves. He could feel her looking at him over her nails, blank as a cat watching some sparrow hopping about. It made him feel trembly, older than he was. He felt he had to grab a book right away, any book, so long as it was heavy and boring.

Up above they must have heard his prayer, since they let him pick a cracker. As soon as he had it in his hand he thought: this'll give Agatha Christie what for. Walter Scott's *Ivanhoe*. He felt a second of pride, as if he'd written it himself. It must be the most boring bloody book in the whole library, he thought.

But now, of course, he had to keep his word. Not that he'd said anything, but when she slid the little chit from the front flap pocket into her file, it was like signing a contract. He didn't say a dicky-bird, just gave her a look which said, Oh yes I will.

'Bye bye, Mr B,' she said.

He said bye bye, but didn't go. He felt his feet had been suddenly nailed to the floor. He stood there looking at her. She was looking at her fingernails again. As he watched he could see the penny drop in her head and her eyes sneak up just a bit, to have a quick inspection of him. Then they went back to her nails while she waited to see what he'd do next. She was even more still than he was, listening, probably not even drawing breath. He could just see the bottom part of one of her ears poking out of the telephone hairdo. It was pale and small with a little bit of pinkness in the lobe. He could imagine its coolness against his lips, the soft and firm and crinkled feel of its surfaces.

'You OK, Mr B?' she suddenly asked, looking up.

'Hunky-dory,' he replied in a small voice. He wondered if he was going mental. I'm soppy on her, he realised. He had a horrible sense of a wasted life. It came over him like vertigo, the thought of how old he was, how young she was. Never the twain shall meet, those were the words he thought of. And what did I do, he thought, in my heyday? Married a pudding on legs.

He made himself turn to walk out. He had to operate his legs one at a time, like a toy soldier. He suddenly thought of a bloke who used to come in the Plough, Harry Colclough, school caretaker with a pot leg that squeaked and two cats he talked about at length. Dead by now, probably. Just stopped coming in the pub, and you don't notice he's not there for years and years, then he comes back into your mind out of the blue.

He turned back to missy. He wanted to say something that wouldn't make sense to her, just to take her down a peg. 'If you got one of them legs,' he said, giving her a nod, 'do you think they put it in the coffin with the rest, when you call it a day, like?'

She didn't seem bothered. Probably wasn't taking it in. Just gave a dreamy look, and said, 'I'm sure I don't know, Mr Bradbury.'

I'll read every word of bloody *Ivanhoe*, he'd told himself as he stamped out. Every last one.

* * *

Rose was so surprised she thought for a moment the knock had been something blowing in the wind. But it came again, and this time she could see the dim pink of somebody's hand through the frosted glass of the window. It was late for anyone to call. And the hand was big, a man's.

She hurried over, all ready to tell him about her dad in the next room. He'll look you to death, he will. And his good pal, the moustache.

Unbolted the bolt, turned the key. Twisted the knob.

She tried to hold the door ajar but the wind thumped it wide. She stepped back, put a hand to her mouth.

On one side a bus conductor was standing. In uniform, a broad leather strap over his shoulder with his notebook clipped to it, and waist-high the ticket machine. On the other side a smaller man wearing the same black uniform and cap with shiny peak, but no strap or machine, the driver, must be. He had furrowed black eyebrows.

And in between, Jack, arm round each shoulder, sagging.

She whimpered with relief. She couldn't think what to say. What she thought was: all my life I've wanted to turn the handle on one of those little ticket things and the once and only time a conductor walks into my house, he's propping up my hubby who's got himself squiffy at the George.

She loved the worn silvery metal of the machines, the complicated ratchetty dials you had to set to print the stop the person got on, the stop she was going to alight at, the fare and all the rest of it, the rapid clicking when conductors turned the handle; also the way the leather strap was always thick and seasoned and well-used, and the convenience of the notebook for writing official things in. The pencil, which had its own little loop, was stubby, as they always were, and you would have to lick it before use.

They thought her not saying anything was shock.

'It's all right, duck,' the conductor said. He had a long bony face, with lots of teeth. He hefted Jack up a bit further, wanting to show her how tall he still could be.

There was a sudden hiss from behind her, as the milk-and-water went over the top.

'Oh. Oh, excuse me,' she said. She said it in a whisper for some reason. She went over and turned the gas off.

'He'll be right as rain in the morning,' the driver said.

'Sleep it off,' she said. She realised why she was whispering: it made her sound posher.

'He's not drunk,' the conductor said.

'He's not?'

'Run over,' the driver told her sadly.

Jack opened and closed his mouth without saying anything.

'Oh my God,' she said.

'Not right over,' the conductor added.

'We hit him,' the driver said in a trembly voice. 'Knocked him down. He went underneath. The front part, like. But the wheel. Didn't.'

'I'll do,' Jack said huskily.

'He's limping a bit,' the driver said.

'He did before,' she told him quickly, as if that was a misunderstanding that needed to be got out of the way. 'He limped already. From the war.'

'Thank God for that,' said the driver. Suddenly he burst into tears. His eyebrows came together in the middle like a pair of thick black knitting needles.

Jack disentangled himself, hobbled over to the cupboard, and leaned against it. He folded his arms and looked back at the bus men.

'I never bumped into anyone before,' the driver said.

'It's all right,' she told him.

He looked a question.

'Nuff said,' she said.

The driver turned off the waterworks and wiped his eyes with a sleeve.

'Come on, Tobe,' the conductor said, resting a hand on

16

his shoulder. 'We got a blimmin great bus waiting in the road.'

She looked at Jack, just to make sure he *was* all right. It was then she realised several of his fly buttons were undone.

How does a bus do that? she wanted to ask. And: did you happen to notice a squashed floozy lying in the road?

She suddenly remembered something her Uncle Herbert had said. He was old when she was young, with side whiskers and a wing collar, a relic of the Victorian age. He was a street cleaner in Congleton. He wore his wing collar when he was cleaning streets. She pictured him in a tail coat too, but perhaps that was wishful thinking. A lot of hedgehogs used to get run over out that way, it being more in the country. They couldn't get used to the traffic. Collecting them up's like peeling silver paper from a toffee, Uncle Herbert had told her.

'Good lad,' the driver said, squeezing Jack's arm. He still had a couple of tears on his cheeks, like small shiny pimples.

'Carry on, mate,' said the conductor, patting Jack's shoulder.

'Bye, missus,' said the driver. They went out awkwardly, doing little bows. She heard them talking excitedly as they went round the side of the house, rags of words in the wind. Big boys now. They were laughing. 'Off the bloody hook,' one of them said.

'I thought my time was up,' Jack told her. He looked embarrassed.

'Nearly was, I should think.'

'It's huge, you know. A bus. Close to.'

He shook his head and sucked his breath between his teeth, as if buses being that big didn't ought to be allowed.

It was like a bright-eyed monster, so big it could gobble the houses. The wind went whoo suddenly and Donald couldn't stop himself from crying out, even though he

17

remembered while he did that it was just the wind and not an animal roaring. Under the wind the bus engine was making the noise the last bit of bathwater makes when it runs away down the plughole, only over and over again.

There were a couple of people sitting in the upstairs part. One of them was a man with a dark jacket and one of those stiff shiny collars only old men wear, that make their necks look as if they have a join in them like dolls' necks do so you can pull the head up and see the prong-thing, with a little hook at the end, and then the start of the elastic band. He was so near you could nearly touch him. He was looking straight forward just as if they were still going along the road, instead of being stopped here in Ash Grove which buses didn't even go down.

There was another man nearer the front, with a cap on his head. He was looking straight forward too.

After he'd looked at them once, Donald didn't look at them again, in case it made them look back at him. He looked to one side of the bus, as if there was something else out there in the dark that he wanted to look at. From the back garden came the sound of one of their chickens bawling its head off.

He looked so long that he had to change eyes, and one of his legs went dead. He wanted to go back to bed but he knew that as soon as he moved, the bus would do something else. It couldn't stay there for ever. Except his staying here might be making it stay there for ever.

Then he heard somebody say something, from the side of the house. It was about a book. Then two men were going down their path to the bus. His eye opened wider as he realised it was the driver and conductor. His other eye was tight shut.

Of course no sooner do you get your concentration going than something comes along and sends it out the window again. Any minute now it would be Rose galloping in with his cup of Camp. In the meantime the hens were raising

18

even more Cain than they did before. *'Dog of an unbeliever,'* *said an old man.* One thing about chickens, two things, they lay you your egg, also act as guard dogs at the same time.

Sure enough there was a kerfuffle in the kitchen. Jack must be back from the George. It sounded like half a dozen of them in there. Must have had a pint or two. Never popped home first and said, how about going down the pub, Dad. Not his way. Probably wanted to jaw with his mates about all the Jerries they'd killed. Still demob happy after years of it. And of course treated like a little tin god because he's got a gammy leg. Gets him more respect than a foot-long willy, what Lionel used to say at work. Everything got you more respect than a foot-long willy, according to Lionel.

Ernie looked back down at his book. Mind you, he thought, I had this to be getting on with anyway, not my day for going to the pub in any case. Keep to a routine, if you're going to get anything done. He remembered missy blowing on her nails. Every bloody word.

'Whelp of a she-wolf!' People in those days didn't coop it up when they had a disagreement with somebody.

Rose came in with the Camp.

'I got a bit behind with it, Dad,' she said. She wrinkled her nose as she said it. When she did that it looked just as if the blessed thing was going to retract, like lipstick when it's wound down the tube, or a propelling pencil. One more push and cheerio. It was her way of saying, you and me are pals together, never mind the rest of them, though why she had to say it with her nose was nobody's business. Probably because it was a fib, doing it to keep him sweet.

'Jack back?' he asked, blowing on the Camp. There was a bit of skin on it already, which folded over when he blew.

'Yi-is,' she said, very high, as if she was busy with thinking about something more important and hardly had room left in her head to say it.

'What's he up to, then?'

19

'Oh. Just having a bit of a wash.'

'Good for him. Nothing like keeping clean.'

'You would too if you'd been working at a hot stove all day.'

'I've got a book to read.' There was a sudden gust of wind, so strong it seemed to hit the house with a bang. 'If the roof doesn't get blown off first.'

The water in the sink sounded more watery than usual, like at the pictures, in a western, when the cowboy scoops up coffee in one of those ladles they drink from, and you can hear how wet it is right across the auditorium. The water made a plinking noise as he rushed it up to his face and it dropped away from his hands, so the droplets sounded as if they were made of metal or china when they landed back on the water in the sink again, that hard china that you make fake eggs for chickens from. The wind was booming round the corner of the house, and on the radio in the parlour a song had come on, 'Now is the Hour' by Rita Williams, one of those songs that seem to come from a long way off or a long time ago. Vera Lynn had the same effect, though her style of singing was completely different, but the way she sang made you feel as if everybody you loved was dead already, up in heaven or wherever it was you fetched up. For two pins I'd blart in the sink myself, Jack thought, mourning my dead relatives even though my mum's still living over the other side of Stockport and Rose is sat in the next room. It must be the shock of nearly being run over by a double-decker bus.

The bulb was dim and behind him, so there was not enough light for a reflection, just the shadow of his head in the water. It looked small and black suddenly, and he shook up the surface of the water to break it up. Vera Lynn, my backside, he said to himself.

Chapter Two

The bus stopped just beyond the Station Café. Jack stood up to get off. It wasn't his pals from last night on duty, just as well. Now he thought about it, he must have looked a proper clown, standing in the headlights like a startled rabbit with his willy in his hand. It was the old story: had a pee early on in the evening and when you start you can't stop, as if there's a door in there which once opened wouldn't be shut. One time he told Ruth that he had to nip out to have a word with somebody. After he said it he drew on his fag so hard that the eye on the same side of his face closed automatically, and he thought to himself, this's how a spiv gives them the wink. He took another leak just before he left the George, and sure enough needed to go again five minutes later.

Doing it in the road had needed all his concentration because of the wind, which also blotted out the noise of traffic, so when he looked up from the proceedings there was a bloody great lit-up bus bearing down on him. As he went under he'd said to himself, double-decker, just my luck. All those years of being scared stiff day in day out in the war, and when he really thought he'd bought it he just felt peeved. And then when he found himself still in the land of the living underneath the engine mounting of the bus the only thing on his mind was putting his dick away. He'd only done up one button of his flies when the bus crew laid hands on him and yanked him out. He couldn't do the rest up after that, it would be like announcing what he'd been up to.

He went round the back of the café, opened the kitchen door and walked slap into a wall of onion. Though it was being fried there was enough sting left to get his eyes going. There was a mound of liver on the side. If nobody was there to stop him, Stan had a tendency to drift into doing liver and onions. He was the kind of boss who needed to be bossed himself.

'We had that Tuesday,' Jack told him.

'We had that Tuesday,' Stan said back. He didn't budge from the cooker, but held his arm to one side and quacked out the words with his fingers and thumb, as if his hand was a ventriloquist's dummy. 'The wholesalers rung in this morning, still no pork, and the liver was ten per cent down from before.'

'From Tuesday.'

'Before. Tuesday. What you want to call it.'

'It's what the customers call it. They'll call it having the same thing twice in one week.'

'They got the choice. Baked fish cakes and white sauce.'

'That was the choice on Friday last.'

'But not against liver and onion. What was the main choice Friday?'

'Mince roly-poly, must have been.'

'There you go then,' Stan said triumphantly.

Jack realised he'd have to do a menu sequence in the memory tickler. Trouble was he needed a new box to put more file cards in. He'd got the tickler system out of a catering magazine. You had record cards with the name of each course on, different sections of the box for befores, mains, puddings, fish, and on the back of each card other information, brief recipes, go-withs, date last served. But if he could cross-refer to, or more to the point, from, a set of cards in sequence, Stan might be persuadable to plan a week at a time. Of course the best laid plans went to blazes when you had constant shortages. But if you couldn't get something you could always flip to the next card in the sequence. Assuming Stan could be bothered.

The funny part of it was Stan had ambitions for the place, despite being a dab hand at the easy option. Stan foresaw the time when they'd have a little band playing on the old stage, and a drinks' licence, cater for an evening crowd, serve Wiener schnitzel.

Jack didn't picture it himself. He said to Stan, it's not the toffs we should be after but the old British Restaurants crowd, ordinary working people who'd got used to eating out during the war, wanted something to bite on while at work or shopping. Those years of sitting in Nissen huts and eating Nissen grub must have created a demand. Half a million eating places in the country as a whole. I suppose you counted, Stan said. I read it somewhere, Jack told him. It's a tide.

You get drowned in them, said Stan, quite witty for a non-drinking man. Stan had seen a high tide once in Blackpool, neap or some word. Churned the sea up till it looked brown as beef stew. That's Stan, Jack thought, sees dinner even when he's looking at the Atlantic Ocean.

The way forward as far as Jack was concerned was snacks. There were snack cars in every lay-by. It was the masses who wanted to eat out now. A long shelf down one wall, with stools at it, get them munching double-decker sandwiches. Scrambled egg and tomato underneath, grated carrot and cress on top. Or savoury fillings on potato cakes. Or oatmeal pancakes. Go for the shoppers, the people off to catch the train or coming back from it. Life wasn't all dinner and tea. You could have enough of living by the clock. People wanted to eat mid-morning or early afternoon these days. Billy Bunter Snacks, for Those on the Go. Milk shakes. Ice cream.

'Mrs Stan's coming in at lunch,' Stan said.

'We'd better take the rubbish down the dump, in that case. It won't wait till the weekend, whether or not.'

'You don't know when you're well off.'

Depended on what kind of well off you were talking about. The Mrs Stan sort was having a dead aunty who owned her own house and only had one niece to leave it to.

'I know, I know.'

He didn't know what he'd been thinking of, telling Stan about his bit of nonsense with Ruth. It was one day when Mrs Stan had turned up, with her face like battery acid. She had a way of looking as though she didn't have any teeth, with pulling her lips in so hard. When she finally went, Stan started talking about another girl he'd gone out with before he got fixed up with her, a pretty one who'd been willing to have some fun. He flushed up as he went into details, and at a certain point Jack decided he'd started embroidering it.

Perhaps it was just the difficulty of picturing a lovely young girl having a pash on Stan. Jack must have switched in his head back to all those nights playing cards for cigarettes in a tent in North Africa. You spot someone bluffing while you've got a hand, and you can't rest till you've seen them. And more to the point, they've seen you. He dropped Ruth into the game as if she was the ace up his sleeve. And the more Stan looked cheesed off, the more he piled it on. Since he and Ruth hadn't got up to anything worth writing home about, he was as bad as Stan, except better at playing his cards.

It was only after a while that he realised Stan had a face on him not because he'd been bested but because he didn't like Jack doing the dirty on Rose. Which Jack didn't like doing either. Nor on Ruth for that matter. Doing the dirty on Ruth wasn't a matter of what they did, because they hadn't done anything. It was talking about it to Stan. A mess, whichever way you looked at it. He told himself, when you've got a gammy leg there's a point to prove, but whatever the reason was for what he was getting up to, that wasn't it.

'What we ought to be cooking is something we use for leftovers the next day,' he said, mainly to get Stan back, because it was just a way of saying trade being like it is there will *be* leftovers. He began on the spuds. 'You can't

24

have liver and onion sandwiches. You thought any more about getting that Crypto-Rotapan?'

'You what?'

'I told you about it. Three in one. Low-pressure steam cooker, conserver and reviver. You take liver, your favourite, the way it goes hard. Bung it in the Crypto, bit of steam through it, good as new. Grind it up tomorrow, shove it in a rissole.'

Stan didn't say anything. Jack could hear him slicing onions testily. 'Just a thought,' Jack said.

'If you're ready to buy in,' Stan said, still chopping as if his life depended on it, 'this might be the right time.'

There was a dead chicken in the run. It was lying on its side, with its legs stiff out. None of them had ever died before, without being helped, anyway. She looked at it in astonishment. Its feathers were very ruffled. Surely it couldn't have been blown to death in that wind last night? It was hard to imagine a hen having a heart attack. Its little beak was slightly open.

She picked it up and took it over to the bin, which was lying on its side. She put the chicken down to leave her hands free to right it, and as she did so she caught a glimpse of white in the hen's rump. She gave it another look, sort of sideways on so she didn't see too much, before dropping it in. The poor creature had died laying an egg. She pressed her hand against the front of her dress and peered down at it once more, lying at the bottom of the bin. The one eye on the top side of its face seemed to be looking back. Its beak was still open, just the same amount. She felt she was looking at it woman to woman. Perhaps she should count her blessings, only having laid the one herself. On the other hand, if another had come along in the time since Jack had been back from the war, maybe things would have been different now.

Dad was in the shed, banging something with a hammer. She went in the door and stood still while she got used to the dim light. He didn't notice her. He was busy pounding a piece of leather on his bootmaker's last. His father had taught him the basics, having been a cobbler by trade. Blimey, she thought, he better not have got up to that game again. Dad used to keep them all shod when she was a child, but for years had contented himself with just doing repairs, since the time when cheaper machine-made shoes came into the shops. He had tried to go back to it during the war, but couldn't get the leather. Jolly good thing too, being that his home-made ones had been like wearing a pair of boats, not just because he always made them too big so your feet could grow into them, which they never did because the shoes grew even faster than your feet did, but because they really were the shape of little dinghies, with a sort of prow or whatever they called it, perhaps a bow, at the front. They had been like court jesters' shoes, except they didn't have little bells on. Not that lark, she said inside her head.

'What are you up to, Dad?' she asked him.

He jumped as if he'd got an electric shock.

'No need to get all of a kay-lie fizz,' she told him. 'It's only me.'

'You shouldn't creep up on me like that. I could have swallowed my nails.' He said it with them still in his mouth, like men in pubs do with their fag hanging out.

'I don't know why you've got them in your mouth to start with, if you're just softening up the leather.'

He just gave her a look. He did because he did, which was the way with him. He would probably have felt naked, making a pair of shoes without nails in his mouth.

'Who are they going to be for?'

'Just a pair of sandals for Donald.'

She had a picture of them full of thongs and straps, like a pair of leather cages to keep Donald's little feet in. 'That'll be nice,' she said. 'One of the chickens has died.'

'I know. I saw it first thing.' He gave the leather one little impatient tap.

26

You could have got rid of it, she thought, instead of leaving it lying there. Him all over.

'What do you – ?'

'Egg-bound.' Another tap.

'Oh, yes.'

'Any laid?'

'I don't know,' she told him, feeling angry, 'I'm not in an eggy mood.'

Tap tap. End of discussion, as far as he was concerned. Blow him. 'What you making sandals for? It would cost less to buy them, wouldn't it?'

He looked up. His eyes seemed to flash. 'I'm not dead yet,' he said.

Dead? she thought, as she left the shed. What's the old blighter talking about?

Donald just had toast. Mum went out for an egg but when she came back she had eggs up to here. 'Have a piece of toast and Marmite,' she said.

'Why do you choo it like that?' mum asked. She said choo in a high long voice. She was pretending to be funny but she was angry really.

'Cherry said, you've got to chew it a hundred times or.'

'Or what?'

'You get a stomachache.'

'Did you ever get a stomachache? Before?'

'Before what?'

'You started chewing it a hundred times.'

'I don't chew it a hundred times. I chew it twenty-eight. It takes too long to chew a hundred.'

'Twenty-eight's too long too. If I see that Cherry I'll Cherry her. What she puts in your head.'

'I got a stomachache sometimes.'

'You'll be late for school and then you'll get a stomach-ache or some kind of ache, telling Miss Matthews you were chewing your toast twenty-eight times.'

He nearly said, that old trout, like dad said when he

27

talked to mum about Miss Matthews once, and mum had laughed. Then he realised mum wouldn't laugh this time. He chewed the next bite twenty. Then the next one after that eighteen. The next one sixteen. That time he felt a little ache just beginning, so he chewed the next one seventeen.

In school Miss Matthews had lost her voice again. Dawn Barton had to stand out in the front of the class, and Miss Matthews whispered the lesson to her, and Dawn said it out loud. She always chose Dawn. Dawn didn't like being chosen. She looked the other way when Miss Matthews came down her row to pick her out, as if she didn't know she was there at all. When she went with her out to the front she looked back at the class as if she was saying she was sorry. And when she said Miss Matthews's lesson she looked like a toy soldier and spoke it very loudly.

They had music on. It was music about the wind last night. They all had to hum for part of it. Then they had to be the wind. Afterwards Dawn told them they had to draw a picture of the wind. They always had to draw a picture when Miss Matthews wanted to go out of the room. When Miss Matthews had gone Donald drew a picture of the bus that came in their road. After a short time some of the children started making a noise and running about. Dawn tried to stop them at first. Her face went red. Then she started making a noise and running about too. Norman Gregg ran up to the front and tried to work the gramophone. He picked the record of the wind up and then it dropped on the floor and broke.

The whole class went quiet. You could hear where the sound of the breaking record had been. They all sat down at their desks. It seemed a long time before Miss Matthews came back. Everybody drew as hard as they could.

Miss Matthews looked through the windows of the door. She looked like a fish looking at you from its water. Donald thought about dad calling her a trout. But he was a long way away now, too far to make her stay one. Donald wished it had been a spell that had turned her into a trout for ever. She looked pleased to see them drawing, which made Donald feel worse, because she would find out the drawing was a fib. A great big smile came on her face.

She came in. She stood by her table. She was still smiling. 'That's what I like to see,' she said. To Donald's surprise she said it in her normal voice. But then she began to lower her face. The broken record was pulling at her from the floor, like a magnet does. Her smile went flat and then upside down.

'Which one of you did this?' she asked. Her voice had gone into a whisper again, but you could tell what she was saying. Nobody said anything. 'Who did it?' she asked again. Everybody looked at each other sideways, just with their eyes while they kept their faces pointing forwards. There was a wobbly feeling in the air, as if any moment the whole class would burst out laughing, even though nobody wanted to. 'Come here, Dawn,' Miss Matthews said.

Dawn got up from her place and walked very slowly to the front of the room. She stood with her back to the class. She joined her hands in front and bowed her head, like you do when you're saying prayers in assembly.

'Did you do this, Dawn?' Miss Matthews whispered.

'No, Miss Matthews,' Dawn said.

'Then who did?'

'I don't know, Miss Matthews.'

'Yes you do, Dawn.'

It was funny to hear Miss Matthews's whispering voice talking to her Dawn voice. Dawn didn't answer this time. She cried instead. Her head began to shake, and little squeaky sounds came out of her, from where she was trying to hold the crying in.

'You've let me down, Dawn,' Miss Matthews told her. 'Stand by the wall.'

Dawn rushed over to the end wall and stood there. She half-faced the class. She was crying properly now, and her face had gone as red as a beetroot, so you could hardly see

29

her eyes and nose and mouth, just a red circle.

Miss Matthews spoke to the whole class. Her voice went so quiet it was like invisible writing. She said, 'Stay in at playtime, and every playtime, until somebody tells me who did it.' You couldn't hear the words, but everybody knew what they said.

The class all began to make whispering noises, just like Miss Matthews did. Norman, Norman, everybody said. It sounded like the wind last night. 'What's that?' Miss Matthews asked, but they knew how to say it so she couldn't quite hear. Donald turned round to look at Norman. His face hadn't gone red like Dawn's. It was white instead. He was grinning as though nothing had happened, but even his lips were white.

Donald began to feel angry. He hated it when things were unfair. Dawn had to stand at the front, and the whole class would miss playtime when it should only be Norman. They were all too scared to say it loud enough.

Suddenly he said it. It sounded like somebody else's voice saying it, but he knew it was his. He said, 'Norman did it, Miss.'

'Thank you, Donald,' Miss Matthews said. She looked just like a fish as her black mouth opened and closed. She pointed at Norman.

It was like old times, getting stuck into a bit of leather again. He'd softened it up a bit first thing this morning, but it would repay doing a bit more, then get on with the job tomorrow. Of course sandals for a youngster were neither here nor there, but they'd do for starters. Ernie could remember the days when he'd knock off a pair of women's boots, little heels on, buckles, the lot, without giving it a second thought. But it was nice to get his eye in again. He hadn't made much use of his shed for a time, not properly, anyway. Come in here, sit at the bench, look out the window, was what it usually amounted to. There was nothing like hitting something with a hammer while you were at it, made you feel you were earning your keep, especially with shoes being twice what they were before the war. That family they had in the *Daily Express*, sample family to show the cost of living, Moffatts or Whipples, some such, they reckoned they spent eight bob a week on being shod. The father spent two quid on a pair of shoes, lasted a year, repaired every three months at a cost of five bob. Mother needed hers heeled once a fortnight, what she do, play football in them? But you could get the message. Whole family sitting there smiling like cream. Even allowing for exaggeration.

The best bit about the shed was the way the window always looked like a picture against the timber-coloured light. It would be bright even when the weather was overcast, as if the day's voltage had been upped. And you got a different angle on things, seeing the backside of the garden compared to what you saw from the house. Not that it boiled down to much, save the hens, some birds, the odd cat, the shelter at the bottom, Mr Prior next door but one poking about at his compost heap, with that face of his that looked as if it had been shut in a door.

The only thing on view this morning'd been Rose clearing away the dead chicken. He'd had to bite his lip to not say I told you so, but he'd told her years back that a drop of castor-oil in the feed from time to time would keep their passages slick. But after reading all the back end of the morning and half the afternoon he was quite happy pulling and pushing at the leather again, softening it up to make the lad a decent pair of sandals for the summer.

He thought about *Ivanhoe* off and on. It was better thinking about it than reading it. Everything happened so slowly that he pictured all the people in the book doing what they did as if they were wading through mud. He remembered years ago, must have been in a pub, some bloke telling him that in the olden days courting couples used to pick each other's noses, just to be friendly. None of them had done it in *Ivanhoe* yet. May have been a yarn in any case. The more delicate kind of woman's nostril would be so small you'd never get your finger in it.

It would be a waste just to do basic sandals. It was a decent bit of leather, and he could make more of a moccasin style of shoe out of it, bit like what he used to do for the girls when they were young. They used to be tickled pink.

Donald came in after school. Opened the door and stepped in.

'Haven't you heard of knocking?'

'He broke the record, and he wouldn't own up.'

'You what?' The lad looked as if he'd seen a ghost.

'Not me, Norman. Miss Matthews came in, and she made Dawn stand in front because Norman didn't own up. She was going to make us all stay in at playtime just because. Norman didn't and didn't. So I did.'

'Wait your horses. This lot's coming out arsy-versy.'

'She said Dawn let her down. So I told her it was Norman.'

'What you saying here?'

'I told Miss Matthews it was Norman,' Donald whispered.

When Ernie cottoned on, rage hit him as if it had dropped out of the sky. 'You pointed the finger at this Norman lad?' He shook. He had so much shake in him he shook his fist so it would have somewhere to go. His hammer was still in it. 'You never, never tell on a mate, no matter what. Never ever. Do you understand what I'm saying?' The rage felt as though it was getting bigger and bigger, crushing him, and the only way he could get free was to use it up. He shouted with all the force in his body: 'You never ever tell on a mate.' He could tell his raised voice sounded phlegmy.

Donald's face went so white it looked as if it had been peeled. His chin was trembling but he didn't burst into tears. Wet his trousers instead, as if he'd mixed up which

32

end was which. His hair was as fine-spun and almost as pale as a dandelion clock. Ernie's rage went away so fast it was like waving a magic wand and what was left behind was an overwhelming love for the boy. He wanted to put his arms round him and protect him, as if his own fury had been coming from outside, from somebody else, from nowhere. But he couldn't move. He knew that if he stretched his arm an inch towards Donald something terrible would happen, the boy would faint or die.

Donald turned, and ran out of the shed.

At the pictures they hanged him. He sat on his horse while they drooped a rope over the branch of a tree. Little clouds of dust blew. One of the cowboys took his hat off and scratched his head with his hand that was holding the hat. Then he wiped his forehead with his sleeve. Another cowboy put the rope round the man's neck. The man was still sitting on his horse, thinking. Perhaps he was praying to God. Then the cowboy who hadn't put his hat back on hit the horse's bottom with the hat, and said Heyer, Beyer, Bah, and the horse galloped off. The hanged man swung.

Woob woob woob.

The big knife went spinning through the air.

Woob. Cut the rope.

For a second, a bit of a bit of a second, the exact same size bit as the one when you switch the switch and the light doesn't come on then it does, the rope stayed in the air with the cut in it. The top half hung down from the tree, then there was a gap, then the bottom half stood up from the hanged man's neck. The hanged man stood in the air.

He fell. He scrunched into the ground like Norman's face when he hit the bottom of the seesaw. He lay on the ground. He looked like a coat.

Then one of his arms woke up and crawled along to the rope round his neck, then the other arm, and the two hands pulled at the loop. When it was loose he sat up and looked around. He shook his head. 'Gold darn,' he said.

The rope was in the little space between the shelter and the garden fence. Donald had put it there so his mother wouldn't see it. It had been left behind when his cousin Eileen last came. It was one of those with little red wooden handles that have a bell on the end, a round one with little gaps in so you can see the ball inside. He didn't give the rope to his mother because she would put it away some-where and he wanted to be able to look at it sometimes. Looking at it gave him that feeling he had when he looked at somebody with her knickers down, in the hedge. Not as big a feeling as that but the same sort, because only girls had a skipping-rope.

Grandad was banging in the shed. Donald went down the path, looking about as if he was looking at the garden. The chickens were in their house. There was a hard chickeny smell as he walked down the part of the path near them. He stopped and looked at their house for a moment, in case grandad was looking at him. One chicken looked out of the window back at him. The window didn't have a window in it, so its beak poked right out. It looked like a pencil that needed sharpening. Donald's underpants went itchy where he had peed but there was a small wind left from the gale last night, and he stood for a time watching the chicken, with his legs apart, trying to let his trousers hang loose so they would dry like washing on the line.

At the bottom of the path was the shelter. It had a curved top like an Eskimo's igloo but it was made of corduroy iron. The metal was in waves, each one the same, like sea when you draw it. Dad had a jacket made of corduroy too, only smaller and softer, and brown.

Donald had put an old chair by the shelter, so he could climb on to the top and slide down again. The chair was one that they didn't use any more in the house because one of its legs had gone smaller than the others and made it limp, even though it never walked anywhere. You sat on it and it limped. It limped when Donald stood on it to climb on to the shelter but he always held on to the edge of the corduroy so he didn't weigh much and that tricked it into only limping a little bit.

He could climb on it now if grandad was still looking. Donald stood and watched the shelter while he tried whether grandad was watching him. Grandad's banging was softer from here, more a tap tap tap. The funny part was you could hear it more clearly than when you were near. There were two parts to each tap, the first part where the hammer hit the leather, and the second part where it pressed through it and knocked the metal shoe-shaped thing the leather was resting on. Donald didn't feel grandad's look. So he didn't climb up on to the shelter.

Instead he went to the far side, where the gap was. Beyond was a wooden fence coloured black like a car. You had to go sideways to get in the gap. There were bits of a brown broken bottle pressed into the ground so that they looked as if they fitted, like pieces of a jigsaw puzzle. Norman said they were shark's teeth. After the teeth there was a metal crate, on its side and leaning against the shelter. It was covered in spiders' webs. Only milkmen had them so it must be stolen. Nobody ever talked about it. Once he had a dream that his father was arrested for stealing it.

In the corner there were some stinging nettles, but before you got to them, after the crate, was the skipping-rope.

It was always a little warmer here than the rest of the outside, as if because of the narrowness the space counted as a room. If it rained when you were in here you only got a little bit wet. The fence smelled of tar and the shelter smelled of metal.

Donald bent down sideways over the crate, as if he was going to do a cartwheel, and picked up the rope. Then he backed out into the garden. Going backwards into the wide space made him feel he wanted to fall.

He held the rope in his arms like a baby and looked at it

as he walked across behind the chicken house past gran-dad's vegetable patch towards the apple tree. As he went he said, 'This is somebody's skipping-rope. They must have left it behind.' Saying the words made him walk along as if he'd just found the rope, instead of having found it a long time ago.

When he got to the tree he stood on the far side, where you could see the edges of the shed but not the window any more because the tree-trunk was in the way. He looked hard at the trunk just to make sure. No window. When you were young you thought that if you closed your eyes the other person couldn't see you but that was a mistake and they all laughed. But a tree-trunk wasn't a mistake. He said it in a kind of whisper to make it true. 'A tree-trunk isn't a mistake.' Then he dropped the rope on the ground under the tree, and walked back towards the shelter.

This time he picked up the chair. It had a kind of hole in the back which he put his head through. The chair seat was against his chest and stomach like a shield, and the legs poked out in front of him. It made him feel a bit like a train and a bit like a tank. It was hard to walk because there was no room to move his arms, so he ran instead, with his arms stiff by his sides. He ran in a curving way to show he was playing, with his cheeks puffed out like when you do train noises, but he didn't do the noises so they wouldn't unpuff.

When he got to the tree he put the legs on the ground, which made him lie on the seat of the chair with his head through the back like the people in the olden days grandad told him about, when they threw tomatoes at them. One came whizzing through the air like a little red cannonball and squelched on his eye. He pulled his head back through the hole in the chair, stood up and wiped it off.

He pushed the chair right up against the tree, picked up the rope, then climbed up on the chair seat. There was a big branch a little bit above his head. He could reach it with his hands if he stretched up. He pushed one end of the rope over it, then over again. He tugged on the long end hanging down. It was like when you pull the chain in the toilet except it didn't sploosh. After a bit of tugging it wouldn't tug any more. Then he got hold of the bottom handle of the rope, and made a loop. He fastened it with the first half of a bow knot. He couldn't do the bow part yet but you didn't need it with rope. The loop hung in the air.

He raised the loop and put it over his head. He looked down at the ground. It seemed a long way away. It was the hard bit of ground near the tree roots where grandad couldn't do gardening, and there was just one lump of grass growing. From up here the grass looked like the woods that the man without a parachute was falling and falling into.

He jumped.

He was at the bottom of the garden behind the apple tree, fooling around with an old skipping-rope.

'Teatime, Donald,' Rose called out. If he did that chewing business again she'd crown him. 'Tea!' What was left of the chickens immediately lined up in a row at the end of the run, thinking she meant them. They clucked. Dad liked to talk about how the sound of clucking made a garden a garden, but in fact when they didn't get what they wanted, which was food, they could cluck quite nastily, in a tone of voice that made you glad they were a lot smaller than you. They probably hadn't even noticed that one of their number had bought it. Be a hen, no funerals to bother with. 'Donald, tea!' she said in a louder voice. He still took no notice. She went on down the garden and called him from the path.

'What are you up to, Donald?'

Silly question, really. He'd bodged himself together a swing. The old chair was still there where he'd climbed on it to hook the rope over a branch, and he was standing by the chair holding on to a sort of loop he'd fashioned at the other end. His little face was as red as a beetroot.

'Playing cowboys.'

'Is *that* it?' Not a swing then. Making out he'd lassoed the tree. We all have to start somewhere. 'I've got macaroni cheese in the oven. If you don't want it I'll have to give it the hens.'

He came trotting over. There was a wet patch on his trouser leg. He couldn't hold it in sometimes when he got excited. She should count herself lucky. There was a boy in his class, Patrick something, who smelled as high as a kite. But she ought to get them off of him as soon as she could. It would make him sore where it rubbed on his thigh.

'Whose skipping-rope is it, anyway? Is it Cherry's?'

'Eileen's,' he said in a whisper. He had a way of telling you something as if he was on his deathbed, making his last will and testament. He must have inherited it from his grandfather, who liked nothing better than to make the most innocent bit of information sound full of doom and gloom.

'Well, don't break it for her before she comes back and fetches it. Why don't you go in the shed and tell grandpa that tea's ready.'

He looked up at her and shook his head. Perhaps he was frightened of the hammering. She nearly said mardy-pants but stopped herself in time, remembering the pants part would be tactless. 'All he's doing is making a pair of shoes for you, silly.'

He still didn't look keen. A gust of wind suddenly caught her under her arms and quite literally gave her spirits a lift. She let herself rise on tiptoe, flapped her wings, turned full circle on the path. 'Twinkle-toes you'll be-ee,' she said, singsong, then bent down level with his head. 'No, you won't,' she whispered. 'Your little tootsies will be in jail. One little jail box for each of them. That's what your wicked old grandfather's making.'

His eyes widened. 'Like dad,' he whispered.

'What do you mean, like dad? Your dad's never made a

pair of shoes in his life. Nor likely to, neither. That's why I married him.'

'In jail.'

'Your dad's never been in jail, Donald, for Pete's sake. Are you thinking about the war? He was in the *war*. So was everybody's dad.'

'In my dream.'

The penny dropped. Last year, the bag of farthings. The things that went on in their heads. They only kept them for card games in any case, newmarket, or canasta if everyone was feeling brainy. When they started cluttering up your purse, fish them out and put them in the bag to gamble with later. There were a few silver threepenny bits in there too, for when you wanted to bet the family silver as dad always said, and to put in the Christmas pudding. And then one wet morning they got up to find the back door had been forced open and there were muddy foot-prints on the floor. It was almost embarrassing, because by the time the constable rolled up on his bicycle they'd had a good look round and the only thing missing was the bag of farthings.

Donald's eyes were like saucers, as the constable told them how he'd keep them informed and all the rest of it. He shook like a leaf, watching him drink his cup of tea. 'Don't let him come back,' Donald asked, after he'd cycled off. 'Nice Mister Policeman,' she'd said, or words to that effect, just to make Donald look on the bright side, but she hadn't taken to him much either. He was a big stiff man, and once he sat in the armchair he looked as if he would stay sat. For a while afterwards Donald had bad dreams. She'd thought it was the burglar, but it wasn't, it was the policeman. Donald had never seen the burglar, after all. Somehow he must have got it into his head that the object of the exercise had been to take Jack into custody. It must have got all mixed up with thoughts of him being away at the war in any case, so she hadn't been far wrong.

39

'Will daddy have to go away?' he'd asked a few days later.

'What on earth for?'

He suddenly croaked, as if he'd got a sore throat out of the blue. 'Because the crate.'

'It wasn't a crate, silly. It was farthings. Where did you get a crate from?'

'Did he steal the farthings?'

'Daddy didn't steal the farthings, darling. They were his farthings to start with. They were all of our farthings. Anyway, they've caught who stole them.' It was the bread man's boy, of all people. She'd never liked him a lot, if truth be told. He had one of those haircuts that went all the way up, leaving room just for a parting and about an inch of hair combed flat either side, showing ears so large and pink and naked they cried out for a pair of ear-cosies. He had big hard spots on his face that never seemed to come to a head. They'd caught him red-handed, breaking into another house on his round. The bag of farthings was still under his bed at home.

She had an idea. 'Would you like a bath before your tea, Donald?' she asked. 'I could turn the macaroni down.' It would be the way to get those trousers off of him.

When Mum turned the Ascot on, a blue sheet came out of the hole and swelled out like a balloon, then went back in again. Then it was just a circle of little points. A fat tube of water came out of the hot tap and a thin one out of the cold tap. There was a little fat man on the side of the bath where the white stuff had come off and showed the black stuff underneath. Donald watched as the water went up to the little man's feet. Then the top of his legs. Then the top of his body. His head was further up the bath. The water crept up slowly. It just touched the bottom of his head then suddenly it jumped like the cat did, and swallowed the whole thing. The man shook a little bit, like you do when you're dead.

40

Mum turned the hot tap off. The circle of flames went away then came back again, and then went away again. Mum pulled his shirt and jumper over his head and he undid his trousers and dropped them down. He stepped out of his pants. She turned the cold tap off. He put his leg over the side and stepped into the water.

'Don't just stand there, Donald, get into it,' his mother said. 'It's not too hot, is it?'

He always had to stand in water whether it was too hot or too cold or just right. He couldn't get under straight away. He had to stand in the shallow part of the swimming-pool too. It wasn't the hot or cold, it was the wetness. It made his heart pound.

'Don't be there all day,' mum said. 'Here's your boat.'

She dropped his little yacht in the water. It swayed, then went still.

'Give yourself a proper wash,' mum said, 'or I'll come and do it for you.' She went.

He put his knees under and the boat bobbed. Then his bum in, as quickly as he dared. A bum-size wave rode down the bath, and the boat rolled far over. He could feel the surface of the water in a ring round his middle. He could feel another ring round his neck, where the loop of skipping-rope had been. The bum-wave hit the end of the bath, folded itself inside out and began to come back. It hit the yacht from the other side, and rolled it towards him, but not as far over as it had gone before. The wave came on and washed the surface of the water further up his stomach. He pulled his stomach in as it did so, but then let it go as the wave folded over and began to turn back again.

Suddenly he felt his whole body soften and become part of the water, except for the faint circle round his neck.

Ruth was a stick. Jack said to her once, you're so thin you're like a drawing of yourself. Her tits hardly showed at all against her clothes. They were just like small folds in the material. And she had a slightly strong smell about her. Jack pictured it as on a scale. Scent, smell, odour, pong, stink. She was just smell, but getting along towards the odour end of it. You couldn't say she smelled of anything in particular. She smelled of herself.

'Port and lemon,' she said, like always. She ducked her head and shrugged her shoulders forward, smiling to herself as if adding, what a naughty girl am I!

'Right then.' He squeezed her shoulder while it was still shrugged. 'I won't be a minute.'

He went over to the bar and ordered the drinks. This is a nice little place, he told himself as Gerald got them. Home from home. They even had that soft fizzy coal on the fire that seemed to melt as it burned. In point of fact that reminded him of school not home, the fire they used to have in the big iron grate when he was in the top class of elementary school. But the little snug was arranged just like a living-room, with a mantelpiece and a little square clock, and a picture on the wall of a woodland path. It never seemed surprising to find Ruth in here waiting for him. In some pubs not far off a lass by herself would be regarded as a woman of easy virtue. That didn't arise with Ruth, no question of anything vampy or tarty about her. She was related to Gerald somehow or other, and did part-time work behind the bar, which made it all right for her to be in here.

Though he'd realised for some time that her virtue wouldn't be too difficult, where he was concerned, anyway.

As he came back he couldn't stop himself exaggerating his limp. Once she'd told him he reminded her of Fred Astaire, and he'd said, except I can't dance. You might as well be like Clark Gable, only ugly. Or Hitler, except kind-hearted.

'You all right?' she asked.

'Got run over by a bus last night.'

Her face went comical with shock. 'You couldn't have.'

'Why couldn't I?'

42

'Well, you'd have been –' She waved her hand. No, she didn't wave it. She moved it flatly, as if she was smoothing an invisible eiderdown.

'I'd have been flattened, you mean?'

She put her hand to her mouth and laughed into it. Her eyes looked up at him as if to say, look at this woman you've made laugh. He suddenly realised it was a moment when he could say something back.

He said it.

Chapter Three

Mrs McMahon didn't go to sleep, she went unconscious. That's what Ruth said anyhow, slitting her throat how you do with your finger. Sits down, puts on the wireless, Music While You Nap.

He stopped on the little front path to look at Ruth in the light coming through the frosted windows of the front door. Her eyelids crawled down her eyes to show Mrs McMahon going unconscious.

'But, ah . . .' he said. He didn't like spelling it out. It made it look as if he didn't trust Ruth not to trap him somehow. Or worse, as if he'd got cold feet. Fearful virgin, like in the war. You a fearful virgin, Tomlinson? You a fearful fucking virgin, Codge?

'What?' They were both whispering.

'She's got to wake up some time, to go to bed.'

'She sits till about half past nine asleep in her armchair, then she wakes up and says I'll go up to my little truckle bed, and off she goes. Not a peep out of her till morning. That's what she says as well. Not a peep out of me till morning. She gets up about eightish, on the dot.'

He pushed up his cuff to look at his watch. It had luminous hands, and luminous dots where the numbers were. Rose had bought it for him. Ten after ten.

'Good-oh. Us two'll peep for all three of us.'

Ruth coloured instantly. There wasn't any colour out here, but her cheeks visibly darkened. He realised she thought of the third being Rose, not Mrs McMahon.

She took her key out of her handbag and opened the

front door. They tiptoed down the hall, up the stairs. He hunched his head and shoulders forward to act as a kind of counterweight to his feet

Her bed was very sharp, very Ruth. Borderline was how he thought about it. Half intimate, half made him want to turn tail and run off. He remembered the motley smells in their tent in Libya. Tommo's got the farts again. Tommo pretending to be asleep, giving out little snores. The desert was one thing, just sand and sky and sun, huge amounts of nothing. But another chap's smell, in the small hours of the night, was a foreign country in itself.

Undressed she wasn't very attractive, quite bony. Her breasts were bigger than when she had clothes on, but narrow and drooping. But the sight of her still resolved his mixed feelings, and made him horny. Maybe more so than if she'd been pretty.

He thought to himself, I'm being crude, not taking an interest in ornamentation. Just want it served up as it comes. Even as he thought it, he knew that was a cruel way of looking at Ruth. Knowing it was cruel made him feel hornier still.

Serves her right, he thought to himself after they'd made love. Not Ruth, Rose. Serves Rose right.

He pictured himself coming home, telling Rose that Stan had given him the chance to buy in. Her saying: what about us getting a house? Of our own.

There's the old man's savings.

Leave him alone, it's his money. I don't want him beggared in his old age.

Not likely, he owns the house we're living in anyway. What difference would it make? Silly old bugger.

He was using Rose's own word for her dad, silly old bugger. But she wouldn't risk his blessed savings, not even to get Jack started once and for all. The fact that living with her old man got her down made her sense of obligation watertight. Hard cheese on her own husband. Gammy leg, Second World War, none of it added up to a half share in a ratty little café when you came down to it.

The one moment of his life. Of course a risk. He wouldn't have been given the opportunity if it wasn't a risk. There were always going to be drawbacks, running a café: rationing, food shortages, national lack of spuds, pay rates gone up by order of the catering commission – good news while he was a worker, bad luck if he became one of the owners. It was a risk. Stan'd manage perfectly well by himself, thank you very much, if there wasn't a risk. But it was an opportunity also. There was a great silent explosion going on in the food business. A café could go either way. When this country got on its feet again, eating at home might be over for good. A risk was the whole point.

And she turns him down.

So, serve her right.

He hadn't been home, and he hadn't asked her, but that's what she'd have done, turn him down. He'd just saved her doing it.

So here he was with Ruth. See, Stan? Want to make something of it, Stan? Served her right.

Albert Pierrepoint, public hangman, catches the London train. In his attaché case he has his private gear. Nothing bulky like the rope, that's provided at the place of execution, all the gallows equipment as such being the responsibility of the prison carpenter. But he brings the hood himself. Not the sort of thing you can buy in the shops. Hasn't got any eyeholes. The man in the street wouldn't think of something like that. An execution hood doesn't just come out of nowhere, somebody's got to make it. Mr Pierrepoint, bent over his work, one eye screwed up, tongue poking out a bit, threading his needle.

Another thing in the attaché case: an extra long tape measure. The standard size, six foot, no good for this job. The drop is nearer seven eight, seven ten, something like that. Depends on the body weight. You have to get the drop just right to make sure you break the neck but avoid the whole head coming off. That possibility wouldn't make a lot of difference to the party concerned, but is likely to distress the onlookers, prison chaplain, governor, Mr Pierrepoint himself. Also, when the guilty party is dead, Mr Pierrepoint has to wind him back up out of the trap, whereas in this case he'd be in a heap down below. Two heaps.

Arrives at Pentonville by taxi. Respect from the blokes on the door. 'How we feeling today, Mr P?' Taken to cell. Shakes hands with the condemned man. Everything done polite. 'Would you mind stepping on these scales, please, sir?' Then off to the execution room to check on the erection of the gallows. Joshes with the chippy. Old pals. Then leaves for a boarding-house, same one as always. Wake me up five on the dot if you please, Mrs Barstow.

Knock on the door. Guvnor's runner. 'Beg pardon, Mr Pierrepoint, condemned man's been reprieved.'

Bound to knock you back a bit. Nothing personal or petty about it. Not there to sit in judgement on the condemned man, but it's natural to take a pride in your job, and be a bit disappointed when it doesn't go according to plan. You want to earn your pay.

Mr Pierrepoint, the public hangman, had to take the night train back to Manchester.

'See that, Rose?' Ernie asked, passing her the paper. 'That Sicilian bloke, the Home Secretary reprieved him at the last moment. They were going to do for him in the morning. Mr Pierrepoint took the night train back up here.'

'I think it's morbid, you take such an interest in that sort of thing.'

'I don't see what's morbid reading about somebody not being hung.'

You don't get run over by a double-decker bus two nights on the trot, it's well known. Maybe there were a lot of

47

hungry people out at Cheadle and he couldn't get away. Catering isn't nine to five.

It was a quieter night, just a faint noise from the fire, which wasn't crackling or roaring like it had yesterday in the wind, but making a kind of general sound, the slight rumble fires give out when burning coal in the normal way of it. Also dad chuntering over the paper, and the clicking of her knitting needles.

Once she heard footsteps going down the street. People must go past day in day out, but you only heard the odd one. It made her think for some reason of those insects preserved in amber. Man's steps, bit too weighty for a woman's. You could hear the longer strides. But not Jack's. You can tell when it's somebody's you know.

Course you can tell. Jack's got a limp, since the war. He goes dee-dah dee-dah dee-dah, even when nobody's looking. Or listening. Funny thing, you always imagine a limp's put on. Probably because you do them so much as a child, makes it difficult to take them seriously. But you only have to look at the way his shin bone turns a corner, ever since his injury in the war.

The footsteps died away.

Dad shoved the paper at her. Somebody let off being hanged. She didn't have the patience. When he saw she wasn't interested he took it back and peered at the item again. Now she knew what he was reading about he had a different appearance in her eyes. His arched neck was like a tortoise's, pointing his intent little face at the page. His moustache was fluffed out like a cat's tail when it's bottled. His mouth moved slightly. There was something indecent about his degree of interest. For two pins she'd tell him: reading about people being hanged, or not being hanged for that matter, makes your neck go scraggy. He managed to make the worst out of whatever he happened to be reading. When it wasn't the *Express* it was his library book, Walter Scott this time round, and the only thing he'd told her about it was that in the olden days when you went spoony you picked your beloved's nose. Give me a bunch of flowers and a box of chocs any time. They must have been even worse off than under rationing, back there in history. Talk about making your own entertainment.

She suddenly laughed painfully inside herself. A bit of it came out, in the form of a snort.

'You all right?' dad asked.

'I'm fine. Thought I might switch the wireless on.'

He nodded gravely, as if giving permission. As long as it doesn't interfere with his concentration on the subject of executions.

She turned the knob until it clicked and the light in the dial came on. She watched through the little holes in the weave as the valves slowly went pink. There was a bit of interference, some squeaks and howls. The tuning never stayed put between the time you switched it off and the time you turned it back on again. You always had to turn the knob a little bit to get back to the Light Programme, even though that's where you'd been before. As always she wondered why Athlone. It sounded like a place in Ireland. She imagined the interference to be strange sad music that they liked over there.

Big Bill Campbell and his Rocky Mountain Rhythm. Somebody singing through his nose, in other words, and banjos strumming along besides. Dad frowned, put the paper down, picked up his library book.

Even the Cheadle eaters couldn't be still at it now, the place closed after tea. She picked up her knitting.

At first she thought the sound was more interference. It was very high-pitched, in the background of the music somewhere. It went on and on. She didn't want to stop knitting and get up to fiddle with the wireless again, so she pretended to herself that it wasn't happening for a while, trying to keep her attention on the mainstream of the music, and then slowly she realised it came from upstairs. Her heart went cold.

49

She dropped her knitting, jumped out of her chair. Yes, clear as a bell, now she'd got her ears round it, Donald. She darted across the room. Dad hadn't had time to look surprised yet, she was just aware of the pale disc of his face peering up at her in her rush. The cry didn't have a beginning or end, but was steady and continuous, so thin and shrill it barely sounded human.

She tore up the stairs. The door of Donald's bedroom was a little bit open. She stopped at the entrance and peered in, hearing herself pant. The noise was still going on but she could hardly make Donald out. She almost switched his light on but thought better of it. Best not to startle him.

She stepped back and switched on the landing light. Donald was sitting up in bed, his head craned forward. Funny thing, he looked a bit like his grandfather had, reading about his executions. Perhaps Donald had been dreaming about one. His eyes were open with a lot of white showing. His face was red and rigid, though his mouth was opening and closing as if he was saying something very slowly. He wasn't, though, he was making that piercing wail, like a whistling kettle that nobody would take off the gas.

She shook his shoulder. Nothing in him answered to the shake. It was like shaking a thing, shaking the branch of a tree. He carried on staring ahead.

'Wake up, Donald,' she said. 'It's only a dream.' She even looked where he was looking, just in case. 'Wake up!'

It made her feel panicky, not being able to get through to him. Some words came into her head, maybe part of a song, one of those Irish ballads that they sing in Athlone: so near, yet so far away.

'I can't get him to wake up,' she said out loud, as if to shame him into cooperating. Then, in a different tone: 'Donald, open your eyes.' She felt herself blush at the stupidity of what she'd said: his eyes *were* open, they didn't

50

even blink. Whispering, mum to son: 'Please, Donald, please, please wake up.'

'You all right up there?' dad called up from the living-room. His voice sounded thick and throaty when it was raised nowadays.

'Yes, Dad. Donald's just had a bit of a bad dream, that's all.'

'All right, then.'

Waiting for somebody to make his Camp for him, no doubt. Must put you out when there's nobody there to watch your little mime.

Suddenly, in a sweet voice like a little bell, Donald said: 'Gold darn it.'

'Yes, gold darn it, my duck,' she found herself agreeing sadly, as if he'd been talking about all life's woes. 'Gold darn it to pieces.'

He still didn't wake, but he didn't seem quite so far away in his dream as he was before. She climbed on to the bed and, kneeling awkwardly, folded him in her arms. It felt strange not to get a hug back, like hugging somebody dead. Her heart banged suddenly at the horrible idea, and then she felt shame at having thought it in the first place, worse than shame, a bleak sense of betrayal, as if by thinking someone dead you could make them it. My little boy, oh my little boy, she said under her breath, don't be dead. The little sweaty curls of his hair tickled her nostrils and his head against hers felt as warm as toast, but she still said to herself, don't be dead.

I was somewhat afflicted to see the grief of the Queen of Love and Beauty, whose sovereignty of a day this event has changed into mourning. And then down she comes with a face like fizz on her.

'He was having such a dream,' she said.

Ernie didn't catch her eye. 'What was it about?'

'I don't know. He didn't tell me.'

He suddenly felt overcome by anger again, he didn't

know why, he wasn't an angry man by nature, surely not. It wasn't as bad as this afternoon in the shed, but the same sort, like that anger's younger brother. I mustn't let fly, he thought, look where it got me last time. Keep it back. 'How'd you know it was a bad one then?'

'He didn't know whether he was coming or going. He was sitting up in bed, looking at something I couldn't see. Looking at his dream, it must have been. Then at long last he settles back and falls asleep in the usual way of it.'

'Probably have forgotten all about it by morning.' His heart was pounding painfully. Getting a bit old to have it pounding like that. He put his hand on his chest to restrain it from going all over the shop. My age, heart's got enough to do just to keep you going level.

'I don't think it's the sort of thing he'd remember anyway. I think he was in another place altogether. Frightened me out of my wits. And there's Jack, nowhere to be seen. First the war and I have to cope with a baby by myself, now he's been demobbed years and I sometimes think nobody's told him yet.'

He put his head back in his book. Not his business to step between husband and wife.

Even though he wasn't looking at her he was aware of her picking up her sewing, putting it down again, tinkering with her hair, getting up and going over to the radio, retuning to the Home Service, back to the Light Programme, returning to her seat, then doing something fiddly without it being the sewing. He looked up, his eyes still holding on to the page till his head was in position.

She was winding something with her hand.

'What you up to?' he asked her.

'I was wondering if you want me to make you a cup of Camp.'

'That'll do the trick.'

She went off into the kitchen. There was a noise from upstairs. He listened. It had gone, but now he thought about it it had only been a cough. His heart was pounding again. He looked back at the book.

Take heed to yourself, for the Devil is unchained.

No thank you, he thought to himself, shutting the book. I've got enough on my plate for the time being.

'Looks as if he got run over good and proper this time,' Rose told dad. He opened his mouth to say something back, couldn't think what, so stayed in a what-do-y'ma-call it, posture, in a posture. A gawping one. Gawp, gawp. Sitting there with his moustache drooping and his mouth sagging open.

They were a couple of rogues, that pair from the bus last night. The way they'd trotted off, pleased as punch, when they realised they'd got away scot-free, no letter of complaint forthcoming to the bus company. You could tell how cocky they became just watching them go out through the door, the conductor clapping the driver on his shoulder. Then their laughter coming back in from outside, muddled up with the wind.

Good luck to them. Serve Jack right, any case. Serve him right if they'd done for him good and proper tonight.

'*You* can talk,' she told dad. 'Mum didn't leave *you* on your own, night after night.'

He shut his mouth then opened it again, but still said nothing. He came so near to saying something, though, that she could tell what it would have been, as if his thought had flown out without its clothes on. What he nearly said was worse luck.

'You,' she said. Men, she thought, they're all the same. Mum came into her head, wearing that dark blue dress with white spots. She always thought of her in that dress. Course she was tubby. She was a lovely fat cuddly mother, who'd be without her? What right did dad think he had to open and shut his mouth and nearly say worse luck? What sort of catch did he think *he* made, scrag-end of nothing?

'I've done nothing,' dad said.

'Not for want of trying.'

They sat in silence for a while. She could feel feeling sorry for him slowly rising to the surface. He'd picked up his book again, with a sigh. There was a faint spot of pink in each of his cheeks. Perhaps the thought still lingered of what he might have got up to, if he'd had the gumption, during his marriage to mum. She'd got on his nerves a bit, certainly in later years. He was a man who prided himself on doing things, whatever the outcome. Mum had never even tried. Doing things wasn't in her nature. In cookery all she'd ever wanted to do was boil. Bit of fish, boil. Meat, boil. Veg, boil. Not a herb in sight. A few shakes of the salt and pepper her limit. Everything came to your plate limp and drowned. Rose could still see the way dad would inspect his dinner, full of indignation. His moustache had been brown in those days. But he hadn't done what Jack was doing, led her a merry dance. Probably the thought never even crossed his mind. He went off to the pub twice a week, on a Wednesday and a Saturday, for one hour only. Still did. Came back on the dot. Only exception to the rule was if Jack happened to invite him, and they went off like a pair of naughty schoolboys.

'I'm going to bed, in any case,' she told him. He looked up cautiously from his book to take that in. 'Don't know what sort of night I might get if Donald has another bad dream.'

He wasn't reading, she suddenly realised. When he read his mouth moved a tiny amount, the way it would if you were chewing some small crumb you've managed to firkle out from between your teeth. It was like the way some people move their mouths when another person is talking, because they're interested in what they say and almost want to say it for them. It would drive her wild to watch it. Even though he wasn't doing it now, the picture she had in her head of when he did do it, made her angry with him.

'I don't know why you don't read something up-to-date,' she said sternly. 'Borrow an Agatha Christie.'

'I'm going to read every blinking word of it,' he told her.

'Oh, pardon me.' Silly old devil. Sometimes she felt she didn't even like him. She forced herself to give him a peck on the top of the head all the same, as she went off to bed.

Sod's law. Tiptoe up the path then kick over a milk bottle. In his panic he even whispered shut up at it. Shut up, you bloody bottle. Hadn't woken up Mrs McMahon even when him and Ruth were at it hammer and tongs, then arrive home like the Queen of bally Sheba. Rose'd think he was squiffy.

Come to think, perhaps it was for the best. Being thought blotto was one up on rogering some floozy he'd met down the pub.

Not that Ruth was a floozy, but that's how she'd look.

No light on, not even in the hall. Ministry of Fuel says switch them off, off they switch.

He groped his way to the sitting-room. The fire had burnt right down, just a couple of bloodshot coals left. He could have fancied a hot drink but thought better of it. It would make him look even worse if he sat about down here drinking a cup of tea when he should be up there going bye-byes. He went out in the scullery, switched on the light, and got himself a cup of water.

As he climbed the stairs he began to feel horny all over again. Perhaps the trick of having a woman on the side was that some of it rubbed off on your missus. He didn't like himself for thinking in that way, but he was in just the mood not to like himself.

Grandad sat like a king, eyes down, saying nothing. Mum poured Donald the puffed wheat. 'Eat up,' she said. 'That puffed wheat was two points. It's too good for the hens. Your porridge is doing, Dad.' She went out to the back kitchen.

Grandad sat and sat. Donald's throat was chock-full of puffed wheat. It wouldn't go down. You didn't need to eat when you were in heaven. He must have known already he was in heaven but only just remembered it. Sometimes you forgot things because they didn't really matter. Other times you forgot them because they were so big they were too big to remember.

His hair went cold as he thought about it. That was why he couldn't swallow his puffed wheat. When he hanged himself yesterday he died. That's what hanging was, dying.

When you were dead you thought everything was the same. You lived in the same house. You had the same mum and dad and grandad. You went to school. But really none of it was true. Back down on earth you had died yesterday, and now your parents were crying about you and there was nothing you could do to make them feel happy again. You could shout and shout and they would never hear. Years and years would go by, and in heaven you would get older, but on earth you would still be dead, and mum and dad would cry about you for ever.

Poor mum, Donald thought, poor poor mum. How can she bear it?

Mum came in with her saucepan. She poured porridge into grandad's bowl. She looked at Donald. 'You all right, Donald? You look as white as a sheet. Doesn't he look as white as a sheet, Dad?'

Donald put his spoon down. His throat was so full of puffed wheat he couldn't speak. He wanted to tell her about being dead, but she was the wrong mother to tell. If only he could tell his real mother then she wouldn't be sad any more, and he could forget he was in heaven and just pretend his life was real.

'Donald, you had a bad dream in the night. Do you remember it?'

He shook his head.

'Don't eat those blooming puffed wheat if you don't want to. A couple of points isn't here nor there.'

She pushed her hand into his hair then went out to the back kitchen again. Grandad looked up at him at last.

'You haven't got to take too much notice of the things I say,' he said. 'Getting on a bit, that's the trouble with me. My brains are coddled, which is what happens to your brains when you get to my age. Makes you say a lot of stuff and nonsense. You need to take the things I tell you with a pinch of salt. Least said, soonest mended, what I say.'

It was like being far up in the sky like the man without a parachute, looking down at the forest. When Donald looked down he saw himself lying dead, and his real mother and father and grandad weeping by his coffin. As long as he lived he would never be able to tell them that he was all right. As time went by, the memory would get fainter. His parents would become distant. They would be living in another time, as well as another place, and up here in heaven it would get different too, so that the two worlds would become further and further apart, and they would never be able to be joined together again.

The potato patties lay on the baking trays like rows of neatly laid eggs. Jack caught Stan's eye and nearly did a chicken noise – baar-bp-bp-bp – but thought better of it. Stan held his hand out palm down as much to say, don't you bother. Then he began to pat them flat with it, still looking back at Jack.

'Makes them stretch,' he said. 'Herself'll be in in a bit.'

'And?'

Stan jerked his head to one side. The movement re-minded Jack of Rose biting and tugging her darning thread. The picture came into his head so vividly that he wanted to say something about Ruth, just to be rid of it. 'You know,' Stan said.

'Night and a half last night.'

'We've got more important things to talk about. She'll want to know where you stand.'

'Where do you think? Same place as usual. No-bloody-where.'

'You talked about it with Rose?'

57

'It's not all a bowl of cherries being married to her, whatever you may think. At least Mrs Stan put up the money for your caff in the first place, she's got that going for her.'

'She didn't put up enough, that's what's buggered us,' Stan said. 'We've got to get somebody else in, fifty per cent to make us straight, fifty per cent to build us up. We can't stay where we are. We're either going to be going up, or down.' He lifted his hand way up for the up, and whacked it down on the next patty in line for the down. It made a sound like flesh being slapped. He stared at Jack the while. He had small brown eyes, nearly black, and the way the lids folded over gave them a long tail each side, so they looked like a pair of tadpoles.

It must be Mrs Stan talking. Stan himself would never think in that clear-cut way, left to his own devices. He was happier taking refuge in vague hopes, waiting for a fairy godmother to wave her wand and change his potato patties and liver-and-onions into lobster thermidor.

'If you can't come in with us, there's this bloke we know,' Stan said. 'Name of Ken.'

'Rose has got one thought in her head, us buying a house of our own when the time is ripe. You're not going to budge her. Believe me, I know,' Jack said.

In the butcher's there was still no word of pork. The paper said it would be back next month but the paper said a lot of things. Even Jack couldn't get hold of any at present. Rose bought some manky-looking mince. There were speckles of white fat scattered over it like miniature snow. The cows must be on to a winner, managing to overeat in this day and age. She had a sudden picture of a field of them inflated like barrage balloons, their feet hardly able to reach the ground, and couldn't stop herself giving a little laugh out loud, like she had last night when thinking about those olden times couples picking each other's noses. She must have sounded like the milkman's horse fetching back its hay. Mr Palmer raised his eyebrows, and grinned like you do when you want to share a joke.

'You seem happy enough, Mrs Willis.'

'You must be seeing things, Mr Palmer. I used up my happy coupons till next week.' He must think she was mental. Making a silly joke about it didn't improve matters. She bought a quarter of corned beef to change the subject. Do for tea. Anyway she didn't have much to be happy about. She was still feeling sore inside where Jack had done his business last night. When he finally got home he'd gone for her like a man possessed. At least it showed he didn't have a floozy tucked away somewhere, but by the same token it made it seem that he wished he did. Not much to do with love anyhow, more like making a point. She'd expected him to be like that in the war when he came home to convalesce, making up for lost time, but he'd been quite gentle on that score, almost half-hearted in point of fact, probably because his leg gave him gyp whenever he made a sudden movement.

She walked home, not having the patience to wait for the bus. Also the sun was shining for once. There was still litter on the pavement from the storm the other day. The trouble with not asking somebody what the matter was, was it got harder to do every time you didn't do it. She pictured the skin wrinkling and puckering on the top of dad's milk drink when he was too busy with his book to remember it. You leave the question you want to ask on one side, and it gets a sort of skin on it. But what question *could* she ask, in any case? Jack, why don't you seem to be you any more? There had been something different about him since he was demobbed. The war must have changed him. She'd always felt, during their courting days, that he was an ambitious person, somebody who wanted to get on. He was still an energetic sort of man, lively and active, but nowadays he seemed directionless. His job in the café didn't show signs of going anywhere much. He wanted one thing, Stan another, and when push came to shove it

59

was Stan's business. She'd suggested they think about trying to buy a house, in hopes that it would make him think about his future a bit more. He put up with dad well enough but you couldn't expect him to want to live with him indefinitely, not being blood relatives.

She reached the uphill bit of Wellington Road and increased her pace. She always went faster up a slope, it seemed less tiring than taking it at a plod. As she got level with Robinson's sweetshop on the other side of the road she crossed on impulse and went in.

Funny how butchers are jolly and sweetshop men are miserable. You'd expect it to be the other way round. Mr Palmer was all sweetness and light as he cut up bits of meat, while Mr Robinson would shuffle pineapple cubes out of the bottle with a despairing expression all the while, shaking his head as if he didn't know what the world was coming to. Also he looked very horrible. He was one of those bulgy men whose underpants elastic always shows.

Having thought of pineapple cubes she nearly asked for them. She loved the dry clatter they made as they went into the scale, like rain on a tin roof.

'Hello, Mrs Willis,' he said. He sighed. 'What'll you have?'

'Have you got a bar of Cadbury's Milk?'

'Children have to take priority, like it says in the adverts. While supplies are short.'

'It's for Donald.' She didn't need to blush, since it was. But think of that great lozzack, standing there all day not selling his customers chocolate. It wouldn't matter if you thought he liked the kiddies. What he liked was saying no.

He sighed again, disappointed. He smacked down a bar on the counter. She picked it up and ran her finger along it, to make sure it hadn't been broken. Everybody knows that's how the goodness leaks out. The nicest part of having a bar of chocolate, or an Easter egg come to that, is that first sense you get of it being intact. Luckily it was. What she would have done if it hadn't been, best not to think about. Given him a bit of an old-fashioned look, in all probability.

Here you are, Donald, she thought to herself as she passed over the coupons, slipped the chocolate into her bag and left the shop, your reward for having bad dreams.

Norman wasn't Norman in the seebackroscope, he was somebody fat. His eyes and nose and mouth were in a little pile in the middle of his face. Everybody went the same. Donald wished he hadn't brought it to the park. He'd found it in his toy drawer, after he came home from school, and took it out because he suddenly felt sorry for it lying there, never being played with.

In the seebackroscope the sunshine went away and there was a fog over everything. It tired you out, everybody being fat, the fog, only being able to see behind you, not in front. He tried opening the other eye, but that made the one in the seebackroscope go dimmer. Grandad had told him about birds having one eye on one side of their head and the other on the other. 'The thing they can't see,' he said, 'is what's right in front of their blinking noses.'

In the seebackroscope you were always walking away from everything. It made you go dizzy. If everywhere got further and further away all the time, soon there would be nowhere left.

When he stopped looking through it the whole park went big.

He let Norman have a go. Norman tried jumping round to face the other way. He was trying to do it fast enough to catch the front while it was still the front. It made him fall over.

While he was still lying on the ground Norman held the seebackroscope to his lips, like one of those tooters you get at a party. He spoke into it and a low, hummy voice came out the end. 'She hit me,' he said. 'She hit me on the hand. Two times.'

Donald felt suddenly happy. It made it seem like another

61

Norman, him talking about what had happened in a seebackroscope voice. The words sounded different from the usual Norman, even though they came out the right way round. 'Did she hit you after the lesson?'

'When everybody went out. Once because the record was broke. The other one for not owning up. When she hit me her teeth all shook.' Norman banged his own teeth together like you do if you shiver very slowly.

That reminded Donald. 'His eyes came out,' he said.

'Whose eyes?' Norman asked. He just said it ordinary, then remembered and said it again into the seebackroscope: 'Whose eyes did?'

'My grandad's. He had a heart attack.'

'Did he raunge?' Norman asked, and raunged himself. He threw the seebackroscope away and grabbed himself in the stomach. He rolled over on to his side, bent in the middle, and poked his tongue out. His throat made that noise it makes when you die. Donald's own throat had made that noise yesterday, when he was hanged. The cold feeling came back into his hair as he remembered being in heaven.

'First of all he raunged and then he died until he was completely dead.'

He couldn't tell Norman he'd died himself, so he said grandad instead. He let his legs go bent and staggered round and round on the grass. It reminded him of when he was an ape the other day, but this time it was being grandad. Then he remembered the rest of the bar of chocolate in his pocket, and pulled it out. Mum had said not to eat it all at once, so he'd kept half till later, but it was later now. He gave Norman some and ate the rest himself. It had melted a bit in his pocket, so he had to eat some of the silver paper as well.

1951

Chapter Four

It always rains on the day you've got to fetch a piano, not that Jack had ever fetched one before.

It was a little back-street place too, off of the main road at Hope's Dale. The road had more of a name than the place amounted to, Marlborough Terrace, and he'd wondered, sitting on the plank passenger seat of Eddie Collins's old van, if it was some outpost of poshness he'd never noticed up till now. If you had to lug a piano, might as well be a white one down marble steps.

No such luck. Marlborough Terrace was a row of four or five houses squeezed between a corner shop at one end and a workshop of some kind at the other, with a cobbled street outside, the stones shining brown in the wet. Bloke in the workshop was thumping something with a mallet through a grimed-up window, and there was a smell of acid hanging over the street, cheek by jowl with the chimney smoke.

Eddie's lad leaned against the van as if he'd been carting a piano about already. He was not the sort of boy you could take much of a shine to, with a short-back-and-sides that met in the middle, and acne or hives galloping all over his face. Jack had come across him before but couldn't place where. He'd nearly asked in the van, but what could you say: I recollect those boils? Probably pulled his tube too often, that's what they put a bad complexion down to in the air force, makes the skin go dry and scaly. Codge had given Dunlop's nose a mighty thump on that score, producing a red Hitler moustache on the poor bloke's upper lip as if by magic.

'Aren't you coming?' Jack asked him.

'Eddie just said drive the van.'

Jack walked up to him. He could see the boy watching his limp, his face going slightly up and down. One thing he'd noticed, if your legs were a bit uneven people assumed you'd taken to a life of crime. He shook out a fag and lit it that way you do. It was a relief to have a drag of it, muffled the sting of the acid on the back of his throat. While his vocal chords still had smoke all over them, he asked, 'What's your name, sonny?'

'Peter.'

Jack nodded over to the front door of the house in question, number three, and walked up to it, Peter following.

He knocked the knocker a couple of times. No one came. Knocked again. Still no one. He muttered his way through a bit of a song, Put Another Nickel In, In the Nickelodeon, as if he was just filling in time.

At last there was a sort of scrabbling sound the other side of the door, and it opened. A wrinkly woman with a dark complexion, almost brown, was standing there, looking as if she'd been shrunk in the wash. Her dress was too big and smooth for her, long and grey with little blue somethings on it, anchors or arrows, and a white panel like a bib at the neck. You couldn't imagine getting hold of one small enough, in point of fact, unless it was from the children's department. The straight-laced effect made her look as if she'd been a schoolmarm in the wild west in her younger, bigger days.

'Come about the piano,' he said.

'So you heff.'

Last thing he expected: she was German. He caught himself straightening up. Something about the accent made you want to click your heels. Funny thing, you didn't expect a woman to have a German accent. You always thought of it as a man's language.

She stepped back to let him in. 'Come on, Pete,' he said,

66

turning round to where he thought he was, but Peter had buggered off and was slouching by the van again. 'Bit shy,' he told the German lady.

'Don't be shy, Pete,' she called out in a surprisingly loud voice, more like the Second World War than you'd ever expect, given her size and that dress. Peter stood where he was for a couple of seconds, as if waiting for it to sink in, then came over towards them. It reminded Jack of when he had a summer job on a farm on the outskirts of Middleton before the war, and had to round the cows up. You went to the far side of the farthest one, and shouted at it. It would take no notice of you for a while, then begin slowly moving off as if it had just decided it wanted to go anyway; and then after a few moments panic set in. You could almost see it thinking, better get out of here, this bloke could be mental for all I know. As it lumbered past the other cows they would do exactly the same in turn, more or less shove a hoof in front of their mouths to stifle a yawn while they hoist their backsides up in the air, then amble along, then trot, then run as though their lives depended on it.

Peter didn't run, but he came over smartish enough. They followed the lady in.

'The piano is placed in the parlour,' she said.

It was dim in there, especially given the rain beating on the window and Eddie's van parked just outside: big wooden furnishings, a mirror with flecks of rust on the silvering, heavy-looking bitch of an upright piano, with the name in unreadable gold letters just above the lid, probably in German.

'I hope we can get it out,' Jack said.

'It came in, it can go out,' she told him.

Maybe, maybe not, he thought to himself. He had a feeling that was one of those things that was true in principle but not necessarily in practice, but he was no engineer, worse luck, or architect, whatever you'd have to be to know.

'First, though, I think you would like a cup of tea. Please to sit down.'

They sat down on a big wooden settee with leather padding and cushions. She went off to get the tea. Peter rubbed his hands on his thighs and looked carefully round, probably for stuff to pinch. From his point of view it would mostly be too big and boring.

'Let's give the piano a bit of a try, see how heavy it is,' Jack suggested. They stood at each end and raised it an inch. 'If you've always wanted longer arms,' Jack told him, 'your time has come.'

Peter just flicked his eyes at the ceiling and said nothing. The ceiling had moulding around the edges, bunches of grapes by the looks of it, and a big brown damp stain in the middle.

The lady came in with a tray.

'I should have introduced myself,' she said. 'My name is Mrs Feltbauer.'

'How d'you do,' Jack said to her.

She gave them home-made jam tarts and a cup of tea. Peter ate his tart in one. It was probably a relief for him to have his gob gummed up for a while. Mrs Feltbauer told Jack she came from Austria. She'd been a Jewish refugee, a couple of years before war broke out. 'We got the chance to leave, so we left. All we could bring were a few odds and ends.' Jack thought of the piano and furniture, maybe trundled on some old cart through Europe. Tough old bird. 'Now my husband has died I have nobody to remember our old life with. It is like a dream.' She took a picture of her husband off the mantelpiece and showed it to them. He was a big man in a suit, with one of those curling-up moustaches. He had a look about him as if he'd died years ago, or never existed in the first place, except in the photograph. 'He was much younger then,' she said. 'That was taken in Austria. Another world. He worked in a bank, the assistant of the manager. Here in England he was just rubbish.

68

Since we come to Stockport he just helped in a bakery, like a piece of rubbish.'

'I work in a café,' Jack said, a bit sharply, but she didn't make any connection.

'Just like a piece of rubbish,' she said. She put down the photograph and picked up her tea. Her cup seemed big compared to the size of her face. 'And now he's dead,' she added, as if that proved it.

The piano was a swine to load into the van. They rested a couple of planks on the sill to make a ramp from the road but they never would have got it up without two men passing by who lent them a hand. What surprised Jack was Peter's willingness to assist in getting the piano into the café. Jack expected him to unload it in the road and drive off. But no, he helped him and Joe, the caretaker, walk it into the dining-room as far as the edge of the stage, then went back to the van and fetched the planks. Stan left his kitchen and the four of them got the bastard into its final resting place. Even then Peter didn't go off. Stan gave him a meat and potato pie but that didn't do the trick either. Peter chucked it down his throat the same way he had the jam tart and carried on leaning against the piano, cooling his heels, like he had against the van in Marlborough Terrace.

Stan went back to the kitchen. Joe returned to the little seat he had by the boiler in the cellar. Finally Jack went off to the toilet for a pee. Just as he came back into the dining-room he was aware of a little bang. Peter was where he had been before, inspecting his thumbnail, but with that look about him of just having moved quickly back into position. Jack went up to him and peered at his face while Peter carried on staring down. There was a bit of white near his mouth, a flake of skin scaled off or possibly of pastry from his pie. Eczema or dandruff bulged around his hair-stubble like fungus in a wood. His skin was dry enough to strike a match on, nothing appealing about him.

'I think Eddie'll be wanting you back,' Jack said.

'No hurry.' Peter put what was left of his thumbnail in his mouth, had a bite, then inspected the damage.

Having settled back in place, his complete unwillingness to budge could fill you with panic if you let it. He had as much inertia as the sodding piano. Jack put his mouth as close to his big taxi-door ear as he could cope with. 'Hop,' he said in a low whisper, 'it.'

Still didn't move. Jack too stayed where he was. You can't say hop it more than once.

Then Peter said: 'Eddie'd split. Half and half.'

'Would he? Good old Eddie.'

'Half for all three of us. Fair's fair.'

'Depart, sonny.'

This time he did, shaking his head at human stupidity. Perhaps there was an element of threat in it too, as much as to say, you don't know what you're letting yourself in for.

As soon as Peter had left the room Jack was at the piano, opening the lid as if it was a Christmas present.

Sure enough, right on top of the workings, a gold cigarette case, one of those that takes around a hundred fags. Peter must have shoved it there when he, Jack, was taking the tea tray out to the kitchen for the old lady. Jack had thought her possessions were safe because they were too hefty to be slipped under Peter's coat. But the piano was another story and accounted for Peter's unwillingness to clear off. If he'd managed to get the case clean away he would probably have shared with Eddie, who'd have more of an idea how to turn it into hard cash. How he thought Mrs Feltbauer wouldn't notice it was missing and put two and two together, was another example of his maths going astray: he *didn't* think.

Before he shut the lid Jack noticed something else, a yellowing bundle wrapped in newspaper in the far corner. He felt no surprise at all. It was as though deep down he'd known it would be there all along. Like as if the cigarette

70

case was just a clue to lead him in the right direction, the way people scatter bits of paper in a paper chase. He even said inside his head: there it is.

He went round and leaned in the piano to fetch it out. It was a dusty old parcel neatly tied up with string. He edged the newspaper to one side to see in. Five-pound notes. He put it back in the piano. He put the cigarette case back in the piano too, shut the lid, took a deep breath. It needed to be a deep one to stop his heart bouncing out of his chest.

Donald whispered it: 'The doctor said. He had to take my eye out. Then mend all its muscles. Then put it back again.'

Cherry looked at him. She looked at each of his eyes in turn, as if they weren't eyes at all, just something you had to look at. Her nose had freckles on it which were browny-white, like those toasted coconut bits on the top of macaroons. She whispered back: 'Which one are they going to take out?' She was happy all over, even her ear, which was pink and looked as if you could nearly see right through it.

'Both of them, I think.' He felt himself go red in the face straight away. He didn't know why he'd said that. The doctor had said his right one. As he thought of it, he quickly wrote with a pretend pen in the air, to make sure which was right. Telling a fib made it sound as if it was all a lie, that no eye was going to be taken out at all. A quick sad look went over Cherry's face as the lie went in. Then she was smiling and excited again.

'Both of them,' she whispered. She put her face right up close to Donald's and squeezed it tight, so her eyes were shut and her nose was wrinkled. Then she opened it again into a huge smile, like when the pigeon came out of the man's hat. 'Bo-oth,' she said from inside her smile.

He shut his right eye and opened it again. 'I think that one is worse,' he said. 'Maybe he'll just do that one.'

She went sad again straight away. She didn't want it to

be just one eye, it had to be both. She looked round the classroom to see if any of her friends were near. Because it was wet play nobody was in their seats. They were playing in little groups and gangs all over the room. As soon as she saw somebody who wasn't busy in a game she'd go. One eye wasn't enough to keep her. If he'd never said two in the first place, she'd still be happy.

'I expect he'll do both, though,' he said.

She smiled again but differently from before. It was like the smile mum did sometimes, when she was thinking about something else and just wanted to make you happy.

'Mrs Cotton looks as if she's crying,' Cherry said.

Mr Washington, the headmaster, came into the classroom at the end of wet play. Donald had borrowed Norman's glasses, to make his eyes seem worse. The optician had said he didn't need any, because it was just a squint. Norman's glasses were only for reading with. But there was writing on the blackboard just behind Mr Washington's head and since Donald had to look at Mr Washington he couldn't stop himself from reading the writing as well, so he put the glasses on. They didn't make any difference to how things looked but they stopped Mr Washington seeming so dangerous.

Mr Washington took out his handkerchief, blew his nose with a loud farting noise that made some of the children laugh then go even quieter than before, wib-wobbed his handkerchief from side to side across his nostrils, folded it into a little parcel and put it back into his trouser pocket.

His eyes zigzagged over the classroom to spot the children who had laughed at the farting noise. Donald quickly turned his head away and looked at Mrs Cotton instead.

She really was crying, just as Cherry said.

'Boys and girls,' Mr Washington said, 'I have something very very sad to tell you all.'

* * *

After a couple of days of rain it cleared up a bit towards noon. Ernie hadn't wasted the sorry conditions, though. He'd fashioned a little footrest out of a strip of metal he had lying about, and rigged it up to the protruding spindle of the back axle of his bike.

The bike had long been a bit of a mishmash. It was principally a huge machine he'd bought for a song donkey's years ago. Must have been ridden by a giant, though when he got hold of it, it was in the hands of a little widow who could only just manage to wheel it out of her hallway into the front garden for him to take a look. Bike and a half he'd told her, not meaning it as a compliment, but her face lit up so much he didn't like not to have it. Its wheels reminded him of that story he'd read Donald a few years back, eyes like saucers. Wheels like saucers. Then they upped the ante, as he recalled, eyes like millstones, which was more the case here. Frame to a similar scale. Over time he'd replaced the handlebars, pedals, saddle and whatnot with parts salvaged from other machines that had come his way, his policy being to try what he could to stunt its growth. The handlebars and saddle were small ones and set as low as possible, giving the machine a pinheaded sort of look about it. Next thing, he built up the pedals. He got the idea from a bloke in the pub, Georgie, who had a club foot. Funny thing, Georgie used to go in the Plough at the same period as Harry Colclough with the pot leg. Some wag sitting between them one day bent down and picked a rivet up off of the floor. 'Has this fell off either of you two gentlemen?' he asked, which didn't strictly apply to Georgie's boot but got the point across. He, Ernie, had offered to sole it for him but that business was all taken care of at the clinic. The long and short of it was he fastened a block of wood to each face of each pedal, so when you were riding along you didn't have to slither your whole body down each side of the bike in turn to enable your foot to reach the bottom part of the arc.

But the thicker pedals weren't thick enough to help him with the problem of mounting the machine in the first place, not now he was stiffening up a bit. He made a joke about it to Rose: 'Now I'm getting on, I'm finding it a bit tricky getting on,' but she wasn't concentrating and just replied, 'Are you, Dad?' with that absent-minded sympathy she occasionally shovelled your way. It was a matter of scooting along with one foot on the pedal, and then hoisting the other leg up so it cleared the saddle. It gave him gyp, cocking his leg that high, and one time he'd failed to get it over and tied himself in all sorts of knots, ending up sitting on his bum in the middle of the road, wearing his bike like a hat.

The idea now was to put his left foot on the footrest, stretch over to grab the handlebars, couple of kicks at the ground with his right foot, then push himself up with the left and more or less land on the bike from above, like cowboys at the pictures do when they jump on their horses from nearby buildings.

Nobody about save a rag-and-bone man fiddling with his nag down the far end of the road. There was a long smooth strip in front of the house where the council had had the cobbles up for some reason and replaced them with a patch of tar, which, ever since, he had used as a runway.

He got in position and was off, nice as pie, except he landed on his left bollock when he arrived in the saddle, firing it about halfway up the inside of his body. Not to worry, hadn't been much use to him for some time, and the tears on his cheeks would soon dry in the wind. The rag-and-bone man was too busy nose-bagging his horse to look up as he went past.

He rode down to the millpond in Reddish Vale, like he did most Thursdays, to watch the ducks in company with a few other old reprobates. Getting off the bike wasn't as much of a problem as getting on, being that gravity went in the same direction, and anyway down the Vale there was a wooden fence you could come to rest against. He lined up on it, came to a halt, and climbed down by means of the wooden rails.

Alf Mulley was already in position, sitting on the one park bench and watching a couple of drakes spar with each other on a half-sunk rowing boat. A train puffed its way across the viaduct in the distance.

'Tell you what,' Alf said without looking round, giving a good view of his three double chins, 'it's a wonder you don't break your neck on that machine of yours. That bird just fetched the other one a fair old swipe, did you see it?'

Ernie was reminded of the way Rose carried on about how nasty the hens were. 'Missed it.' Anybody'd think there was a plague of violent poultry.

'You must have a charmed life.' Alf shook his head. His dewlaps flapped out of time with each other, like washing on the line. He had a nose like a potato. Funny thing, Ernie could picture him a few years back with a nose no different from anybody else's. Who'd think it, you have a particular face on you the majority of your life, get to the age of seventy and your nose suddenly chooses to inflate. 'Better luck than my nephew, anyhow,' Alf said.

'He got in trouble again?'

'Climbing up the drainpipe of the furniture shop down Underbank, Neil and Garrods. Aiming to get on the roof and pinch a bit of the lead flashing. Drainpipe comes adrift, he swings out, swings back again, goes smack through the big front window. Tell you one thing, he wouldn't have gone through before the war, they had proper plate glass in them days, would have bounced off. Oh, I see what was the cause of all that malarkey, one of them drakes is doing its business with a duck now, hammer and tongs, look at them go. Not a scratch on him, which was the only good point about it. If it had been good quality glass, and *had* give way, he'd have known about it, as I told him. Along comes a police constable, heard the crash. Dougie gets to his feet and says, "OK. It's a fair cop.

Shake." Shakes hands, copper shakes back. But the worst part of it was, he got arrested for burglary. Breaking and entering. Stripping stuff off of a roof's only robbery, because you're not illegally entering the premises when all's said and done. I said to Dougie, plead not guilty, explain it wasn't burglary, you just had an accident befallen you while on the way to commit a robbery. You broke and entered right enough, but not with intent, that's the case you want to put.' Suddenly he wiped his eyes with his hand. His fingers had gone podgy of late like his nose. He shook his head as if in irritation at the wind, but it wasn't that, Dougie's goings-on were getting too much for him, that's what it was.

Luckily at that moment the other two rolled up, Pat and Arn. They all talked about this and that. Ernie mentioned his reading, having gone back to Walter Scott which he did from time to time, *Guy Mannering* this time around. But he didn't have much to say. He'd come over melancholy, truth to tell. It was Alf's grief over his nephew Dougie, and the fact that Alf himself was swelling out the way he was: a feeling about time passing, and things happening that couldn't be gone back on. Didn't help reading about the olden days, in all probability. He thought of his grandson Donald, not exactly as he was now but a year or two ago, that head of hair like a dandelion clock, the way he'd run out of the shed when Ernie had gone for him on the subject of telling tales out of school – in school, as it happened. Donald had probably forgotten the whole episode by now, but it was the sort of thing that never completely went away, like when the ostrich swallowed the tin can.

It had been a silly argument, like all their arguments. Over tea last night. Rose could tell that something had happened that pleased Jack. All three of them, dad, Jack and Donald, had the same way of striding in when they had good news, swollen out with it like an egg about to hatch. Rose would wait for their little door to spring open and a cuckoo to pop out, like the one in mum's old clock used to before she secretly strangled it. So she sat in suspense while Jack ate his sardines on toast. He didn't have a big tea as a rule since he usually had something at work.

When he'd finished he took a sip of his tea, scratched his nose, sighed, and came out with it: 'Bought a piano today.'

Her first reaction was disappointment. She'd expected something big but vague, a career, a business, a house. A piano was just big. Then she thought, he means well, something for Donald, give him credit for wanting to be fatherly, doesn't happen that often.

'That's nice,' she said cautiously. Jack looked lost in his own thoughts.

'Dorothy was a poor pianist,' dad said. 'Used to give me earache. It's not a subject I know a lot about, but all her notes sounded on the sharp side to me.'

'The only problem is space,' Rose went on.

'That's why we got rid in the first place,' dad said, 'when the family came along.'

'Oh no, not here,' Jack said, quite impatiently, as if they were being obtuse.

'Not here?' Her heart thumped. Silly, when she thought about it behindhand, imagining that somebody, even somebody as impractical as Jack, would buy a piano first and a house to fit it into after. Sillier still to think that this might be his romantic way of making the announcement, a rigmarole to go through because you couldn't wrap a whole new house up in crêpe paper. But once upon a time he used to draw her pictures of oases.

'In the café, where d'you think?'

'The café?'

'You know how Stan's always wanted to use that stage thing? What he'd like most of all is a little band, and put on supper dances. You look in the paper, they have pages of them advertised every week. You charge half a crown a

77

shake just to go in the door, then they buy something to eat and take a smooch round the floor. Larry Mendoza and his Musical Maniacs. Stan knows Larry, he's done a bit of business with him, you know, when supplies have been hard to come by.'

'Black market, you mean?'

'Larry said he'd do it on spec, just to see whether it takes off.'

'I would have thought musical maniacs wouldn't have much use for a piano.'

'No, no, Ken talked him out of the Maniacs. He said he shouldn't run before he could walk. Ken said, why not try having a piano, and getting a bloke to play in the background for the afternoon tea crowd. Maybe leave a bit of floor space in case the odd couple wanted a spin. Test the water. You know Ken.'

She knew Ken. Ken said this. Ken said that. She had grown to hate Ken. Whenever his name was mentioned she always thought the same thought: Ken could have been Jack. He'd bought his way in when Stan was going through hard times just after the war, not long after Jack first started working there. She wished Jack had had the wit to raise the money somehow and do that himself. It got on her nerves, the way he just let things happen. Even Stan had enough ambition to want to have a dance band. What did Jack want?

'I thought you were thinking about Donald,' she said. 'I always wanted him to learn music.'

'There isn't room, like dad said.'

'If you want room, you can make room,' she told him in a heavy-handed way that made him flinch. Hypocrite that she was – she'd never even thought about a piano before. He stamped off, as she knew he would, down to the pub, the solution to all life's problems. While he was out she sat with dad as he moaned and groaned over his new library book, wondering to herself why Jack'd been so excited about the piano in the first place. Just because Stan had wanted music and now would have it? Because he, Jack, had been the one to collect it from wherever he'd collected it from? He was like a child, pleased with so little. So content to live other people's lives for them. The thought of his weakness and passivity made her feel a sudden shock of love for him. Her face went so pink dad looked up from his book at her.

And now, this morning, rain again. She'd wanted to rush out to the shops and buy Jack some haddock. You couldn't give flowers when you'd been nasty to your husband, and he did love fish, always complaining they never had it enough. Her fault, but after years of watching her mother's boiled rock salmon come apart flake by flake in a saucepan of scummy water she tended to shy clear of it. Dad was no help, having suffered the same diet himself. When she did serve fish dad would look at it long and hard, much like a fish himself, or at least a walrus, then fork it up in tiny amounts and chew it that way he had when he wasn't enjoying his grub, so his upper and lower plates didn't quite meet.

The rain gave her time for second thoughts. Sure as fate if she bought fish he would turn out to have eaten a meal before he came home, and not have the appetite. Then she'd be miffed at him turning it down, and the outcome would be a haddock as well as a piano lying between them.

A jacket. He needed one. He looked like a badly-wrapped parcel, going to work. He ought to dress smartly, or at least tidily, to counterbalance that limp of his. Like an old tramp otherwise. He hated buying clothes. As a rule she waited for the sales, but they were months off. And the whole point was to surprise him, be attentive.

Late morning it began to clear. Dad climbed on that monster of a bicycle of his and wobbled off in search of a broken neck. It looked like a penny-farthing, except both wheels were pennies. As he turned the corner a ray of sunshine caught his moustache and made it seem dazzlingly bright. She left the house and walked down Wellington Road towards the town centre.

It was then that a terrible thing happened. She bumped into Mrs Singleton.

How could she have forgotten? How *could* she?

'Where've you been, Mrs Singleton?' she asked, by way of being polite. She didn't really like Mrs Singleton, who was one of those competitive women, always had a new radiogram or fridge. She was very pushy about her son, Victor, too, in those conversations that took place at the school gate. She'd bought a television set to keep him amused.

Afterwards Rose cringed when she thought about asking that question, especially when she recalled the tone of voice she'd used, that bright and breezy one you adopt when you don't like the person you're talking to.

'I'm just coming back from the funeral parlour,' Mrs Singleton said. Even then it still didn't sink in. Rose was busy noticing that Mrs Singleton looked pale and drawn, with lustreless hair, and remembering that it was only a few weeks ago that she'd been talking about a personal hygiene course she'd been on at the town hall. Rose had seen the advertisement herself: Miss Madeleine Marshall will cover care of hair, skin, hands and feet, also make-up and deportment. In fact it hadn't been all that expensive but was the sort of thing Rose didn't have the nerve to enrol on herself, grown women walking across the floor with books balanced on their heads. Much good it had done, Mrs Singleton being stood here with wisps of her hair blowing in the breeze. Perhaps she was having one of those Trying Days, as the Baxen advertisements called them.

When she heard the words funeral parlour, what Rose thought was that it must be something to do with Victor's fancy dress.

That was what she and Mrs Singleton had discussed last time they'd met. The Chamber of Commerce were organising a fancy dress party. Mrs Singleton asked what Donald was going as. Rose hadn't thought. Mrs Singleton had looked surprised at hearing that, then all smily while she waited to be asked in turn. Rose obligingly asked.

'Don't tell,' Mrs Singleton had said. 'I don't want anyone else to have the same idea.' What she'd meant was: I don't want *you* to have the same idea. She leaned forward, and whispered: 'I'm thinking of sending him as "I tawt I taw a puddy tat." '

A puddy tat: that fat thing Victor? had been Rose's thought. No wonder personal hygiene with Miss Marshall held no fears for Mrs Singleton, if she was willing to make a fool of her boy like that.

Now her mention of a funeral parlour made Rose jump to the conclusion that Mrs Singleton had changed her mind, as any mother who had any feeling for her boy would, and was going to send him as, who knows what went through Rose's foolish head, a pall-bearer, a funeral man, an undertaker?

'Victor died yesterday,' Mrs Singleton said.

There are two mes, Rose thought. I'm like one of those Russian dolls. The outside one which has been talking to Mrs Singleton has no brain at all. Also no human feelings, no kindness, no niceness. It's like a hollow statue. The inside one, which is just a bit smaller, and nearly fills the space, has a mind, and a memory, and some idea of other people's concerns. The inside me remembered being told a week or so ago that Victor Singleton had been taken to hospital with inflammation of the brain. It tried and tried to communicate this information to the outside one, but to no avail.

Rose had been in a rush when told. It didn't sink in properly. She intended to think about it later, but later hadn't come. Perhaps it was because she had never particularly taken to Victor in the first place. Neither had Donald for that matter. In fact Victor had fetched him a proper smack on one occasion when they were quite little. Maybe the reason why it hadn't sunk in was because it was a different kind of news from what she had ever heard about another child before. Perhaps the news was too serious, too grave, too *big*, to remember.

But the inside me had known all along.

All these thoughts shot through her head in an instant. And immediately after, she did the terrible thing.

She burst into laughter.

She would never know whether Mrs Singleton realised. She converted it into a cry of shock, of pain, as soon as it came out of her mouth, as if noise was like clay, you could pat it into what shape you wanted. A fair-minded person would understand that the laughter must mean shock and pain in any case, a sort of sudden hysterics. Secretly she knew, in her inner me, that the laughter had been laughter, caused by a sudden picture of plump gawky Victor, being dead as if it was fancy dress. I tawt I taw.

The confusion of her thoughts and feelings made her weep in earnest, big shuddering sobs, and she could feel poor worn Mrs Singleton's hand patting her shoulder, deep sympathy and gratitude in her eyes. That didn't prove she'd got away with it, of course. If Mrs Singleton *had* realised, she'd have to pretend for always that it hadn't happened, the same as Rose would.

Last night when Jack went home he couldn't stop talking about the piano. From the way he talked they must have expected him to sit himself down in front of it and flog out a whole symphony for the benefit of the general public. What you called inoculation. Back in the café the piano was sitting there through the night with a cigarette case inside it worth God knows what, and a bundle of fivers worth much much more, and there he was talking about it as if he had nothing to hide in the whole wide world. While he was speaking he couldn't help thinking to himself how much easier it was to push the piano in and out of a conversation than it was to manhandle it out of Mrs Feltbauer's parlour and into Eddie's van.

Today, time to do something. Stan was talking about a tuner. 'Play that thing as it is,' he said, 'you got the sound coming at you from all angles.'

'The fact you don't know how to play doh ray me may have something to do with it,' Jack told him.

'You don't have to be able to play it to know when it needs seeing to.'

'That piano's been pushed over the Alps for all we know. And on its travels again yesterday. One way and another it's had a right mauling.'

'There's no need to make excuses for it, Jack. I'm not *blaming* it. All I'm saying, needs a blinking tuner.'

'Please yourself,' Jack said sulkily. Of course it needed a tuner. He just didn't like being forced to make a decision so soon.

But as soon as Stan's back was turned he took both items out of the piano and hid them under an old sack in the outbuildings at the back of the café.

Chapter Five

When Donald woke up he tried to move his legs but they wouldn't.

He got himself half up in the bed by pushing with his hands. It made him go like when he was in Uncle Dick's sidecar, half lying, half sitting up, his legs flat ahead in the little pointed front bit, his face level with the tiny wind-screen. Then Uncle Dick pulled the roof over and fastened it into place. He looked huge, bending over to look through the soft side-window to check if Donald was all right, with his big goggles like a panda, and leather helmet. He put his thumb up in its gauntlet, and Donald put his thumb up too.

Uncle Dick went round to the motorbike part. Through the sidecar windows he seemed to be walking at the bottom of the sea, like a diver. He got on the bike, kicked his leg, twisted the hand-grip, and suddenly there was a roar as the engine started. There was a roaring inside Donald's head to match. Then there was a click which was softer than the roar but you could still hear it, and the bike and sidecar jerked forward a bit, like when Mrs Dobson lets you unfasten Sally from her lead but you still hold on to her collar for a minute, and then they were moving off properly, the road sliding down the sidecar windscreen, the little crinkles and wrinkles of the tarmac becoming suddenly sharp and close to, just at the moment they rolled down out of sight. Donald was so glad that he shouted out loud, not a word just a shout, but nobody could hear because of the noise.

The road came faster and faster, the same as the hill did when he was on his sledge, and he could feel the wheel of the sidecar spinning and its tyre biting the road as if in some thin stretched-out sort of a way it was a part of his own body.

It was raining. Drops settled one after the other on his bedroom window, fat and round like ladybirds that haven't been coloured in yet. Donald pulled his sheet and blankets right up to his chin and imagined how it would be if you had a motorbike and sidecar waiting for you on a rainy day, going out of the house without a mac on, walking down the garden path with the rain sprinkling down on your head, getting into your own tiny indoors and driving off, while all the poor wet people walk up and down on the pavement.

'Time to get up, duck,' mum said.

'My legs feel funny.'

Her eyes went a little bit closer together. 'What do you mean, funny?'

'They've got an ache in them.' They had the same ache in both of them, not an ache each.

'What kind of ache?'

'Just aching.'

Mum said: 'Do you remember something, Donald? Do you remember that day? When it snowed?'

Donald remembered. It was when he was young. He went out of the house to run down the road to school and a snowflake went in his eye. He hadn't known it was snowing but when he blinked it away he saw that there were other snowflakes scattered all over the air. They weren't falling down thickly the way they do sometimes, so many all at once you can nearly hear them landing on the ground. At Christmas dad made snowflakes out of little balls of cottonwool and hung them from the ceiling with thread, some high, some lower. These were more that sort of snowflakes, hanging between the sky and the road. He wondered whether one would go in his mouth if he walked along with his mouth open, so he did.

In morning assembly it was hard to sing the hymn. The words felt spiky as they came up. He told his teacher when they went back into the classroom, and she looked down his throat and then told him to go home. It was snowing proper snow when he left the school.

His house was empty. He could see it was, just by looking. It was a different house. It looked like a house does when it's lived in by other people who you don't know. The windows were black, the same black as the pupil of your eye. Walking out of the gate and down the road were the big footprints of grandad, and walking out of the gate and on to the road were the thinner footprints of mum. There was a little flick of snow in front of each of her footprints where the pointed front of her shoes must have kicked the snow while she walked.

He went round the back of the house just in case the door had been left unlocked. No. Grandad's shed had its padlock done up too. He stood waiting by the back door. The snow stopped suddenly and a little bit after that a hole came in the clouds and the sun shone through, white as snow itself. The cat from Mrs Oogeeflip's house jumped down from the fence and came over, very slowly, sliding each paw in turn into the snow as if it was putting on wellington boots.

They waited. A bird jumped about in the snow on the lawn, a robin. The cat looked at it, and then turned the other way so it didn't have to chase it. The cat tried to sit down but its bum didn't like the snow so it stood up again. That was the trouble with snow, nowhere to sit.

Donald began to feel sleepy. He had read a story about when they got very cold they felt sleepy, and after that they died. The cat looked up at him and blinked with very slow eyelids. Perhaps it was getting sleepy too. Or perhaps Donald just saw the blink happening that slowly because he was getting more sleepy still. He realised he couldn't feel his body, and his heart began to pound with fear. He told himself that you don't feel your body except if something's touching it, even just a bit of wind touching it. Anyway, he could feel the tops of his socks holding on to his legs, and the beating of his heart. The cold didn't feel cold enough, but he didn't know whether that was good or bad. Maybe it meant it wasn't cold enough to kill you, or maybe it meant you were half dead already.

'What –'

Donald cried out: 'Ah!'

The cat ran off.

'– doing, Donald?'

'I didn't hear you coming round.'

'That was because of the snow, I expect. *I* could hear me coming but I was listening to my feet. When they press the snow down it makes a funny squeaky scrunching sound. It reminded me of something but I couldn't think what. Then I remembered what. Do you know what it reminded me of?'

He shook his head.

'When the dentist filled my tooth, and he pressed the filling stuff hard down with his presser thing into the hole he'd drilled. That went scrunch too, just the same, and squeaked with it. I suppose school's run out of coke for the boiler again?'

'I've got a sore throat.'

'Have you just. Fat lot of good it'll have done it, you stuck on the step for half an hour while I was over at Mrs Shaw's. Your teacher should have more sense than just sending you home on the off-chance. Let's get you inside.'

When they were inside she made him say aaa.

'There's nothing wrong with that throat of yours.'

'It was sore before.'

'Perhaps you were shouting too much.'

'I didn't shout. I went to school with my mouth open. I was trying to catch the snow. You can't shout with your mouth open.'

She had looked at him without moving for a second.

Then suddenly she burst out laughing. 'You little imp,' she said. She made her fist like a hammer and banged it gently on the top of his head.

Donald looked over at his bedroom window. The rain was beating against it now. Why had she asked him about that day when it snowed? 'I was thinking about the rain,' he told her.

'I didn't mean the *snow* snow, I meant how you got your sore throat. What I want you to think about is if you've done something to make your legs ache. Run a lot, things like that. Played football. PT.'

Her eyes went still closer to each other, and suddenly he saw they were big and fearful.

'Think, Donald,' she said.

'Just walked around on them, same as usual,' he said.

'I fear from your looks,' said the father, 'that you have bad tidings to tell me of my young stranger.'

You could say that again. Thing about these characters, Ernie decided, they were quite poor at taking a hint. *The guest had spent a part of the night in ascertaining the position of the heavenly bodies, and calculating their probable influence; until at length the result of his observations induced him to send for the father, and conjure him, in the most solemn manner, to cause the assistants to retard the birth, if practicable, were it but for five minutes.* Cork your old lady, in other words, while she's in the last stages of labour. Couldn't be done, of course. *The answer declared this to be impossible; and almost in the instant that the message was returned, the father and his guest were made acquainted with the birth of a boy.* Whoopsa-daisy. But hubby still doesn't cotton on that this whole palaver must mean bad tidings, till next day at breakfast.

Young stranger, that's the right name, sure enough. They come into the household out of the wide blue yonder, you never know for sure where you are with them. With Donald, at any rate. Nice little chap but you couldn't have the faintest idea what was going on inside that circular head of his. Certainly he never confided in him, Ernie. His head was as round as a football but delicate-looking at the same time, especially before, when it had had fluffy curls all over the top of it. These had died down of late, or been removed, more to the point, with receiving more regular haircuts. Course Donald was hardly likely to confide, was he? given what had happened to him last time he did confide. Goes into the shed to have a word with his old grandad about a spot of bother he's got himself into, and made to feel he was the scum of the earth.

The Author of Evil was present in the room with him in bodily shape, and, potent with spirits of a melancholy cast, was impressing upon him the desperation of his state. You had to hand it to Walter Scott, boring he might be, make your toes bunch together, but he knew a bit about how it feels to have things go to pot on you.

He put the book down and pulled out his pocket watch. She'd been gone fifteen minutes, no more. On the other hand, if she'd let him go on his bike he could have been back by now, but she would have none of it. 'It's got to be me. It's got to be me,' she kept saying. Maybe she was right. If he'd gone instead, possibly the doctor would have thought to himself, it's only the grandfather, what would *he* know? Though being a doctor he was quite likely to say the same thing about the mother. The way doctors regarded it, nobody but themselves had the sense to know anything.

He could go up and tell Donald his mum had nipped out but there was no point in jumping the gun. If he asks, would be soon enough. The trick was to not let any anxiety show through.

He didn't want to read *Guy Mannering* for the time being. He hadn't been reading it this morning anyway, only looking over the bit at the front where Walter Scott says how the idea of the story came into his head. Ernie had gone back to it because he recalled how it seemed to have a bearing. In point of fact last night, and the night before, he'd got some way into the story proper, which was quite interesting once you got hold of the dialect the Scottish characters had, which sounded like English that had been put through a mincer. The best part so far was the scenery.

He picked up the book again and found a bit that had stayed with him. *It was now very cloudy, although the stars, from time to time, shed a twinkling and uncertain light. Hitherto nothing had broken the silence, but the deep cry of the bog-blitter, or bull-of-the-bog, a large species of bittern; and the sighs of the wind as it passed along the dreary morass.* Bog-blitter, that was the bird: not many of them to be found here in Stockport. He wondered how he could work it into a conversation with Sylvie down the library.

He went out into the scullery to make himself a cup of tea. Perhaps the lad would like something. Again he decided it was best to let well alone for the time being. A chicken in the run must have spotted him moving around through the windows in the back door, because it started making a racket, and some of the others joined in, but however hard they tried they were never going to pack the wallop of a bog-blitter in full cry.

That was no answer, because he'd have to find some way of talking about hens to start with, and a girl like Sylvie wouldn't be seen dead having a conversation on that subject. Fingernails was more her line.

He held the kettle below the tap and turned the water on. It occurred to him that it didn't come out exactly dead-square. It looked as if the tap wasn't set quite plumb. As he bent down to peer at it more closely, he must have moved the kettle off-centre so the water started missing the hole and hitting the kettle's shoulder, which gave it the exact angle to bounce off and drench his groin. In the shock he jerked the kettle the wrong way and got on the receiving end of a bigger salvo still, which saw to most of the front area of his trousers.

He cried out half a word at the sudden wetting, but

stopped himself in time. There wouldn't be any satisfaction in it with nobody about to listen except the little chap upstairs, and the other half of that word was the last thing *he* ought to hear. Any luck, he'd be sleeping through.

The water had shot right through to his underpants. It was like an ice-cold hand giving you a feel. It located parts of his privates that were so private he hadn't known they were there in the first place. The trouble with these old-style stone sinks, they were set so low on the wall. He'd plumbed it in himself, but that was the way it was done in those days. A modern one, the sort he'd put in often enough in the later part of his career, was more up level with your stomach.

He tried to walk but just putting one leg in front of another released more rivers down his lower half. The cold seemed to go right through his body and enter his heart. In the plumbing trade you got used to a drenching from time to time, it was a hazard of the job, but he didn't seem to have sufficient resistance for it now. The pain in his heart got so intense it felt like the next best thing to an attack. The sensation also rose up through his shoulders and gave him toothache, of all things, despite having no teeth of his own.

Nothing for it. He took off his waistcoat, slid his braces off his shoulders, undid his fly-buttons, and let his trousers drop. Give those chickens something to cluck about.

She made her business known to the receptionist, a woman called Mary Butler who had in fact been in the same class as Rose's older sister, and who suffered from tombstone teeth. Never married, perhaps for that reason. Being a receptionist was husband and kiddies for her, according to Margery.

'He's got other patients to see,' Mary Butler said.

'It'll take him two minutes in the car. I think Donald might have got inflammation of the brain. One of the children in his class died of it the day before yesterday.'

'If he's that bad you should send him directly to the hospital.'

'I don't know whether he's that bad or not. That's what I want the doctor to tell me.'

'Is he running a temperature?'

Rose nearly pointed out that she hadn't come this far to get a diagnosis from Mary Butler, but stopped herself in time. No point in being unpleasant, especially when it was liable to be counter-productive. Instead she told her the highest temperature she thought she could get away with: 'A hundred and four.'

It was like saying abracadabra. Mary Butler's face cleared. She looked almost cheerful. Rose realised she'd not been being the big I am, but the opposite: fretting at the responsibility of taking it upon herself to interrupt the doctor in mid-surgery. The fib about Donald's temperature had let her off the hook. For all she, Rose, knew, it might not even have been a fib in the first place. Donald's forehead had felt quite hot when she rested her hand on it.

A few minutes later she was in the doctor's car, whizzing homewards through the rain. The doctor was a small lean man with a pepper-and-salt moustache and a dry look about him, like when you bite into an old apple. Perhaps she thought of that because his car smelled musty.

'Does he have a headache?' the doctor asked.

Already she was beginning to feel a fool. It was one thing having to get to the doctor at all costs, but when you'd succeeded you had time for doubts to set in. That was what Mary Butler was there for, she realised. She was like an obstacle in an obstacle race: only the illest people were allowed to scramble over her and arrive at the finishing line. She, Rose, had cheated, so now she didn't know whether she'd deserved to reach there or should have been weeded out.

'No,' she said. 'That I know of.' She hadn't dared ask, for fear of putting the idea into Donald's head that he might have the same thing Victor had. It was bad enough having that idea in her own head.

'Ah,' said the doctor, as if he had thought as much. Rose suddenly found herself wanting to burst into tears.

'He's got an ache in his legs. A bad ache. He could hardly move them.'

'You know that song,' the doctor said, 'one of those Negro songs. I can't remember how it goes.'

He didn't say anything more, and there was an awkward pause for a moment. It didn't seem much to go on. Rose racked her brains, feeling more of a fool than ever. Then the doctor said: 'The knee bone is connected to the thigh bone, that song.'

' "Dem Bones",' Rose said, relieved.

' "Dem Bones", that's the one. It's some time since I studied anatomy, of course, but I can't remember anything about the leg bone being connected to the brain bone, can you?'

To her humiliation a tear actually sprang out of each of her eyes. She coughed, to distract attention from them.

'I know you can get a brain injury, and it stops you from walking properly,' she said in almost a whisper. 'It happened to men in the war.'

'Your husband's got a limp, as I recall.'

'Yes, but that was a leg injury,' she said, and went bright red as she realised what he was driving at. She wanted to cry out in her vexation at how unfair he was being: whatever she said he seemed to be able to prove her wrong, and he hadn't even taken a look at Donald yet.

'So Donald's legs ache, and he's running a temperature?'

'Yes.'

'That's normally what we call influenza.'

There was another silence. What we call influenza, as if influenza was a word ignorant people like herself might not have heard of. She bit her bottom lip to stop a sob bursting out. It rattled about inside her instead, making her jump slightly, as if she had hiccups.

'Here we are,' she said at last, as they came abreast of the house. Her voice was trembly.

They got out of the car. It was still raining steadily. She remembered that in her rush she hadn't brought her handbag with the key in it. She could knock, of course, but she didn't want to knock on her own door, with the doctor being like he was, and have dad shuffling along to answer it. Let the doctor get rained on a bit. She led the way round the back.

The garden looked tidy enough, though sopping wet. She opened the back door, the doctor right behind her.

How *could* he? 'What on earth?'

Dad was standing in the middle of the scullery, his trousers round his ankles, dabbing at his spindly thighs with a tea towel.

She put her fist to her mouth, bit it, moaned aloud.

'Bomb gone off?' the doctor asked.

'Had myself a wetting,' dad said.

'Right-oh.' He said it in that tone of voice when you say, good *boy*.

'No, no, I didn't – filling the kettle, and it got a bit out of hand.'

'I see. Well, you get yourself decent, while we go off and look at our young patient.' The doctor sounded pleased as punch now. He must feel he'd got the upper hand once and for all. Rose led the way. She gave dad an old-fashioned looking at as she went past, though doing it through her tears felt a bit like glaring out at somebody through a net curtain.

Donald was propped up on his pillows playing with a little cannon dad had given him last Christmas, which let out real sparks when you fired it. Or did sometimes. Jack had tried to light a cigarette with it once, but gave up. 'Worse than a blasted lighter,' he'd said. But, as luck would have it, quite a big flame shot out of the barrel as they walked through the door.

'You better be careful, young man, or you'll have the

whole house afire, won't he, Mum?' the doctor said. Donald's face looked almost as white as the pillow, and there were dark circles under his eyes. Rose felt relieved to see him looking so ill, and then a sense of shock that she could play fast and loose in such a way with the health of her own child, just because she was embarrassed at fetching the doctor.

The doctor put his hand on Donald's forehead. Then he shook his head and slid a thermometer in his mouth. After a minute he took it out, shook it, looked at it, shook his head again and put it back in his mouth. The next time he looked at it he muttered something under his breath but she couldn't make out what. She began to feel panic rising.

He pulled back the bedclothes, showing a big label on one of the blankets. Even while he pulled Donald's pyjama legs up to look at his knees she saw his eyes lingering on it. It said: *A Present to the People of Great Britain from their Friends in Australia.* Jack had had it over his legs when he was sent back to convalesce during the war. You couldn't explain how you'd come by something like that, it would only make it look worse. The doctor felt Donald's knees, waggled his legs for him. Donald groaned with the pain of it. Then the same with his arms.

'That'll do, young fellow. You just lie back, now, and have a bit of a rest.' He clapped Donald on the shoulder, turned to Rose, and nodded towards the door.

As they got on to the landing dad came out of his bedroom, snapping his braces on to his shoulders. The doctor must think he had a gift for popping out at you just when he wasn't wanted, along with an inability to put his trousers on in the morning and let them stay there for the rest of the day like ordinary people did.

For some reason it was the doctor who led the way down the stairs, and instead of turning off into the parlour, where she would have taken him given the chance, he went back into the kitchen. Dad's discarded trousers were

95

draped over the draining board, legs apart, like the bottom half of a giant gingerbread man.

'You're to keep him in bed for the time being,' the doctor said.

'In bed.'

'In bed, yes. This afternoon I'll arrange for a nurse to come round and take a sample of his blood.'

'Of his blood.' She nodded wisely, as if she was testing the doctor, and he was doing all right.

'Just a small amount. Enough to fill a little bottle. It's so that we can test what's wrong with him.'

'What *is* wrong with him, doctor?'

'That's what we've got to check.'

'Is it . . . ?' She couldn't say any more. She looked out of the door windows at the wet garden. She pictured, not Victor standing there, but his mother, dim and grey in the rain that was still tipping it down, looking as though *she* was the ghost rather than that son of hers, the ghost of being a mother. Think of that woman going to the under-taker's, alone. Where was her husband? Perhaps he was dead, or had run off. Rose had never pictured her as having one in the first place. Only Victor, getting podgier with each year. Like a tree, when you cut through the trunk, those rings they have. His thick pink thighs filling the legholes of his short flannel trousers. Too many sweets, too much cake, mounds of jelly. Rose felt a sort of comfort imagining Mrs Singleton to be a bad mother, spoiling her child. And now, no more Victor. And if he'd passed it on to Donald, there'd be . . . Oh God, she thought, as fear clutched her heart, it's just like 'Ten Green Bottles'. She sobbed so sharply it felt like retching.

'No, it's not inflammation of the brain. I've got a good idea of what it might be, but I want to be certain. In the meantime you have an important job to do: not worry. Not worry, that's what you've got to do.'

The doctor insisted on leaving by the back door, the way

96

he'd come in. As soon as he'd gone, dad appeared.

'You're a fine one, you are,' she told him. Where he'd got his dry trousers from, lord only knew. They looked to have been made for somebody much bigger than him, and sagged in a horribly old-mannish way between the legs. 'I can't imagine what you thought you were playing at. It's beyond me.' She couldn't sound as angry with him as she wanted to be. It was her own fault, when all was said and done. She'd wished a serious illness on her own little boy, so as not to feel a fool for fetching out the doctor. If dad had made a fool of her in any case, serve her right.

'That tap's a bit skew-whiff,' he said.

'I told you about that, years back.'

'What is it?'

'The doctor doesn't know.'

'There, what did I tell you? Blessed doctors.'

'You didn't tell me anything, Dad.'

'Well.' He looked around with a sheepish smile on his face, as if trying to get support from somebody else.

'I think he thinks it's something serious. He said he's sending somebody round to do a blood test.'

'Oh,' dad said. He smoothed one side of his moustache. 'If he thought it was that serious he'd have him straight in hospital.'

'I suppose so. I was wondering if you'd mind nipping out and getting him a bottle of squash, with him being so hot. The doctor said fluids. If you don't mind getting wet all over again.' She flapped a limp leg of the rogue trousers. It was the nearest she could get to saying let's be friends again.

'Good idea,' he said. 'Won't be two ticks. Do you think it'll be all right if I get the little bloke some sweets as well?'

'I don't see why not. The doctor didn't say not to.'

He went on foot down the road. It was no joy cycling in the rain, not with all the rigmarole of putting his cape on, and sou'wester. It would take more time this way, all to the

97

good. He could hardly bear the thought of Donald up those stairs, with goodness knows what wrong with him, that fuggy smell of a hot boy under blankets. Let it rain, it reminded you you were outdoors. The only thing was the way it hit you in the face, made your eyeballs feel raw.

He thought back years, to that day in the shed, the shock on Donald's face when he blew his top at him, made him feel small, out of his depth. Maybe something had got into the lad's system at that moment, a sort of germ of worry and misery that couldn't be shaken off. Course you could tally up lots of good times Donald had had since then, but that didn't prevent something inside eating away at him.

If that lad cops it, he thought, it'll be me to blame.

You knew where you were with an A-board, even if it was sometimes a bit of a squeeze.

> Soup
> Haricot Mutton/
>   Fried Whiting, Parsley S'ce
> Cabbage, Baked or Boiled Pots
> Raw Veg Salad
> Almond Rice Mould, Peaches
> 2/6

Jack liked opening the alphabet bag, and slowly forming a balanced meal out of the jumble of white plastic letters. Now, though, Stan had had menu cards printed, with LUNCHEON on the top then First Course, Main Course, Dessert, so you could write in the day's dishes under each heading. The cards were stood on the centre of each table in a little red plastic holder. Luncheon, it would give their customers the willies sure as fate. It wasn't even spelt wrong. Rhymes with bunion, Joe said, and sang: I'll raise a bunion on his Spanish onion, if I catch Alphonso tonight, bom bom. Dessert instead of pudding was asking for trouble. They'd desert all right. Last thing they wanted was anything posh. Their idea, most of them, was to come in here and gobble some dinner, like in a works canteen. If Jack had had his way, there'd be an A-board one side of the room for midday dinner, and a servery at the end with Bunter's Bar in big letters over it, and boarding behind showing a list of snacks and beverages that you wouldn't have to change much because most would be on offer all the time. There'd been something in the paper the other day about a television serial to be made on Billy Bunter, all grist to the mill. The tuck-loving sluggard what they described him as. You could make him like one of those patron saints they have for going on a journey or when your loved one's not feeling too brisk, Saint Bunter for all bolters of food. Get somebody who knew how to draw to do his big fat face on the wall above the boarding.

But it washed over Stan. He still had this hope of one day serving snails to toffs. The piano was a little step in that direction. Ken took the view that his own preserve was building and equipment, leave the catering decisions to his partner. He'd made a difference in that sphere since he'd bought a share of the café, no question. Got the curling linoleum off the floor and put down brownish-red rock asphalt, had a Warerite plastic-laminated serving counter built, with a Heetaerator to keep food warm without withering, not the same kettle of fish as the Crypto-Rotapan Jack used to lust after but a good steam conserver all the same, installed a brush type plate-washer, only cub-size but adequate for their turnover, and an electric gravity-feed food-slicer with a slice deflector that meant you could cut meat wafer-thin without breaking, perfect for sandwiches and salad meat. Multipots for volume tea that doesn't stew every five minutes. All in all, they had just about all the appliances needed for a snack service, but Stan still dreamt of his bain-marie and setting crêpes suzettes afire at people's tables even while in actual fact he was standing over the stove softening onions for twenty pounds of liver.

Once the main rush was over Stan asked Jack to take his car over to the vegetable wholesalers to see what he could pick up for tomorrow. Jack slipped the two items from the storeroom into brown paper bags from a pile Stan kept there, old ones that supplies came in, that he hoped to reuse some day, tight bugger, and popped them in the boot of Stan's Austin before he set off. It was pouring with rain so there was nobody out in the yard to watch him go.

He stopped a bit up the road from Mrs Feltbauer's house so he could have a think without her noticing him, before going in. He tried to picture Mr Feltbauer back in Austria, where he'd been a bank manager's deputy or whatever it was, before he arrived in Stockport and got demoted to a piece of rubbish like everybody else. Because Jack had only seen him in an old photograph it was hard to picture him as anything but brownish black and white, like what they called Randolph Turpin in the paper: the slayer in sepia.

The thought of it made him laugh out loud. If the bloke in the workshop had looked out at the right moment he would have imagined he was going round the bend. Mr Feltbauer, the slayer in sepia, with his curled-up moustache. But he was a hero to Mrs Feltbauer, that was the point. As far as Jack was concerned, Mrs Feltbauer herself was the hero. He pictured her in silhouette, an old woman on an Alp, pushing that piano. And what had become of it? Turned into a hidey-hole for funny money. If the money had been honestly come by, it would have been in a bank account, or at least under the mattress. Mrs Feltbauer didn't know of its existence or she wouldn't have sold the piano with it still inside, and that showed she wouldn't have approved of the way it had been got hold of. In fact she wouldn't have had to sell the piano at all, because she wouldn't have been short of a few bob. If he gave the money to her now it would break her heart. Every fiver in the bundle would be another nail in her husband's coffin. Kinder to throw the whole lot away.

Knock knock.

Once again it took a time for her to come. He waited in suspense. At last she opened the door. She looked a bit raggle-taggle today, an undone-up cardigan over a blouse, and a long stiffish black skirt almost down to her ankles, like something from the Victorian period. He realised she had taken trouble to dress up last time, because she'd been expecting them. She was wearing little leather slippers, one of which was coming slightly adrift between upper and lower. Be balm to the soul of Rose's dad, something to stitch up.

She looked up at him rather blindly through her spectacles. 'Yes?' she asked.

'It's me,' he said. 'You know. I fetched the piano.'

'Oh. Oh yes.' Her face went pink suddenly. 'It is all right, I hope. It needs to tune, as I said.'

'Oh, it's fine. No problem with the piano.'

'Ah, that's good.' She looked at him worriedly still, then suddenly smiled. 'I do not have another piano, if you need two.'

'No, that's all right. One's enough. Just the job.'

She nodded, then shrugged her shoulders.

'Can I step in a minute? I've got something I want to show you.' He let her see the paper bag he was carrying.

She led him back into the parlour and sat him down on the settee. She sat down on the armchair beside it. She rubbed her knees, which showed knobbily through her skirt. She looked nervous.

'It's a bit of a facer,' Jack said. 'You know what it's like nowadays. Bloke who had a meal at the café said to me, these times will go down as the golden age of spivs, drones, eels and butterflies. JP, he was. He said he gave somebody a month for pinching a meat pie. Thing is, I found this in the piano.' He pulled the cigarette case out of its paper bag.

Her face lit up at the sight of it, then darkened as she realised what it meant. She glanced over at the mantelpiece where it must have been before. He caught her quandary. She didn't know whether to be happy or sad, upset or relieved.

'How did it get in there?' she whispered. She suddenly seemed quite frightened.

'Guess,' he said.

'Pete? Oh.' Shocked, that was her reaction. No way on earth she could have coped with the news that her husband had been storing his ill-gotten gains in that piano as well, cheek by jowl, so to say. He felt a sudden sweat spring up on his chest and down his spine. That wad of money was all by its lonesome in the big wide world, an orphan looking for a good home.

'I think he's that type of boy. Can't keep his hands off other people's property.'

'Is he ill?'

'It's a kind of illness, if you look at it that way.'

'No, I mean an eel, like that man in the restaurant told you.'

'Oh, I see what you're driving at. I suppose he is. More an eel than a butterfly, any road, whichever way you cut the cake.'

'Would you like a cup of tea?'

'Better not, thanks all the same. I must do an errand and go back to the café.'

'It is very kind –'

'I was wondering if you intended to go to the police about it?'

'My husband's cigarette case is returned. I do not think there is anything to go to the police about.'

'All right then. I better be off.'

Back in Stan's car he was shaking with relief, as if he'd had a narrow squeak himself. The last thing he'd wanted was to have policemen crawling over that piano and, even worse, to be made to appear as a witness in court. He felt sorry for Peter for some reason. How could he have expected to get away with it? His idea must have been that if you could get your swag off the premises, you'd done the trick. The fact that once Mrs Feltbauer had noticed it was missing there would be no problem in tracking him down was probably too complicated a consideration for him to take on board.

But the main thing was that the remaining package seemed to belong in a dark world, dark as a piano with its lid down. Only he, Jack, knew it was there. That's the way he wanted it to stay.

You could see your face in the table-tops, if that's what you really wanted to do. Little flower in a little vase on each one, a few fronds of lavender or a sweet william, just picked out of the garden most probably, but nice in a pub, at least during the day: you wouldn't necessarily want them around late evening. Brass andirons winking. Place as a whole polished to such a shine it hummed.

The Swan was a small building in a bunch of old houses that looked as if they'd been shoved together any old how one side of the hill that led up to the market. They sometimes bought vegetables for the café from the stalls on a Friday. It was as cheap as the wholesalers often enough, occasionally cheaper, and gave more choice. Jack had stepped in the pub one day a few months ago for a pint before going the rounds, since like the other market pubs it had an all-day licence on Fridays. Just on spec. He'd tried most of the pubs in the vicinity, of which there were plenty, but never happened to go into this one before. And who should he see but Ruth.

It was the best part of two years since he'd last laid eyes on her. Everybody said Gerald had done a flit from the George, he'd cleared off so sudden. One minute there he was, next there he was gone. Ruth as well, Gerald being her uncle or cousin or godfather, whatever it was. People said he'd been spotted in Ireland, had fled to relations in Dorset, any amount of different theories. Then one day Jack had just happened to say something about wondering

103

about Gerald's whereabouts, and the bloke he was talking to looked at him as if he was mental, and straight away set about broadcasting it to the whole pub: 'Jack here thinks Gerald did a flit.' It turned out Gerald had simply got himself the tenancy of another pub in Stockport, in a more central location. That had happened once or twice in the war, an idea or a story goes the rounds of you and your mates, and then you go back to it at a later date, and as far as they're concerned it had never happened, leaving you stuck out in the cold. They had a way of saying 'You what?' sometimes that would make you believe black was white.

Ruth was helping Gerald out a bit behind the bar as before. She had switched too. Just as well. Jack and her had gone back to her room on a few occasions and then suddenly they didn't any more. At the back of his mind he must have been worried about the situation getting out of hand, Mrs McMahon waking herself up with the noise of her own snores and coming in on them, Rose finding out, calamity ensuing; must have been in Ruth's mind too. Anyway they'd talked together a few evenings without anything coming of it, sort of leading up to going back to her place and then not quite getting round to going there, then the next few times he came in they chatted together more casually for a shorter time, and before you knew, it was as if they'd agreed it had never happened in the first place. And all the time he knew she knew, and she knew he knew she knew, and it all got a bit edgy. So when she flitted he'd breathed a sigh of relief.

When he bumped into her again in the Swan all that difficulty had blown over. They were just old acquaintances. You could notch it up on a scale, two years being exactly long enough to get going to bed with someone out of both of your systems. They talked about this and that with no pressure behind it. He told her about how the café was getting on, she gave him news of Gerald's latest antics. Like uncle like niece he could have said, but it wouldn't have been true. She wasn't a good-time girl, whatever kind of times she had. She just took life as it came along. He didn't become a regular, the Swan was a bit too far to nip out to in the evening, just dropped in when passing.

He went there today, after he'd been to the wholesalers, trays of produce piled up on the back seat of Stan's Austin. He hopped out and ran across the pavement through the rain. The pub felt a bit damp inside, the same air as out in the weather only with the rain removed. Not many customers as yet to warm the place up. Ruth was behind the bar on her own, as luck would have it. She had a thick woollen jacket on. From his side of the bar he could smell the wool, plus that Ruth odour inside it.

He'd bought some brown paper and string, and done the money up in a proper parcel which he placed on the counter while he had a drink. Ruth told him some yarn about her doctor being found dead. He'd left his practice a few months ago and gone off as a cruise doctor. Had seemed perfectly all right, so the story went, went to some shipboard do wearing a false nose, happy as a skylark, then a few hours later they found him slumped in a deckchair with a hypodermic syringe dangling from his arm. 'Goes to show,' Ruth said.

'It does that,' he said. 'Ruth, you still live in that place of yours at Mrs McMahon's?'

Her face straight off went brilliant red as though somebody had slapped paint over it. That was another time, another place, another pair of people having a spot of how's your father.

'What's it to you?' she said, not very graciously.

'Just wondered if you could stow this there for the time being.' He slid the parcel across the bar towards her. 'I want it to be out of the way for a while. Not got room for it at home.'

If you believe that you'll believe anything. He hadn't liked to look her in the face while he said it. She fiddled at the string while she thought. Funny thing was he knew for

105

certain she'd never open it when his back was turned. In her own way she was honest as the day is long, one of those cross my heart and die types. Which is more than I can say for me, he thought to himself. But he didn't exactly believe it. This all wasn't a lie, it was just separate business, that was the name for it. He found himself in a position where he'd got hold of something that he couldn't give back, for Mrs Feltbauer's own sake. She would feel she was being widowed all over again if she discovered her husband had been up to something.

But at the same time it didn't exactly belong to Jack, either. Rose wouldn't understand how he'd come by it, any more than Mrs Feltbauer would have understood how *her* husband had. It was money that needed a new home.

'I hope it's not for too long. I don't like being responsible for other people's things.'

'No. It's just for a day or two, till I've made some arrangements. Buy you a dri-ink,' he said teasingly.

'All right then,' she said with a bit of a pout. Her bottom lip went readily to that position, she was a girl who'd grown used to giving in.

'Talk about cats and dogs,' the nurse said.

'Oh, I'm sorry.'

'It's not your fault.'

It felt as if it was, all these people getting wet on behalf of Donald. Dad's word for it was peeing down. Mind you, given he could drench himself from head to toe inside the shelter of his own home he was a fine one to complain. He'd bought Donald a quarter of japs. Rose had stood by the bed holding her breath in hopes that Donald would eat them. He'd hardly touched his lunch. He had put his hand in the bag, and she watched as if it was a bag of jewels. They were pretty sweets in any case, yellow, red, orange, brown, white, simple bold colours. Then he started gobbling away, and ate the lot. She'd shuddered with relief.

You're not about to die if you've just polished off a bag of sweets, surely.

'Can I get you a cup of tea?' she asked the nurse, who was plump and jolly to the point of hugeness, with a moustache and those bosoms that seem to be part of the uniform.

'No, I'll go up and see the little tinker, if that's all right.'

Rose showed her upstairs.

'What have we been up to, then?' she asked Donald.

'Nothing,' Donald said.

'Ooh, that isn't what your mum's been telling me, is it, Mum?'

'No,' Rose said half-heartedly. The last thing she wanted to do was start blaming him for things he hadn't even done.

The nurse whipped up his sleeve. 'Just a pin-prick,' she said. 'Mum, take his other hand. Now, Donald, my love, you just look at your mum. What I want you to do is count. Count to twenty. One, two, like that.'

He began to count. He was looking in Rose's eyes unblinkingly, as if trying to hypnotise her. His eyes were huge and wobbly when seen from this close. His pale face tapered down below them, from this angle almost coming to a point. He was awfully thin. Now she thought about it, he was so little he hardly made a bump in the bedclothes. Had he always been like that? She hadn't stood him on a weighing machine since she didn't know when, he could have lost pounds. He could have been ailing for weeks. What kind of mother was she not to know? What chance did Donald have if the person who was supposed to take care of him wasn't taking care of him?

'All done,' the nurse said. The phial on the end of the hypodermic was black with Donald's blood. Donald gasped softly when he saw it.

'It didn't hurt, did it, Donald?' Rose asked.

'Course it didn't hurt,' the nurse said.

Donald tried to smile but it made his mouth shake.

107

Rose pulled his bedclothes up to his chin and gave him a kiss. 'I'll come up and sort you out in two ticks,' she told him. What that meant she couldn't have said. It was as if he was a drawer that needed tidying up, but in actual fact he looked as neat as pie, lying there in his bed. His big eyes when his blood was being taken reminded her of how he'd looked once upon a time a year or two back, when he'd had a horrible dream he couldn't wake up from.

That's what she meant: tidy away the fright in his eyes, the trembling of his mouth. She felt her own eyes go suddenly wet and had to blink them a couple of times.

'How you can read that blessed book of yours, with Donald lying upstairs.'

Dad looked up at her. When his mouth was closed his moustache covered his lips. You almost thought its two halves would draw apart to let him speak, like the curtains at the panto. They didn't and he didn't. He looked back at his book. Then without looking up again he said: 'I thought I'd get Donald a little wireless set.'

'Oh. Did you?'

'So he could have something to listen to, while he's stuck in bed.'

'We could take this one in, during the day anyway.'

He looked up now he'd got the main part of what he had to say over with. 'It would be a mither, day in day out. And you like to listen to it during the day, in any case.'

'Cost a bit of money.'

He shrugged. 'The boy's got to have something.'

She almost cried, not at him being so kind in itself, but at the thought of Donald being serious enough to make him as kind as that. And meanwhile Jack hadn't even bothered to come home. There was no reason why he shouldn't be back by half past six or so, but day after day he arrived at more like seven, having stopped off at the pub for a drink first. As luck would have it, today he chose to be even later than usual, since he didn't turn up till getting on for eight.

He would come bursting in with a kind of snarling cheerfulness, daring you to say anything to him that contradicted it, all smile and swagger. Sometimes it would have the desired effect on her for a different reason than he thought. She would soften because his bravado seemed so schoolboyish. Not today, though.

'Here I am,' he said. He wasn't a big man but when he was in this state he seemed to fill up half the room, hopping about like a bug on a rug. 'What's for tea?'

She said nothing. Dad got out of his chair, muttered something, and left the room. She didn't look at Jack.

'Would you believe it,' he said, 'it's still pouring down out there.' He shook himself like a dog does to get the wet off.

'What a day,' he went on, changing tack a little as he began to realise she wasn't having any of his nonsense. The funny thing was, when you feel very far away from someone you can suddenly get a glimpse into his mind, more easily than when you are dancing along hand in hand. She could see Jack trying to decide whether to make out he'd had a hard day and had only this moment got out of work, or come a bit closer to the fact of the matter by saying he'd had a hard day and so had needed more beer than usual before he could manage to get himself home.

Save him the bother of deciding.

'Donald's seriously ill.'

You could watch it sink in. He was busy getting ready to say the next thing, and then he suddenly froze. He looked just as if cold water was trickling down his spine. With all that rainwater on him, maybe it was.

She was glad to wipe the silly grin off of his face. Then fear caught hold of her heart as she realised she'd done the same thing as she had before, when it had become clear that Donald was ill enough to justify having fetched the doctor in the first place, and she'd felt relieved. It was like wishing his illness on him. All right, that was back to front, he being ill already, but she'd still wished it. Jack might have used his smile to beat and bash her with, but in return, in revenge, she'd used that little sick son of theirs to bash him back.

Chapter Six

My hobby is digging holes. Sometimes I dig them in my garden. Sometimes I dig them in somewhere else. I dug one on the beach once, but it is dangerous. They can fall on you so you can't even breathe. I dig them with my friend. He is called Norman. Once we dug one that deep your head just came out the top. Another, we dug a den. We put a roof. We made it with sticks and a sack. And a blanket mum said we can borrow it. It had a seat. And it had a bottle of beer. Which was water in it but it tasted like beer from the beer that was in before. There was some dirt in it. Once we dug a boat. We made sides from the ground we dug out of the hole part. We had a pole. It was a washing-line pole to make the clothes hang higher. It was its mast. We had a flag on the top. Grandad gave us a plank to sit in it on. I had a broom to row it along with and Norman had a rake. The rake got stuck because of the points.

Donald's bed was like the sea. There were cold parts where the big fish were, the big cold cods and octopuses and sharks, and warm parts you could paddle in where only small fish swam. The eiderdown was the waves. The pillows were an island. Donald held on to them as you hold on to the steps of a swimming-pool, letting the sheets swish round his legs. Then he sat on the island with his feet in the white part of the water, the bit which went white and bubbly when it hit the shore, which was the folded-over sheets at the top of the blankets. Dad had brought him a table that stretched over the bed like one of those little docks you go down to your boat on. It had one long leg.

You could write on the table part or have your dinner. He was writing on it. His teacher, Mrs Cotton, said if he was well enough he could write a composition about his hobby. Sometimes his arm ached and he felt tired, but he didn't know whether that was because he had rheumatism in the blood or because he was writing a composition.

Mum brought him in his dinner. It was tomato soup and bread and butter. While he ate it, or drank it, he watched the sunlight coming in through his window. Sunlight was sad when you were in bed, except first thing in the morning when you could lie there and hear the milk bottles clinking and the children screaming on their way to school and all the noises you were not supposed to hear because you should be out in the middle of them instead of listening to them. But as the morning wore on the sunshine became sadder and sadder and made you feel as if you had been left behind by everybody and forgotten about. It wasn't your sunshine at all any more because you couldn't go out to play in it. It belonged to all the rest of them.

Then mum came in and took his plates away. She gave him a fairy cake and a cup of milk. She turned on his wireless. *Listen with Mother* was for the little children but you could listen to it when you were ill. People at home could listen to it. Grown-ups at home could listen to it, even old ones. Grandad did sometimes. But mum had to listen to it downstairs. Otherwise Donald would be listening *with*. That was for the young children to do, not for when you were nine. Down she went.

The music to *Listen with Mother* was beautiful and horrible at the same time. It wasn't like the sunshine, it was like stars in a black night coming out one by one. He loved to hear it, and it made him feel lonely enough to weep. When he listened to it he remembered how he'd been hung years and years ago and was long dead in his grave. He felt panicky at the thought that all the usual little children were listening to the programme, and even though he was old he would never be able to listen to it properly like them, because the programme he heard was a different one, one you listened to when you were in heaven. The one he was listening to was *like Listen with Mother*. Everything he did in his whole life was like itself only it wasn't itself. It was like living in a story.

Ernie had the feeling the whole world was going to pot. At the pond Alf was still in a state of gloom over his nephew Dougie getting himself in hot water for breaking and entering Neil and Garrods' furniture shop by accident. Alf kept saying, it's the point of no return. He obviously felt responsible, having brought Dougie up, more or less.

Going down Reddish Vale to watch ducks had got like listening to a sermon in church. The point of no return for young Dougie, Alf said over and over again, shaking his head with his three chins lagging behind then overtaking and flapping out beyond his jawline like a cockerel's wattle. Good six months in clink, his future down the plughole. Impossible to get a job. No choice but carry on with a life of crime. If he can get caught when he isn't committing a burglary, imagine how quickly he'll be nabbed when he is. And so the whole miserable business will go on going round and round. It didn't seem polite to Alf in his distress to be anything but miserable as sin to keep him company, so they sat in a row like so many wise monkeys, glaring at the pond.

Then home to the little fellow upstairs seriously ill with rheumatism in the blood and Rose about to go off to visit the mother of one of his classmates who copped it last week from inflammation of the brain. It made your head spin. Ernie tried to remember the little lad who died. He'd been around to the house apparently, in his time, a fat little chap, but Ernie couldn't picture him. Not being able to made him uneasy, as if the boy's death had gone to waste in some respect. You couldn't get whatever it was you got out of it, if you didn't remember the dead person in the first place. Morbid satisfaction, he supposed people would say. But not being able to recall the person who'd passed on left the situation untidy, somehow.

After Rose left, he went upstairs to see if he could cheer Donald up. Some hopes. The lad had been sitting up in bed writing a composition for school and somehow managed to prick himself in the arm with a sharpened pencil. Must have been trying to shuffle himself into a more comfortable position and a buttock gave way. There was a little pimple of blood on his inner forearm, with a pencil mark leading up to it. Donald looked quite weepy.

'Come on, lad,' Ernie said to him, 'there's worse happens at sea.'

What was upsetting the boy was that the point of the pencil had broken off. That was when Ernie said something daft, which only served to make matters worse. He said: 'That's all you need, my son, lead poisoning.'

He meant it as a joke, to get things in proportion, but try telling that to Donald. He spent some time explaining to him there was lead and there was lead. Funny thing, the way lead poisoning was a particular set of words, as if it was a recognised way of dying, like heart attack.

He went to the bathroom and got a flannel to wipe the wound. There was a bruise on the inside of Donald's elbow, where the nurse took blood. Probably the pencil had been the straw that broke the camel's back. You can take just so much at that age. He didn't like to think of him being a cry-baby, but the important thing was not to sit in judgement. He'd done enough of that in his time already. Certainly there was very little to Donald's injury. You could hardly have a more piddling little wound if you tried. He felt around as best he could but no trace of the pencil tip. Somewhere in the bedclothes, as like as not.

He put a plaster on the place, more to make Donald feel better about it than because it was needed. 'Tell you what,' he said, 'plasters have a sucking effect. It's a well-known fact. Anything in there, it'll be drawn to the surface.'

The boy looked at him, wanting to be convinced.

114

'Not that it's of any account, either way. Tell you what,' he said, leaning down towards him, 'if I had my own teeth I'd eat the rest of the blimmin pencil and be as right as rain tomorrow morning.'

That seemed to cheer Donald up a bit. 'I need it for my composition,' he said, which was at least practical.

Ernie had got to the part in *Guy Mannering* where Guy's daughter, Julia, is staying in the Lake District with a family friend, name of Mervyn. Guy writes Mervyn a letter. *Why will you still upbraid me with my melancholy, Mervyn?* Melancholy Mervyn, good name for old Alf. *Do you think, after the lapse of twenty-five years, I am still the same lively, unbroken Guy Mannering, who climbed Skiddaw with you, or shot grouse upon Crossfell?* No, am I buggery, because I got myself into a right old fix, same as most people do sooner or later.

The fix had happened when in India. A bloke called Brown joined Guy's regiment. Somebody put the idea in Guy's head that Brown had gone soft on Mrs Mannering. *He called my attention to what he led me to term coquetry between my wife and this young man.* Upshot, a duel of course, and Brown left for dead. Afterwards Guy finds out he had hold of the wrong end of the stick. Another soldier who wanted Brown's job had been stirring things up. Mrs M dies of shock, in the general sort of way women did in those times. *Now that you know my story,* Guy tells Mervyn, *you will no longer ask me the reason of my melancholy, but permit me to brood upon it as I may.*

A bit later Guy has to shoot off down to the Lake District, where his own daughter is getting involved with a mysterious suitor, much to Mervyn's consternation. And guess who it is? Guy doesn't find out at first, naturally, but we get to see, because we look at the young girl's letters to her pal Matilda. Brown, of course. Not dead after all. Turns out he had young Julia in his sights all along, not her mum.

Walter Scott was all right if there was no one in the room to watch you reading it, or listen to you, rather. You could get through quite a wodge as long as you were private enough to be able to let out a little moan now and then. That seemed to relieve the pressure and allow you to carry on. After a while, though, nothing could stop you developing trouble in your feet. Toes bunched together, first symptom. Then a sort of itchy sensation in the arches. Then fully-fledged St Vitus dance, your feet hopping about as if electrified. The only solution to which was to put them on the ground and walk on them. Make a cup of tea, might as well, at the same time, if he could avoid drenching himself from head to foot in the process.

He went into the kitchen and put the kettle on. He thought about that fix Guy Mannering got himself into in India, when he thought Brown was after his wife when he was really after his daughter.

He froze with shock as that situation sank in, his spoon exactly halfway between the caddy and the pot.

It was an aluminium teapot with a white knob on top and a flower grooved on the side. Standing beside it like a little woollen house was its green tea cosy. The cups were thin china and they had flowers on them too. There was a cake plate to match them, with four Banjo biscuits on it. Two were side by side on the plate, and the other two lay on top of them, like when you set kindling in the grate. Beyond the table, over by the window, was a television set.

'How do you like your tea?' Mrs Singleton asked.

'Oh. I don't take sugar, thank you,' Rose said.

'Would you like a biscuit?'

'I've not had one of these before. I've seen the advertisements for them. The biscuit with the thrilling filling, as they call it.' She did a little laugh and that movement of the head she sometimes made when she felt shy and coy, pushing it forwards and downwards as if she was going through a low doorway, the way a chicken does. She disliked herself for simpering, but at the same time it was so difficult to work out what you could talk about and what you couldn't to someone in Mrs Singleton's position.

'Victor liked them.'

'Oh, did he?' She took a bite. 'They *are* nice, aren't they?'

Mrs Singleton ran a hand through her hair distractedly. 'I suppose so,' she said.

She won't be able to taste them in her own right, Rose realised, she'll only be able to taste Victor tasting them. Everything she does these days will feel second-hand. If she watches the television set she'll be Victor watching the television set. If she . . .

Rose tried to picture other things that Mrs Singleton might do that Victor used to, but couldn't. She could only imagine Victor eating Banjo biscuits with their thrilling filling and watching the television.

Oh yes: suddenly she had a picture of Mrs Singleton, in the night-time silence of her house, walking from room to room in Victor's puddy tat outfit. There was a horrible half-frightening funniness about it, like you get from a clown. In the half-darkness Mrs Singleton's shadow would be fierce and huge, not a pussy cat at all.

'I think you have a lovely home here,' Rose said.

'Thank you.' Mrs Singleton poured the tea. Rose was conscious of the sound of the cups filling up, of her own breathing, of the ticking of the clock on the mantelpiece. Home, she thought, what on earth made me say home? What sort of a home is it when you're all by yourself?

Mrs Singleton replaced the cosy on the pot. 'How's *your* boy then?'

'Oh.' Her boy. My boy. How's *my* boy, as opposed to hers, hers being in his grave. It was one of those questions you had to answer exactly right, like the eleven-plus. If she talked about how ill he was, it would seem as if she was trying to compete with Victor being dead. If she talked about how well he was, she would sound smug. Even worse would be using Donald's illness for her own ends, as she'd done a couple of times already. There could only be one punishment for that, and she knew what it was. The only way to avoid all these dangers was to tell the truth.

It suddenly struck Rose that when you speak about anything to anybody almost every single word is a little bit of a lie, because it was so difficult and would take so long to say things exactly right.

'The nurse says he's on the right road. We were very worried about him at first.'

'I expect you were.'

There was a pause. Mrs Singleton took a drink of her tea. Rose remembered those moments when you are in school, and the teacher is sitting at her desk looking thoughtfully down at her register while she's waiting for you to own up.

'We were frightened it was the same thing Victor had,' she said at last in a tiny voice.

Mrs Singleton shut her eyes, as suddenly as if she'd been smacked, then opened them again and shook her head in a quick doglike way, as though to shake the smack off.

'Of course. You would have been.'

'Yes. We were.'

'But it wasn't, as it turned out.'

'No, it wasn't. It was rheumatism in the blood, that's what the doctor called it.'

'Rheumatism in the blood, eh?' Mrs Singleton said. She was trying to sound lively. Game, that was it, she was trying to sound game. 'What's that when it's at home?' she asked gamely. Her eyes weren't game. They didn't keep quite still. They reminded Rose of those maddening toys you get in Christmas stockings, where you have to steer a little silver ball through a maze into a hole by tilting the box it's in this way and that, and it never ever goes where you ask it to.

'I think it's the same as rheumatic fever, only a mild type.'

118

'Oh yes,' said Mrs Singleton, and nodded.

Rose reached over the table and patted her hand. 'I'm so sorry, Mrs Singleton,' she said.

This time Mrs Singleton's eyes held hers. After a moment she said, 'You must call me Vera.'

'And Rose,' Rose told her in almost a whisper.

'He was much older than me, Rose. Much older.'

For a moment the room seemed to swim. Rose opened her mouth to speak but Vera spoke first.

'Ray. Ray was.'

'Oh, Ray.'

'My husband.'

'Yes.'

'He was much older than me. I was a girl of twenty. He had hair going grey at the temples, very distinguished, I thought. It was in the war, of course, and he was in uniform. Swept me off my feet. He was a lieutenant. I never expected to attract the attention of somebody so important. In the air force. He never flew, of course.'

'My husband was in the air force. He didn't fly either.' She forbore to say he'd only risen to corporal. Vera would know anyway. Just looking at their respective houses would tell her. This house was a large semi-detached in Cedar Grove. If you could give houses a rank it would be a lieutenant too. Not that Rose envied it particularly. It was rather old-fashioned and gloomy for her taste. She would prefer one of the new ones they were building in Heaton Chapel, made of modern light brick that seemed designed to catch the sunshine.

'He was twice my age. A different generation. I'll tell you something about him, Rose.'

Vera leaned forward over the table and spoke so quietly she was almost miming the words: 'He never let me see his willy.'

Rose looked back towards her, too shocked to speak for a moment. Her eyes felt circular in her head. 'Didn't he?' she asked at last.

'Never once.'

Where did Victor come from then? Rose wanted to ask, but didn't dare. 'Good lord,' she said.

'Well, once, I suppose.' Vera's eyes were still fixed on Rose's face, unflinching now, almost as if she wanted to hypnotise her.

What a relief – once was enough, when all's said and done, was what Rose thought.

'And that was after he was dead.'

Oh no. 'Was it?'

At last Vera dropped her eyes. She rubbed a hand over her forehead, as if the memory had suddenly given her a headache.

'He had his attack as he was coming in from the bathroom. It was all a big kerfuffle. His pyjama trousers came adrift. He passed on with them round his ankles. That was the only time. The only time they were ever round his ankles.' She looked up again, but to Rose's relief didn't catch her eyes this time, just looked forlornly ahead.

'But, Vera,' Rose asked, 'how did you –'

'Every night of our married life he would march off to the bathroom with his pyjamas under his arm. Then when he had washed his face and cleaned his teeth he would march back in in his pyjamas. He always had his clothes stacked in a folded pile on his arms, the way a waiter carries a tray. As far as I was concerned, his willy was just something that lived under the bedclothes, like a rabbit in its rabbit hole.'

Suddenly Vera made a high-pitched sound, over and over again. Rose looked at her aghast. Because of the word rabbit the words of a poem she'd had to learn at school came into her head:

> I hear a sudden cry of pain
>   It is a rabbit in a snare.
> Now I hear the cry again
>   But I cannot tell from where.

This must be what happens when you have hysterics, Rose thought. Then she realised the noise was Vera laughing.

Rose found herself laughing too. The two of them sat on opposite sides of the table, not looking at each other, laughing on and on. Rose felt as if only her mouth was laughing, while her brain could sit still and carry on thinking. Maybe Vera felt the same. She certainly looked serious enough. What Rose thought was: I've been wanting to laugh about poor Victor dying, and now I've got the chance to laugh about his dead father's willy instead.

When she could speak, Vera said, 'I only knew what they looked like because I had Victor.'

They laughed again, more gently this time, sharing the laughter. 'You didn't miss much,' Rose told her. 'You know what, when the doctor came to see Donald, my dad was standing in the kitchen without his trousers on. It's funny how something happens or you talk about something, and it's nearly the same as something else that's happened.'

Suddenly Vera's face seemed to glaze over. Rose realised straight away what she was thinking: it's like poor Victor getting inflammation of the brain, and then Donald falling ill too. She could have bitten her tongue off.

'Oh well,' Vera said. She was still looking a bit stiff of face, but her eyes were intently on Rose again. Slowly she began to do something very strange. She seemed to hunch her shoulders together. Her dress was dark blue but not very much of a mourning one. It had a slightly scooped neck, nothing immodest, just enough to show off a neck-lace, though she wasn't wearing one. As she pulled her shoulders forwards she bent towards Rose over the table. Her stare suddenly seemed terrible, but it seemed equally terrible to leave her eyes. Nevertheless, Rose couldn't help herself. She felt her gaze move down Vera's face. Nose and cheeks. The cheeks slightly red, but that could have been the laughter. Mouth a little open, so you could see the edges of her top teeth resting on her lower lip. Neck, craned towards her. Shoulders. Shoulder bones. The ribs, tailing off into darkness, a gentle swelling just beginning on each side.

All the blokes in hats like before the war. Outdoor work, Ken said.

Perhaps sometimes you needed to see someone out in the fresh air to see what they looked like. Ken, any road. It struck Jack that he'd always kept his gaze averted from Ken ever since he'd invested the money Jack himself should have had to invest in the Station Café. Couldn't quite bring himself to catch his eye. You'd say it wasn't possible that you could avoid looking a bloke in the eyes over a period of near enough three years, but why not? Do it for one day, then multiply up. He only came into the café once or twice a week in any case.

One of those pencil-line moustaches like David Niven, but there the resemblance ended. Sagging cheeks even though he couldn't have been more than in his forties, useful as handles if his head needed wagging from side to side. Eyes bright and watery, though that might be due in part to the breeze from the Welsh hills blowing over Chester race-course. He had on a camel coat with big pointed lapels, a silk scarf in green-and-yellow check dangling down outside it, and a small trilby type of hat perched on the back of his head at an angle you'd have to be a younger, handsomer, man to get away with, and which on him just appeared as if it had been half blown off in the wind and was hanging on by the skin of its teeth. His head as a whole looked to have been patted into shape with the back of a spade. The odd thing was, looking a bit comic made him seem amused too, as if the joke was on him. Jack realised how jealous of him he'd been, and was glad he'd plucked up the courage to ask him for advice on setting up in business.

In the second race, one of the horses keeled over and died.

Jack assumed it had just tripped up, or maybe fainted. Boxing was his game, when all was said and done. The horses had been bobbling along over the far side of the track, with the doomed one, a horse called Diamond Light with a jockey in pink, in mid-field, running along with a gap fore and aft. Suddenly its front legs gave way and it was down.

'Goner,' Ken said.

'How'd you know?'

'You get to know.' He put a big puffy hand behind his little hat and pushed it forwards, almost over his forehead, as if he needed to keep his brains warm while he thought about it. 'Thing about horses, they don't have the margins to play with that humans have got. They're strong enough animals but they go beyond a certain point and it's curtains. You have a person, he can be ill as all buggeration and crawl back to life again. You don't get a horse doing that.'

'Oh. Tell you the truth my nipper's poorly at the moment. Gave us a bit of a fright.'

'That's what I'm getting at. You ever performed really well at a sport?'

'Did a bit of schoolboy boxing in my time.'

Ken gave him a quick glance with those uncooked-looking little eyes of his and lit a cigarette. 'You don't say. I wouldn't have you down as a pugilist.'

'Only as a kid. Got a bit of an injury in the war, duff leg. Put the kybosh on it.'

'I don't suppose you'd put me down as a tennis player neither, but that was my game. Schoolboy likewise. Just played on a court in the local park. Then I got myself signed up for a county tournament. I was drawn against a lad, rumoured to be the best player of his age in the country. Way out of my depth, I was. On the morning of the day in question I went on court, bounce in my step, on top of the world. You know when you have days like that?'

'I suppose I had them once upon a time.'

'There you go then. It was as if everything happened very slowly. He'd give the ball a fearful swipe, whack it like buggery, and it would come drifting over the net so I had all the time in the world to play it. I felt like a bloody ballerina, prancing about. Each time I could get my racket at just the right angle to make the return I wanted. I won the first set six three, somewhere on those lines. Then the first couple of games of the second set. And then I suddenly thought to myself, what am I doing here? And that was that. Back to normal. Didn't win another game. Same as that horse. He ran right out of himself. Only difference was, he couldn't get back.'

'But he was halfway down the field.'

'That's what I mean. Should have been last, got no form at all. Galloped his little socks off, poor old sod.'

Jack lit a cigarette of his own. It was true enough. They'd strapped Diamond Light to some sort of winch, and were hoisting him on to the back of a small lorry. Because of what Ken said about the horse running out of itself, he pictured it in mid-stride, giving birth in a manner of speaking, another ghostly horse galloping out of the front of it and away, until it vanishes into thin air and leaves the real horse with no option but popping its clogs.

'Tell you what,' Jack said, 'why don't you go for a combination?'

'I didn't think you followed form.'

'What's form got to do with it?'

'Giving advice on betting.'

'Form,' Jack said, and shook his head. He suddenly felt confident in a way he could hardly remember, in a way he hadn't been, perhaps, since before the war. The war knocked the confidence out of a lot of people. He recalled doing a soufflé at technical college, light as a feather, buoyed up by sheer will-power, the only one in the class that rose. That was one of those moments, like Ken and his tennis match. He'd known it was going to rise from the word go. There were occasions when for two pins you

124

could talk in a foreign language, just out of the air. He'd thought at the time he could build a whole career on that soufflé, more fool him, rise up with it. Instead, the war: dried eggs, dried milk, aluminium trays of toad-in-the-hole that you could never prevent going hard on top if it was going to be cooked through to the bottom. That was his war, and his post-war. And now he suddenly had the sense something new was going to start happening. 'I just remembered what we used to sing when I was doing my catering course,' he said. 'The tune was from some opera or other. It went: "All bones and jolly great lumps of fat, All bones and jolly great lumps of fat, Dee-dah dee duddly dud dee dah, Dee duddly dah dee duddly dah, Dee daah dah." ' He sang it, in an undertone so as not to attract the attention of the other punters. 'Something on those lines. Funny how it comes back to you, all of a sudden.'

'What I meant was, boxing being your line.'

'No trouble using form there, you've only got to pick one out of two. But when you have a bunch of them . . .' All he was talking about was trying to get a return from backing a couple of horses, rather than putting your money on just the one. Nothing clever about it, save that he was able to do the combined odds calculations in his head. He did them for some of the possibilities in the next race, one set of odds against another. Before he did each one he had the same feeling as with the soufflé, he could do it without even knowing how, just work it out fast enough that there's no time to think. He'd been good at maths, back in his school-days. He felt something give, as Ken decided to make room for him in his range of concerns. With Jack's senses sharp it was as definite as somebody shifting a bit of furniture. The sun was shining; he felt braced by the breeze. This was a lovely race-track: you could follow it all the way round. Suddenly Jack felt at home. No, not at home. What he felt was that he was at home away from home.

'Our tom-cat's swallowed a load of bricks,' Ken sang, or rather muttered in a singsong voice, 'Our tom-cat's doing the blinking shits.' His bright little eyes twizzled round at Jack, then flicked back towards the far side of the course, where the next race was assembling.

Mrs Onslow had a Riley with a bootful of champagne. There didn't seem to be a Mr Onslow, just a Michael instead, who poured the drinks and served little sand-wiches, the triangular sort with their crusts cut off. Smoked salmon and cucumber. When Michael offered the plate he kept his eyes fixed on the food, minion-fashion, so maybe he was a chauffeur-butler type, though he could have been a ground-under husband at a pinch. Ken had said, as they strolled over to the parking area, 'Now you'll see for yourself how some people have man-aged to make themselves a bit of money, even in this day and age.'

Jack could live without smoked salmon as it happened. It had a tendency to stick to the roof of his mouth. But he stuffed it in while he had the chance, champagne the same. It'll come in for a rainy day, he thought to himself, as if you could save it up like money in a bank account. Or in a piano. He remembered old Tomlinson in the tent in Libya, dreaming of a pork pie. Tommo had never liked pork pies, that had been the funny part about it. He didn't like anything about them. He didn't like the raised high-baked pastry that was traditionally used, crusty on the outside, a trifle sludgy within, the pinkish meat which gave him the heebie-jeebies, it being pork, and above all the gelatine, which reminded him of snot. He was very detailed in his dislike, went through it aspect by aspect. But in Libya he couldn't get the thought of pork pies out of his head.

He'd worked out the explanation: his constitution must require a certain minimum amount of them, say one a year, and before the war that need had always been satisfied, even without him choosing. Every so often a pork pie had come his way willy-nilly. Perhaps visiting an elderly relative, and she puts a quarter of one on your plate, along with a lettuce leaf, a slice of tomato and a pinch of mustard and cress, and you had to get it down so as not to hurt her feelings. Or you go into a café, and that's all they've got left. Without ever exactly choosing to, you end up eating sufficient so that you're in no danger of suffering from pork pie deficiency. Then you find yourself in the Second World War in Libya, and not a pork pie to be had for love nor money. And as time goes by, you develop the need. A bit like the cows licking the salt lick on that farm in Middleton. Jack asked the farmer how they could put up with it, and he said when you need salt it starts to taste good to you. Applies to humans as well, though Jack had never experienced it, even in the Sahara Desert.

Another funny thing about Tommo: he used to say, if I ever get any trouble with my teeth, the lot are coming out. First twinge, every last one of them. He always said it as if it was a matter of principle, as though everybody else was too lax on the subject, let their teeth get away with murder, and he was going to show his who was in charge. Yet in other respects he was the sort of bloke who wouldn't say boo to a goose.

One thing you had to say about a smoked salmon sandwich: it wasn't a pork pie. Also the fizziness of the champagne helped to unglue it from the roof of your mouth. Any rate, Jack stowed them down himself while he had the chance. He had the sense he was saving himself money, not that he'd ever have spent out on smoked salmon and champagne in the first place.

There were other people at the trough, of course, tweedy types in three-piece suits and waistcoats. Women with furs draped over their shoulders, fox the minimum. Some were probably mink. As luck would have it Rose had bought him a new jacket only the other day, so he didn't feel as if he stuck out like a sore thumb. Rush of blood to the head, he'd thought at the time. The men around him talked about horses and business. He kept quiet himself, which was another reason why he gobbled the provisions. Ken came and went. He was hobnobbing, as he called it.

After a while somebody came over and began chatting. He was a small bloke, weedy you could call him, with a very thin, skull-like face. Difficult to give him an age, because your first guess would be he'd died a year or two ago. The problem was compounded by the fact that his hat seemed too big. It had a ribbon round the bottom of the brim with a feather sticking out, but it seemed to rest sorely low on his forehead, giving him that shrunken look that the old and dead have. Also his jacket, yellowy-green flecked tweed, was a bit long in the sleeve. Down among the lower classes he would look to be wearing passed-ons, maybe from some relative who'd got himself properly kitted out just before unexpectedly kicking the bucket, but in this company the effect was to make him appear too fragile and high quality to fill out the fabric, as if the flesh he was made of had been charged for by the ounce.

'Harkness,' he said, offering his hand. 'Call me Bernard.'

Jack thought of a day when they were on the outskirts of Tripoli, and a certain lieutenant came into the tent on some pretext or other. 'Ah, Coughlin,' he'd said to Codge, 'seems silly to be formal when we're off-duty. What do you call yourself when you're at home, so to speak?'

'Veronica,' Codge had replied, quick as a flash. Survival instinct, he explained afterwards, being as the lieutenant posed no threat whatsoever to the opposite sex. The lieutenant coloured up, and looked for a moment as if he was going to make something of it, but then realised how impossible that would be, and sloped off.

Not that there was anything obviously pansyish about Bernard. But there was something insinuating about his manner. His hand felt cold and damp at the same time.

'Ken tells me you're very interested in gadgets.'

'Does he?' Jack asked, feeling suddenly at sea. Perhaps his first notion had been correct. 'Am I?'

'So Ken said.'

'Well. I suppose.'

'Kitchen.'

'Kitchen?'

'Kitchen gadgets.'

'Oh, them,' Jack said, relieved.

'He said you're always wanting to get the latest thing.'

'A Crypto-Rotapan, that's what I set my sights on. But you can't have everything you want in this life.'

Bernard put a finger up to his mouth and pursed his lips as if he was blowing on it. 'Oh, don't say that, whatever you do,' he said. 'The way I look at it, if you want something enough you make sure you get it.'

'I think our Heetaerator may have been a better buy, all ways round.'

'That's not the point. It's how it captures your imagination.'

Jack tried to imagine a Crypto-Rotapan capturing anyone's imagination. That wasn't how he looked at things. The question was, how useful something might be. It was the way things fitted in together that captured his imagination.

'Oh well.'

'I was wondering about bigger gadgets than your Crippo thingummyjig. Car engines, for instance.'

What it was, Ken explained on the way back, Bernard believed that someone in a business always ought to have sympathy with the product. Not Bernard himself: he wasn't a sympathetic type. Or at least, his sympathy was confined to business as business. That was his contribution.

Ken had a way of making life seem like a game. Jack hadn't understood that before. When he talked about things and people they became more humorous and less threatening than they were originally. Bernard didn't seem as skeletal and creepy, more like one of the lads. Ken called everybody lads.

What Bernard liked to do was go partners with people. Jack would have thought he'd have enough loot to invest just off his own bat. You'd be surprised, Ken told him, meaning not so many readies around as you might think, being that when it was on hand, it was put into something. Bernard was a man who'd started from rock bottom, in any case. 'Pulled himself up by his fingertips,' as he said. Jack thought of his fingertips, at least the one finger he'd had raised in front of his mouth like a candle, to shush on. It was thin and bony, but with a pad on the end like a frog's. Spatulate the word for it. Jack must have got that from somewhere, come across someone with those sort of fingers before, though he couldn't think where. Sometimes you'd imagine you must have had another life, the information you seemed to have picked up. 'Lucky he's not that heavy,' he'd said back, trying to be amusing, but Ken took it quite seriously: 'No, he's not. He likes to travel light, type of thing.'

They were driving through Sandiway, halfway home. It was a sunny evening, shadows from the tree-lined pavement lying across the road in stripes. Suddenly an old man stepped off of the kerb, right in front of them. Nothing Ken could do. There was a thump, and the old man flew suddenly in the air. He was wearing a mackintosh, despite the sunshine, which fluttered like a sail. 'Oh shit,' Ken said, but he didn't raise his voice. The old man travelled through the air very slowly, or seemed to, like a tatty bald-headed vulture looking for somewhere to land. Ken braked so hard Jack hit his head on the windscreen.

The old man was sitting in the road, hands in his lap. 'Just on me way to the pub,' he said, by way of explanation. Jack and Ken helped him to his feet. 'Not hurt your car, has it?'

Ken looked at the front of the car. 'Not that I can see.'

'Thank your stars you hit me and not a lamppost. You'd know all about it then.'

'I was run down by a double-decker bus, once upon a time,' Jack told the old man.

'Car'll do me,' the old man said.

'Have a fiver,' Ken said.

'What for?' the old man asked him, a bit dignified.

'You might need your coat cleaning.'

'Oh, in that case,' he said, stuffing it in his coat pocket like an old handkerchief.

'He could buy three coats for that,' Jack said, when the old man had limped off.

'Cheap at the price.'

Which was how it went for Ken, he realised. Life didn't seem to have to be taken so seriously, when he was around. What Ken was, was a man who could make things happen, when he set his mind to it. In this case, unhappen, as near as dammit was to swearing. Avoid the tragic view, was the trick of it.

He told Rose and dad about going with Ken to Chester races, though he had to keep his mouth shut about the fact they'd gone there to talk about how he could invest the money he'd found in Mrs Feltbauer's piano. Jack couldn't have discussed it with Stan around, that was the point. And Ken was his boss, having to keep him company on a day out was the most natural thing in the world. It's not lying, he thought to himself, it's just a matter of not going into all the details. Those details didn't belong here, back at home. They belonged somewhere else. He knew where. He had a word for it: Austria.

Rose was in high spirits but didn't approve of horse-racing. 'Jockeys are horrible little things,' she said. 'They should find an island to live on, where they can all be small together.'

Dad didn't have anything to say. He just looked into

space for most of the evening. Perhaps somebody had been strung up today. That always seemed to send him into a brown study. Jack didn't even know whether the old man was for or against. Possibly it was like a road accident. People liked to look, even though in principle they wished they hadn't happened.

What he, Jack, wanted was bed, so he could lie in the dark and think it all out. Even side by side with Rose, that seemed the one place where he could be on his own. It had been the same in the tent, with all the other blokes. If you waited until they were all asleep the place became yours. He'd get the feeling that his mind was swelling till it filled the whole tent. Not that he was getting any cleverer, some hope, but that he had room to think all his thoughts through. You could go through them one at a time instead of having them all heaped up on top of each other, packed tight inside your head.

The first thing to think of was tomorrow, meeting Bernard after work at Shaw Heath to look at possible premises for a garage. He knew nothing at all about car engines, that was a fact. You don't power an Austin 10 with a Crypto-Rotapan. For that matter he knew nothing about Crypto-Rotapans. All he knew about was kitchens. But he was in sympathy with gadgets, which was enough for Bernard. He pictured a car engine. He'd not seen many close to, never having owned a car himself, though of course people were always tinkering with broken-down jeeps in the war. Thing about an engine, you were never really looking at it. All you could see was the housing of the different parts of the mechanism, boxes inside boxes. Still, he thought, sympathy, that's what I feel. For me, an engine is soft and tender, something that needs caring for. Stroke it, like a cat.

He recalled the cat they'd had in the desert in the war, a stray that had taken to hanging about near their tent. Codge had adopted her. She wasn't a pretty cat. 'Big fat donkey of an animal,' Codge said she was. He called her

Mrs Cat. Mrs Cat liked eating their leftovers, and also cockroaches, which she crunched noisily like you might a raw carrot, while the cockroach would wave its legs and tendrils out of the side of her mouth even when most of its body had already been swallowed. One day they found Mrs Cat dead, just outside the entrance to their tent. Perhaps she'd eaten one cockroach too many. Could have been bitten by a snake, though they didn't find any bite marks. Tomlinson suggested that maybe she just died of death. You've got to die sometime, perhaps this was her moment. There doesn't always have to be a reason, he said, which seemed shaky ground, but he unexpectedly got on to his high horse, like he did sometimes on the subject of teeth. Whatever the cause, Mrs Cat had died with her eyes open. Codge tried to shut them, but each time he did they sprang open again.

Jack lay with his own eyes open, remembering the sand pouring on to Mrs Cat's open eyes as they buried her. It made his own feel grainy. Perhaps that was just fatigue. That could have been why he was remembering Mrs Cat in the first place, like when you dream about your alarm clock and then it rings. He had other more important things to think about, such as the matter of investing the sum of one thousand eight hundred pounds, the most money, by a margin of almost one thousand seven hundred pounds, that he'd ever laid hands on in his whole life. You could get the cold sweats thinking about that lot going down the plughole. Bernard wasn't the man he'd ever have pictured himself dancing hand in hand with in any case, particularly with the sort of hands Bernard had got. On the other hand, Ken seemed to know what was what, and Bernard was Ken's suggestion. Perhaps the best way to look at the whole business was easy come easy go.

Suddenly Jack was grabbed. It was so swift and unexpected that he forgot where he was for a moment, thought one of the men in the tent had turned funny, or maybe that lieutenant. He gasped with shock.

'I think I've caught myself a little rabbit,' Rose whispered.

Chapter Seven

She burst into tears with such force and speed a drop hit him on the cheek. What a waste, Ernie thought, a beautiful young girl in distress, me all alone with her in the library, chance of a lifetime; except in my case the lifetime is the best part over. Knock off half a century and it would be the moment to make my move.

It was beneath him, wanting to take advantage like that, which was exactly what he wanted to do, do something beneath him. That's where all the treasure lay buried, beneath. It takes you a lifetime to learn the things you needed to have known when you were twenty. Him, any rate.

He'd been talking to her about the manure on his vegetable patch for want of a better subject, telling about having to get it dug in pronto because it began sprouting a weed called fat hen soon as his back was turned. Then all of a sudden: splash.

He wiped it off with his finger. He would have licked the finger if he'd dared, caught the taste of salt. The thought made him look at her ear, peeping out from underneath her hair. That girl had ears the way other people had private parts, so delicate and trembly in shape they could have you crying out loud if you didn't watch it. She had small earrings on, golden with a tiny dangling lozenge of blue enamel. He felt his forehead go hot.

'What's got you down, my duck?' he heard himself saying. Duck, that's where I've arrived, grandad talk. No darling, no true love, for me.

She opened her handbag, head bowed, and took a hanky out. She had long fingernails, which meant she had to hold everything with the inside of her hands, so to say, so that her fingers made fluttery movements when they lined up to grasp whatever it might be, humble snot rag in the present case, as if they were lapping round it like the tide does when it's coming in.

She bunched it in her palm and pressed it just below her nose. Her eyes were red. Even her nose had developed a bit of a shine. There was a small dot of light on its tip, from the library windows. He could tell straight away that what was on her mind for the moment was how her face had gone to pot. He felt for once in his life in touch with a woman's feelings. The message must have winged its way across the ether inside her tear, like the way a radio wave carries Charlie Chester and all the rest of them miles through the air until they land up in your wireless.

'Tell them to wait a mo,' she said. She got up and scuttled off, to the staff lav, no doubt.

Nobody came in, luckily. It was the quiet time of day, mid-afternoon. All over Stockport the old folk were dozing in their armchairs. More fool them, this was real life.

When she returned, her foundation was back on. He thought the best move was to pretend nothing had happened. 'My chickens wouldn't give you a thank you for it,' he said. He'd been explaining that fat hen was called fat hen because chickens were supposed to like tucking into it.

Sylvie said: 'We've been courting for two years now. Over. Everybody thinks we're going to get married. I feel such a fool.'

'Doesn't matter what people think. You need to do what you think best.'

'But it's not what I think best, is it? It's what Mr Lovey-Dovey Popham thinks is best. Now he knows what true love is. I'll tell you what true love is, so far as he's concerned. It isn't me, that's what it is. It's a girl who's a secretary where he works, called Shirley Cook. They sat next to each other on the bus when they went on the works outing to Southport. Her eyes, he said, were what made him fall in love with her. He said he didn't know it was possible to feel the feelings he felt.'

'If it was eyes he was after he should have taken a gander at yours,' Ernie said. It struck him as he said it that Sylvie's eyes at present were the colours of the Union Jack, blue irises, a touch of red still there from where she'd been crying, and of course white.

Sylvie wasn't in the mood to take a compliment. 'He pretended he was being noble and honest, telling me all this. "We've never lied to each other," he said. He talked as if breaking it off with me was something to be proud of. It's her eyes, her eyes, he kept saying. I thought to myself, her eyes, my Aunt Fanny. Her bosom more like.'

Ernie wanted to say, what's wrong with *your* bosom, I'd like to know, or words to that effect, but decided it would be too personal.

'He doesn't even know if she's willing to start seeing him. She keeps blowing hot and cold. She said she doesn't undertake this sort of thing lightly.'

'I know that type,' Ernie said. He tried to remember if he did know that type. Somewhere deep down he seemed to, sort of girl who goes into courtship the way other people might set about laying a garden path. Probably never met such a female in his life, but when you got to a certain age you had the feeling you'd come across near enough everybody in your time. Like when you get on a bus and there's not a person on board who seems like a stranger even though you don't in fact know any of them. After a time you get so you recognise *every*body. Which either meant that only a few different types had ever been manufactured to start with, or that all possible people were inside each one of us. 'Beginning to sound like a parson,' he said, then wished he could bite his tongue. It was what he'd been thinking that was like a parson, not what he'd said.

Water under the bridge. She had too much on her mind to take any notice of things he was saying.

'They're brown, apparently,' she said. 'And big.'

Wasted opportunity from one point of view. He could have launched in about her bosom and got away with it. Never mind. 'Yours are big too,' he said, which she could take either way.

'Oh well, Mr B,' she said, suddenly snapping herself out of it, 'and what can I do for you?'

'Brought this back,' he said, passing over *Guy Mannering*.

'Oh, one of your Walter Scotts. I don't know how you've got the patience, really I don't.'

'That's one of the best books it's ever been my privilege to read,' he said, and immediately wished he hadn't, sort of thing you say at Christmas after a glass of port, or when some bloke's retiring from work, far cry from more or less mentioning her bosom a bit ago.

'If you say so.'

'Tell you what,' he said, feeling the need to explain why he did say so, 'that book is about what happened to me. It's a prophecy. In part, any rate. Quite a small part, to tell the truth, but very sharp when it does.'

'Big but ugly.'

'I beg your pardon?'

'You can't fool me, Mr B. My eyes aren't anything to write home about. Not at the moment, anyhow. Comes of blarting. Makes your eyes bulge. Not the same thing at all as Miss Shirley Cook's lovely cowy eyes.' She suddenly looked at Ernie sideways on, or rather, it wasn't her, it was the Shirley Cook woman looking at Sylvie's fellow, fellow-as-was, giving him the old come-hither on the Southport charabanc. It was uncanny. The red had gone, the white glistened, and he could have sworn Sylvie's irises had changed from blue to brown. One thing you could say about Sylvie: she knew exactly what she was up against.

The business had been in Garland Road, Hazel Grove, on the side of the street that was always in shadow, Peach and Son, Plumbing. They say you always remember blue skies from when you were a lad, but those tended to be across the road. The sunshine would make you blink when you stepped over to it. The street was cobbled, of course, with horse manure trodden into the gaps between the sets, like old food between somebody's teeth. Fifty years ago there was a pong of horses hanging over every street, what people nowadays forget. Harold Peach *was* the son, his dad having retired years before Ernie even joined as an apprentice. The building was a detached house at the end of a terrace. They had a yard at the back, and a shed stuck on the side, where all the supplies were kept. The front room was an office, and the Peaches had the back parlour and kitchen and the upstairs to live in. The Peaches were Harold and Hilda, the Haitches as Ernie and his mate Albert used to call them, and their daughter Dorothy.

The bit of Walter Scott that happened to Ernie was when he'd been at Peach's some years, he would have been twenty or twenty-one. Albert was three or four years older, and considering setting up on his own at that stage. Harold had made it clear he could do with one of them leaving so he could take on a new apprentice in his place, to do the dogsbodying and to not cost so much in wages.

Harold's Hilda, Mrs Peach, was a looker, that was the whole point of what happened. Well-rounded in the way women were in those days. It wasn't just the clothes, they seemed to be made in a different fashion from top to bottom, big bosoms and hips, small waists, lazy curves from one part of them to the next. So different from men they could have been another type of animal altogether. He came across a word once that seemed to sum up the shape of women about the turn of the century: pulch-ritude. Their daughter Dorothy was more a boxy type of figure, seemed to have her mouth open a good deal, with hair a bit thin and straggly. She had sinus trouble, in other words a blocked-up nose. You could hear her breathing from a way away. Hilda probably thirty-seven or thereabouts, Dorothy eighteen.

One day after work Ernie went to the public house with Harold. This happened from time to time. Albert never joined them, being from a teetotal family. Harold had a few and became maudlin, which was his way. 'One of you's got to go, I hate to say it,' he said. 'Dun't add up otherwise.'

'I believe Albert's got plans, in any case.'

'Let's hope. Just need that slice, make all the difference. Since you've been fully time-served we've been one too many. This is a two men and a boy business. We take on a little apprentice, he can hump the cart, save your time, and Albert's.'

'There wouldn't be an Albert.'

'Save more time still.'

Harold didn't have nice eyes. Shiny enough, especially when in drink, but with a look about them like pieces of gristle. They went beyond shiny on that occasion, and filled with tears. It was while the potman was bringing them new pints.

'Whatever's the matter?' Ernie asked when he'd gone again.

'Nothing's the matter.' Harold's little wet eyes looked bleakly across the table, as if he was looking right through Ernie towards Siberia or somewhere.

'I can see there's something the matter. Either that or you need a couple of washers changing.'

'Bit of trouble in the back,' he said, by which he meant, back of the house, family in other words. 'My Hilda,' he added, to Ernie's surprise.

'What's she up to now?' he asked.

'It's what she's not up to,' Harold said, taking his eyes off of the faraway and giving him a very direct look, ending with one of those little nods which mean yes, I *am* talking about what you think I'm talking about. That was probably about as far as a married man would be prepared to go in those days, at least with a younger bloke, particularly one in his employ.

'Oh,' Ernie said. He looked at the suds crawling down the sides of his glass.

Harold gave out an odd little noise, a sob that had been changed to a cough at the final moment. He pulled his pipe from his pocket and began to light it. Nothing like having something to shove in your gob when you got to a sticky patch. When he spoke he had that sort of reduced voice you could blame on having taken a large inhale. 'I think there's maybe another fellow in the picture,' he said.

'Not Hilda,' said Ernie, truly meaning it, but when he thought later it seemed likely enough, lovely woman shoved into the back of a poky house, husband a nice enough sort but with those knobby eyes of his and absorption in the plumbing trade hardly going to set your heart racing, so how was she going to make the time pass? A little house-maid to help with running the place. The sound of Dorothy breathing on the far side of the room. It was little wonder if Hilda's attention turned elsewhere, given half a chance.

Not any of his business. Wouldn't his life, other people's lives, have turned out so differently if he'd remembered that!

Probably would have remained not his business if it hadn't been that a customer he was working for had a funny turn a day or two later. Ernie was installing a lavatory with overhead cistern, and telling the bloke about how the water closet had been invented by a Mr Crapper, when the man's legs seemed to melt away under him and he landed up on the floor. Ernie and the grown-up daughter helped him to bed and she sent off for the doctor. She asked Ernie if he'd mind coming back to finish the job another day, being that she didn't want the doctor to find him putting the systemic syphon one-pull flushing cistern on to its angle brackets, though she didn't say so in so many words. She did find time to question whether the rising and falling pipe work was at ninety degrees to the horizontal, however, which got his goat. Given the joints had ninety degrees built in, this would have meant that the horizontal piping was skew-whiff as well. Funny how you remember something like that over the years.

The long and short of it was he found himself walking back into the office in mid-afternoon. No one about. He sat at the desk in the corner of the room and looked at Harold's worksheets to see if there was anything he could be getting on with. Then he became aware of laughing, a certain particular kind of laughing, first a woman's, then a man's, then both, coming from the back of the house. The woman's laughter was sharp and high, fresh as a daisy. Just listening to it gave him a pang. Then there was a bit of a squeal, then a distinct smack, then the man's voice laughing again, then lowered voices, then the door opens and out comes Albert, cocky as you please, waistcoat undone, hands in his pockets, whistling away. Straight across the office and out to the front. Doesn't clock Ernie at all.

Perhaps if that woman hadn't said about the ninety degrees. Certainly if her dad hadn't been taken with a fit of the collywobbles. Who knows? Perhaps it would have happened whether or not. Walter Scott had written about it nearly a hundred years before.

Harold comes home in due course. Wants to go to the pub again. That's a sign he's not himself, twice in one week. Ernie obliges.

Harold at his wit's end, sure something is going on. His beer shakes in its glass. 'I want Hilda to be happy, that's the long and short of it.'

A cockle seller came the rounds, and Harold bought himself a portion, in a twist of waxed paper. There's nothing more forlorn than a sad man eating, like watching a pig nibble grass after its throat's been cut, which Ernie had seen once upon a time when visiting his uncle's farm in Northwich during his childhood.

'What I think,' Ernie said.

'And what might that be?' asked Harold, with the testiness that comes with grief. Misery doesn't bring out the best in people on the whole, as Ernie noticed on a number of occasions later in his life.

'You know Albert is thinking of starting up on his own?'

'So you've told me.'

'What I think is you should let him go.'

Harold stared at his beer while he took this in. His mouth was still chewing the latest cockle. After a while he slowly raised his head to look towards Ernie, but his eyes were focused inwards, where he was doing a calculation.

'What do you mean?' he asked in the end. What he was asking was, do you mean give him permission to go, or boot him out?

'Let him go,' Ernie repeated. There was a pause. Harold finally swallowed his cockle the way you swallow medicine, Adam's apple to the fore. 'Then maybe it'll all blow over,' Ernie added.

Albert was packing up his gear by the end of that week. He was so hang-dog he looked almost comical. 'I bin with Harold ten years, near enough,' he said. 'I can't get to the bottom of it.'

'I thought you were aiming to set up on your own in any case.'

'This year next year some time never. You have to have enough put by for supplies and tools. And a place to work from. I'm still living with me mam and dad. Tell you what, I wanted to ask you something.'

'What?'

He leaned towards Ernie and whispered, 'Harold's not said anything about me canoodling, has he?'

'Canoodling?' Ernie felt himself go red.

'I been a bit sweet on Dorothy. I think she was a bit sweet on me, to tell the truth. It was only a bit of fun.'

'*Dorothy?*' His head felt on fire now, so much so that even Albert, with all his worries, noticed it and laughed.

'Yes, Dor-oth-y. Haven't you ever seen a young girl and

143

wanted to try your luck? You're old enough and ugly enough, for goodness sake.' He made a grasping movement with his hand, and winked. Miming a canoodle. 'A bit of a spoon from time to time, keeps the wolf from the door. They're no better than us, you know, what if they do have a niminy-piminy way of going about the shop.'

'Who aren't?'

'Who do you think? Dorothy. And all the rest of them. That's who.'

Half a century went by before Ernie read what Guy Mannering had written to his friend Mervyn about what led up to his duel: *an acute friend of mine gave a more harmless, or at least a less offensive, construction to Brown's attentions, which he conceived to be meant for the daughter, though immediately addressed to propitiate the influence of her mother. This could have been no very flattering or pleasing enterprise on the part of an obscure and nameless young man; but I should not have been offended at this folly, as I was at the higher degree of presumption that I suspected.*

Offended, however, I was, and in a mortal degree.

Ernie's obscure and nameless young man, by name Albert, disappeared. So, as far as Guy Mannering was concerned, did his obscure and nameless young man, by name Brown, at least for the time being. Brown came back, but Albert never did. Ernie guessed he'd left the plumbing business or he'd have heard of him in the line of work. He didn't ask after him, and nobody mentioned his name. Perhaps he'd joined the army, gone to South Africa. Perhaps he was still in the service when the Great War came round, stringy old warrior by then, pushing forty, face brown and creased by the sunshine on the other side of the world from the shadowy half of Garland Road. Then died like everybody else down some mudhole in Flanders or Picardy, the last faint memory of canoodling with Dorothy in the back of Peach and Son snuffed out along with all the other things he'd done, or had done to him.

That's what came of telling on a mate. Not that that was the end of the story, by a long chalk.

I will sit quite still by the window and watch the chickens pecking in their run. Just for ten minutes. Peck peck peck. They must eat a dreadful amount of earth. They peck and peck and I will sit and sit.

Be a good girl, Rose told herself. Inspect the hens.

Mrs Dobson next door had told her a funny story about travelling with her brother-in-law in his car. They were going through the outskirts of Birmingham when he pulled up suddenly near two women who were chatting over their garden wall. He stepped out of his car and walked up to them. 'Would you two women stop gossiping and get on with your work,' he said, 'I'm a government inspector.' Then he got back in and drove off.

It was funny to think of the two biddies staring at the car as it whizzed away, and then trotting back into their houses to get on with their chores. He *was* a government inspector of some kind, to do with factories. They must have concluded there was such a thing as housewife inspectors.

What she, Rose, was for the time being, was an inspector of chickens. Get on with being chickens, she ordered them, don't waste time. She said it inside her head of course.

She inspected one hen in particular, only an ordinary one, with its big brown backside in the air and its tiny head pointing down at the ground. They were all ordinary ones, that was the thing about chickens. It was so busy pecking that it accidentally walked into another one, and they both flapped and scuttled sideways in fright, though it seemed silly to be frightened of something when you were as like each other as peas in a pod. Then they carried on pecking again.

Rose remembered Vera Singleton leaning forwards over the table with the front of her dress gaping open, like a dark tunnel. She thought of riding on the ghost train with

145

her sister when they were staying at Pontin's before the war, travelling down a long dark tunnel, things jumping out at them from either side, making them squeal.

Rose had looked sharply away, towards a bowl of apples on the sideboard, a small bowl, four apples, just for Vera, four apples quite a lot when there was only one you. She'd looked at those apples the same way as she was inspecting the chicken now, feeling her face go bright red. What a terrible idea to come into my head, she'd told herself, hoping the apples would calm her down, get everything back into proportion. Instead she thought of those puzzles Donald liked, where all you have is numbered dots speckling the page, so you join dot number one to dot number two and dot number two to number three, and slowly the shape of something, a dog or a rocket ship, becomes apparent. She'd joined the dots of Vera's eyes, her nose, her lips, her neck, the top of her dress, and finally two last shapes had started to appear, slowly becoming visible in the darkness of the dress.

Rose had turned back again. Vera was still sitting as she had been, the top of her dress still gaping. Rose could feel Vera's gaze fixed on her face while her own eyes followed the dark tunnel. Her heart pounded. It's the last thing in the whole world I'm interested in, that kind of nonsense, she thought, but she also thought, poor Vera, she's had so much to put up with, I must make allowances, I have to be gentle with her. She felt Vera's hand grasping her own on the table-top.

They both rose to their feet, still holding hands. The table was between them. Rose felt posed and awkward, as if on the stage. Vera's face was downcast again, not daring to catch her eye. Her dress had flattened itself against her body as she'd stood up. The fact that she'd been forward, the way she had been, and then become shy once more, made her seem oddly childlike, and Rose suddenly felt strong and confident. She stepped round the table and took Vera in her arms.

146

It had been a hug, the hug of new friends. A hug by one woman consoling another who had lost her son. It had been more than that too. Not very much more, but more. Other things had taken place, silly things. It wasn't worth giving them names. Not that the situation had gone out of control. In fact Rose stayed calm throughout. She had thought to herself, this is like rationing. We're all experts on that subject, nowadays. Let Vera go so far, have so much, and no more. She felt she could gauge exactly what was necessary to make Vera feel better without the two of them reaching some point of no return.

She didn't feel calm now, thinking back on it. While she sat watching the chicken she began to shake all over. She thought: I'm clutching at that chicken like a drowning woman clutching at a straw. She was no longer the person organising what was taking place but an onlooker, swept along by the excitement of the occasion, not knowing what was going to happen next. Not knowing how *much* was going to happen next.

Not that anything did. Not that anything could, anything that mattered. Two women together, they hardly had the wherewithal to do something final, drastic. Something and nothing, it had to be.

What *was* final and drastic was what had happened in bed that night, and the night after, and the night after that, all the nights since. She hadn't been able to keep her hands off Jack. It was as if Vera's story about her poor late husband's willy had given her the secret. She no longer had to worry about the way that part of him looked like uncooked sausages, or a length of bowel which had become exposed in some terrible road accident. When felt with your hands its outline became definite and understand-able. You didn't have to think of it as a threat, it just had a particular job to do. She knew men sometimes described it as a tool, and now she understood why. She didn't call it a tool, though, she called it her rabbit.

Perhaps also that foolish business that had taken place

between herself and Vera had helped, given her the chance of seeing all these shenanigans from the man's point of view.

Jack didn't know what had hit him. Once she tugged at him so fiercely he seemed to fold in the middle, in a way that reminded her of when you pulled down your umbrella. Another time she became so carried away with excitement she bit him, quite hard though not enough to do any harm, which made Jack cry out, and she had to scramble up the bed and put her hand over his mouth to prevent him waking Donald or disturbing dad, keeping her laughter bottled up inside herself as she did. She grasped him by the hair and pulled his head to places on her body where she wanted it to be. Talking of tools, a head could be a useful tool as well. A mouth could be a useful tool. What a useful head, she said in the depths of her lust, while Jack's head made remote feathery sounds from far down in the sheets where it had been put.

She sighed as she thought about all that had happened. It had been a week of madness, beginning with that peculiar half-embarrassing half-thrilling business with Vera – Banjos, the biscuit with the thrilling filling – and carrying on during those nights with Jack. I should be in an advertisement for Banjos, she thought, they've certainly cleared my complexion, and my eyes have never been brighter.

And all the time she'd been sitting here shivering with excitement at the memory of her silliness with Vera, shaking with hidden laughter at the thought of giving Jack that big big bite right on the end of his rabbit, all that time the chicken in the run had carried on being a boring brown chicken, peck peck peck.

But she wasn't the same old Rose. It was at that moment she understood something had happened to her, that a change was taking place inside her very body.

First, small rain fizzing in the air, like on television.

Whenever Donald watched Norman's television it always looked as if it was raining, even indoors. Then thin rain like the bristles on a hair brush. That rain is white. The next bigness of rain is normal rain. This one makes you wet. You can't say what it looks like because it just looks like rain. Only the other ones that are bigger or smaller than it look like things that aren't rain. The one up from the just rain one is like commas or tadpoles, drops with a tail. These ones splash on you but leave dry bits in between. The one on top of that is lines, and the biggest rain of all is called a storm. He wished it would do a storm. It wasn't even doing small rain. The sky through his bedroom window looked like when you've done a lot of drawing in pencil then rubbed it all out.

It was a composition again, but he hadn't written it down yet. Norman came yesterday and said Mrs Cotton said do one called A Rainy Day. She sent back the one about holes. She wrote on the bottom, *This is very good, Donald. I hope you don't dig all the way to Australia!*

Norman had been on the way to Cubs. He wasn't dressed in a Cub uniform but just in his ordinary Norman clothes. He had his bow tie on that he always had on. He was the only person in their class who wore a bow tie. All the other people who ever wore bow ties were grown-ups. Norman's head was square like a box. The only round part of it, except when he put his reading glasses on, was the smile he always had on his face. The only time Norman didn't smile was years and years ago when they were in Miss Matthews's class and he dropped her record of the wind. That time Norman had gone very white. Even that time Norman smiled but it wasn't a proper smile.

'Well, little fellow, not feeling too hot, are you?'

Dad. Donald kept his face pointing away from him. He tried to pull his tears back into his eyes but they wouldn't go. One went loose instead and trickled off down the side of his cheek on to the pillow.

'Bit achey, is it?'

Donald nodded.

'Shall I get you an aspirin? What does mum give you, half or a whole one?'

He shook his head. 'I have to do another composition. One about a rainy day.'

'That'll be right up your street,' dad said. 'You like doing compositions, don't you?'

'It rains all different kinds of rain. I don't know which rain to do.'

'Why don't you write a composition about all the lot of them?'

'How can I do that?'

'It's just a matter of sorting them out. You can sort rain out same as anything else. You make yourself a list, starting with drizzle at one end, and ending up with a bally great cloudburst at the other. That'll do the trick. It's just a matter of getting them in the right order.'

'But the composition said a *day*, a rainy *day*.'

'Well, write about a day when there's every sort of rain. Goes from bad to worse type of show. You don't live in Stockport for nothing.'

The place had gone to buggery, and Jack was in no position to put it back to rights again. It was as if a massacre had happened there some time in the past, guts everywhere, floor thick with sludge, horrible empty headlight sockets with grinning bumpers beneath and radiator grilles showing missing teeth. It brought back into Jack's mind the airstrip in Libya, the plane scorched black, pilot in his seat shrunk to about three foot tall, eyeballs fried to nothing, quite white teeth fixed in a big grin, must have been protected from the ravages of the heat by his lips while they lasted.

Only cars were dead in this repair shop, but they gave Jack a turn just the same.

'Money to be made here,' Bernard said.

'*I* can't do it,' Jack told him. 'I don't have time on my hands any more than you.'

'As long as you've enough time to do the books.'

'Do the books is one thing. Tidying this lot up's another. Black hole of Calcutta.'

'I wouldn't argue with black hole. Or even better, another one we learned at school, by name cleansing of the Augean stables. I can't remember if the g is hard or soft.'

'These stables are hard, I can say that for nowt.'

'The point being, the place is going for a song. We just pay somebody else to tidy it up. Do you know anybody?'

'Bloke called Eddie and a lad. But they'll pinch anything that's not nailed down.' He felt his chin tingle, like it does when you need a shave, at accusing them of stealing considering what *he*'d done. The fact that it had probably been for the best not to give the money back somehow made it seem worse rather than better, brought the whole business of excuses into it, compared with straightforward pinching of a cigarette case.

'All the better. It'll mean they'll leave this place clean as a new pin. Take away everything that can be moved, which will be exactly the outcome we're looking for.'

'Lot of pillars.' The garage had two rows of cast-iron pillars supporting the ceiling. They ran in parallel down the length of the building, positioned at intervals of ten feet or so.

'They're quite delicate considering this is basically a warehouse type of building, or was when it was built. You imagine, my son, putting a lick of paint on them. Blue up to those little ledge things, halfway up, then maybe yellow to encourage that bit of light up at the top.' Bernard pointed a spatulate finger up towards a dim skylight in the roof. 'Nothing like getting the place looking light and airy to make your employees work like blacks.'

'What I'm getting at is, driving the cars in and out. Manhandling the ones you can't drive. It'll be a pig, getting them in between without giving them a scrape.'

'The last lot must have done it.'

'The last lot went bust.'

'It's just a matter of how you look at it. What we've got is a series of workshop bays marked out by the pillars. It'll keep everything shipshape. Men at work with spanners on car number one, men at work with spanners on car number two, all the way along the line.'

'You're thinking a bit far ahead.'

'That's the only way *to* think.'

They ended up buying the business, which included a long lease on the premises. A bit of a chance, given the whole place had gone down the swanny. But that didn't perturb Bernard. Night in armour, thought Jack, if such a tortoise-looking bloke could ever be. Posters, leaflets, adverts in the local paper, Bernard had it all worked out. But just getting the lease for that price was a bargain, that was the point. Even Jack could see that.

They needed a name. 'Bunter's,' Jack said.

'Far be it from me,' Bernard told him, with a bit of a constipated expression on his face, 'one handle being as good as another, I suppose. But since you've got to use a pen name, so to speak, couldn't you use one that brings cars to mind?'

'I promised myself if ever I had a business, Bunter's would be the name over the door.'

'Oh. Fair do in that case.'

Jack wished there was something else beginning with B to go with it, cars, repairs, a word like that. Bernard was no help. Buzz up to Bunter's was his thought on the matter. Jack made the point that the word which buzz usually went with was off. He himself wondered about remove. Have the Fat Owl of the Remove remove your . . . but he couldn't think what. Best to leave it simple. Bunter's for all your Vehicle Repairs. He could be called Bunter himself, for all anyone knew. Jack Bunter.

Bernard said he could start a business account at the

bank under that name, no reason why not. You could call yourself what you liked, as long as there was no intent to defraud. But as far as Jack could see, calling yourself a false name *was* an intent to defraud. Bernard was the type to sail close to the wind. Jack contented himself by using a different bank from his other one, Martin's instead of Lloyds, and in a different part of town, a little shopping area in Shaw Heath itself, not far from the repair shop. It had a wooden sign outside with a grasshopper on the bank's badge for some reason, no more point to it than Billy Bunter for a garage. The sign creaked in a slight breeze. You could almost imagine Shaw Heath being a place on its own, separate from Stockport altogether. A dog had been tied to the grasshopper pole and was curled up on the pavement, snoozing in the sun.

In the bank he told them he wanted all correspondence sent to his business address. The young man behind the desk said they would still need his home address. He felt like saying, this is my home, out here in Shaw Heath, my home from home. He gave Bernard's address instead.

Ruth's landlady, Mrs McMahon, had gone out shopping. 'She takes at least two hours,' Ruth said, 'always gets back around four o'clock.' Four being an hour and ten minutes after the time she left the house, which had happened just as he arrived, stumping off down the road past him with a shopping basket in each hand, like a cross between Giles's grandma and the scales of justice. Luckily she looked right through him.

Subtracting wasn't Ruth's strong point. Having a strong point wasn't her strong point, for that matter. He didn't even know for sure whether she'd timed his visit on purpose. He'd gone in the Swan on his way home from work yesterday to ask her for his package back, now that he'd opened his Martin's bank account to put it in, plus had a business that needed paying for. She said she'd bring it to the pub next day but he told her he'd prefer not to have to go down dark streets with that on him. She blushed pink. She'd dyed her hair blonde, which brought out the blush, bit of a tarty look, quite short but coming out at the sides like little wings. It made her thin face look thinner, and maybe a bit older too, but more inviting for all that, as if she was saying, there's a bit of life in me after all. She was blushing because he was all but admitting the package was money, which made it an imposition for him to have given her the responsibility and risk in the first place. Blushing on his behalf, in other words. When he thought that, he had a pang that she wouldn't need to blush on her own consideration, being that she would never take advantage in the first place. You don't get to be pushing thirty, and working in your uncle's pub, and still living at Mrs McMahon's, by taking advantage. She had on cherry-red lipstick and when he'd got a couple of pints down him he told her she looked like a hot coal, red underneath and gold on top, but she'd been a barmaid long enough to take that with a pinch of salt. She'd suggested he came to her place round about three, so he told Stan some story about an offer he'd had from a supplier, and drove the Austin in from Cheadle.

When they had their affair a few years back, he used to tell himself: my wife's not interested in that side of life. He couldn't remember ever saying it to Ruth, it would have come out like a lie despite being the truth. He'd have sounded like every other bloke who's ever been to bed with a barmaid. Best to keep your trap shut on that topic.

And he certainly couldn't say it this time around. When he got into bed these days he took such a mauling he was hard put to it to walk to the bus stop the next day. Made him glad he already had a limp, saved suddenly acquiring one.

What had got into Rose, who could say? He'd tried to be understanding before, not that the matter had ever been mentioned. When he was sent home to convalesce towards the end of the war it had all been a bit of a disappointment.

She'd always been so loving in her letters and was gung-ho enough when he arrived, tucked up in blankets, but after his leg was finally out of plaster and usable again she'd looked at him more like something the cat had coughed up. You could sense a shudder, like when you swallow a spoonful of cod-liver oil. It was disheartening, no dispute about that, but he'd done his best to be fair. He'd probably changed, too. War was bound to have an effect. Hard to picture why a woman would go for a man in the physical sense in any case. There wasn't much to appeal when looked at from their point of view. Probably the best way for them to get themselves in a lather was not think about the bloke as such, but how desirable they were themselves, as women, how the whole set-up looked from the bloke's point of view, in other words, which was a bit of a long way round and made it hardly surprising when they didn't always hop off at the right stop. The alternative motive was just them wanting to be nice, which of course Rose usually was.

But now, suddenly, Rose couldn't keep her hands off him.

'Blimey,' Ruth said, 'you haven't been getting your rations this last year or two.' Which was wrong, as far as the last week or two were concerned, anyhow. More oats you have, more you want, seemed to be the secret of it. Even while he was at it with Ruth, the thought went through his head that maybe the same applied to Rose, perhaps she was spending on him what she had come by in another place. The idea went away as soon as it came. Rose wouldn't be Rose, getting up to that sort of nonsense. It only compounded the felony, putting his behaviour on to her shoulders.

1955

Chapter Eight

They had baked beans and sausages, fat soft ones that floated in the beans. Like turds, Murd said. Murd's name was Marston but at school they'd started calling him Turd because he talked about them so much, but then it changed to Murd because you couldn't shout out Turd without the teachers flapping their ears.

The trouble was, once Murd had said it, Donald could see the turdy look of those sausages bobbing in the pan of beans. He tried to change them to something else, water-logged logs in the sea, nearly sinking just the same way the sausages were nearly sinking in the beans. When he reviewed the fleet at Spithead with Uncle Len and his friend Alec, a big log had bumped into the side of the yacht. It was a whole tree-trunk but so wet that its knocking against the boat was soft. And turdy. Dad told about when he was in Tripoli in the war he went to a café and had a cup of tea and when he was drinking it he felt something bumping against his lip, and he looked into the cup and there was a dead cockroach floating there. In the tent they lived in in the desert there was a cat that ate cockroaches, but it died.

Akela doled out the grub just like in the cowboys, with a big ladle, one scoop on each plate. Norman was the bread butterer, or Echo-margariner, worst luck, spreading it on two sliced bread slices and bunging them on each plate as it was passed to him by Akela. Akela had said shall we make scout bread but everybody called out sliced. Because Norman had to do each one in a split second to keep up with Akela, the pieces of bread had a hill of marge one end and were empty the other. Donald spread one of his slices a bit more with the back of his spoon, not because he really wanted the Echo everywhere but to prevent having too much of it in one place and making himself sick with it. He couldn't spread the other one because it had slid into the beans and gone soggy.

They only had spoons, no knives and forks, so whatever you ate was like eating pudding. Akela said they'd forgotten them. 'Whoops, lads, guess what we forgot,' he said. When anything went a bit wrong Akela pushed out his bottom lip and curled it down, so it was one of those inside-out wet lips that Donald's little brother Peter did when he started to cry. When kiddies cried they looked as if they were putting it on even though they weren't. Then Akela went oooh, and screwed his finger into the side of his head. Harty said he was just pretending he forgot, because really they didn't want them to have knives and forks in case they started killing each other with them. He said people in prison had to just have spoons too.

Murd cut one of his sausages with the edge of his spoon and the cut-off bit shot off and landed on the ground. He just puffed out his cheeks, picked it up, wiped it on his sleeve, and ate it. Donald looked at his. You got two each. The one thing that made them not turds was they were too pale, pinky-grey. They looked a bit like seals. One of them had a black fleck near the end, where the seal's eye would be. Donald thought: if I can only get them to just stay sausages for a minute, I'll eat them.

He cut a curving slice off with his spoon and put it in his mouth. It was the bit with the eye in it. 'Lot of bread in them,' he said with his mouth full.

'You *what*?' Emb said, sarcastically. He had eyebrows like forked lightning which he could make go right down almost into his eyes.

'Bread in them.'

Emb did a pretend laugh, very high, like a girl laughing. He rested his plate on his knees and put his hands on his hips so he'd look as if he was laughing more. His ha's dried up almost straight away, but he carried on doing them silently, with his mouth doing a big laugh like people do when they've been shot.

'My dad's a cook,' Donald said. 'He says there's always some bread in them. Just depends, a lot or a little.'

'Great cook, makes sausages out of bread.'

'They put bread in them to pad out the meat.'

'What you think they make sausages out of, Embley?' Hart asked.

It was nearly dark, and a breeze blew past the camp-fire, making the flames bend over. The breeze smelled of water as though a little bit of the lake had been folded into it. Donald remembered his father the other Saturday, making bread in the kitchen at home, his powdery hands in their big yellow bowl, folding the dough into itself. Stupidly the suddenness of the picture nearly made him cry. Dad had lived in a tent, he told himself, lived in it for years and years in the war, not just for a couple of days in the Easter hols.

'Sausage,' Emb said. His eyes sneaked from one side to the other. 'Make them out of sausage.' You could tell he thought he'd got it wrong, and was trying to decide if he should take over being the idiot from Donald.

'Sausage!' Hart said. He started to laugh the exact same way that Emb had, except that he had a different face to do it on, bigger and handsomer, with his teeth white in the firelight.

'Meat pies out of meat, sausages out of sausage,' Emb said, in the sulky voice he used for answering questions in class.

Murd put his plate down, being it was empty in any case, and lay on the grass to laugh properly. After the first bit of sausage had flown on the grass he'd dropped the rest down the back of his throat like a sword swallower. As he lay he smacked his forehead with his hand. He had one of those uck-uck type of laughs.

'What? What?' Emb said, still not decided whether to be pleased to make people laugh, or hope he was right after all.

'You're thick as shit, Emb,' Murd said, sitting up again. 'There's a farmer farming this farm, right? In his first field he's got cows, for the milk. In his next he's got sheep for the wool. In the one after he's got sausages, for the sausages. What they look like, Emb? Great big turds on legs?'

'You make them out of pigs, stupid,' Hart told Emb.

'Quack said bread,' Emb said.

'Put bread *in* them, I said,' Donald told him.

Ballou and her friend came over from their tent. It was a new Ballou, not the one who'd been it when they were Cubs. She took a little dollop of beans with one sausage in it. Her friend just nibbled a piece of bread.

'What they come for?' Hart whispered. 'Ballous are supposed to do just Cubs.'

'She wants to shag a few Scouts,' Murd said.

'Rather do her friend,' Emb said, putting his tongue out and panting like a dog.

The friend wasn't in uniform. She had a skirt and blouse on, and a jumper, with her hair in a ponytail. She kept her eyes down, to not look at them all. She was about the same age as the Ballou, maybe seventeen. Then she suddenly looked up, right at Donald, and smiled over her bread. His heart thumped.

It smelled of grass in the tent. He liked the smell but not in bed. Hart's sleeping bag was right by his, and Murd's and Embley's the other side. Hart whispered: 'We got chucked out of Reddish Baths.'

'Did you? Who?' Donald asked.

'Murd and me.'

'What for?'

'Got caught. In the changing rooms.'

'What were you doing there?'

'In one of the cubicles. We were doing it. Having a go. Joe.'

There was silence, except for the sound of Emb and Murd whispering, then suddenly laughing, across the tent. Donald could see the camp-fire through the tent canvas. When he half-shut his eyes it looked as if the flames were burning the tent itself.

'Do *you* do it?' Hart asked.

Donald felt a shiver of fear run over him. It was like when a teacher asks you a question in class and you have to decide whether it's best to answer and maybe be wrong in front of everybody, or say you don't know.

'I saw you got a big one, when we stripped for PT,' Hart said. 'When you do it, something happens at the finish. Good happens. You know what it is what happens?'

'Yeh. Yes, I know,' Donald whispered.

'Give him the money, Mabel,' Hart said.

'What happened in the baths?'

'This swimming-pool bloke come in, one of the life-guards. He just opened the door and came in. He must have seen Murd and me go in the same cubicle.'

'You were doing it, when he came in?'

'What you think? Having a wank, is what we were doing.'

'You both?'

'Yeh. It's better together. You can talk about what you're thinking about while you're doing it. You got a sister?'

'No. I've just got a little brother.'

'I tell Murd about my sister. She's fifteen. When my mum and dad are out, we go into the bathroom and she lets me undo her bra, to practise. I tell Murd about her tits.'

Donald wondered what he said. They must be hard to talk about. They were hard to draw, even though he'd seen some too, his mum's when she was breast-feeding Peter, and some in photographs in a magazine that he'd found

163

some pages of. When he drew them they looked like guns.

'What did the swimming-pool man say?'

'He said get your clothes on and bugger off. Don't let me see you here again. What he said. He was a horrible bastard. I though he was going to belt us one. He's really tough-looking.'

'I know the one.' He did, too. Small, but with a big chest and a level face, like boxers have. Donald had a sudden picture of what had happened, as if he wasn't a boy or a grown-up himself, just an eye, like one of the cameras they have for television. One minute them in the cubicle talking about Hart's sister's tits, with their big dicks in their hands, the next all white arms and legs and bums as they tried to pull up their pants double-quick while the lifeguard stood looking at them with his arms folded and his face flat as a wall. He couldn't understand how come Hart could even talk about it. If it had happened to him the shame and horror of being caught would have been so bad he wouldn't have wanted to live any longer.

But he felt jealous, despite them being found out. He envied Hart having a sister who let him practise. It must be like having a real-life facts of life book. All he, Donald, had was a little brother who was still nearly a baby. What use was that? And Hart daring to ask Murd to come into the cubicle so they could do it together. Or Murd asking *him*. All the sex Donald had ever thought about was in a little cubicle deep inside his own head. He'd never even imagined about sex being something you could have with somebody else. The best thing he'd ever done was find a dog-end his dad had left in an ashtray, quite a long one, and go in the toilet with the box of matches from the stove, and smoke the rest of the cigarette while he was doing it. At the time his heart had bounced in his chest so much he thought it might fly out.

Ballou's friend got off the coach in Bolton, miles and miles before they reached Stockport. It was a relief. All day Donald had felt that smile she had given specially for him yesterday sucking at him like the suck you get when you put your foot over the plughole in the bath. Once when he was little his foot had got sucked so hard he couldn't move it at all and had to call for help. Grandad came rushing in. All he said was, 'Your feet must be flat, to get as good a seal as the one you've got there,' and then there'd been a horrible cacky noise like somebody being sick and his foot came loose.

She hadn't smiled again, not even been near him. When they walked round the lake she was up at the front with Akela and Ballou. But when she looked back her eyes always touched him, made him separate from the other boys. The lake was silvery. The funny thing about it was it was brighter than the sky, so sometimes Donald felt he was walking upside down, and went giddy. He told Embley about the people in Australia walking upside down, and Emb nearly believed him. He said, 'They wha-at?' that angry way you do when people are doing things and you don't understand why. 'Der, der,' Norman said and rolled his eyes up. Even here Norman managed to wear his bow tie. He'd told Akela a story about how his mum had put his neckerchief and woggle in the dustbin by mistake. He didn't go to Scouts very often and when he did he never had his neckerchief on. The funny thing about Norman was, when he was doing PT at school, and wasn't wearing his bow tie for once, he looked fat, as if it was his bow tie that kept everything in, like when someone does up a parcel and it suddenly becomes neat.

It began to rain in the afternoon. There was a bit of wind too. Akela said when you were in the hills the wind was all over the place because of the corners it had to go round. The rain got jumbled too. It fell sideways, even a bit up, so it went in your nose. They came to a little town by the lake, and Akela said they could go in a shop. Donald bought a bar of Kendal Mint Cake and some goofy teeth and afterwards they had fish and chips in a café.

It got dark while they were on the coach. Ballou and her friend sat on the back seat. Norman, Murd and Hart were on it too. Donald had got on the bus too late because of the queue in the café toilets, and was sitting on the seat but one from the back, with Embley. There was a lot of noise and talking at the back and Donald felt a bit left out, especially as Emb was so boring to talk to. He looked out the window at the darkness going past. His own electric head looked back at him, and Emb's kept wagging backwards and forwards into view, like Noddy's head on a spring which Donald read to Peter sometimes.

When the bus stopped in Ballou's friend's road in Bolton she went down the aisle without looking round at Donald. Having Emb sitting on the outside was no help. Emb got on most people's nerves, though Akela seemed to like him and called him the jumping bean. A girl of sixteen or seventeen going by is like the lifeguard going into Hart's and Murd's cubicle: it makes you suddenly smaller. Especially Emb, who only looked about ten anyway. The worst thing about being with somebody who looks young is it makes you look young as well, like catching a disease.

Akela helped Ballou's friend get her rucksack out of the flap thing at the side of the bus. Donald wiped the condensation off the window to see better. Akela patted her on the shoulder and got back on the bus. As she went past Donald's window she suddenly looked up. She began to smile and to give a little wave of her hand but had walked on before she was doing it properly. Perhaps she was doing her smile and wave for Ballou, but she started it when she saw Donald so maybe it was for him, and Ballou just had what was left over.

As the coach drove on towards Manchester in the night Donald could almost see the faint image of Ballou's friend beginning to smile and wave in his window, lying beyond the reflection of his own head peering at it. The throbbing of the bus engine made him sleepy as he looked, and he dozed off.

When he woke up again the bus light seemed to have become dimmer and he had a sudden panicky sense that things had changed. He turned towards Emb and nearly cried out with fright. Emb had grown much bigger, so his head was further up the back of the seat, and he now had a podgy froglike face.

Donald jumped off his seat, ready to dart over the changed Emb and run off up the aisle, but the very moment he did so he realised what had happened, and sank back on to the seat again. It wasn't Emb at all, it was Norman. Donald tried to look as if he was only now waking up, that his jump had been one of those you do in a dream, when you fly out of your sleep as if you've been given an electric shock. Now he could see it was Norman, Norman looked his usual self, not like a frog at all. He had his smile on his face to say hello with. It was funny how his smile and bow tie seemed to match.

'Where's Emb?'

'He's gone to the back, to have a French kiss with Ballou.'

Donald looked at him in amazement. '*Emb?*' he asked.

'She's doing it with anybody who wants. She lets you have a feel as well. She let me do it with her, but I got fed up with it. Murd did it. And Harty. I don't know why everybody makes such a fuss about it.'

Donald screwed his head round to look through the V that separated the two halves of the seat they were sitting on, and through the same V in the seat behind. Ballou was partly visible, with a boy kneeling on the seat beside her and kissing her. Donald could see part of his hand feeling her breast through her Guide blouse but it wasn't Emb, it was a boy named Derek Cousins who was in Norman's class at grammar school.

Donald turned back. Emb was standing in the aisle. His face was red.

'You're back quick,' Norman said.

'Near enough shagged her,' Emb said. He put his hands in the air and did a sort of jive.

167

'Are *you* going?' Norman asked Donald.

'You want to go, Quack,' Emb said. 'It's good. She lets you near enough –'

'Might do,' Donald said, 'might not.'

He turned back to the window. He could hardly breathe at the thought of French kissing and feeling Ballou. At the same time his legs felt like lead. He didn't want to stand up and walk to the back seat like Emb had, following in his footsteps, getting younger and more little with each step. Be in a queue. What would Ballou think? She wouldn't mind, he supposed, since she was letting them all do it. Suddenly he had an idea which made him blush. He could make out the blush even in his reflection in the breathy window. Perhaps Ballou let them do those things to her as a way of making fun of them all. To make them feel more little-boyish than they had before.

'Quack's getting ready for it,' Emb said, 'I saw him go puff.'

'Go *puff*?' Norman said. 'What's go *puff*, Emb, Emb, what's go *puff*?'

Emb did panting. 'You know,' he said. 'Puff puff. What you go.'

There was a sound of pushing and shoving from the back seat, somebody complaining. Perhaps Derek Cousins had tried to have more than his share, or Ballou was getting fed up with the whole thing. Emb scuttled off to see what was going on. Donald carried on looking out of the window. All at once who he wanted to see there was his brother Peter. He felt a second of panic as for a moment he couldn't remember what Peter looked like, except small. Then he pictured his little trousers, made of stuff a bit like towels are made of, sort of pimply material, and the way he walked, a bit swayey, like the toy cow he had with big feet that walked down a slope. Peter fell down a lot, like the cow, and when he did he would bawl his head off, and after he'd done that enough he would just stop and be quite happy again. Now Donald could suddenly see his bobbing curly head. He wanted to make the wheels of the coach turn faster, to get home.

Thing about working on an allotment, you can let your mind wander. Ernie thought about what that Mrs Lloyd said, according to the newspaper, when she was being tried for murdering the woman who lived next door to her, Mrs Aldridge. It had all started with Mrs Aldridge's son. Did something a decent person wouldn't. That would get on the neighbour's wick. A disagreeable personal habit. Could be a lot of things, Ernie thought to himself, but you have to remember he was no spring chicken, so probably rule out the usual rum ti tum. Ernie saw him in his mind's eye. Moon-faced. A proper Herbert.

Widdled in the back garden before going to bed.

Night after night, big fat shadow, noise of the grass being sprayed, sighs as he gives a final shake, perhaps lets out a little belch or fart, to leave no stone unturned. Even both together, Ernie'd heard it done.

Nothing worse than the way blokes give it that shake. It beat him why they did it, always had. When he turned his tap off, off it was, even at his age. All those years standing in line watching them wag it up and down before they shoot back their backsides and retract it into their trousers. One night in the pub, must have had a bit extra on that occasion, he said to the young beezer at the next stall, 'What's the trouble, washer gone? You want to get a stopcock installed.' It had been on his mind to say that over the years, the stopcock part being a joke familiar to plumbers. The bloke said nowt, just looked at him while giving it a couple of final shakes. Kept on looking as Ernie went off. Ernie glanced back as he was going out the door, and he was still standing up against the porcelain, buttoning his flies, his head screwed completely round like an owl's, looking.

Mrs Lloyd perhaps went out one summer's night to take the air before retiring to bed, and heard a splashing though

169

no rain fell. Same game the next night, to check. She'd soon get to the point when she couldn't let it alone, like jabbing your tongue on a wonky tooth. On hot nights kept her quarter light shut to prevent the sound, then at the appointed time put her ear to the window so as to not miss it. On cold winter evenings opened the back door to hear him piddle in the snow, maybe write his name.

The worst part of it was, he never left home. Just grew older and older. Like the speedo on Jack's car, clocks up to thirty, thirty-five, forty. Fifty. Fifty-five. His mum was eighty-seven when she copped it, for heaven's sake.

Mrs Lloyd sent Mrs Aldridge a poison-pen letter about him. You could picture the sort of thing she would have written in it. Big fat lummock that he is. Time he was taught some manners. Wants to get off his bottom and go out in the wide world. Tell him be a man, not a shirt button. Mrs A takes umbrage. Knows Mrs Lloyd must have written the letter, even though it's anonymous. She's the next-door neighbour. Who else could have heard those tinkles? Pressure builds.

Another thing that came out at the trial: Mrs Aldridge let the butcher leave Mrs Lloyd stale meat. How that came about was not so easy to understand. The butcher calls, Mrs L out, has left a note saying leave the meat next door, he goes next door and drops off iffy goods. But it was difficult to see how that would bring about a wall of silence lasting for two years.

Mrs A trots round with the chops, Mrs L has a smell of them, asks what are these doing when they're at home, Mrs A says what do you mean, they're *your* chops, Mrs L says you took them from him, you eat them, give them to that eerie son of yours. At least I got a son, what about you, whatever happened to that Mr Lloyd of yours, he must have cleared off pretty quick, rat leaving a sinking ship. How *dare* you bring my personal life into this, no wonder you took them chops in, wouldn't notice the whiff. What you mean wouldn't notice, you saying I smell?

In this life one thing can lead to another, that's the point. It's never a case of just chops.

The soil being soft Ernie could eschew Alf's dibbler. What he did instead was keep his right middle finger ramrod straight as if it wasn't a finger at all, just a tool, and push it in the ground at intervals of three inches. Only drawback was that little grains of soil forced themselves under his fingernail till he had a crescent moon of dirt on the rim, occupational hazard on an allotment. Always puzzled him why it showed green when the colour of dirt was brown. Probably never struck Alf even after all these years, him not having an enquiring mind. Ernie didn't use a row marker either but got the line straight by eye.

Once the row of holes was complete he dropped a beetroot seed into each one and closed them up. Then the next row. Then a row of broad beans. After that he had to straighten up for a while. Going erect gave him gyp, made him feel he was breaking in two. Halfway up he reached a point of rest where for two pins he could have remained, walking round the place at ninety degrees to the vertical like an angle bracket. Meanwhile Alf was showing his prowess by sitting on an old kitchen chair at the entrance to his tarpaper hut. A good amount of huff and puff but not much doing was the mark of his character. He preferred to sit on his chair worrying about the latest escapades of that nephew of his. Being the size he was these days didn't help matters, the main job of his clothes to stop him rolling all over the shop like a bag of marbles. That conk of his had gone a shade somewhere between maroon and blue, and shapely as a monkey's bum. As he bent down to do the next row, Ernie couldn't escape the sensation that he was being watched not by Alf's eyes, which were more or less buried beneath his cheeks, but by his nose instead.

Help, help! Mrs Aldridge cries out in her quavering old voice. Mrs Lloyd hears it. She's hanging out the washing. She starts to run on a reflex, then she thinks but it's that

171

old so-and-so, then speeds up once more. When push comes to shove you don't have a choice.

Up beside her own house, down beside Mrs A's. There Mrs A was, on her tufty lawn, prone. Mrs Lloyd runs up to the body. No movement. Kneels down. Puts her hands on the ribcage. Can make out big flaps of breasts but in for a penny in for a pound. Presses down.

Mrs Aldridge's eyes open as suddenly as a doll's do, when it's tilted.

Suddenly down came the rain. It made a slight fizzing sound as it hit the soil. Ernie straightened up again slowly, dusted off his knees, and went over towards Alf's hut. Alf had retreated within and was sat looking out at the weather. He shook his head as he saw Ernie approach so his face flapped and cracked like washing in the wind. What will become of us all, thought Ernie, first his nose shot and bolted, then his whole head followed suit, after which his body, to the extent of hardly being able to walk.

Alf pointed behind into the shed. By comparison with what had become of the rest of him his arm looked short and stubby. You can eat till the cows come home but one thing it won't do is make your arms any longer. Ernie went past him and pulled another chair out of the darkness. Funnily enough he still kept his dibbling finger straight while he carried it out. The chair wasn't anything to write home about, the seat lifting and half the back gone missing. Also, with Alf's bum drooping over the edges of his, there wasn't a lot of room to sit side by side towards the front of the hut. But Ernie installed it best he could and sat. The rain was making a dreadful racket drumming on the roof of the little shed.

It was almost like being at the pictures, the two of them seated there looking out the door. Boring film though, just rain beating down on a bunch of allotments. Men were sitting in the doorways of other little huts like so many guards at Buckingham Palace, save for their collarless shirts and open waistcoats.

172

'What you think?' Alf asked.

'What about?'

'Having took on Ted's allotment.'

'Oh, all right.'

'Never easy, filling dead men's shoes.'

He was talking as if Ernie was a novice, instead of having had a lifetime of gardening behind him.

'I'll make do.'

'Got a tip for you. Tie a stick to each end of a bit of string, that'll give you a line to work with when you're planting out rows.'

'I'm happy to trust this here,' Ernie said, pointing to his right eyeball. 'Stood me in good stead over the years.'

'Suit yourself. From where I'm standing the naked eye is never going to be as straight as a length of tight string.'

'Any news of Dougie?' Asking that was asking for trouble, but anything to stop Alf being Adam the gardener.

'Only bad,' said Alf with a sigh. 'He's got himself in prison in Argentina.'

'Oh. Least he's seeing the world.'

'I can't help but blame myself. I told him he needed a new start. After that spot of trouble he had in Leicester, when he stole a portable typewriter thinking it was a gramophone.'

'Funny mistake to make.'

'It was it being in a carrying case which fooled him. Got six months for it whether or not.'

Ernie suddenly cottoned to the point Alf was driving at. Another miscarriage of justice. Dougie was always getting done for crimes he didn't commit, or rather, committed by accident.

'I thought, him having done his National Service in the navy,' Alf continued, 'he'd take to the merchant service like a duck to water. It'd give him a new start. But not to be. A group of them were granted shore leave, one thing led to another and it all got out of hand. You can't stop young people wanting to enjoy themselves. That's where

173

those hula-hoop girls come from, don't they, that way on? The worst part of it is, his ship has sailed, so I don't know where that leaves him.'

'Argentina, that's where.'

Alf gave him a fishy look and fell silent, which was the idea. They watched the rain a bit more.

Mrs A. looks up, blank as a statue.

'You all right, Mrs A?' Mrs L asks, leaning over her, hands still on the old girl's bosoms.

No answer.

'You all right, Mrs A?' Higher and louder than before.

Still nothing. Mrs L gives another shove downwards. This time there's a thundering great caterwaul, nearly frightens her out of her wits. Then she realises it's Mrs A laughing.

Who's to judge? Maybe Mrs A genuinely had a bit of a turn and fell down in a faint on her back lawn. At eighty-seven you've got to expect to be unconscious some of the time. Then woke up and decided to take advantage. Or maybe the whole episode was a nasty trick, devised to make Mrs Lloyd feel foolish.

Either way, something snapped. That woman laughing her socks off on the lawn, while Mrs L had been applying artificial respiration in hopes to save her life, too much to bear after years of the son's nightly widdling, the stale meat, whatever else.

Recoils. Looks about her. Spade nearby. Hard to imagine the Aldridges as gardeners. Probably been stuck there for years, robin sits on the handle round Christmas-time. Mrs L grabs it, turns, and swings.

'Something wrong with that finger of yours?' Alf asked.

'No. Just –' Ernie was going to say about dibbling, but thought better of it. It suddenly struck home he couldn't bend it in any case. 'Tempus fugit.' It must have locked somehow.

'You never said a truer word. You'll find it a blimmin nuisance, stiff out like that.'

174

Bash bash bash. *And she carried on laughing.* Even when her silly face was flat. Even when there was blood every-where. That's why Mrs L didn't stop. She couldn't, till the laughing ceased.

Face like a piece of stewing steak. Some kind of laughter still gurgling out. Mrs A had one thing on her mind as she died and died and died: got to have the last laugh.

Mrs L can't lift the spade any more. Her shoulder and arm are worn out. Also there is the horrible sludgy sensation at the end of the spade as it strikes. Funny how you can feel things at the end of an implement, as though it's part and parcel of your arm.

Mrs L staggers off. There is just a low moaning but as she nears the house the laughter starts up again full volume. Horrible to think of it coming out of that wrecked face. She stumbles into Mrs A's kitchen, casts around for something to bring it all to an end with.

On the cooker there's a pan of boiling vegetables.

She picks it up and carries it out to the garden. There's the meat, here's the veg, splash, now we have stew. Mrs A shuddered like a salted slug and settled back again. Her face was dotted with diced carrots and potatoes. Her laughter stopped.

'That woman going to be hanged, Mrs Lloyd,' Ernie said to Alf.

'Oh yes, what about her?'

'Been reprieved. It was in the paper this morning. Now there's only Ruth Ellis left. She's due to go next week.'

The copse gave her the collywobbles. She said as much to Jack. He said, Ruthie, it's only three trees deep.

Only when he'd gone did she think of a reply: you can drown in three inches of water. She usually thought of a reply once people had gone. It was a saying of Uncle Gerald's – he was always telling people how easy it was to die. Unless you've got a very big nose, he said.

Jack said maybe the copse was what was left of the grove

part of Hazel Grove. Maybe the trees were hazel trees for all she knew. She didn't know what hazel trees were like. A tree was a tree as far as she was concerned. There was a little stream going through the middle. Some boys had tied a thick rope to one of the branches of a tree so they could swing out over the water. Only snag was, when they swung back they went straight into the trunk, which fetched them a horrible smack, dropping them off on to the bank like windfalls. They would get to their feet quite dazed, then show off all the more, to save face. The copse was all right when the little boys were there, a bit of company, though they were often enough cheeky. One of them even shouted give us a kiss, on one occasion. He must have been about eight.

This morning, though, when she took Gyp for his first walk of the day, there was nobody else about. Gyp was happy enough. He just sniffed around and wee-ed against the tree-trunks. He was a plucky enough dog, though not very big. Mainly a terrier in all probability, though, as she told Jack, he was a dog of no fixed abode. He would bark like billy-o at dogs much bigger than himself.

Suddenly, though, he froze in his tracks. His fur all stood on end. She froze too. She had the exact same feeling, of *her* fur all standing on end. The path turned right past a specially fat tree-trunk. She waited for whoever or whatever it was to come round the corner. Nobody did. When bad things were happening she always imagined telling about them afterwards. 'I didn't mind if it was just a murderer, I was frightened it was something *much* worse. Just because a murderer is a murderer, he may be quite nice the rest of the time.' Murderers might pass the time of day or go shopping. They couldn't be murderers non-stop.

She walked towards the corner, one step at a time, Gyp the same way, two paws at a time. Sometimes he would stop with one front paw raised. It would be more sensible to turn and run, but she was too frightened to do that, leaving the thing around the corner to come bubbling along after them.

She got to the corner and peered round the tree. Gyp was behind her by now.

Standing in the path, looking straight back at her, was a fox.

She'd not seen one before. She was surprised how large it was. Also, how red its fur. There'd been a boy at school with very red hair who everybody called Ginger Nut, and the fox was his shade near enough. Its eyes were the same colour.

'Not much you can say to a fox,' she imagined saying. It didn't seem frightened, but then, quick as a flash, it turned and went. 'It was just as if somebody'd switched it off.' She would forget that idea by the time she had the chance to tell it to someone.

Gyp ran barking along the path a few feet, then stopped in case the fox took it into its head to come back again.

She turned back, and Gyp followed as if he had a new lease of life. It was something to talk to Mrs McMahon about, at any rate.

Out into the daylight, along the footpath between the wire fences of people's gardens, then down the white cement road. A window cleaner was singing Que sera sera while washing the bedroom windows of one of the houses, what will be will be. It was a nice estate, some little ordinary houses, then a row of semi-bungalows like hers. She didn't know if semi-bungalow meant joined on to the house next door, which it was, or with two bedrooms upstairs, with dormer windows, which it had. She asked Jack if bungalow meant to do with being low, but he just laughed. He said it was a French word. He knew some French with training as a cook before he went into the car repair business. He didn't say what it meant, though. She guessed it was one of those words that nobody knew what it really meant.

What she liked about the bungalow was sunlight and plants. At Mrs McMahon's her plants had taken one look at their surroundings and withered up and died. She'd had a goldfish once that Jack won for her when they went to a fair, but it did the same. It had looked miserable from the moment she brought it back. Jack said don't be silly, what do you expect a goldfish to do, smile? What had worried her was the way it swam about opening and shutting its mouth. She kept imagining it was gasping for breath. Of course, that was silly being that it breathed water. Sometimes, as she sat by its bowl, she would open and shut her own mouth too, to see what it felt like. It swam more and more slowly until after a few weeks it just bobbed over and died. Although it was only a goldfish, she often felt sad about it dying, even years later, almost a kind of homesickness for times gone by.

When Jack had got the bungalow for her, he'd bought her Gyp at the same time. Be company for you, he'd said, at least until. Not much of a guard dog was her thought, but she was wrong about that, in one way. He'd bark at anything. The only snag was he wouldn't be much good at frightening somebody away, though willing enough. He was like a mad caterpillar, as Jack described him, but on an estate like hers just making a racket might be sufficient to do the trick.

She clicked her fingers and Gyp sailed into his wicker basket like a horse jumping a fence. 'Be good,' she told him, and he obediently curled up to go to sleep, but kept one eye open to watch her while she got ready to go out. It was Thursday, her day for seeing Mrs McMahon before going into the pub for lunchtime.

Mrs McMahon's smelled beddy, the whole house, including Mrs McMahon herself. When people spend a lot of their time in bed they seem to go off slightly, like food does when it's been around too long. She was always up when Ruth visited, but goodness knows how much time and effort it took her to get dressed and down the stairs. Ruth had told her to stay in bed and leave the key somewhere but she insisted. Perhaps it was good for her.

178

A nurse visited nearly every day, and Mrs McMahon's sister brought round most of her meals.

Ruth made them both a cup of tea. She told about the fox. 'It ran off as quick as anything,' she said.

'That's not the only fox you'll set eyes on today, I'll be bound,' Mrs McMahon told her. Mrs McMahon was funny to look at nowadays, both fat and thin at the same time. She had lots of bosom and suchlike but at the same time her shoulders poked bonily through her cardigan and her face was gaunt. Ruth coloured at what she'd said. Mrs McMahon gave her a cunning little look to make sure it had struck home, then started to talk about a friend of hers, Miss Bowker, who had just retired from having sold tickets at Reddish Baths since more or less the first war. 'I don't know how she put up with it,' Mrs McMahon said. 'That entrance hall has been green-tiled all my lifetime for a fact. It's just like working all those years in a public lavatory.' Because Miss Bowker was at home during the day nowadays she had started to see a hedgehog in her back garden.

'I thought they just came out at night-time,' Ruth said.

'I hope you're not saying Miss Bowker is seeing things,' Mrs McMahon said quite nastily. Saying something snide about Jack had put her in a bad temper.

'No, of course I'm not. I expect there are night-time ones and daily ones.'

'The one you've got yourself landed with is a night-time one, unless I'm much mistaken.'

'Jack is not a hedgehog, thank you very much,' Ruth said as sharply as possible, but it did no good.

'No, he certainly is not a hedgehog. For your sake, my girl, I only wish he was. Let me tell you something, I've seen the Jacks of this world come, and I've seen them go, and more often than not, they go.' Mrs McMahon nodded, very hot-eyed. Because she'd got herself so worked up her breath whistled in her throat when she finished speaking.

'He isn't going to go. He'll be moving in to stay.'

'And when will that be?'

'This summer. We're going to be wed the beginning of August.'

'I'll believe that when I see it.'

'We are.' Stupidly her eyes filled with tears. She always did that when people didn't believe what she said, and it made her mad because as a result they didn't believe her even more, and then getting mad made her crying worse. She felt like that poor dying goldfish in its bowl. 'We are,' she said again. She felt her lower lip poking out like a little girl's. 'He's just waiting for his divorce to come through.'

'Oh yes? And where's he living in the meantime?'

Stupid stupid stupid, she thought to herself on the bus to the pub. Stupid. She even whispered it out loud to herself. When she was tired of that she busied herself hating Mrs McMahon. Silly fat lump, she thought, I hope she dies soon. No, oh God, don't let her die soon, take no notice. But she's still a silly fat lump.

One two-three, one two-three. Old girls with their hand-bags dangling from their elbows, too fashed to leave them behind on their chairs. Trembly old fellows in blazers. Sometimes Jack felt like Armand and Michaela Dennis, driving their jeep into a clearing and coming upon some strange tribe, witch-doctors the lot of them, jitterbugging slowly around the place in hopes to make it rain. Waving stiff limbs about: Rain, blow you, rain!

And, by gum, it rained all right. The Cheadle drought was broken. First water to be seen since day before yesterday. In between the one two-threes you could hear a pitter-patter on the front windowpanes.

But they danced on, through the sad afternoon, tea dancing with Larry Mendoza's Musical Matinée, two fat men and one thin one, each in a frilly shirt and cummer-bund, one of the fats on violin, the thin on double bass, Larry on the piano. Mrs Feltbauer humping that thing over the Alps so that Larry could tickle the ivories from three o'clock onwards every Tuesday and Thursday afternoon. Stan had got what he wanted, wallpaper with flecks of glitter on it like you have on Christmas cards, only more discreet, artistically draped curtains where there weren't even any windows, parquet flooring on top of the rock asphalt in the dancing area, marble topped café tables and wrought-iron chairs in the cafeteria part. He hadn't even bothered to upgrade the menu. It was still meat and two veg for lunch, and the tea-dancing tea consisted of one slice of toast and relish (known to its chums as Marmite), two quarter-round sandwiches of tinned salmon or ham, two of cucumber, a scone with jam and confectioner's cream, an iced fancy, and a pot of tea. Set you back three and six, or your grandmother, whichever came cheapest.

The worst part of the afternoon chores was replenishing the teapots. That was a selling point, as Stan had explained, his ears quite red from excitement. Ken's suggestion, needless to say. As much tea as you can drink, and some of the poor so-and-sos made a serious attempt to put away their three and a tanner's worth. So Jack had to scuttle from table to table, feeling the pots for warmth, weighing them in his hand for content, and hoiking new ones out of the multipot as necessary.

By four fifteen the place was packed. The air smelled of talcum powder, lavender water, sweat. It made Jack feel sad to see people become happy so easily. Maybe he was just jealous because of his limp, which caused him to waltz even when there was no music playing. Anyway, not everybody was happy. One couple seated at a table were having a terrific row. She had been left stranded in Bournemouth. He hadn't behaved like a gentleman. He shook with rage at being accused. Jack leaned over to feel their pot. 'Thank you very much,' the old codger said, nice as pie. 'Thank you,' his wife said as Jack took it away. He could hear them start up again as soon as his back was turned.

As he skirted the dance floor there was a thump, a sudden buzz of voices, and then the music fizzled out. People seemed to be fusing together in the middle of the floor. He put the angry couple's pot on a nearby table and made his way over. As he pushed into the throng somebody said, 'Make room, he works here,' there was a murmur of agreement, and a path opened up in the crowd. Oh yes, he thought to himself, Me to the rescue, I'm official, I make the tea. Last time he'd approached a calamity he had been stepping along that plane wing in North Africa, only to find the pilot burned to a crisp in the cockpit, and shrunk to half-size. At least he wouldn't be seeing and smelling that again. Nor having to go through what had happened next.

A little circle in the middle of all the people, like you used to get in the school playground when a fight was going on. A woman was lying on the parquet, her arms flung up above her head. In her fifties, probably, her hair thinning a bit. She looked plump, almost puffy, very white. Her eyes weren't quite shut. It was queer standing by her with an audience looking on, people expecting him to know what to do. He had to stop himself prodding her with his foot, like you do a dead dog.

He knelt down and moved her face round to face his, squeezing her cheeks in doing so, so her mouth became a figure eight. Her eyes went fully shut. Again he wanted to do something wrong, to say, 'Give us a kiss, duck,' not out of malice, just to lighten the atmosphere. He tried to run through the possibilities in his mind. Artificial respiration. But she was breathing all right, almost snoring. Loosen her clothing. Asking for trouble. Cart her off somewhere quiet to recover. Too heavy.

Suddenly Joe appeared, as if he'd popped up through the flooring from his chair in the cellar by the boiler. He put his arm under her shoulder. 'Come on, love, uppity up,' he said. He looked up at everybody standing there. 'Where's hubby?' he asked. Why didn't I think of that?

Jack wondered. A weedy bloke stepped forward. Cowardly sod had been trying to merge into the background. 'Your missus has gone and danced herself to a stop,' Joe told him. The hubby grinned embarrassedly back, and there was a bit of a laugh from the rest of the crowd. Some of them began moving away. 'Give us a hand, get her up,' Joe said, and he and the hubby took a shoulder each and hoisted her to her feet.

She came to as soon as she was upright, but went floppy straight away. She'd realised it was best to stay fainted while collecting her wits. Both the blokes supporting her were littler than she was, which didn't help. But at that moment Larry and his merry men struck up a new tune, and people obediently began to fall into couples once more. Time to move. She had the choice: walk her legs across the dance floor, or slump to the ground in a threesome, so she walked her legs. The three of them staggered towards a table, Jack following.

They helped her into a chair, she looking porky and clumsy as she lowered her bum, not at her best. 'Didn't know where I was for a minute or two,' she said. You and me both, thought Jack.

Edwin Slack put a fag to his lips with an inside-out hand as mechanics do, took a pull, lowered it, shook his head. He had an oily nose which made his face look like a liquorice allsort. He looked out of the big double doors at the falling rain. 'Your oil's not circulating,' he told Jack, counting off on the fingers of his cupped hand, the fag still poking up from the middle like a plant in a plant pot, 'you've got a knock, loss of power, what you're looking at is the big fucking end. Cost a few bob.' He turned his hand over and rubbed the tip of his cigarette against the windowsill doodah of his little office, gently as a cat rubbing its head on your leg, shaping the end to a tiny red cone.

The office had been Bernard's idea. Jack had suggested a KarriKabin prefabricated one to save building from scratch, being that the business previous to Bunter's seemed not to have had a proper office at all, which was probably why it became a dead duck. Bernard meanwhile sent away to some gardening place and came trotting along with a catalogue of garden sheds. He was full of beans as he leafed through it with Jack.

'These have so much more charm than those other things,' he said. 'They're made of wood, not those horrible panels of enamelled metal, I don't know what they're called, caravan I call them, not made of *caravan*. You can even get little summer houses with verandahs.'

Jack persuaded him they didn't want a little summer house with a verandah. 'What you think we are?' he asked him, 'Bill and Ben the Flowerpot Men?' But they agreed on a large garden shed which cost half what the KarriKabin would have been. The catalogue was catering to the private citizen, as Bernard pointed out, people who needed to watch their wallet. It had little windows with sills, and came ready creosoted, but they'd nevertheless had it erected inside the building, in the first bay on the left, where there was plenty of room and it would last indefinitely.

Time had gone by, though. Now there was a trade calendar on its wall, showing a platinum blonde wearing an aertex sort of blouse that was gathered up under her bosom so you could see her belly-button, which had been deepened with a fingerprint, and Edwin always left his papers beaked up on the little desk, held in place with spanners.

'What I mean, cost Tom, Dick and Harry a few bob,' Edwin said.

'Cost Jack, as far as that goes,' Jack told him.

'Please yourself.' Edwin obviously thought he was potty to shell out when he owned the place.

Keep what's separate separate, that was the point, more than a point, a belief, a religion. More than a religion, a necessity.

In any case: you have a business, you make money, assuming the wind blows in the right direction. You own a car, it costs you money. Two separate arrangements. Just because the business is car repairs doesn't mean that your car repair is free. That was just muddled thinking, an inability to keep the arithmetic involved clear.

The business concerned here and now was the job at the Station Café, not part-ownership of Bunter's. It was his wages from the café that would pay the bill. The car was the family car. His job at the café paid for his family life. His garage was separate.

He collected the books and invoices, put them in the attaché case Ruth had given him for his birthday, and turned to go. Edwin had started locking up. It was his job to run the garage day to day. All Jack did was sort out the paperwork of an evening.

'Car keys,' Edwin said, 'if you want us to get going on it tomorrow.'

'Forget my head,' Jack said, and passed them over. Edwin put them in his overall pocket that casual way mechanics do, cars being all in a day's work. Jack couldn't see them in that light, not even as part-owner of Bunter's. When you'd not had one before, you couldn't take for granted the way they'd ferry you wherever you wanted to go. The fact they ever worked at all seemed a miracle, not that he'd ever learned much about how. But Ken had been right to tell Bernard he was the man for this investment. He might not be able to make a car go, but keeping a repair business on the road was the thing he'd turned out to be good at.

Having to get up to Ruth's on the bus made him behind, so he started on his paperwork at her kitchen table without a lot of chitchat. Poor idea. This was a night for noses, Edwin's black with oil, Ruth's red. Perhaps I'm the only person left in Stockport with a common or garden, vanilla-flavoured nose, Jack thought. But he'd missed the point. Ruth's was a sad and sorry little nose, that was the point.

'Me and Gyp saw a fox this morning,' she told him while he was in the middle of his accounts.

He made that noise you do when you don't want to be disturbed: you don't say a particular word, just the stuff words are made out of. The nose sniffed. He kept on working.

'Mrs McMahon's got a friend who has a hedgehog come in her garden.'

'Three cheers,' he said this time.

Sniff again – no, this time a sob. 'There's no call to be sarcastic,' Ruth said.

He gave her a look. Funny how when somebody's sad and you want to comfort her you give her a cold look for a moment or two, prolong the agony. 'I don't know, you,' he said then, softly patting the top of her head. 'You're not as green as you are cabbage-looking, are you?'

She shook her head impatiently and looked out the window.

'What is it?' he asked.

'If you're getting a divorce –'

'What you mean, if? It'll be coming through middle of next month'

'But you have to go to court.'

'I've done that part.'

'I haven't.'

'For heaven's sake, Ruth, you're not married.'

'I'm the other woman. There's always one of those, isn't there? You got to have the other woman.'

She made it seem like some advert on a billboard.

'What do you think I am? I wasn't going to drag you into it. That's not what you do nowadays. What you do, you get a private detective to arrange it all. He puts some woman you've never even met into a hotel room. Co-respondent, what they call her. Then you go along to the same room. He takes a photo of you going in. Then you sit inside for an hour or two, the two of you, have a nice cup of tea. Then you and the co-respondent shake hands and you leave, and the detective takes another photo of you coming out. That's all there is to it.'

'When are you going to do it?'

'I've done it.'

'When?'

'Last year.'

'Oh.'

'What you say oh for?' He made his oh sound just like hers, small and disappointed, and she did a little smile as she recognised it, then went sad again.

'I didn't know you went last year.'

'I didn't tell you.'

'Why not?'

'Didn't want you to worry.'

She sat a while, chewing that one over. 'Why didn't you tell me after?'

'I told you the divorce was coming through. I said about it lots of times. That was telling you.'

'Which hotel did you go to?'

'Not here, you need to be a bit discreet. You don't have a naughty weekend in your own back garden.'

'Where then?'

'South of England. Bournemouth. Nice place. Got cliffs, and a pier. We ought to have a holiday there some time, when we've got ourselves sorted out.'

'Perhaps we could go for our honeymoon.'

'My idea of a honeymoon'll be moving in here. Do me for the time being.'

Ruth slapped the side of her head. 'That's what I was going to ask you,' she said. It was that nasty thing Mrs McMahon had said to her. 'If, if all what you say,' she went on, rolling her eyes at the divorce business they'd just been talking about, 'why're you still living at home?'

'Where else would I be living? I can't hardly move in here, can I, as things stand? Do you a fat lot of good on the estate to have them all saying, see that Ruth? Got her lover-boy installed.'

'Lover-boy,' she said, amused at seeing him in that light.

He leaned over towards her. Phew, maybe some of that fox had rubbed off. Perhaps it was just she'd got herself worked up. Makes the glands get to work. Push through it, that was the trick. Something arousing about it in any case. He kissed the pink nose.

'It doesn't sound decent,' Ruth said softly.

'Oh, it's decent enough. It's us two who're not decent.'

'You know what I mean.' She pushed a hand through her hair. Its blondeness riffled through her fingers like sand. He remembered pushing his hands into dunes to catch a feel of coolness inside. Not too many ways to keep yourself amused in the Sahara Desert. 'Her soon not being your wife.'

'Doesn't stop us being friendly.'

'How can you stay friendly with a man who's getting divorced from you so he can go and marry somebody else?'

'Maybe she never thought I was that much of a catch in the first place. You've got to remember something about her, Ruth. She was never very interested in, you know, from the start. Now she's got her children, she's glad enough to see the back of it. She *likes* just being chums.'

Ruth sat very still, with her eyes cast down towards the table-top. 'I'm interested in it,' she said.

'Attagirl,' he told her. 'Music to my ears.'

'It's not the same as when we had our own chickens,' dad said, making soldiers for himself and Peter.

He always used his penknife for that purpose for some unaccountable reason, when a table knife would do every bit as well, and at least would be guaranteed clean. Rose asked him what he'd last used it for, but he couldn't tell her. Instead he made an elaborate business of wiping the blade on his trouser leg, which was not the solution she wanted. She could hardly ask him what he'd last used his trousers for, but the state of the knees meant she could

188

make a shrewd guess. He'd been so gleeful about taking over that allotment of his chum who'd passed away.

It was funny how unsympathetic the old seemed to be about people dying. Certainly dad didn't take the view that there but for the grace of God. He regarded anyone he knew popping their clogs more on the lines of personal victory, another scalp to hang on his belt. Perhaps his interest in people being executed was an example of the same attitude.

'The days of chickens in people's back gardens are over with, Dad,' she told him.

'I don't see why.'

'It's old-fashioned.'

'How can you say chickens are old-fashioned? You may as well say cows are old-fashioned while you're at it.'

'People don't have cows in their back gardens either.'

He opened his mouth to say something but couldn't think what. He had made quite a few soldiers by now, neatly piling them on top of each other like a miniature stack of scaffolding planks or railway sleepers. For some reason the middle finger of his right hand poked straight out while he did so, like a fat pink cigar. Why chickens were old-fashioned was they put people in mind of the war and rationing, all that palaver. Those days weren't as far behind them as all that, given the fact that you still couldn't buy bacon for love nor money. Perhaps what they ought to have in the back garden was a pig. But the point was, people wanted to feel they'd moved on. She wanted to feel *she*'d moved on.

'I like chickners,' Peter said. He had a funny way with him sometimes of saying part of a word backwards.

'You don't want them with a little one about the place,' she told dad. 'You never know what they'll pick up from them.'

'You must be thinking of parrots. I've never heard of anybody catching chicken disease in all my days.' He divided the soldiers and passed Peter's share over to him.

Peter immediately put a handful in his mouth. 'Hold your horses, sonny Jim, they're for dipping,' dad said.

He could have cut the top off Peter's egg instead of making speeches about why it would have been better had it been laid in the garden and been brought in with its little blob of chicken mess stuck to it, along with a feather or two for good measure. The time she'd spent cleaning eggs at the sink, scrubbing them delicately so as not to break the shell. 'Thieves break in and steal the gold,' she said, doing it herself.

'Thieves break it,' Peter said, hitting himself on the ear with the hand that held the soldiers. He must have been picturing his head as an egg.

'He's gone and buttered his hair,' dad said. 'Are you not having one?'

'Ha!' Peter said. One thing you learned about small children: they could do false laughs as well as anyone else.

'I'll have something a bit later, when Donald comes back from Scout camp.' It would be more than life was worth to tell him that she'd realised she only had two eggs left after having suggested them for tea.

'I watched *Harding Finds Out* on the television last night, while you were putting Peter to bed.'

'Oh yes.'

'He was saying that some children fail their eleven-plus on purpose.'

She stared at him a moment. He opened his egg with his penknife too. Perhaps it had a special egg blade. Yolk pulsed out and ran down the side. He glared at it with his intense old man's eyes. She was watching him in detail because what he'd said had made her too angry to speak for the time being. When she did speak her teeth were gritted as tight as lockjaw. 'What would they do that for?'

He used a soldier to mop up the dripping yolk and popped it into his mouth. She noticed how he arched his upper lip to keep his moustache away from the food. 'For fear of having to work too hard at the grammar school,' he said when his mouthful had calmed down. 'That's what Gilbert Harding said. He'd looked into it.'

'So you think Donald's lazy, is that it?'

'What I think is Donald's brainy, that's what I think.'

She scooped out some of Peter's egg with a spoon, put it on the end of a soldier, and passed it to him. 'Donald got behind with that rheumatic fever business, that's what happened to him. It just put him off his stride. He's not the sort of boy to be sneaky, you should know that well enough.'

'There's sneaky and sneaky.'

'I *beg* your pardon?'

'We're all sneaky some time or other, that's all I meant to say.' His face had gone bright red all of a sudden. Silly old man.

'He's settled down well at secondary modern,' she said. 'I think it suits him. He's a practical boy. It's the place for somebody practical. Woodwork and metalwork, and technical drawing. He likes all those. Takes after his grandad. You're practical.'

'I've got a new egg,' Peter said. He'd turned his egg upside down in its cup. He always loved to do that but he tended to be a bit premature. She picked it up quickly and peeped in. Most of the yolk had gone anyway. She replaced it. Peter politely pretended not to notice she'd interrupted the trick. 'Thieves break it,' he said, and hit it with his spoon.

'Oh dear,' she said, looking at the hole in surprise. 'Thieves have stolen the gold already.'

I won't get angry with him, Rose told herself over and over as the clock crawled on, it'll only spoil Donald coming back. As long as Jack comes in time for us to get to the bus station I'll say nowt.

He came just in the nick of time, and she did get angry with him.

'Just this once, that's all I asked. I've been on pins all evening.'

191

'I tried –'

'Trying isn't good enough where our lad's concerned.' She knew she wasn't being exactly fair. Jack's job had changed since the early days. The Station Café had become more of a young people's place, from what he told her, more or less a milk bar, and stayed open till eight, and on Fridays all evening when they had jiving to records. She worried about Teddy boys, but business seemed to be booming and Jack's pay had gone up. It meant he worked dreadful hours, though, and she didn't see much of him nowadays.

'I've had a day of it,' he said. 'We had a spot of bother. A girl got knocked down.'

'*Girl?*'

'One of those things. You have to allow for a bit of daft behaviour when there's a lot of youngsters about.'

'It'll be you getting knocked down one of these days, that's what *I* dread.'

'They were just jostling, that's all there was to it. There's no harm in them.'

'Try telling that – Your hair's wet.' It was caked on his head. She looked at it in horror, realising. 'What's happened to the car?'

'Big end. I told you I was going to get it looked at.'

I'm going to panic now, she thought. It seemed funny to be able to choose. It was better to panic than to be bad-tempered and resentful. She let out a little moan and rushed for her mac. 'We'll never get there in time. Damn, damn and blast it.'

'For heaven's sake, Rose. Donald's perfectly able to come home from the middle of Stockport under his own steam. He's done it plenty of times. He's getting to be a big boy now.'

There were a couple of buses drawn up at the platforms with their lights off. Like fatted oxen, Rose said to herself for some reason. That must be the panic talking. Their own bus sped off. It could go as fast as it liked now they'd been set down. It had ground its way unwillingly to the centre of Stockport with them on board, insisting on stopping at stops where no one was waiting, where no one had ever waited.

'The first time he's been away and we weren't here when he got back,' she said. 'All the other mothers and fathers were here, oh yes, but not us, that would have been too much trouble that would.'

'How do you know all the other ones were here?'

'Where are they now, I ask you? There's nobody about at all.' She waved forlornly at the absence of everybody. The bus station, with a drizzle still falling, had a look about it as if the Scouts and their parents must have left hours ago. How you can tell that, who knows? As if people left a shadow, an echo of their hubbub, when they went, something that faded with the passing of time. 'Oh God,' she said, 'what will he have thought?'

'He'll have thought, oh they're not here, I better get home, that's what he'd have thought.'

'Hello,' came a voice.

She turned. All along she'd been just pretending to be panicked, and she still was. She recognised Donald's voice straight away, she was his mother after all, and it had just got to that raw grating stage that boys' voices go through. But she still felt herself looking round fearfully, wanting to prolong the agony.

When she saw him, he did make her jump. Sincerely. Serve her right. His eye was right over, and he looked grotesque. She felt a pang. He'd been supposed to have his squint seen to a few years ago, but had got himself into a state about it. He kept talking about them taking his eye out. She told him that was stuff and nonsense, but when she'd asked the surgeon he'd said, yes, that's what they would have to do, to get at the muscles or whatever they were. Then pop it back. He'd actually told Donald that in the first place. Why on earth? Because he asked, was the reply, children have the right to know. He might have been good at eyes but he didn't seem to have much of a clue about how children's minds worked. She'd pictured little ones in bed all over Manchester, waiting to have their eyes taken out. He hadn't even told her he'd told Donald. Which had put her on the spot by giving her the lie. So she'd asked the man if the operation was strictly necessary. It was only for cosmetic reasons, he said, the squint would probably correct itself as he grew older. Donald's rheumatic fever had meant postponement in any case, so she'd called the operation off altogether. He'd been through enough.

But she hadn't been able to stop herself doing a little jump at the sight of him squinting now.

'It's all right, Mum, it's just goofy teeth,' Donald said, and took them out.

'I was so frightened,' she said. 'I didn't know where you were.'

He just shrugged. She realised he must have secreted himself behind a pillar to put those teeth in. Her heart suddenly melted at what a baby he still was.

'Let's have a shufty,' Jack said, taking them from him. He put them in himself, bulged his eyes, and bent down so his arms dangled. Talking of which, Jack was still a baby too.

Chapter Nine

It was funny to be cleaning the kitchen for the first time. They weren't able to get a new house just now, according to Jack, but he'd said let's have a new kitchen to be going on with.

It had been a bit tricky persuading dad not to do the plumbing. The worst part was that he knew in his heart of hearts he wasn't quite up to it. He'd given over his leather work, and that had been a straw in the wind. When Donald was smaller he'd made him sandals on a couple of occasions, which the little chap had valiantly worn, though they'd turned out cockeyed, especially the second pair. Donald had funny little-toes, cone-shaped with a scrap of horny nail on each, and they had a tendency to come out through a gap in the straps, looking naked and out of place, as if each foot had grown itself a tiny willy. After that dad had used his shed mainly for reading in, until the allotment had come along, when he'd rigged up a shelf under the window to use for seed trays. 'You're retired, Dad, you've done your share of plumbing,' Rose had told him.

'I put this sink in when I got married,' he said, looking a bit tearful. You could obviously get soppy about practically anything, including long-ago sinks.

'All the more reason,' she said, which she'd realised afterwards could be taken either way.

The long and short of it was she'd got a steel sink, with new taps and a proper draining-board, also a kitchen cupboard for utensils, all the shelves renewed in the pantry, the cooker replaced, and to top it off a yellow enamel Bendix washing machine, just too late for all the nappies Peter had produced, but a godsend all the same. Good quality lino on the floor instead of bits of matting. The difference between a scullery and a kitchen as such, as Jack said. The wireless dad had bought Donald when he had rheumatic fever was on the windowsill, having lost its charms for him now dad had rented a television for the front room. Next thing on the list was a fridge, though the pantry had always been cool. I'm getting a new house from the inside out, Rose had thought to herself rather wistfully.

The kitchen had just had time to get mucky, a month. She'd wiped over the surfaces and mopped the floor in the meantime, of course, but now it had reached the point where it needed a bottomer. The wireless had *Music While You Work* on and she was deep in the oven, Peter sitting on the floor behind her doing some crayoning.

Then, rat-a-tat-tat on the front door.

'I don't know. Who can that be, eh, Peter?' she asked, as she backed out on to the floor beside him. He didn't look up from his drawing. He tended to get very absorbed in it, even though everything he drew, whether a human or an animal, came out looking like a spider. She sometimes wondered if kiddies were good drawers despite appearances, just saw things in a different way. Perhaps what they saw, poor mites, was spiders everywhere.

She got to her feet, dusted herself off. She was wearing a tatty cardigan over an ancient dress, a forties thing with askew shoulder pads, and trodden-down slippers. 'I hope it's not my sailor, home from the sea,' she told Peter, and went out into the hall. Rat-tat again.

'Mind your hurry,' she said. Funny the way you chunter on for a three-year-old's benefit, as he sits with his tongue poking out, scribbling his circles, adding matchstick arms and legs and horrid deformed heads with unkempt curls, taking no notice whatever of your goings-on. She opened the door.

Oh dear.

One thing she'd realised: things didn't get simpler with the passage of time. Awkward situations didn't become less awkward.

It was Vera.

It was like one of the stories she told Peter. A long time ago there was a very sad lady, whose husband had kicked the bucket. Whose son had also kicked his own little bucket. Which had left her all alone in that gloomy, empty house of hers.

And then along came Rose.

They had been silly together. But perhaps you can be forgiven for being silly in certain circumstances. Vera had plenty of excuse, and Rose had too for that matter, with Donald having been so ill.

The trouble was, what happened afterwards.

Hand on heart, she had to confess that what happened afterwards was: Peter.

Perhaps she'd felt the need to convince herself that she was normal. Perhaps she'd been given an appetite by what had happened. Perhaps it was just time. Whatever the reason, before she knew it she'd found herself pregnant again.

After that, when she met Vera, she never knew what to say. There was a warmth and expectation in Vera's eyes, a desire for something more. Rose felt that her own eyes in response were as hard as pebbles. She would thrust her bulging tummy out as far as possible, using it as a wall to separate them from each other. But it didn't seem possible to hurt Vera's feelings: she'd just look hopefully back.

The arrival of Peter made life a lot easier. She absorbed herself in him, let everything else, except Donald of course, take second place. The perfect excuse. Nevertheless, several times she met Vera in the street while she was out pushing the pram. Vera would inspect the baby, then her eyes would rise, as they had done in her dining-room, and meet her own, and there was still a soft unpushy need in them, a kind of love, Rose supposed it was, that wouldn't go away however much you wanted it to.

But in the last year or so they hadn't happened to bump into each other. Perhaps they'd begun to go in different directions. Perhaps Vera was deliberately avoiding her. Anyhow, it had been a relief. Or not exactly, because you don't seem to notice when things stop happening. If they had kept on bumping into each other that would have been the opposite of a relief.

But now, here she was again.

'Hello, Rose. Can I come in a minute?'

Rose blushed. Vera's eyes were the same as usual, fixed on her own, no embarrassment or guilt or difficulty in them, nothing but simple need. Full of that. Topped up, like Jack said when he put oil in the car. But her voice was quite different. There was something wheedling about it, an edge to her tone. The way she said 'minute' was almost sarcastic.

Rose couldn't say anything in reply for a moment. It was like having to talk to two different people at once. When she did speak it was in a whisper: 'Come in.' She backed against the door-frame to let Vera pass without them touching, then followed her down the hall into the kitchen.

'Hello, young Peter,' Vera said. She bent down to ruffle his hair. He looked up at her with beady eyes. 'My word, that's a good picture,' she said. 'Is it your mummy and daddy? I think I can see which one's your mummy.'

She looked up at Rose, and winked.

Suddenly a terrible idea crossed Rose's mind.

Could Vera possibly believe that she had had Peter for *her* sake? So that he could take poor dead Victor's place in the world?

As soon as she thought that, something occurred to her which made it even worse. She had an attack of mental snobbery. How *dare* Vera imagine that Peter could have been brought into the world as a memorial to that podgy lad of hers. It seemed like an insult, though even as the shock of indignation struck her she was aware that Vera could hardly be expected to see it as such. But Rose wanted to tell her not even to touch Peter, if that's how she saw him.

She blushed all over again, for having such unworthy thoughts.

'Would you like a cup of coffee?' she asked her.

'I'd love one. If you've got time.'

'I've been giving the kitchen a bottom. I could do with a rest.'

'It's a lovely kitchen.'

'We've not long had it done through.' She put the kettle on.

'I haven't had anything done to my house since I don't know when,' Vera said. She started patting Peter's head once more. He didn't look up this time. He was deeply drawing again. Yes, Rose hadn't been imagining it, there was something clingy about Vera's pats, like the way Donald's wrists went when he was playing with his yo-yo, a soft wavy motion that brought the yo-yo back like a magnet into the palm of his hand. She recalled what that policeman had said years back about the baker's boy who'd stolen their bag of farthings: 'That's a lad with sticky palms.' Well, if Vera's palms were sticky they'd better get unsticky soon enough. Peter's little head was not going to be allowed to attach itself to them.

'What I've been doing,' Vera said, 'I've just been faffing about, these last years.'

Rose spooned Nescafé into two cups. 'No one can blame you,' she said, 'after what happened.'

'It's all in the past, anyhow. I've sold my house.'

Rose froze, halfway through pouring the kettle. What she felt she wasn't certain. Partly a weight lifted from her shoulders. That silly moment, packed in its box, was being sent off to the wide blue yonder. But also a twinge of resentment, as if she had the right to expect Vera to guard what had happened for ever more, not let it fall into the hands of strangers.

She resumed her pouring. I want to move on myself, she thought, but I want Vera to remain exactly where she was, where we were. Since when did playing fair come into it?

'Where will you live?' she asked.

'Newcastle.'

'Newcastle?'

'Upon Tyne.' She gave Peter's hair one last ruffle and straightened up. 'I've met someone. He's a nice man. We're going to get married. He's a company representative. He's going to be based in Newcastle. We are, going to be.'

'I see. Congratulations.'

'Thank you. I knew you'd be pleased.'

'Oh, I am. You deserve – some happiness.'

'Oh,' Vera said, 'having seen what I've seen, I don't think any of us deserves anything. What I think is, things just happen to you. Or they don't. I was beginning to think nothing was ever going to happen to me again.' She gave a nervous smile, shrugging her shoulders.

'And now it has.' Rose put the milk in the cups.

Vera gave a comical look, pursing her lips and widening her eyes, like a naughty schoolgirl.

Makes Vera laugh. Well, I should jolly well kayko. He wouldn't have to be *very* funny to be funnier than she'd been used to, the last few years.

But Rose couldn't stop wondering just what way he might be funny. I can be funny too, she thought. I can make Peter laugh. Of course he's only three. I could make Donald laugh once upon a time, but he knows all my funninesses by now. I could make Jack laugh, but he's never at home. And dad, if only he had a sense of humour, and wasn't so interested in executions. Come to think of it, Donald hasn't got much of a sense of humour either, now he's older, serious little lad. Perhaps he's inherited that from dad, if you *can* inherit not having something.

What makes Vera's fellow funnier than me? she kept on

wondering. In her mind's eye she saw Vera laugh. She had never seen that in real life. The only emotion Rose had seen on her face since Victor died was sorrow, coupled with that lovey-dovey expression.

Her fiancé was quite handsome. Well, not very, perhaps, to another person, but handsome enough for her, Vera. What he had, she said, was a nice face. Gentle.

Gentleman? Rose asked, thinking that that was the word Vera had used.

Not *too* much of a one, I hope! Vera said: you can take being a gentleman too far. She reddened as she looked at Rose, and the picture went through both their minds at once: the march to the bathroom with pyjamas carried aloft, the return with them on, the rabbit shooting out of its burrow in the darkness of the bed.

Rose reddened in return and they both nearly laughed, holding their top lips buttoned over their teeth. Not too much of one, Rose agreed, but even as she said it she felt resentful: funny, quite handsome, not too much of a gentleman, why can't that be me, she thought to herself deep down. Why can't I *be* those things, though the strangeness of that idea made her flesh creep a little. But while it was a strange idea, it wasn't an impossible one. She had seen in those eyes of Vera's that she still felt the same, that however her mouth talked about this beau of hers, nothing had changed. Rose had only to say the word.

But what word was it? And what would it lead to? How could it possibly be said? It must be a nonsense word, like abracadabra. She felt she had been given a glimpse of a never-never land, a place where you couldn't possibly live.

Not quite never-never. An only-once land, a never-again land.

In bed that night, with the lump of Jack asleep beside her, she thought: nothing good or new or exciting is ever going to happen to me again, and she wept.

Lovely June day, hot enough to fry an egg. Perhaps as a

result, Alf didn't turn up at Reddish Vale, which was a relief, being that Ernie saw him enough at the allotments these days. Mind you, if you didn't have Alf mithering about his Dougie, you had Pat on the subject of his dead dog, Patch. It had been a tedious enough animal in life, one of those small white dogs with a brown head and very short legs, simply your basic dog, more or less lacking any distinguishing features. As far as Ernie could recall it didn't even have a patch as such, despite its name, far less a personality. It was friendly enough, wagged its tail to say hello, and would run for a ball, though didn't have the brain to fetch it back afterwards. The last year or two it had stiffened up with old age, and then got something wrong with its stomach, so eventually Pat had had to have it put down.

What a fuss he made: talk about the condemned man ate a hearty breakfast. Bought a tin of chicken breasts and cut them up, so its digestion could cope. Dogs just bolt their grub when all's said and done, don't know what it tastes like until tomorrow. Took it on a last walk, or rather hobble, down this very place, Reddish Vale, then was driven off by his pal Malcolm to the vet's, where the deed was done. Humans should be so lucky, was Ernie's verdict on the proceedings. Ruth Ellis should be so lucky.

The long and short of it was Pat spent his time moping. Ernie only said, 'Nice weather,' but that was enough to start him off.

'Feels wrong,' Pat said, 'with Patch not being here to enjoy it.'

'He'd only have got himself fashed,' Ernie told him. 'See dogs on a day like today, they have their mouths open like so many crocodiles.'

'Better being like a crocodile than not here at all.'

'The world is full of dogs, Pat,' Arn said. Arn would sit and think about something and then say the obvious, like a hen laying a very small egg.

'No,' Pat said.

'It's worth thinking about,' Ernie told him.

'It's not the same thing as getting a new pair of trousers, you know. I'll never have another one.'

'Suit yourself.'

'Patch'll do me.' He looked out at the ground beyond the millpond, as if he could still see Patch over there, not fetching his ball.

Ernie had brought his paper with him. He didn't have a saddlebag as such, because the width would have impeded his method of mounting the bike, but there was a little leather case holding a puncture repair kit fastened with straps to the eyelets on the back of the saddle, and he could slide the *Express* in tube form part way into it, leaving room for his leg to swing over the far side, then centre it when he was safely on the go by reaching one hand back and working it towards the mid-point, so it poked out equally both sides like a pair of trafficators. He got it out now and shook it open. Let Pat think about his dead dog, and Arn about not much. The sunshine was almost dazzling on the page.

'You read about the Home Secretary?' he asked after a moment or two.

'What about him?' Arn asked.

'Only went to visit his sister at the weekend.'

'What's wrong with that?'

'Lady Megan, her name.'

'Lady Muck, of Dishwater Hall,' Pat said, not normally a bitter type.

'It says here that when he went out into his sister's garden to sniff the roses, a burly detective sergeant sniffed alongside him.'

'Not what you might call news,' Pat said.

'The point is, he spent the weekend considering whether to give Ruth Ellis a reprieve. Fat lot of good sniffing the roses did, from her point of view. He's left her to hang, in any case.'

'I don't see why people should be let off, just because

203

they're a woman,' Arn said. 'She emptied her gun into that fellow of hers, what's that when it's at home if not murder?'

'Women always empty their gun into them,' Pat said. 'It's because they only kill somebody when they've got themselves into a state. When Patch died I could have killed somebody just like swatting a fly, if they'd crossed me in any way.'

Ernie gave Pat a bit of a look. Something about him, his narrow shoulders, shrunken jacket, glum physog, made you think that if it came to him swatting a fly you might put your money on the fly.

'In that case,' Arn said, 'you should go for a Burton and all.'

'She had a miscarriage three days before the murder,' Ernie said.

'What I tell you?' Pat said, looking cheerful for the first time in a week or two, now he'd got Patch being put down and Ruth Ellis's young man getting shot going along side by side.

Ernie let Pat and Arn get on with it: he didn't have the patience. Maybe Ruth Ellis hadn't had the patience either, and that's why she shot David Blakely. Like Mrs Lloyd hitting Mrs Aldridge when Mrs Aldridge laughed at her. Something snaps. Ruth Ellis had got her patience back now. There was a letter she'd written to someone from her prison cell published in the paper. She said: *No doubt you have heard, I do not want to live. You may find this very hard to believe but that is what I want. I am quite well and happy under the circumstances, and very well looked after. I have plenty to amuse me. Well, Frank, this must be all for now.*

It struck him that Arn and Pat were missing the point, thinking it mattered which side they were on. Same as the Home Secretary sniffing that rose. Ruth Ellis was beyond all that. What you thought when you read that letter was how calm and peaceful it must be being in the death cell.

She was so polite, didn't want to hurt anybody's feelings. What it was, she was in the position of advantage. She didn't have to worry about herself any more. She'd come to terms. Everybody thought she was in a terrible predicament, and some people gloated over it and other people were sorry. But Ernie realised he envied her.

The sun came through the window. On the television it was *Bill and Ben*. The Bill and Bens had hats on their heads. One of the Bill and Bens came out of his flowerpot. He went in a wobbly way. The other Bill and Ben said the long word. He tried to catch the first Bill and Ben but his arm was too wavy. So he came out of his flowerpot as well. When the Bill and Bens walked they danced. The weed grew. The weed had a sun for its head. The weed's head didn't have a hat. You could look at the weed. The weed said weed. The Bill and Ben that came the first said the long word. That made the weed laugh. The Bill and Bens laughed too. Then the weed was frightened. The weed said weed. The Bill and Bens said globbalob. The weed said WE-eed. The weed said weed weed weed. The Bill and Bens danced to their pots. Globbalob weed globbalob weed. One Bill and Ben tried to jump in his pot. He fell over. The other Bill and Ben pulled him up. Both the Bill and Bens shook their arms. They flew up into their pots. The weed clapped her leaves. Then the man came in. The weed was only a weed. The Bill and Bens were safe inside their pots.

Mummy didn't watch *Watch with Mother*. She washed up instead. Peter went into the kitchen but she wasn't washing up any more. The back door was open. He went out into the garden. Mummy was talking to the lady in the next garden. There was grandad's shed. There was a bit of open in the door. Peter got inside the open and pressed the door with his bottom and more open came. It was night in the shed. Under the window was a table. There was a chair. He pushed the chair to near the table. Then he lay his front on the chair seat and waved his legs until his bottom went up and his knees fitted underneath. Then he kneeled up.

There were flowerpots on the table. They were like a dead Bill and Ben.

Mummy came in the shed. Peter said weed to the dead Bill and Ben.

There was an old mill down Hope's Dale that had gone into upholstery supplies, and Stan had asked Jack to pick up an order of moquette which was going to be used on a couple of settees for the café. Come in useful for laying the ladies on that had passed out with the excitement of tea dancing. After he'd done that he drove on impulse down Marlborough Terrace, where he'd got the piano a few years back. Pay his respects. But who should answer the door but a nasty-looking bald bloke with those rimless specs that seem to glitter at you even in a poor light. It seemed dim and dank in that hallway of Mrs Feltbauer's, despite the hot day.

'Who might you be?' the man asked.

'I could ask the same about you,' Jack told him. 'I came to see Mrs Feltbauer.'

'She's in the hospital. I'm the landlord.'

'That doesn't give you the right to poke about among her things.'

'She'll not be coming back.'

'She better not be,' Jack said, which wasn't what he intended to say, but he moved a bit forward towards the landlord to get the point across. The eyes looked back through their little windows.

'Stepping Hill Hospital,' the man told him.

'I hope you're not pinching her things.'

'If you must know I'm giving this place a clear-out for the next tenant. You a relation?'

'No.'

'In that case, bugger off. I've work to do.'

206

Should have thumped him, messing with her things, Jack thought as he got back in Stan's van. 'Can't, when they've got specs on,' he told himself out loud as he drove off. That thought calmed him down a bit.

It was coming up to the end of afternoon visiting at Stepping Hill, and the ward nurse was in two minds to give him the elbow.

'Are you a relation?' she asked him.

'Yes. Nephew.'

She thought about it. That was all right. When they think about it you're home and dry. What with the hot day, and the way they always heated hospitals, it was stifling in here. 'Just ten minutes,' she said. 'She hasn't had any visitors that I know of since she's been here.'

Mrs Feltbauer hardly made a bump in the bed. Poor old girl, Jack thought, she's not the princess, only the pea. She'd aged a lot since he'd last seen her. Her brown wizened face reminded him of the burned pilot, as if dying itself had a cooking effect. There were screens round the bed, presumably to give her the chance of popping off in peace.

'Hello, Mrs Feltbauer.'

She opened her eyes, but just looked straight up, not at him. Even her eyes seemed dried out, almost furry. He took out his handkerchief and mopped his forehead with it. You could hardly breathe. There was a smell of piddle and decay and disinfectant in the thick air. 'I'm sorry you've not been well.'

'The old ladies,' she said.

'Oh yes,' he said. 'I suppose we're all getting older.'

'They wore their hats. Very serious ones. With cloth flowers, or a netting. They were happy to be.'

Hats. And she'd ended up in Stockport, hat capital of England. Joe at the café had a son who worked in a hat factory, making bowlers for city gents. You had to mould the head piece in boiling water. Your hands got acclimatised, according to Joe. Jack had pictured a factory full of men with hands like gammon.

'People don't wear hats like they did,' he said. 'Since the war.'

She seemed to take that in, gave a little nod, had a look as if he'd put his finger on it. Old like she was, she must see lack of hats as a sign things had gone to pot, but what a thing to pick on, for heaven's sake. Then she started talking about some other nonsense, lemons, also a kangaroo. Maybe she'd been listening to Shirley Abicair and her zither. He didn't understand most of it, some didn't sound English even, but he didn't think it was German, not that he knew any, except from war films. He didn't think it was anything in particular. She was looking at him now, her face skewed sideways on the pillow. It was as if she had a message she had to get across and was watching intently for signs it had sunk in. It gave him the creeps to see her like that.

The little town she came from resembled itself so much you might think it was only one very large spread-about building, all neat grey stone and tall slate roofs, with the shops with their small panes and their smells of bread and ham and their fat shopkeepers in aprons, leather or white linen, almost all men, and the old ladies in their long black dresses and serious hats, with big wicker shopping bags, fat too because nobody minded being fat in those times, it meant there was more of you to enjoy your life with. There was the smell of apples and cinnamon in the kitchen in midwinter, while mother was cooking her apple cake. In summer a smell so sharp it made your cheeks suck in when she boiled whole lemons for lemonade. There was a proper river that you could skate on and swim in and fish out of, and a fat bridge that carried the main street over.

Here in Stockport how could you become fat, except maybe by drinking too much beer? All her old age she was so thin she was like only half a person, living half a life. No fish swam in the river, only foam and scum from the factories, and in any case most of the river was now hidden with a sort of road on the top of it, and shops built on the road. She had been young in the town of her youth, and the town was the sort of town you see with young eyes, like one in a fairy tale, and she was old in Stockport, and this was a town you see with old eyes, grey and dull and without promise for the future. The two towns were like the names of the two parts of her life. Anyone would think that, for example, having motorcars and lorries about everywhere was no more than the sign of old age.

When she thought of her husband she thought of him in the old place, not here. Perhaps that was why she could not bring his name to mind, because she could not remember the name of the old place either. She used to think in their young marriage that he had a look of exploding bones, because although he was big it seemed he might become suddenly bigger at any moment. Sometimes you see a growing tree like that, pushing at the air above with its shoulders. He had a curling-up moustache that when he first grew it it looked like a joke aimed at the older people because it was one of their moustaches. Also he had a stomach but not a general one. It rested in the front of his trousers like a kangeroo's baby in its pocket. It was useful to have a moustache and a stomach for working in the bank.

At the weekends they liked to go to the woods and eat a picnic. Sometimes he would fish. She remembered how he would catch small ones no bigger than his finger, shrug his shoulders comically, click his tongue and sigh. He did the same actions later, when the problems were serious, and those early days came back into her memory so sharply and surprisingly that they made her cry even though she was trying her best to be brave. She loved the sunshine coming through pine trees, pine light she called it, the colour of lions. Her husband had big white teeth which became visible when he laughed or smiled. After the last war he developed gum problems and had to have them all removed. Big teeth shining in the pine light, small silver fishes dangling from his hand, that was how she remembered those summer days.

'You remember me,' he said, when she paused for a bit. 'I was the bloke that took off your piano.'

'Piano,' she said, as if trying to remember what a piano was.

He felt he was on *Animal, Vegetable and Mineral*, needing to give her a clue. What to say? Big bugger: you humped it all across the Alps. Kept the music on tap, even when there was a war on and you'd been booted out of Austria.

He played pretend keys on her bed, going doh ray me as he did so. Good job the screens were in place, not that the other patients were in much better nick than Mrs Feltbauer, one of them, he'd noticed on the way in, being a nasty shade of blue. Not a tooth on the ward, far as he could make out, not even a denture. Just a row of dark gawping mouths, struggling to keep the air coming in and going out. Mrs Feltbauer watched him play. Something about her expression reminded him of the way Peter would watch when you did something, could be the most ordinary thing in the world, like tying your shoelace, as if you'd just invented how to do it. 'Playing – the – piano,' he told her.

All at once the penny dropped. She suddenly pulled a hand out of the bed and grabbed his arm with it. It didn't look like her hand at all, knobby and big out of all proportion. He hadn't noticed that when he met her before. Must be rheumatism, swelled it up. He felt embarrassed to look at it, as if it was a hand she'd stolen from somebody else. 'The piano,' she said in a harsh whisper.

'That's right, the piano.'

'Mine. My piano.'

'It was, true enough. You sold it, remember?'

She seemed to say his words over again with her lips,

as if needing to feel her way around them.

'It's at the café. Tell you what, *I* can play it now. I don't know what there is about it, it's a piano that lends itself. We have these dinners, Wiener schnitzel, that sort of jobby, wine with, the whole caper, and I play on the piano while the diners dine. If we're not overbusy, like. Put on a white jacket, to look the part. Just a bit of music going on, helps the grub go down. What I'm getting at, it didn't go to waste, hoiking it over here in the first place. Serves its turn.'

She was looking at him, still trying to interpret. Then she shook her head briskly, waved her king-size hand to stop him saying any more, and spoke. No: she'd waved her hand to make him look at her hand, or whoever's it was. 'Fingers,' she said. 'Silver,' she added. Then she was lost for words. She said silver a couple of times more, looking around with her small slow head for her drift.

He looked at his own hands, played a few more notes, then nodded his head and shrugged his shoulders a bit, as to say, Got you, even though he didn't have a clue what she was on about.

Hot day meant lettuce. Lettuce was one of those things you didn't want to eat but wasn't too bad when you did, specially if you put sugar on it. It was grandad's lettuce now he had an allotment. Donald could tell they weren't shop ones because the wickies seemed to have had a good munch of them first off.

Grandad grew beetroots as well, though very small ones, like marbles, except with long tails. Mum snipped off most of the tail before cooking them, so there was only a stump left, like a boxer dog's tail.

Salad was all right when you had hot potatoes with it. You needed something hot to stop it being too salady. Peter was allowed to not like salad. He had toast and Marmite and a carrot instead. He sucked the carrot like you suck a lollipop. Even though his food always looked grubby and mauled about, as if it had been sat on a couple of times, the way he sucked it made you want to have a carrot yourself. Mum had grated some up and put it in with the other salad stuff but it wasn't the same because it didn't taste of much except being grated. Could have been grated wood. Once when they'd gone for a walk at Alderley Edge they saw a donkey eating a thistle, and it made such a juicy noise eating it mum said she'd eat one herself for two pins. Peter had called the donkey donk, not because the rest of it was hard to say, just too long. He was little then.

Grandad said, 'It's all up with Ruth Ellis tomorrow. All but if someone comes forward with this new piece of evidence they keep talking about in the paper. Somebody drowned himself today, in protest. In a canal somewhere.'

'More fool him. That's nonsense, in any case,' mum said. 'If he drowned himself, he did. Just stuck Ruth Ellis's name on it for the effect, make people imagine there was something more to it.'

'Be that as it may,' grandad said. He suddenly went bright red. There was a bit of lettuce poking out under his moustache, from where he was too angry to finish putting it in his mouth.

Donald hadn't seen him get in such a rage for years and years. Suddenly, stupidly, he wanted to pee.

'Can I leave the table?' he asked.

'What on earth for?' mum said. 'You've only just started.'

'I want to go to the toilet.'

'Honestly, Donald, you're as bad as Peter. Peter broke into your shed this afternoon, Dad. You must have left the door open. He could have done himself an untold injury with your tools. I found him standing on your chair. He might have broke his little neck. He told me he'd wet himself, but I couldn't feel anything, could I, Peter love?'

Peter shook his head, and carried on sucking his carrot. Donald went upstairs to the bathroom. Even though it was a hot day he shivered while he was having his pee. When he came down again grandad was in the same position, just as red as before. Mum was messing about with Peter.

Grandad said: 'People aren't going to stand for it. Not commit suicide in every case, I'm not saying that. But they've had enough. There are crowds standing outside the gates of that prison. Evans, Bentley, and now Ruth Ellis. You have to add it up.'

'And what does it add up to, then?' mum asked.

'People being hanged who shouldn't be hanged, that's what it adds up to.'

'I thought you liked executions.'

'I beg your pardon.' His eyes looked glaring in his boiling face.

'You rabbit on about them enough, the way other chaps do about football.' Mum was still looking at Peter, not at grandad at all. Donald, even with his heart pounding, was amazed she could talk so calmly with grandad's rage just across the table. 'Just like a hobby. Mr Pierrepoint arrives at the prison in a taxi. Mr Pierrepoint has to catch the train home because the reprieve came through.'

'Fat chance this time,' grandad said. Like a miracle, he'd suddenly gone quiet and sad-looking. 'Albert Pierrepoint is the only one of us whose conscience is clear.'

'How do you make that out? Peter, take that carrot out of your gob –' when she said gob she made her mouth go round like a gob and her eyes shine at Peter '– and let me put a bit of this toast in instead.'

Peter looked back at her, not taking the carrot out. Then he laughed, which made his gob bigger than the carrot, so mum pulled it out and shoved the toast in.

'How I make it out is, when somebody is hanged, they're hanged on behalf of the country at large. Which is you and me and all the rest. Hanged on our behalf. But the person who does the hanging is Albert Pierrepoint. He is doing it at our behest. He's just a tool himself. He's the only one in the country who *isn't* responsible for the hanging.'

'I don't know how you make that out,' mum said. 'He gives me the ooh-jahs, is all I can say about it.'

It was so long since Donald had cried he'd forgotten how hot tears were. As he lay on his back on the top of his bed they ran out of the wrong corner of his eyes down the side of his head, beads of heat. The same hotness as those times when he had a go, Joe, before he went to sleep at night.

You do sort of hiccups while you cry. He kept his mouth tight shut so it wasn't loud.

All those years. Not thinking he was dead the *whole* time, just remembering it now and again, almost as though he was two people, one alive like normal, the other dead. Having a horrible worry like a ball inside you, not in your head, more down in the pit of your stomach, and every so often you remember it's there and feel yourself being sucked towards it.

Grandad shouting. Him peeing his trousers. Going down to the bottom of the garden.

When he thought about it nowadays it was like being on the television, everything in black and white. Perhaps that was to do with dying. Or maybe it was because when you went back so often in your mind the colour drained away in the end, like looking at old photographs in grandad's album. The other thing he remembered in black and white was when he went down to Aunty Eunice's funeral in Gosport last year and all the fleet were anchored off Spithead to be inspected by the Queen because of her being crowned the year before, and he went out in Uncle Len's yacht with Uncle Len's friend Alec to inspect them. Alec was a cripple but he could swing around the little deck with his crutch, holding on to rigging. Even though Alec had given him a Davy Crockett hat Donald didn't like him much, he was so quick, a bit like a monkey shooting through trees. Because his legs were short his arms looked too long. He got about better on the boat than he did on dry land. Inspecting the fleet was all black and white because it had really been black and white, grey sea, grey sky, grey hands and legs in the cold watery wind that blew over the tops of the waves, big grey battleships in long lines, staying dead level while their little yacht jumped like a bucking bronco.

Putting that old chair under the tree. Getting the skipping-rope his cousin Eileen had left behind out from where he kept it behind the shelter. He still had it. She never asked for it so he never gave it, but it wasn't the same any more. The rain and stuff made it go dim, until it became like an ordinary skipping-rope, grey rope, paint flaked off the handles and their wood gone split and grey, a black and white skipping-rope like the other black and white things of that day, its little bells rusted so they wouldn't ding.

Stood on the chair. Tied the skipping-rope to the tree and round his neck. Tugged at it to get the feel on his throat. Then half jumped half slipped off the chair so he didn't have the chance to make his mind up if he was really going to do it or not, and then landed on the ground with his throat just a bit squeezed so he had to stand on tiptoe to untie it.

He wished. He wished he hadn't untied it so quick. He wished he'd given himself time to think. To remember each thing that had happened one by one while the rope was still round his throat, while he was still joined to them all. To check them all in turn. To make sure.

Tied the skipping-rope. Tugged at it to get the feel. Half jumped half slipped. Landed. Just a bit squeezed. Just a bit. Enough length to go the whole way.

He undid it, to get rid of it. And ever after he couldn't quite remember. He couldn't be sure. One of him was an ordinary boy who'd jumped off a chair with a rope round his neck that had enough length to go the whole way. The other him died when he was six. Had been hanged by his grandad because he had done what you must never

215

ever do. Never ever. Never tell on a mate.

What grandad said at tea kept going through his mind. People aren't going to stand for it. There are crowds standing outside the gates of that prison. He remembered the names grandad said: Evans, Bentley, and now Ruth Ellis. You have to add it up.

His chest felt shuddery with crying as he thought about it. In his mind he pictured himself leaning over the table at teatime and saying: what about me, Grandad? Why didn't you add *me* up?

Why did you forget about me?

I tell you, even the retainers of the law, who course life as grey-hounds do hares, will rejoice at the escape of a creature so young – so beautiful.

Yes. And I'm a Dutchman.

Ernie had been reading *Heart of Midlothian* half the night. Not gone to bed. He didn't like reading in bed, made his arms go to sleep. Never could get himself in a comfortable position. He didn't like bed much at all. It was a young man's game. Not just the tomfoolery, that was a young man's game no argument at all, but even going up to sleep: one moment going about on your legs, the next dead to the world. Being old bones was a different story altogether. As soon as you got under your sheets your rheumatism would come out to play, sure as eggs were eggs, a low dull ache in the shoulders and the shins. Then acid in the stomach, moving slowly up towards the chest like the tide coming in, that kind of lippy motion, inch by inch. Next thing your heart would start bouncing about like a jumping jack. Then you'd begin to wonder if your indigestion was heartburn or heart attack in disguise. The aching would reach down to the tips of your fingers, a combination of aching and numbness, even though you'd have thought with any justice the one would be a let-off from having the other. The very last thing on offer was sweet dreams.

Sitting up in his armchair reading Walter Scott bore no comparison. No symptoms at all except occasionally his heart would go pitter-pat, like in the song. Goose walked over my grave, he said to himself when it did that. But he could stretch his arms a little, expand his chest, and it would calm down. It didn't seem to go on the rampage like it did when he was in bed.

This young Scots lass, Effie Deans, had gone off as a servant girl and got herself in bother. Must have happened a thousand times. The baby is born in strict confidence, then disappears, done away with. Part of the midwife's service but little Effie gets the blame. So she is arrested for the murder. Back at home her sister Jeanie still lives with their dad, one of those grim old Scots gents with grey bushy eyebrows, nothing but God the Father from dawn till dusk. Young man seeks them out. A friend of the family, vicar style of bloke, comes across him. Young man says to him he must see Jeanie. *'Tell her, she must meet me at the Hunter's Bog tonight, as the moon rises behind St Anthony's Hill.'* The vicar thinks this is a bit of a cheek. *'Who or what are you, who charge me with such an errand?'*

'I am the devil!' – answered the young man hastily.

No answer to that. *'Call me Apollyon, Abaddon, whatever name you choose,'* he goes on, by way of getting on friendly terms. Never thought of the devil having first names before. The long and short is the message is delivered, and off Jeanie goes to Hunter's Bog.

They must have their fair share of bogs up in Scotland. You get the idea that the young man must have had a hand, or more likely some other part of the body, in the disaster that had befallen little Effie. He says Jeanie must tell the trial that Effie mentioned to her having a bun in the oven.

In Scotland in those days, if you could establish a pregnancy had been concealed by the mother, then the case for infanticide was considered proved. If not, not. Trouble was that Effie *hadn't* told Jeanie she was pregnant, and Jeanie had had too much of a bellyful of keeping to the straight and narrow from her old man to have any truck with fibbing in court, even to save her sister's bacon.

But since Apollyon or Abaddon, whoever he is, knows so much about what really happened, why doesn't *he* bear witness? He could do it with a clear conscience, when all's said and done.

'To whom do you talk of a clear conscience, woman?' said he, with a sudden fierceness which renewed her terrors, – 'to me? – I have not known one for many a year. Bear witness in her behalf? – a proper witness, that, even to speak these few words to a woman of so little consequence as yourself, must choose such an hour and such a place as this. When you see owls and bats fly abroad, like larks, in the sunshine, you may expect to see such as I am in the assemblies of men.'

Not one to shilly-shally, you could say that for him. *'Your sister's fate is in your hands.' So saying, he turned from her, and with a swift, yet cautiously noiseless step, plunged into the darkness, and was soon lost to her sight.* Swift yet cautiously noiseless, funny how you could imagine it all, running off tender-toed, like a cat on hot bricks.

Ernie read on, not daring to look at his pocket watch. The trial was held. Jeanie could not tell a lie. Effie was found guilty. In those days they had the public executioner act as Doomster, to read out the death sentence in court, and save the judge from sullying his lips. *He gabbled over the words, which condemned Euphemia Deans to be conducted back to the Tolbooth of Edinburgh, and detained there until Wednesday the – day of –; and upon that day, betwixt the hours of two and four o'clock afternoon, to be conveyed to the common place of execution, and there hanged by the neck upon a gibbet. 'And this,' said the Doomster, aggravating his harsh voice, 'I pronounce for doom.'*

Pitter-pat.

Ernie got up to stretch his legs. Must be gone midnight. The house was warm as toast. He undid his waistcoat. That gave his heart more room to pitter-pat in, also cooled him off a touch. His shirt stuck to his chest where his waistcoat had been pressing it. He unlocked the back door and stepped out into the garden. This time of the year it never got completely dark. Or more to the point, the dark looked dark enough, but you could still see through it, even without a moon.

There was the bit of lawn and the big square shed. He stepped out under the apple tree.

Missing witness, just like the Ruth Ellis trial. Only difference was, in the story Jeanie Deans was going to save the day. Walter Scott never minded giving the game away in the bit he wrote at the beginning of his books, when he says where the yarn came from. There was a real Jeanie Deans, by name of Helen Walker, and off she trotted to London, to petition some duke or other to get her sister a pardon. Gets her off the hook in the nick of time.

Nobody was going to do that for Ruth Ellis. The paper said Mr Pierrepoint, the doomster, was to spend the night at the prison. Probably couldn't get in through the crowds if he stayed in a guest house. He would be woken first thing in the morning, have his cup of tea and go off to do his business. No witness would turn up on Ruth Ellis's behalf.

She had three last wishes.

1, that candles should be lit in her cell while she received communion from the prison chaplain before her execution.

2, that a crucifix should hang from the wall in the execution room where she could see it a few moments before her death.

3, that she should have some brandy before walking from the condemned cell.

People usually die any old how. This was formal and final, more like a wedding day.

No witness would turn up to say call the whole thing off. No owls and bats would flit about in the sunshine of tomorrow morning. They wouldn't fly about even at night, come to that, at least not here in Stockport.

Chapter Ten

It got hotter and hotter until it burst. That's how it felt.

In the lunch-hour he'd gone over to the school playing-fields. There was a rough patch of ground beyond the football pitch. It had a clump of nettles where Chris Chell had been pushed after his trousers were taken off, but most of the area was long tufty grass, with some big holes in it. Emb said he'd told his dad about them and his dad said bombs probably did them in the war, but Hart said the German bombers must be rotten aimers if that was true, dropping bombs in the middle of nowhere. Donald tried to imagine Emb's dad, a bigger Emb. The school was quite new, though, so maybe what was there before was something the Germans would have wanted to drop bombs on.

What they liked to do was sit on the edge of one of the holes, with their feet in it, in a circle, and throw their caps on each other's heads. They had to wear caps even though it was a secondary modern school, grey ones, and grey jackets. You could put a spin on the caps so they flew level through the air like quoits, and if you got it just right they would drop suddenly out of the sky and land bang on top of the target head like a flying saucer. Usually the person whose head it was was watching it approach and would tilt their head just the right angle to get it landed neatly.

When they got fed up of that they dug for pignuts with Murd's penknife, taking turns. Pignuts were quite nice but they didn't taste of anything. The best part of them was peeling them so all the skin and dirt came off and they were white as a Ping-Pong ball inside.

On this hot day it was Murd, Hart, Fleck and Donald, no Emb, which made a change. Emb was the worst cap thrower of the lot, and he always took extra turns when he did a dud till he finally got there, which messed up the whole thing because the idea was to just do it without any fuss and talk to each other at the same time. With Emb not being there they talked about Emb.

Ever since they'd gone with the Scouts to the Lake District at Easter Emb had been obsessed with sex. He talked about French kissing day in day out. It must be because of that Ballou letting people do what they wanted. There was another Ballou at the Cubs now, according to Murd's little brother, so perhaps the Ballou on the coach had been sacked for being a sex maniac.

If she was one, Emb had caught it off of her, that was certain sure. He'd told them he was going out with a girl who didn't go to their school, called Patricia.

Fleck said it was a bit fishy that with four hundred girls to choose from at their school he had to find one nobody'd ever seen. Hart said it was because no girl at their school could stand the shame of going out with Emb, but if that was right it still meant that maybe there was a real girl called Patricia who was really going out with him. When you were with girls at your own school you could guess what they'd do, and what they'd think of anyone, how far they'd let you go, if anywhere at all. They were real girls, and real would be enough for them. But a girl from somewhere else might be completely different, might even be interested in Emb.

Murd had asked him if she let him go the whole hog but Emb thought he meant something to do with pigs and was sarky at first; afterwards he said yes, she did let him do the lot. She had a mole on one of her tits.

How do you prove it, Fleck said now, while they were talking in their hole, when we've never even seen her, let alone her tit?

It was good fun talking about Emb having sex or not, it felt like as if you were having a small bit of sex yourself. I'm surprised Emb didn't think moles were those things that dig in people's gardens, Fleck said. Perhaps he does, Murd said. Donald imagined the triangle head of a mole poking out of that Patricia's tit.

He's not got a completely little one, Hart said, but he hasn't got a proper-size one either, prolly still growing, halfway between big and little. Hart seemed to have everyone's dick arranged in order in his mind, titchy one end, massive the other. Maybe it's got to as big as it's going to get, Hart said, that's the other possibility.

There was something Donald was dying to tell the others. Emb had told him about it yesterday. They were walking home from school. Emb said he had to go some-where tomorrow evening, at seven o'clock. He didn't sound as boastful as he usually did, in fact he seemed almost frightened about it. He didn't tell what it was to Donald for quite a while, then suddenly did.

It was this man. Not a man, more about twenty. Maybe seventeen or eighteen. He had a car, however old you have to be to drive. Banger kind of car, which made this screechy noise, like cars do when they're skidding round a corner or something, only this car did it when it was just going along as slowly as anything. It wasn't the type of car what could go fast, any case, more like a sort of van.

One day it stopped by him while he was going home, and the bloke asked him if he knew where somebody lived, Mr something or other lived. Emb said no. Another day he stopped and said you're the boy the other day. Emb asked him if he found Mr thing and he said the bloke lived up in Levenshulme not in Stockie at all. Been told it wrong by someone. He gave Emb a fag.

I never seen you smoke, Emb, Donald said. I smoke, Emb said, looking snooty. Emb's nose curled up because it was such a big deal he smoked this cigarette the car bloke gave him. Donald nearly told him about smoking cigarettes while you're wanking, but you couldn't tell Emb things like that because he'd probably laugh till his head fell off. But Donald told about it to Hart. Hart had done a slow nod, like as if he was saying, you're beginning to get the idea, chum.

The bloke asked Emb what school he went to, what he liked to do, did he have a girlfriend, all things like that. Emb probably told him a lot of tosh about Patricia with the mole on her tit. Then the bloke started talking about this girl. She was a year or two older than Emb, but not as old as the bloke.

He kept telling me just little bits about her, Emb said. Donald could almost hear him doing that, sort of wanting to tell Emb about her and not wanting to at the same time, and Emb listening with his ear growing bigger and bigger like a rose or a daffodil or something, making sure he didn't miss a single scrap of it.

She likes boys, the man said, she goes like this for them. He lolloped his tongue out and panted to show how she went. Emb did it to show how the man went and the man did it to show how the girl went. She has a crush on you, the man said. But I've never seen her, Emb said. But she's seen you, we drove past you in the van one day. She looked at you and she said that one would do me OK. She said he's my type, I could go for him.

Emb shut his eyes and showed his top teeth and made them keep biting down on his bottom lip with his nose screwed up, like doing how a rabbit twitches. The man must have done it to show how the girl more or less wanted to eat Emb, and Emb remembered it exactly, same as remembering someone's exact words. Donald could see the man doing it even though he'd never seen the man.

You know I said about looking for where the bloke was who turned out to live in Levenshulme? the man said, I made it up because she wanted me to get to know you, like. It was just an excuse. But if she's your girlfriend, where do I come into it? Emb asked him. She's not my girlfriend, she's my sister, the man said. You know, Emb said to Donald, like Hart's sister, like the bra and that.

Bloody hell, sisters, Donald said. All he had was a brother, and Peter was more or less still only a baby, anyhow.

I said but she's older than me, Emb said. That's what she likes, the bloke said, she likes doing it with boys a bit younger. That's the best part about it. She's pretty bossy, he said, you haven't got to mind her being bossy. I don't mind, Emb said, she can be bossy all she likes.

Tell you what, Emb said to Donald. He lowered his voice in case anyone was listening, even though they were just standing in dog muck park by now and nobody at all was near them, who I think is his sister, I think it's that Blue what went camping with us. I think she's his sister.

What you got to do, Emb said to Donald, is not tell anybody. Anybody at all. I won't say a dicky-bird, Donald said. No, I mean it, Emb told him. No, I mean it as well. Cross your heart. Cross my heart.

Donald crossed his heart then cut his throat to prove it, then asked is it because of Patricia?

Patricia? asked Emb. He did a little jump as he said it, as if that was the last word he expected to hear, then moved his lips as if he was saying it to himself over again, Patricia, like some word he'd forgotten the meaning of. Maybe he was so busy thinking about this van bloke's sister that he couldn't remember who she was, or maybe it was because there'd never been a Patricia in the first place. He had a look about him which reminded Donald of Peter when he was waiting for you to jump out at him and say boo.

Emb said, in a grumpy voice, all what I'm saying, not tell a thing to anybody.

I told you, Donald said, I never tell on a mate.

Murd dug out a pignut with the knife. He peeled it and cut them all a bit. They ate it. It was almost too hot to move.

When the thunder began to roll it felt like thunder

225

inside your head. Then the light went away, one minute blue sky the next fat purple clouds everywhere. It made you feel like as if your body was falling to pieces. 'Bloody hell,' Murd said, 'it's going to piss it down.' But they didn't run back to school while there was still time, they just sat there chewing their bits of pignut.

'I think he's not just got Patricia,' Donald said.

'Who?' Murd asked. 'Not got what?'

'Who'd you think? Emb. Not got. Patricia.' Thing was, you couldn't keep the ideas in your head on the go. It was like being in the gap between a sunny day and a storm, like that funny bit in-between carriages on a train, sort of inside a concertina. It made you feel you were sliding away.

'I don't think he's got her, neither,' Fleck said.

'No but, I think he's got another one on the go and all.'

'Come on,' Hart said, '*Emb?*'

'Who?' Murd asked. 'Who's he got on the go?'

'Don't know.'

'That's a fat lot of good.'

It was just as if it got hotter and hotter till it burst. There were two or three splashes in the long grass, then it was bucketing down. It rained so hard down their hole that it bounced up again when it hit the ground.

'Fuck a duck,' Hart said.

They all stood up and put their caps on double-quick. Fleck pulled his jacket up over his head, cap included, so he looked like a hunchback with little dinosaur arms dangling at the front.

'Oh shit,' Murd said.

Soaked as he was, Donald didn't mind it. He liked all the different sorts of rain.

Here she was, arm in arm with Jack, talking about their wedding day. If any children come along, I'll make sure they walk *beside*, Ruth thought, not tag along behind, like we used to do.

First dad, then mum scurrying along about ten yards

226

behind, then Janice, then Ruth herself. When they went off to the bus stop to go shopping they practically took up the whole street, they were so spread out. Dad was a little bloke like a ferret, but those legs of his could zip along. Mum next, hell for leather, her bosoms jangling and mithered. She had a brassiere big as one of the great catapults they used in days gone by, two, more to the point. Janice next, like one of those water things that walk on the top of water with their long thin legs, water buffalo Ruth wanted to call them. Then Ruth, so far behind she was almost a member of the public, but still had to go along with the others, no escape.

It would have been so nice to be one of those families that stayed clustered together like a bunch of flowers. Nothing flowerish about *them*, their house ponged to high heaven, used to hit you like a wall whenever you'd been out of it a while.

Worst thing about her dad was the way he'd come into bed with her and Janice when mum was having one of her bad days. 'What's the odds,' he would say if they complained, 'it's all the same, in't it? Don't think you got anything different from anybody else, my girl,' which was the last thing she thought. 'You got to remember, there's a war on,' he liked to tell them, too.

In front of her and Jack, Gyp trotted on his lead. His little legs could zip along as well.

'I booked the registry office for August the second,' Jack said, 'the Tuesday. They couldn't do us on the Monday. I don't know whether it was fully booked, or whether they don't have weddings on a bank holiday. Eleven o'clock. Then I thought we could go to the Griffin for a little celebration. Not a lot. A few sandwiches and a cake. Then drive off to Bournemouth in the afternoon, stay there the rest of the week. I booked that hotel I went to last year for the divorce. It seemed a nice enough place.'

'A hotel,' Ruth said.

'Course a hotel. You only get married the once. Well, a

227

couple of times in my case. Sentimental attachment, the way I look at it.'

'I've not been in a hotel before. I thought we were just going to come back to our house.'

'You've no need to worry. You're a ladylike person by nature. You'll fit like a glove.'

'I won't know which fork to use, that type of thing.'

'Don't forget, catering's my trade. I'll see you're all right.'

'Oh yes,' she said, relieved. She pictured his big hand coming across the white tablecloth, sliding the fish fork into hers while nobody was looking. And even if they were, who cared? They would just think to themselves, love's young dream. Not too young of course, but that made it all the nicer. 'That's where the lads swing,' she said, pointing at the rope which dangled over the little river.

'I didn't think it was where they hanged theirselves.'

'Oh, you.'

'Tell you what,' he said, 'I'm not having my Donald along. If I had him, I'd have to have Petey, and he's still glued to his mother, see what I mean?'

'I should think not,' she said, shocked at the very thought.

'Just a couple of pals. Bernard, who I own the garage with.'

'I thought he was a bit of a toff.'

'He's all right when you get to know him.'

'I would have liked Mrs McMahon, if she still had the legs. I'll have to tell her all about it after. Who I'll invite, I'll invite Uncle Gerald. He can get somebody in, to keep an eye on the pub.'

'I don't think he likes me much.'

'He's family.'

'I'll take your word for it, duck.'

'All the family I've got, nowadays.'

'You've got me. You'll be Mrs Willis soon.'

Little Gyp pulled on his lead so hard his eyes nearly

popped out of his head. 'Why don't you let him off?' Jack asked.

'This is near where we saw the fox that time,' she said.

'Well, the fox won't eat him.'

She let Gyp off his lead and he rushed away up the path. 'He'll soon be Gyp Willis,' she said.

'If you say so.'

'Tell you what, can you change somebody's name after they're dead, Jack?'

'What do you mean?'

'Well, say a woman has a baby, and the baby dies. And then after a bit she gets married again. Then she would have a different name from her own baby.' The thought of it suddenly made her eyes fill with tears. 'The baby would be all by itself.'

They walked on a while without Jack saying anything. It was stifling hot. Then he asked, 'Did *you* have a baby, Ruthie?' He said it in one of those careful voices, so she would know he was taking trouble to not go angry or upset. Dad had done that sometimes, talk polite to you, at his most frightening when for all the world he was being so niminy piminy pop.

'Of course I didn't,' she said, shocked at the idea. She couldn't imagine what she'd been thinking of. It's me being on my monthly, she told herself. The only living creature she'd had, before Gyp, had been that blimmin goldfish.

Fat lot of good changing *its* name to Willis. She remembered how sad it had been in its bowl, how it had opened and shut its mouth, with its lips sort of curved down. It hadn't even known it had a name in the first place.

'I don't see as how it makes a lot of difference,' Jack said. 'When you're dead, you're dead.'

'It might have its name on its gravestone.'

'All the more reason for doing bugger all. You can hardly do crossings out in solid marble, put a line through the old name and chip in the new one on top of it.'

'I suppose not,' she said. She knew her voice sounded

trembly. 'I'm worried where Gyp's got to.'

'We'll probably come upon a pile of little bones, where he got himself munched by Mr Fox.'

'Don't say that, Jack, even in joke. You gave me Gyp, same as you gave me that goldfish that time. It's always you what gives me things.'

'Maybe I'll be giving you something else, before too long.'

He said it as if it was something and nothing. She looked at him out of the corner of her eyes. Maybe she'd hinted to him too much. She didn't mean to, but when things were in her mind she couldn't stop them tumbling out. Best to talk as if it was about something else.

'Will you bake it your own self?'

'You what?'

'The cake.'

'My word, I call that a bad case of the willies.'

It was Gyp, just round a corner of the path. He was crouched down low, with his hair all standing on end, and his teeth bared.

'That fox must've come back,' Ruth said.

'Or he's got the smell of it, from before.'

'Gyp,' she said. He took no notice. 'I think he can see him,' she whispered to Jack.

'Fox worth its salt would have buggered off by now. Be long gone.'

'Oh.' She looked around but there was no sign of the fox. 'Come on, Gyp,' she said, but he still took no notice. 'Tell you what,' she said to Jack, 'I don't think I'd want Mrs McMahon there, even if she did have the use of her legs.'

'We could put a sofa on the pavement outside the registry office, and let her sleep through it, same as usual,' Jack said, 'that'd be the way.'

Ruth did a bit of a laugh, but not too much of one, because she suddenly realised it might turn into crying again. Mustn't let Jack see how soppy she was, at least till after the wedding, when it probably couldn't be helped. 'Come *on*, Gyp,' she said.

Jack bent down to pick him up. 'Little bugger's stiff as a poker,' he said.

At that moment there was a crack of thunder. Gyp jumped on to Jack's shoulder as if there were springs in his feet. '*That's* what was up, was it, little feller?' Jack said. 'Thunder coming on.'

Maybe that's what was up with me as well, Ruth thought, not just my period but the weather building. Maybe I'm not as daft as I thought I was.

'It'll be pissing down in a moment,' Jack said, 'We better get back.'

'I'd like it to have two what-do-you-ma-call-ums,' she said. She really couldn't think what you did call them. With a house you called them storeys. 'Even if each one is a very small one. Sooner than having only the one, only bigger.'

'What you on about, Ruth?'

'The cake,' she said. 'Cakes. With those little pillars between.'

'I'm not baking us a cake.'

'Oh.' She didn't need rain, she could rain all by herself. The tears flew into her eyes and straight down her face. It's me who's pouring down, she thought. She wouldn't say the word Jack said about the rain even in her head. She didn't like the way he used bad language to her sometimes. It was different when you were in the pub.

Luckily Jack had his head tucked to one side, choo-chooing at Gyp, so he didn't see her blart. The funny part was, Gyp was curled round his neck just like when a woman wears one of those fox stoles. 'You being a chef, I thought –'

'I can't bake a cake for our own wedding,' Jack said. 'It's my wedding too, you know. It would be like making myself my own birthday cake.'

'Oh yes, course it would.' She took a big sniff as if she was sniffing the approaching storm, so he wouldn't pay attention to her weepy eyes. 'I'm sorry, I didn't think.'

231

'What I'll do, I'll order one from a bakery for us. How about that?'

'Oh yes, please. And will it have –?'

'Have what?'

'You know.'

'Have what, Ruthie?'

'An upstairs and a downstairs.'

The rain came. Funny thing was, the first thing you noticed, before you even felt the wet, was the noise. Wuff, Gyp said, angry at the weather.

What you don't always spot is what isn't there any more. When did the telephones go? Silly question, people hadn't worn their hair that way for many a long year. It was just a fashion. But nobody said Sylvie had to have her hair cut sharp round just below her ears and across her forehead, like an olden days sort of head cover she'd just pulled on to her head. You could hardly see her ears any more, and when you did they didn't have earrings on. As if she was saying, they're just ears, want to make something of it? She smelled nice enough but of cologne water, not cachous. Clean was the look she was after. Who'd be clean? Ernie wondered. Not me. Dirty old man, me.

Her blouse did up all the way to the neck, despite the heat. A bosom was a bosom when all was said and done, but hers seemed far off now, far off and long ago. Just a couple of bumps in the material and no one any the wiser.

'You been here some years, Sylvie,' he said.

'Don't say that, Mr B. Gives me the collywobbles.' She didn't even have enough vim to be snooty to him any more.

'I was just recalling that spot of bother you had a year or two back, with that young man of yours.'

Bull's-eye, for what it was worth. She reddened up. Even her white blouse seemed to go pink. Her eyes took on a hot look that reminded him of how Donald's went when he'd gone a bit feverish with rheumatism in the blood.

'What his name was,' he said, not so much to press the point as to give her a moment or two, 'Popeye, or there-abouts.'

'Davy Popham,' she said.

'That's the one.'

'Married his Shirley and lived happy ever after. They have two kiddies. A lickle boy and a lickle girl. Trust old Davy to get his cruet set.'

Ernie didn't know whether she said lickle to be sarcastic or whether she was one of those people who couldn't say it any other way. He once had an apprentice sicked on him who said frikened, despite being strong as an ox and half as brainy. 'Plenty more fish in the sea,' he told her. Blimey, he thought, she's got to the point where her old boyfriends are family men. If *she*'s getting past it where does that leave me?

High and dry, where I've been since the year dot.

He sat down at the newspaper table. The year dot. Well-named. Must be all those books I've been reading. Year dot. O-one, if you want to put a number to it. O-one or o-two, somewhere about then. The year I got myself fixed up with Dot Peach.

It wasn't that he felt he had to take Albert's place. Or had the chance of taking Albert's place, had the opportunity to take advantage.

Of course, it could have looked like that, from one point of view. Albert had been spoony on Dorothy. He, Ernest, had thought that who Albert was gone on was Dorothy's mother.

He'd mistaken the one for the other and as a result, no more Albert.

Young girl, lost her beau. Most natural thing in the world to make it up to her.

But he hadn't been up to working it all out in that fashion. At least not that he could remember. Thing about reading Walter Scott, or any writer come to that, his people always seemed to know their own minds. Bad or good they woke up in the morning knowing how to behave. Ruth Ellis similar. In point of fact she was so relaxed she didn't even bother to wake up yesterday morning, the day she was hanged. Slept till eight forty-five, due to go to the rope nine o'clock. Not a trace of panic.

Made your head swim, the thought of her knowing what she was about to that extent. She seemed more a person in a book than a real woman, especially now it was all over and done with.

For his part all Ernie ever seemed to do was muddle along.

Dorothy had been on hand. Day in day out. You could hear her breathing, even from the next room.

In those days you didn't have a lot of opportunities to mingle with the opposite sex, not like now. No pictures to go to, or dance halls. You couldn't take a young lady into a pub. But there Dorothy was, back of Peach and Son, breathing away.

He wasn't trying to make it up to her. But from one point of view you could see it as a vacancy, like when they advertise a job in the paper, sit vac.

One day, not long after Albert left, Hilda Peach appeared in the office. Harold was out with the new apprentice, watching him work. What his name was, gone with the wind. You have apprentices by the cartload in a working life. Ernest doing something with the books.

Hilda in her full regalia. Hair stacked up on her head with a hat on top of it at an angle, like a small boat in a typhoon. That's how he remembered her, anyhow. Parasol with tassles. Little tapestry-work bag with a loop round her wrist. What she would do with herself in Stockport in that get-up, who could think.

Half a century later, the answer came to him. Nothing.

She would have just walked down the road, gone round the local park, killed time. Left him to do the business with Dorothy.

'I'm just going out for an hour, Ernest,' she said.

'Right-oh, Mrs Peach.'

'Annie's not in today, remember.'

'Oh. Yes.'

'So . . .'

So what?

'So, listen out.' She crinkled up her nose, as to say, you understand. He even recalled her raising a white gloved hand to her little ear and giving it a wag, to illustrate listen.

He hadn't understood at all. What did he think she meant? Dorothy being an eighteen-year-old female left to her own devices, she was bound to do something foolish, fall down the stairs or stab herself in the palm of the hand with a kitchen knife, is that what he thought she meant? Listen out for screaming, as disaster struck?

It was like reading one of those letters that take fifty years to deliver. Here he was, sitting at a table in the library, heat like a blast furnace, sweat dribbling down his back, and at last he understood her.

What Hilda Peach meant was, you've got an hour to canoodle away to your heart's content. What she meant was, listen out for *me*, coming back.

What she meant was, this is my chance to get Dot off my hands once and for all.

The sniffs and snuffles from out back had sounded less and less annoying as Ernest sat in the office and *listened out*. He stopped thinking of them as coming from Dorothy Peach, with her blocked-up nose and sagging mouth. They sounded more like the scurrying about of some animal. Anyway he was beginning to breathe a bit himself. All he could think of was: there's a girl in the next room, and nobody else in the house.

He stood up. He walked up and down the room a turn or two, almost as if he was trying to put somebody who wasn't even there off the scent. Probably thought he was being so cunning, trying to take advantage while Hilda's back was turned.

Thought never struck him that she'd turned her back on purpose. All he was thinking about were the words of poor Albert: they're no better than us, you know. It better be true, he thought. He knocked on the door.

Me and Sylvie are in the same boat, Ernie realised. She didn't marry Davy Popham. I did marry Dorothy. Both of us marooned. Not just us. What about Dorothy herself? Spent a lifetime being married to a man who didn't even like her much. Not that she liked him much in return. What a thing for a married couple to have in common, not liking each other much.

She had liked Albert, he could tell that by the way she talked of him from time to time. Perhaps Albert had liked her. Which meant he, Ernest, had diddled them both. He'd pinched Albert's girl from him, and Dorothy's young man from her. He'd mucked up the lives of all the three of them.

That's what came of telling on a mate.

He didn't even end up inheriting the business. After Albert went, it limped on for a year or two, then folded. Ernie ended up working for a big plumbing firm based on the other side of town.

There was a crack of thunder, and shortly after Ernie saw through the library window that it had started chucking it down.

You can eat snails. Daddy said. Donald said he ate a worm. Worms have a head like a crayon. The snails nearly have a proper head. They are not like a crayon. They have bumps on their head. The bumps grow. On top of the bumps they have eyes. Their eyes can look. They have eyes like the man in the circus with long long legs. And they have a little mouth that can only eat small food. When you eat them they have a crunchy part then chewy. The crunchy part is called the shell. You can suck it. The snaily part tastes like snot.

A snail you silly, mummy said. Peter said daddy said you can eat them. Mummy said daddy. She took the shell and threw it. She said a day like this and then the sky broke. It was so loud Peter put his hands over his ears and ran away. Mummy ran and picked him up. He liked feeling her big steps as she carried him along.

Nowhere like a garage for watching the rain fall. Jack stood in Bunter's all afternoon like a spare leg while the stuff dropped on their cobbly access road, the old mill opposite, the VD clinic a bit beyond. It was so hot there were wisps of steam.

Behind him Edwin was chuntering on to himself. Naturally, he didn't like Jack here during the day, thought he was being checked up on, being as Jack usually didn't put in an appearance until after he'd done a day's work at the café. There wasn't anything for Jack to do in any case, given the books were up to scratch.

The only person who would spare a word was Cliff, the clearer-upperer, and he was a grumpy so-and-so, not surprising after years of having the living daylights bashed out of him in the boxing-ring.

Jack had seen him once, late in his career if it could be so called, at Stockport Town Hall, matched up against Ray Tartura, the human windmill. By that stage Cliff had a stomach on him and his legs were on the spindly side. Maybe he'd always been like that. He took a horrible pasting, blows raining down. Tartura wasn't big built but he could cluster his punches till there was no escape. The local rag said Cliff's face assumed gargoyle proportions, which summed it up, though funnily enough when it deflated again the opposite was the case: his features had been boxed pretty well flat.

Apart from some part-time life-saving at Reddish Baths, Cliff was practically on his uppers when Jack came across him. Jack gave him some work helping Eddie and his lad sort out the garage when it was first bought, and since then had had him in a couple of days a week to keep everything ticking over, fetch spares, that type of caper. With that and the swimming-pool job he eked a living of sorts.

'You don't know of a nice cakeshop round about, do you, Cliff?' Jack asked him.

'You what?'

'Cakeshop.'

He only really asked to dumbfound Cliff. Cliff stared out at the hot rain with those miserable eyes of his that probably hadn't taken in anything fresh since they saw Ray Tartura's fists approaching like a couple of cannonballs. 'One round the corner,' he said eventually.

'That where you go to get your iced fancies, is it?'

'Ha ha,' Cliff said. He slid a finger the size of a sausage up his nose, which had been squelched to such an extent his nostrils lay flat against his face at ninety degrees to the usual layout. His nose swelled with the finger like a snake swallowing its prey.

'My dad-in-law told me once that people in the old days used to pick each other's noses as a mark of true love.'

'Oh yeah?' Cliff pulled his forefinger out and held it aloft, completely unembarrassed. There was no trophy on the top of it. Funnily enough Rose's dad had had a finger sticking up the last few days, middle one in his case, done something to cause it to go rigid while working on his new allotment, but he tried to conceal his, walking about with his hand behind his back as if he had a present for somebody.

'I'll give it a try,' Jack said.

'You can keep your fucking finger to yourself.'

'I mean the cakeshop.'

'Please yourself.'

One point about Cliff, you didn't need to fear being buttered up.

There was nothing refreshing about the rain, so warm it was almost sticky. When Jack got to the bakery they were just clearing up for the day, nice jolly-looking woman, do for Mrs Bun in Happy Families, her hair in a kind of parcel tied up with a blue scarf, the husband a little worried type of bloke with brylcreemed hair slicked back. It must be four o'clock, near enough. Jack had forgotten that in the bakery trade they've done all the business they're going to do by mid-afternoon.

'Sorry,' said the bloke, 'we've just cashed up.'

'That's all right. I wanted to place an order.'

'Better ask the missus.' He was stacking aluminium trays.

'What can we do for you?' the missus asked. Funny thing about her being Mrs Bun, there was a white sprinkle on her cheeks which looked just like icing sugar or flour, but could have been pale face powder.

'What I want to ask about –' At that moment out from the back of the shop strolled Bernard. 'Bloody hell,' Jack said.

'I thought it was you,' Bernard said.

He was his usual self, suit a bit long in the sleeves, tortoise lips in a grin, attaché case clutched in one of those froggy hands of his. When you see somebody in an unexpected place you see them fresh, and Jack suddenly thought: he's a simple sort, Bernard is, that's why he's clever at what he does. Doesn't let complication get in the way. He's pleased as punch catching me on the hop.

'What are you doing here?' Jack asked him.

'I could ask you the same thing. I would have thought you'd still be at the café at this time of day.'

'Day off.'

'You don't say?'

'We're opening on Saturday this week. In the evening. Stan's organised a gourmet night. Wiener schnitzel, the lot. He's wanted to try it since the year dot. People can bring their own bottles. If it's a success he wants to aim for the evening trade and apply for a licence. Big nobs coming, we've all got to show our faces. Stan, Mrs Stan, Larry

Mendoza on the joanna, even Ken's going to be there. I've got today off in lieu.'

'Ken might not be at his best.'

'Is he ever?'

'What I mean is, he might still be steaming a little.' Bernard had a look as if he was carrying a present, so thirsty to give his snippet of news.

'Oh?'

'I got a phone call from him, just before I left home. He's at Ascot.'

'What's he doing there?'

'Royal Ascot, what do you think?'

'He didn't say anything. About going.'

'It was a last minute do. I was due to go. With that pal of mine, Mrs Onslow. You remember her.'

'Oh yes.'

'But something cropped up this morning, so I had to drop out. Ken went instead. Maybe it's kismet, or whatever they call it. He's gone and got himself struck by lightning. The whole bunch of them have. Even while he was phoning me, he said his hair was standing on end.'

'Blow me.'

'Nasty do. A thunderbolt struck the stand. He said for a second he thought the lot of them were going to be fused together in a solid block. Then they were rolling all over the shop like so many ninepins. I suppose poor Mrs Onslow's hair stood on end as well. It won't do her any favours. She'll look like that woman in Greek tragedy whose hair was made of snakes. What went through my mind was, if I'd gone instead, maybe I'd be done for. I don't think I'm the sort to put up much resistance to lightning. I have this picture of myself lying in the paddock, twitching.'

'*Did* anyone cop it?'

'One person did, Ken thought. If I'd been there it would probably have been me. I once tried to change a light bulb and got such a shock I must have lit up the whole room. Ken says the tips of his fingers have gone black. He thought they were charred at first, then realised it was soot. But it makes you think.'

'Yes,' said Jack. 'It does.'

Mrs Bun and her hubby went through to the back of the shop, with a pile of trays each, and the leftover loaves. 'Pig bloke comes and picks them up in the evening,' Bernard said.

'I didn't know you had an interest in a bakery,' said Jack. 'Specially it being so near Bunter's.'

'Oh well, I haven't got much interest in it to tell you the truth, except money. You don't get the margin in this sort of business. The lady of the shop worked for a friend of mine in earlier days, so I got to hear. They were going to sell and got let down at the last minute. A few years ago. This German chap had arranged to buy them out lock, stock and barrel. Cash in hand, no nonsense about it. He'd been saving up for years, unbeknownst to his missus, meant it for a surprise. He was going to make those German cakes a speciality, apple strudel and Black Forest gateau, that type of caper. Then he passed away just before the exchange of contracts, and that was the end of that plan. By name Fartblower, or words to that effect. I put some money in the business, to keep the wolf from the door. I get my percentage, so I can't complain.'

Jack opened his mouth but couldn't say anything. Bernard noticed, and gave a sharpish look, but before he had time to ask what was up, Mrs Bun came back in.

'Was you saying you wanted to place an order?' she asked Jack.

'Yes,' Jack told her.

She looked at him, waiting. 'For what?' she asked in the end.

'Oh,' he said. 'A cake.'

'A cake.'

'Yes.'

'What kind of cake?'

'Fruit cake, I should think.'

241

'What I mean, is it for a birthday or what?'

Jack paused. Then he said, nearly in a whisper, 'Get Well cake.'

'A Get Well cake?'

'That's the one.'

'Sometimes they're on a diet,' she said, 'you've got to be careful.'

'She could do with fattening up,' Jack said.

Jack was home for tea for once. 'To what do we owe the honour?' Rose had asked him. Apparently it had been a slack day at the café, and Stan said clock off early. Donald was telling him about doing algebra.

'It's when you put a instead of the number,' he said.

'A what?' Jack asked him.

'An *a*,' Donald said. 'A. Or b.'

'But if it's fourteen,' Jack said, 'you can't put eighteen. So if it's a, how can it might just as well be b?'

'Stop pestering him, Jack,' Rose said.

'It's just algebra, that's all,' Donald said.

'It's beyond me.' Jack shook his head. 'Never was any good at mathematics.' He had a crafty little smile on his face. He liked to tease, but was one of those teasers that never bothered to say fooled you. He left his teases in mid-air, which Rose thought was a bit mean of him. 'I've got some news,' he said next, using the same little smile as he'd had for Donald.

'Oh yes?' she said. She was past getting herself aerated when he made his announcements. Once, some years back, he'd done a big tarara-boom-de-ay which had made her think he was about to say he'd bought them a new house to live in, and all it turned out to be was a piano for the café. So she sat there quite ready to tell him to stick whatever-it-was up his jumper. It won't be a new house, that's for sure, was her thought.

'I fixed up for us to go to Bournemouth,' Jack said.

'You *what*?' She looked at the others for some sign of a

response. Dad was miles away. He'd been much shaken at hearing on the news about a bolt of lightning that had struck a hundred people at Ascot. 'The day after they hanged Ruth Ellis,' he'd announced, as if there was some connection between the two events. Donald was still muttering to himself about algebra, and Peter had stuffed a whole corned-beef sandwich in his mouth so his cheeks were inflated like balloons and he had to press the heel of his hand against his lips to stop it popping out. Jack could have said he'd fixed up to go to the moon for all any of them noticed.

'First two weeks of August. The lot of us. It's about time we had a family holiday.'

'You could have said something about it first,' she said in an icy tone. 'I would have quite liked to be consulted.'

'I thought you could do with a break. I saw this place advertised in Stan's paper. Holiday chalet. Vacancy had come available due to cancellation. It was a bit of luck, being how hot the summer's turning out, and the short notice. I thought I better look sharp. I used the telephone in the café. Otherwise I'd have had to come home, talk to you, and ring them from a phone box, by which time it would have been too late likely as not.'

'It's raining today,' dad said.

'Rain, rain,' Peter added.

'Don't talk with your mouth full,' Rose told him. In reply Peter opened his mouth hugely wide and sat with it like that. Sure enough it was clean as a whistle inside, not a crumb. It could have been hoovered. He must have swallowed the sandwich whole, like an oyster.

'But still hot,' Donald said quickly. The penny had dropped about going to Bournemouth. 'Hot as hot.' Rose realised he feared dad and Peter might argue them out of the holiday.

'Hot all right,' she said. 'I didn't know where to put myself.'

'You'll give yourself lockjaw if you're not careful,' dad told Peter. Peter shut his mouth pronto. His milk teeth clashing together made an oddly high-pitched sound, almost a ping.

'I didn't intend to sneep you,' Jack said, quite humbly.

Now she thought about it, they hadn't had a proper family holiday before, not as such. What they'd tended to do was go down to visit Len and Eunice in Gosport, but since Eunice had died it wasn't the same. Not that Len was unwelcoming, he just seemed different without her about, turned in upon himself. Also he insisted in taking Donald out in his horrible leaky boat, along with that crippled friend of his who'd be a fat lot of good if they sank, waving his crutch one last time before disappearing under the waves. It had given her the cold shivers, entrusting Donald to that pair. In any case, Peter had put a bit of a dampener on it. Holiday hardly seems worth the bother when you have a babe in arms.

Dad cleared his throat, for all the world as if he was going to make a useful contribution. 'There was a queue a mile long for the train back to London from Brighton last Saturday evening,' he said. 'There'd been that many day-trippers. Teddy boys tried to shove their way in. There were a few scuffles, according to the paper.'

'I don't like Teddy boys,' Peter said.

'There won't be any Teddy boys at Bournemouth,' Donald told him.

'I don't like them,' Peter insisted.

'Also girls,' dad said. 'I don't know what the name for *them* is.'

'I ate a snail,' Peter said in a loud voice, looking off into the middle distance. He obviously wanted to change the subject.

'That was your fault,' Rose told Jack. 'He said you said you could eat them.'

Jack looked at Peter in surprise and then laughed. 'Well, the Frogs do,' he said.

'I didn't eat a frog,' Peter said, shaking his head. 'I ate a snail.'

'He didn't eat much of it,' Rose said, softening. 'I told him it was dirty.'

Jack sang:

> 'Baby doppy poony
> On the duddy floor
> Daddy say he will not pick
> That poony up no more
> Ickle baby cy cy
> Daddy bery soon
> Bendy down on duddy floor
> And picky up dat poon.'

'I think Peter's getting a bit too old for that,' Rose told him.

'*He* might be. I'm not.'

Rose thought: I'm being mean to Jack, making heavy weather of this holiday. It's not his fault he has to work such long hours at the café. She had a tendency to jump down his throat at the slightest thing. It would be nice for Donald to have a seaside holiday. And for Peter to see the sea for the first time.

'Well, everybody,' she said, 'won't it be fun, us all off to Bournemouth?'

'I won't like the teddy bears,' Peter said grimly.

'*Boys*, you twerp,' Donald said.

'He thinks Bournemouth is plagued by man-eating teddy bears,' Jack said, laughing, but Peter just stared off into the middle distance. Donald wasn't amused either, too worried that the holiday might go off the rails, in all probability.

Donald could see Peter was seeing something that wasn't there. His eyes were moving but not to look outside. Peter's eyes were looking at a picture inside his head. Donald said twerp to him but he took no notice. Donald didn't say twerp because Peter was a twerp but because he didn't like how he was looking. Dad said man-eating teddy bears and laughed but you shouldn't laugh. You shouldn't laugh and you shouldn't say twerp.

Seven o'clock was when Emb was going to meet the man in the van. It was a quarter past six now. There was three-quarters of an hour left, till it was too late.

He used to have a book when he was young, about a man who fell from a plane in the war for a mile without a parachute. When he began to fall he could see the forest far below, and then it kept on getting nearer. Once Donald asked grandad how long it would have taken the man to fall all the way. Grandad was interested in everything to do with people dying. Grandad said a few numbers, muttering them and closing one eye as if he was looking along something to check it was level, looking along the calculations he was doing, maybe, and then said a minute, which seemed about right. You could imagine it being a minute. When mum and dad bought Donald his Ingersoll watch with a second hand, same sort as dad's, he tried holding his breath for a minute. He held it for thirty-two seconds and then he could feel himself beginning to die. When you were holding your breath the second hand crawled around the watch one tick at a time, and seemed to take a little rest when it got to the blob of green luminous paint by each number. But the trouble was that when you want to start breathing again after you've stopped for thirty-two seconds you can't do it at first, as if that's a long enough time for you to have forgotten how. Donald had stood there telling himself to breathe and not breathing. He thought to himself: this is the daftest way of dying anybody ever did, just standing here until I drop dead because I've forgotten how to breathe.

Then suddenly a whole load of air came in at once. It sounded like a big snore, one of those wallopers dad did sometimes when he came home late from the pub.

The man without a parachute must have known for certain sure he was going to die even though he didn't die.

246

The minute of his falling must have seemed like for ever.

All his life Donald had remembered that forest tilting towards him, had lived through that man's minute. Those Christmas trees shooting upwards like rocket ships, coming and coming, fast and yet slow at the same time.

That was how seven o'clock was coming towards Donald now, fast and yet slow. Donald felt he was falling down towards a great forest called seven o'clock; only when he landed there it would be Emb who died.

Donald asked: 'Grandad, have any kids been killed lately?'

Grandad looked up from his book. Then he looked round to check if mum or dad were there, but they'd gone. Mum had taken Peter off for his bath. Dad was washing up the tea things, first time since the kitchen was done. He'd said he wanted to give it a try.

'Kiddies're being killed all the time, same as everybody else,' he said.

'Any in the paper today?'

He thought for a moment. 'It said about a boy of six, killed by a shooting coal.'

'Shooting?'

'It would have been that slaty kind, which is liable to jump. Burnt to death, poor little lad. Only had his pyjamas on.'

'But it's too hot to have a fire in any case.'

Donald realised as he spoke it was a soppy thing to say, as if that should mean a let-off, like a goal not being allowed. He thought of the way they used to come alive again playing the war in the playground at primary school, Nelstrop School, when you got killed and had to count up to fifty not to be dead any longer.

Emb, going to be killed at seven o'clock by the man with the van thingie. Count fifty, Emb, and you can be in the land of the living again. Emb being Emb would probably believe it was true.

Hung from an apple tree when you're seven: count fifty.

Then be alive once more, not let some other boy you've never met live your life far far below while you sit up in heaven and wait for ever.

'Happened last winter, I expect. What it was, it would have been the coroner's report, must have been the report of the inquest, saying how the lad come to cop it.'

'What I meant, any died *yesterday*? Any murdered yesterday?'

'What's the matter, little feller? You got a touch of the willies?' Ernie asked. Maybe he *had* been grinding on too much about the Ruth Ellis case, created a morbid atmosphere. Young chap like Donald broods about it all, next thing he thinks he's going to be done away with in his bed. He's not too old yet awhile to get such ideas in his head. None of us are, for that matter. And he always was a sensitive soul.

Saw him once upon a time go white as a sheet, eyes like saucers. Dandelion-clock head he had in them days.

'Ruth Ellis didn't kill any children. She had children of her own. Who she killed was a grown-up. Mind you, her kiddies've been left in the lurch.'

'I didn't mean her. I meant anyone. I meant someone they haven't caught yet. A man who goes round collecting children in a van, then he goes off and kills them somewhere.'

'You have been thinking it through.'

'Is there? Someone?'

'You get a case like that from time to time. I don't know of one at the present.'

'But what they want to kill children for? If people hate somebody or want to wipe out their enemies, who've done them wrong, I mean that's fair enough. Is the children part for practice or what?'

Donald thought of Ballou French kissing all those Scouts because some sex maniac part of her liked doing it, and

248

of that stuff the van man said about his sister wanting boys younger than herself. He wanted grandad to say something about that as well, to prove it was true. It was so screwy it seemed like the sort of thing you just dreamed might happen when you were having a go, Joe, or that you made up while sitting round the hole, throwing caps. Or like stuff Emb said: 'Shagged her, near enough'; that mole he talked about on Patricia's tit. He hadn't said Patricia short, hadn't said Pat. If he'd really known a Patricia so well to have seen a mole on her tit, he'd have called her Pat.

Ernie realised Donald must have a picture in his head of killing a child being only fifty per cent of killing a grown-up, so you do two or three of them till you get the hang of it. 'Some people don't need a reason,' Ernie told him, 'they just kill for the sake of it. Doesn't matter who. Big or small.'

'Like as if it's a hobby of theirs, sort of thing?'

'That's about the size of it. I'll bet you're looking forward to going to Bournemouth, aren't you? Only a couple of weeks, then off.'

Last thing Ernie himself wanted to do. Bounce around in a car for hours on end. Sit on the beach with sand in his bum. Palpitate in his bed inside a stuffy little chalet. And back here, in the meantime, all his carefully planted plants going to seed on the allotment. Thank you very much, Jack.

Donald tried to sort it out in his head.

First one: tells mum.

What does he say? Emb's going to meet a man in a van. 'Oh yes, dear.' The man might kill him. 'Oh, lovie. I'm sure he won't.'

Second one: goes to the police. Don't waste our time, sonny Jim.

Third one: somebody understands the danger.

249

But Donald doesn't know where the man with the van in going to be. So what?

Fourth one: they catch them.

But all that's going on is Emb French kissing the van man's sister. Near enough shagging her. Thank you very much, says Emb. Thank you very much, the bobbies say. Even thinking about it made Donald go red.

Fifth one: they catch them.

This time Emb is in the middle of being murdered. Saved at the last minute. The van man and his sister go to prison. Or just the van man if the sister part is a lie.

The fifth one was like things Donald thought when he was on the bus going to school. He never wanted to talk to anyone in the mornings. He just wanted to look out of the window. Then things happened like in *Jeff Hawke* or the *Eagle*, big complicated stories that had hardly any story at all except him saving people. The bus journey was only a few minutes but sometimes he seemed to have been in those stories for hours. He had a feeling as if he'd just woken up after a long sleep when he got off the bus.

The fifth one was one you only dream.

Blow the list. Panic came over him, like when you wake up and wonder what time it is, think you missed everything. Twenty-five to seven. Suddenly he wanted seven o'clock to come more than anything. Then it would be too late and he wouldn't have to choose any more.

Grandad was sitting in his chair, reading a book. His moustache was as white as snow. Donald remembered how he'd gone the other day, same as that time years ago when he'd shouted about never never telling on a mate, face all red, neck stringy, his voice loud and bubbly. You could hardly believe he could go like that. That grandad seemed like one in a dream as well.

Chapter Eleven

It wasn't properly light when they set out, and there was a bit of mist in low places on the road. Rose thought how pleasant it was travelling when there was so little traffic, just the occasional milk float buzzing along and some men riding bicycles to an early shift.

It seemed to stay early for a long time. After they'd got through the Potteries and were in the Staffordshire countryside they took a turning off the main road on to a lane which wound down to a ford over a small river.

Jack liked to do things properly – it must be the cook in him. He got out the Primus and a frying pan and began making bacon and eggs. Meths was a smell that was horrible most of the time but nice when you were having a picnic. Dad was making a bit of a fuss, needless to say.

'When you're my age,' he said, not once but twice, 'there's nowhere to sit.'

She offered him a corner of the blanket that they'd spread beside the water but he said that once he'd got down he'd never be able to get up again. In the end he sat in the car with the door open, muttering to himself. He was peeved because a bit earlier they'd gone past a newsagent's that seemed open and he'd wanted to stop for his blessed paper, read about more hangings like as not, or fights involving Teddy boys so he could scare Peter out of his wits.

There was still a scrap of mist over the water of the ford, and an early-morning-in-the-country smell, now mixed up with meths and breakfast and enginey fumes from the car. She thought to herself: yes, we really are on holiday.

'I could do with a cup of tea first,' said dad, glaring at the frying pan.

'Tell you what,' Rose said to Jack, 'I looked at two church clocks as we went past and they were both an hour slow.'

'That'll be because they've never been put on summer time,' Donald said. He was a bit of a know-all these days.

'Why not?'

'Too high up, probly.'

Jack was squinting for all he was worth at the stuff in the pan. Suddenly Rose felt a little pang of fear.

'Jack,' she said, 'what time have you got?'

He pretended not to hear for a second.

'Jack.'

He glanced at his watch, then said, very quickly, 'Twenty past.'

'Twenty past what?'

He began busily shovelling the eggs. Donald peered at his own wrist. 'Eight,' Donald said.

'Twenty past *eight*?'

'Yes, eight.'

'My watch says nine.' Her fear turned to anger. How silly, to be angry about the time, but she was. For two pins she would have taken her watch off and flung it into the ford.

'Must be fast,' Donald said.

'You did it, didn't you?' she asked Jack.

'Grub's up!'

'*Did*n't you?'

'Yes,' he said. He plonked an egg and a rasher of bacon on a plate, and held it up. 'Who wants first go?' he asked.

'I suppose so,' dad said.

'I thought you wanted a cup of tea first,' Donald said.

'Beggars can't be choosers,' dad told him.

'It's OK, Donald,' Jack said, 'there's enough here for you too.' He made up another plate.

'How did you do it?' she asked.

'When you were asleep. You were dead to the world.'

Peter had climbed up on to the wooden footbridge that went over the ford, and was looking down into the water, his head poking out between the fence rails. 'There's a fish!' he called out excitedly.

'Let me see,' Donald said. He put his plate down and rushed up beside him. 'That's just a stone,' he told him.

'It's a fish,' Peter said. 'It's a fish what looks like a stone.' He sounded a bit half-hearted as he said it.

'I thought you were in a hurry for it,' Jack said, wagging the plate at Donald.

She *had* been dead to the world last night, not what she'd expected on the eve of a holiday. She'd had a very vivid dream. It was about that time years ago when Jack was brought home by a bus driver one side and a conductor the other. He'd had a pint or two and been knocked over by the bus.

In her dream the two busmen were laughing and joking. She seemed to know them very well, as though they'd been acquaintances from way back. They were going to go driving off into the wide blue yonder on their bus, and she was all emotional about it. She kept looking at the conductor's little ticket machine. It seemed special and twinkly, hanging from his middle like a present on a Christmas tree. Jack must have been put down somewhere by the men and forgotten about because it was all between her and them. She pecked each one on the cheek but they wouldn't take parting seriously. They were too busy joking and yarning between themselves.

The driver one climbed up into his little room at the front of the bus. The conductor got on at the back, and suddenly they were far off and he was a little doll-like figure on his platform. The bus had gone. Never again, she'd thought in her dream, never again in this world.

She'd woken up with that one word in her mind: never. Never, she said out loud. There Jack was, sleeping peace-fully at her side. Her heart was pounding. It must be to do with holiday nerves, also with the thought of Vera going to live in Newcastle upon Tyne. She hadn't asked her when she was leaving. Perhaps she would be gone by the time they came back from Bournemouth.

'How did you manage it?' she asked Jack.

'Your watch was on the side, where you always put it. I just wound it forward an hour.'

'Why, Jack?'

'It looks like a stone but it's not a stone,' Peter said. 'It's a fish.'

Donald came down from the bridge and took his plate back from Jack. From the car came the sound of dad choking. Rose deliberately took no notice. Let him choke.

'Why?'

'I wanted us to be off in good time.'

'But I did as well. Since when did I argue about that? If you'd said an hour earlier an hour earlier it would have been. You didn't need to muck about with my watch.'

'You could eat that fish,' Peter said, 'but it might be a bit hard.'

'That's because it's a stone,' Donald said.

'Only a *bit* hard.'

From the car dad made a loud roaring noise, then a couple of more moderate coughs. 'Thought I was a goner,' he said. 'Bit of bacon stuck in my throat. Fetched it up again in the end, thank the lord. Some of that bacon's quite hard.'

'It's using a thin pan,' Jack said. 'You can't stop it catching a bit.'

'My fish is hard,' Peter said excitedly, as if dad's bacon had proved him right. 'It's quite hard. It sticks in your froke as well.'

'Throat,' Rose said.

'Better not eat my fish,' Peter said, and came down from the bridge. 'My fish is a bit hard.'

'You must have done the alarm clock as well,' Rose told Jack.

'Do you want the same?' Jack asked her. He was holding an egg poised above the pan. 'Egg and bacon?'

'As long as it doesn't choke me.'

'It's probably all right if you've still got your own teeth,' dad said.

'What do you mean, *if*, Dad?'

'When, then. When or if, what's the odds?'

Jack broke the egg one-handed on the rim of the pan, the way cooks do, and dropped it beside a rasher of bacon that was already sizzling there. 'You deceived me,' Rose said. She could feel her lip trembling. How stupid. What did it matter? It was nothing. It was a silly joke. But being an hour adrift of everyone else gave her a panicky sense of being left out, that feeling you get when you're little and you lose sight of your mother in a shop. She had been going along thinking everything was fine when in reality she had been all by herself ever since they got up, living in a different part of the day from the rest of them.

'Oh well,' Jack said. 'Look on the bright side. At least we've got the time to have a nice breakfast.'

Back in the car they sang Ten Green Bottles, Hanging on the Wall. Peter managed to get it wrong, even though it was the easiest song you could ever sing. He sang: hanging on the floor. Maybe it was because he was thinking about if one green bottle should accidentally fall. Mum laughed, so of course he sang floor even louder next time.

As the green bottles fell, one after the other, Donald felt his stomach go tight. It was just like when he was waiting that time for seven o'clock to come round, on the night Emb was going to meet the man with the sister. The last green bottle was like a small green Emb, hanging on the wall.

Next day, there Emb was, at school. Just like normal. Except he wasn't normal. He was about a couple of inches smaller, and was hunched up like slugs go when grandad put salt on them. The thing that made him most different from usual was he didn't look like a big-head any more.

'What happened, Emb?' Donald asked him.

Emb didn't say anything. His eyes swayed off to one side. The old Emb would immediately have started exaggerating and making stuff up.

'Did you?'

'Did I what?'

'Do her?'

'Who?'

'Oh, Emb, you know who. The bloke with the van's sister whosit, that who.'

Emb didn't say anything.

'Shagged her or what?' Donald asked.

'I don't want to tell about it,' Emb said.

'Don't you? You used to love telling about it.' Even if there wasn't always much of it to tell, a lot of the time. It was like as if Emb was telling himself about it, same as the rest of them.

Emb was walking about the school grounds as if he was a bit broken, as though somebody had wound his clock-work up too much. At lunch-break, when they sat in the hole, Emb just threw the cap gently and carefully like everybody else. After a few times it missed but instead of insisting on another go he made a funny little disappointed noise and wandered off.

'Blarty-farty,' Murd said.

'Near enough,' Fleck said, which made Donald think about how Emb always liked to say about near enough shagging everybody in sight, 'near enough blarting his eyeballs out.'

'What's he want to blart for just because he missed Donald's old bonce?' Murd asked.

'Thing about Donald's head, he's got the biggest head of the lot of us,' Hart said, 'so if you're going to blart about missing a head, his is the worst one.'

Flipping heck, Donald thought, does Harty line our heads up in order of size, same as our dicks? Maybe they

256

match up. Some hope. But when Hart had said about Donald's one that time he said a big one. Emb's was pretty little, was what Hart had said as well. Maybe that's what this sister of the van bloke thought about Emb's and all. Maybe that's all it was, just laughing at him for being titchy.

The trouble was, Emb carried on being as miserable as sin. Emb being Emb, Donald would have expected him to start the usual stories after a few days, as if he'd just remembered what a great time he'd had. But he stayed sad and small, shuffling about as if his walking springs had all got bust.

They got round Birmingham, no trouble, but where they jammed up was approaching Newbury, mid-afternoon. It reminded Jack of being in a convoy once in the desert, when it rained out of the blue, and lorries kept getting mired in the puddly sand. 'It's enough to drive you blinking mental,' Codge had said over and over again, and finally Tomlinson said: 'What you bothering yourself about, Codge? You afraid you're going to be late for an appointment? It only matters going slow if you're going somewhere, but there isn't anywhere to go to here. It's all the bloody same, which way you look.'

That was the difference, this time they were going somewhere, Bournemouth by name. When you mounted a bit of a rise you could see the black cars queuing for miles. Something about the way they looked from behind made you think of old ladies hunched over their knitting.

Jack's old lady had copped it.

He'd gone off to Stepping Hill Hospital bearing his cake. It was a nice one too. It had Get Well Soon in fancy writing, little tails to the ls and strokes going across the S, a bit like a dollar sign. He was a good enough icer himself but not so strong on lettering. Your handwriting seemed to lose its way a little travelling through an icing funnel, and he wasn't up on other styles. He had a book on cake calligraphy he kept meaning to work through, but hadn't got round to it so far. Until quite recently there hadn't been much call at the Station Café for celebration cakes, but since the opening of the tea dancing that had begun to change, old geezers wanting to use the sessions as a birthday party for their wives. With evening dinners you could expect more of the same. He'd been using bought-in Happy Birthdays in silvered confectioner's sugar but felt it was a bit of a cheat. And he still had to pipe in To Muriel, With Love, or whatever it might be. Where he was strongest was putting sugar roses in icing-sugar cages round the rim. Stan loved those. 'Tickles me to death,' he would say, and shake his head, but the cake he wanted for Ken's birthday, after Jack came back from Bournemouth, was on a different plan altogether, with flashes of lightning, thunderclouds and flames leaping up, to celebrate him being struck at Ascot. Jack had said he wasn't about to do the human form, especially Ken's, nor horses neither. It struck him thinking about it in the traffic jam at Newbury that what he could do was the words Happy Birthday with the individual letters on fire. Kill two birds with one stone that way. Ken had said smoke came out of his ears for a couple of hours after, made him look like the devil incarnate. Stan said, same as usual then, Ken, and winked at Jack. Funny thing, Jack even envied Ken his thunderbolt. Even Mrs Stan seemed to look at Ken with more respect, so far as you could tell with her loose face.

He'd parked in the Stepping Hill car park and got the boxed cake out of his boot. Carting it into the hospital gave him an odd sensation. His face felt shiny, like when he used to go to Sunday school when he was a kiddie. No, more like one of those choirboys in procession at church, carrying their open hymn books and singing their pansy faces off. Used to make him feel like taking a swing at them as they went past, squelch those cherry lips of theirs, make the heart-shaped nostrils bleed. He took the box up the hospital steps just as if it was something religious, and what was inside could put everything to rights.

He skipped past the desk in case it was no visitors, looked a bit downwards and faraway, like a delivery man might look. Got to the ward. There was a big blank-looking nurse in the sort of cubicle by the door, guarding the inmates was how it appeared, all face and no features, with frizzy ginger hair and a couple of freckles on her tiddly little nose to match. Then suddenly she smiled at him. Teeth a bit gingery also, but it somehow made her look quite pleasant, friendly any road.

'That looks like a nice surprise,' she said.

'Cake.'

'Ooh, I like cake.'

'Tch tch tch, not for you, my darling.' He wagged a finger at her. She sort of wiggled in reply, like a snake, bit of a porky one.

'I've got a sweet tooth.'

'Well, you'll have to watch your hurry then, won't you?' She did a pout. 'It looks big enough to share around.'

'You'll be surprised how big it is,' he said confidentially.

'Takes a man, not a shirt button,' she said huskily. She arched her sandy brows and looked him straight in the eye.

'It's for Mrs Feltbauer. I came to visit her the other day.'

The oomph went out of the nurse like puff from a burst balloon. 'Oh, I'm sorry,' she said. 'Mrs Feltbauer's gone.'

'Has she then? I'm surprised by that. She didn't appear too well when I saw her.'

'No, she wasn't, poor thing.'

'I hope she's got a roof over her head. Her landlord looked to have taken possession. Bit of a nasty piece of work, far as I could see.'

'Oh no.' The nurse went pink with distress. 'I mean *gone* gone.'

The cake suddenly felt heavy as a cannonball. 'You mean she's –'

The nurse mouthed the words without saying them:

'Passed on, yes.' Then out loud: 'Poor love.'

'Oh bugger.'

'Was she, um? Are you . . . ?'

'I brought her a cake.' He meant: that's who I am. There didn't seem much point in pretending to be Mrs Feltbauer's nephew any more.

'That's nice,' she said, just as if it had never been mentioned before.

'Might as well give it one of the others in that case. It's got Get Well Soon on it.' He shoved it into her arms.

'That'll suit the lot of them. Only trouble is some'll need a magic cake if it's to do them any good.'

'You never know. I paid enough for it.'

She looked down at the parcel. Her arms were big, mannish, with the blotchy pink skin ginger people get sometimes. 'Abracadabra,' she said as if she was magicking the cake. She looked up at him and shrugged her shoulders the way women do to say aren't I a silly. It made Jack think about what Rose's dad had said to him about her mum, once upon a time, on the subject of her way of being intimate: like a carthorse learning to dance. The nurse became businesslike again: 'We've got one or two things of Mrs Feltbauer's, if you're next of kin.'

'Oh no, her stuff's nowt to do with me. Somebody else'll have to sort that out.'

'Nobody else has turned up, as yet.'

'But it's not my business. I only –'

She'd put the cake on her little desk, flap of wood more like, fastened to the panelling of her cubicle, and fetched over a notepad. 'I'll just put your name, anyhow.'

'Cake,' he said, finishing what he'd been saying before, then skedaddled off fairly smartish.

Sitting in the jam on the outskirts of Newbury he thought: maybe that's what she wrote down, Mr Cake.

What Ruth didn't need, when she went to visit somebody on a hot summer's day, was for them to talk about their bottom for hours on end. It didn't help that Mrs McMahon smelled like Ruth's butter did, before Jack fixed her up with her own fridge, when she used to have to keep it in a little meat safe, and in hot weather it would go a bit over, rancid was the word, and to top it all talks about bottom this, bottom that.

Mrs McMahon had constipation because of what she could eat and what she couldn't eat, and all the things going on in her insides, and then of course straining away with constipation for hours on end led to piles. Hanging piles, Mrs McMahon said in a whisper, and did a wink, so to say that's between you and me, my duck. Hanging piles reminded Ruth of somebody they did years ago in school, a horrible judge in the olden days who killed people all the time, Hanging Judge Jeffreys his name. The thought of him being all mixed up with piles made her almost laugh, but that was only because you would laugh at more or less anything after an hour or two of Mrs McMahon's bottom. TCP ointment hadn't succeeded in shrinking her piles. The doc was going to have them off soon as he could but she wasn't up to the operation in her state of health. It's a no-go area for the time being, she said, till such time as I get back the use of my legs.

Ruth thought: Mrs McMahon is harping on this one string because there's something else she doesn't want to talk about. No prizes for guessing that would be Jack. Even when she was in full flight she had a thoughtful look in her eyes as if she was going through all her health problems from memory while other matters occupied her brain. It made Ruth feel tense, like when you go to the dentist and he says what a nice day it is and how are you before he gets round to telling you to open up.

She got Mrs McMahon her bit of lunch, just a poached egg on toast. Mrs McMahon tried to get her to do one for herself but she didn't feel hungry. She wondered if Mrs McMahon ought to eat eggs at all, the state she was in, but Mrs McMahon said she didn't have patience with that sort

261

of old wives' tale. Ruth thought perhaps she was just saying that because there wasn't anything else in the house, putting a brave face on it. Certainly her pantry seemed very bare.

'Do you want me to do a bit of shopping for you?' she asked. 'After the weekend?'

'It's a bank holiday,' Mrs McMahon said sternly.

'Oh yes, I forgot.'

'And after it's over you'll have enough on your plate without running about after me.'

That was true. Ruth didn't say anything.

'Tuesday, isn't it?' Mrs McMahon asked. How she knew, Ruth couldn't guess. She nodded. She felt ashamed, as if Tuesday was the day when she was going to do something wrong. At the same time she was angry with herself for thinking such a thing, just because Mrs McMahon disapproved.

'I've bought you a present,' Mrs McMahon said, to her amazement. 'It's over there, on the sideboard.'

Sure enough, there it was, a parcel wrapped in brown paper, and tied with a ribbon. It was half-hidden behind the biscuit barrel.

'That's so kind of you, Mrs McMahon. Can I open it?' Her voice was trembly, and her cheeks were burning. Even her nose felt as if it was shining all of a sudden.

'Course you can open it.'

'I thought I ought to wait till . . .' Even though Mrs McMahon had bought her a present to celebrate it she still couldn't bring herself to say Wedding Day.

'You open it, my girl,' Mrs McMahon said.

The ribbon was green for some reason. I expect I'm getting a bit too old for pink, Ruth thought.

She undid the bow. White box inside. She opened it. Tissue paper. Inside, some metal, and china.

'Oh, Mrs McMahon,' she said. She wasn't sure what it was, but hoped she sounded so pleased with it it didn't need saying.

'It's a cake stand.'

'A cake stand,' she said, as though Mrs McMahon had taken the very words out of her mouth. The metal was a frame, and you balanced two plates on it, one above the other. She put it together. Her first thought was, I can put my wedding cake on it, it's got two floors.

Then she remembered the wedding cake would have pillar things of its own in between. This stand was for small cakes, one sort on the underneath plate, another on the one above, or maybe biscuits or even little sandwiches, the triangular ones with their crusts cut off.

She wondered how on earth Mrs McMahon had managed to get out and buy her a cake stand without the use of her legs. The kindness of it, especially with her not even approving of Jack, made Ruth nearly burst into tears.

'It's just what I want,' she said.

Mrs McMahon gave her a long look. 'I hope this husband of yours is just what you want, and all.'

Just when you feel all grateful to somebody, you have to go in again and do battle. It didn't seem fair. 'He is, Mrs McMahon,' she said.

By mid-afternoon everybody had settled down a bit. Peter went straight off to sleep, sitting on the back seat in his little towelling trousers and striped T-shirt, legs straight out in front of him. He was of an age when you could still see the dimples in his knees. Probably fatigued from playing I-Spy. He'd been at that game like a dog with a bone, surprising really since he hadn't a clue what it was all about. Not just that he couldn't spell, he didn't know what spelling was at his age. He'd said, 'I spy with my little eye something beginning with per,' and they spent must have been near enough half an hour trying to get it, peacock, peas, pigeon, pears, pig, park, the whole caboodle. Ernie knew that at his tender age Peter couldn't be expected to be reliable, so tried other words on him too, cows, grass, hill, all to no avail. They took a few rests from time to time, but Peter wouldn't give in and tell them.

Donald got the answer in the end, more or less by chance. It was snail. Donald said, 'Remember when you ate that snail that time,' and Peter suddenly let forth 'Snail! Snail!' The fact that you can't see a blessed snail from a moving vehicle, and if you could it wouldn't begin with p didn't matter a jot or tittle to him. 'I spy with my little eyed a snail, I did,' he'd said, pleased as punch.

They were going through uppy countryside now, called the South Downs for some reason, so p for snail was not the only one. The air wasn't quite so sweltering as it came in through the window, though it was hot and steep enough on the road to put paid to a few car radiators. The scenery was nice though, hardly a tree but sheep scattered like so many maggots over the distant hillsides. You could hear their bleating in the wind coming in, faint but hysterical as if they were being massacred. Alf had said to him yesterday, when Ernie was trying to make arrangements for the tending of his allotment while he was away: 'Sometimes I think I can hear Dougie, crying for help.' You must have sensitive hearing, all the way from Argentina, Ernie wanted to tell him, but instead said, 'I don't think they'll be using thumbscrews on him, just for getting blotto on shore leave.' Of course that made matters worse by putting ideas in Alf's head, since he wasn't a bloke to have many of his own to start with.

Ernie opened his book, *The Bride of Lammermoor*.

'I wouldn't read that, if I was you,' Jack said.

'I beg your pardon?' He wasn't used to being put right in that sort of a tone. 'I'll read whatever I please. It's Sir Walter Scott.' He fastened his eyeballs on to the page as if he was looking at the crown jewels, no nonsense about it.

'What I mean, it'll make you sick as a dog.'

'I don't see how you make that out. I would have thought I was old enough and ugly enough.' He still didn't shift his line of vision from the book.

'I'm not arguing whether you're old enough and ugly enough, for heaven's sake. I'm talking about the motion of the car. It creeps up on you without you knowing it.' Ernie saw Jack do a little smile to himself out of the corner of his eye. 'All I'm doing, I'm just saying.'

'If you want my opinion,' Ernie told him, 'that's my eye and Betty Martin.'

'What it is, your eyes are going from side to side, and the car is taking you up and down. It's like being in a blimmin cocktail shaker.'

'I'll take my chances.'

'Suit yourself.'

Of course, now it had been said, Ernie straight away got an uneasy sensation as he began to read. He kept thinking the car was dropping downhill, but when he looked up he could see it was keeping more or less level, going across a plateau affair along the top of the downs. But still, a page or two to be going on with, wipe the smile off of Jack's face.

The opening of the book, as usual, was Walter Scott telling you the whole story. Fat lot of good if he'd ever tried his hand at detective novels, the show would be over and done with by page six. This one was about a love tragedy. Young girl of posh birth falls for a bloke and he gives her a gold sovereign, which signifies they're engaged. Bit different from nowadays, when it takes a bun in the oven to do that trick. When the family find out they'll have none of it. They've got another lad in mind who's from the aristocracy like themselves. Tell the daughter to make the man take his coin back.

Brings to mind Wilfred Pickles on the wireless: 'Give him the money, Mabel.'

Girl does what she's told, doesn't utter a squeak of protest. The betrothed-as-was is fairly peeved, however, and slopes off. Meanwhile the parents fix up the wedding with the young chap they approve of. Girl goes along with it. Everything appears hunky-dory. They have the ceremony. She's quiet but co-operative. The rejected suitor has cleared off abroad by now, and is wandering glumly all over the shop. The couple trot off to the bridal chamber. Didn't seem to go in for honeymoons in those days. Bit later on there's a commotion.

The family break in and all hell's been let loose. The bridegroom's been stabbed to death, and the bride is burbling away like one possessed and covered in blood from top to toe. She dies three weeks later.

Something Pat said, down in Reddish Vale, on the subject of the Ruth Ellis murder came into Ernie's mind. They always empty their gun in them. They only kill somebody when they've got themselves in a state. The bride had gone through the preliminaries nice as pie, then when it was finally time to get down to the serious business she'd turned her marriage bed into a charnel house.

Having told the true story he'd based his book on, Walter Scott went on to explain how he'd altered some of the details, just in case the reader might be tempted to feel any suspense. He had decided to make the bridegroom survive the murderous attack, and send him off to wander round foreign parts rather than the suitor, presumably with stab wounds all over him.

Once that was explained away, it was time to begin. Chapter One.

It was difficult to concentrate, however. Ernie couldn't help but think of his Dorothy and the way she'd been during that interval before *they* got wed. She'd been very quiet. She'd been very quiet after they were wed for that matter. Whenever they were alone in their courting days she let him get on with it, no complaint. She didn't exactly join in but she didn't make any fuss either. He didn't know what to expect from a girl in any case. Poor Albert had said women are no better than us, when he talked to Ernie that day after being given his cards by old Harold Peach, but Ernie had had no way of knowing how that showed itself. Not telling you to push off when you had your hand down their front was how he'd chosen to interpret it. What you had to say about Dorothy's approach to the whole business was: matter of fact. She tried to join in a bit when they were married and going the whole hog, but it was like a carthorse learning to dance. You got the feeling her attention was elsewhere, or nowhere.

It was the same as her attitude to pain. He remembered one time she got stung on the foot by a wasp. She made so little of it he didn't quite believe her. He thought perhaps it had only been a gnat, or maybe a wasp that had recently stung some other poor so-and-so and hadn't got its sting back yet to full force. Then that night when she took her shoe and stocking off, her foot was as swollen and pink as a cow's udder. It reminded him of one of those rubber gloves which some joker's filled with water. But not a peep out of her, not a dicky-bird. She had just accepted having one big foot and one little foot as though it had been ordained that way from the start.

Having babies the same. Quiet as a lamb, according to the midwife. Dying the same. She died well, the chaplain-johnnie told him when Ernie came back from the toilet and discovered she'd passed away, for all the world as if it was his job to assign each patient a mark out of ten for it.

What Dorothy had never done was run amuck with a knife and stab Ernie to death. But perhaps that maddening way she had of plodding through life had been the calm before the storm, except that the storm never broke. Or even . . . Ernie couldn't quite put his finger on it. That way she walked. Some women moved their hips, let their walking flow through their whole body. Dorothy just put one foot in front of the other. Same with cooking, boil, boil, boil. She boiled cabbage till it lost its green and began to turn yellow, also peas. Perhaps her tendency to always be disappointing *was* the storm. Perhaps she'd guessed somehow what he'd done to Albert, and was taking her revenge, day in day out for the rest of her life.

Never once had she worn perfume the way Sylvie in the library used to, catch your breath and make you think, this is a woman I've got on my hands here, better or worse, it's a woman all right, what do I do about it? Read blinking Walter Scott, the only hope. Show her that there's something to me as well.

Never once. What he remembered was that way she had of sniffing.

Of course, Sylvie had been left high and dry in turn. She didn't wear perfume nowadays, not that you could notice, and that telephone hairdo of hers was long gone.

He particularly shone in painting horses, that being a favourite sign in Scottish villages; and, in tracing his progress, it is beautiful to observe, how by degrees he learned to shorten the backs, and prolong the legs, of these noble animals, until they came to look less like crocodiles, and more like nags.

It was no good. The words were going swimmy on the page.

There was Jack, fixed up the holiday, steering the car: he even knew when people ought not to read *The Bride of Lammermoor*. Ernie glanced at him side on. He still looked to be grinning a little grin. No, on second thoughts, maybe that was just how his lips arranged themselves, the way the one on top happened to come to rest on the other. Not too often you looked at someone from side on.

Change the subject, that was the answer. He turned back to look at Donald. Well, as much as he could. Ernie didn't have enough neck these days to get his head round the necessary distance. Not with old joints, anyway.

'That pal of yours,' he said. He sent his eyes round as far as they would go but still couldn't look Donald square in the face. It felt as if they were getting stiff in their sockets same as all the rest.

'Norman?' Donald asked.

'No, not Norman. Saw you walking home from school with him the other day. You don't come home from school

268

with Norman, do you these days, more's the pity.'

'Dad,' Rose said, 'if you're going to start up about that grammar school business again, I'll crown you.'

'Murd?' asked Donald.

'Little chap. Lives over in Gower Road.'

'Oh. Emb.'

'Emb, that's the one. I knew it was something I couldn't remember. Emb.'

'What about him.'

'He looked as if he'd seen a ghost. White as a sheet, he looked to me.'

'That's the way he is. He always looks as if he's seen a ghost.'

'That so? I didn't notice before. I thought maybe he was sickening for something.'

'You can't expect everybody to be laughing their heads off all the time. Just because old Nor-man does.'

'Oh dear, it's like that, is it?'

'Like what?'

'Old *Nor*-man.'

'Wherever are you taking us, Jack?' Rose said, a bit sharpish. Sure enough Jack had turned off the road into a driveway.

'Hey-up,' Ernie said, 'we're not here already, are we?'

'Thought we could do with a spot of grub,' Jack said.

Rose felt so angry she couldn't speak for a moment. Of all the ways to waste their money. Right at the start of the holiday too.

'We've still got plenty of picnic stuff left,' she said finally.

'Be nice to have something hot. Set us up for when we arrive.'

'Hot?' she said. 'Jack, it's like a furnace. What on earth do we need something hot for?'

'Look,' Jack said with satisfaction, 'they've got an A-board out. Plaice, new pots, and peas. How's that for a game of soldiers?'

269

'I notice you didn't read out the cost,' she said, 'five bob a head.'

'That includes the pud.' He'd stopped the car and was sitting still holding the wheel, like a kiddie pretending to drive. 'Being in the trade I can tell you it's not a bad price for this sort of a set-up.'

'Not if you're cooking and the customers are feeding, it's not. But where we are we're the wrong side of the counter here, that's the trouble with it.' The funny thing was, she normally got over a bout of bad temper in a moment or two, but his time she felt herself getting more and more furious. It must be that business of the watch, festering away inside her the whole day.

Suddenly she felt her arm go up and back and then come flying forward to hit Jack a slap on the back of his head.

His head went forward and he clasped his hands over his neck to protect himself. She could tell by the exaggerated way he hunched himself that for a moment he'd thought it was a joke, but then the sting filtered through and he was realising she'd smacked him really hard.

Dad sort of hoisted himself around. His face had gone as red as a brick, so red it made his white moustache look like a little neon light being switched on.

'What in heaven's name's got into you, Rose?' he asked. He wasn't looking her directly in the eyes. His head looked wobbly with fury. Funny thing was, he seemed ferocious and fragile at one and the same time. Also what was strange, he had got himself so angry at the idea of *her* being so angry.

It was very bad of me, she thought, fetching our Jack such a biff on the back of his head, but I feel as right as rain having done it.

'Well,' she said. 'Sometimes it drives you up the bally wall. Plaice and new potatoes and all the rest of it, it seems so unnecessary.' She didn't feel angry at all, it was only a matter of explaining. What they used to say in church:

cleansed. Only they meant doing away with sin, whereas what had cheered her up all of a sudden was having committed one.

'Plaice is a fish,' Donald explained to Peter.

'My fish was a bit hard,' Peter said. 'My fish what I fished yesterday.'

'I'm sure this fish will be a soft fish,' Jack said. He looked a bit like a fish himself, surfacing from beneath the dashboard. Trust him to be making conversation with Peter, after the sky had just fallen on his head.

'No,' Peter said impatiently, as if he was tired of people getting hold of the wrong end of the stick, 'it was a hard fish.'

'We've got just so much money,' Rose said. 'If you spend it all now, we won't have anything to enjoy our holiday with.' She felt she owed him an explanation for her act of violence. She tried to make herself still sound bad-tempered so he wouldn't feel offended at how quickly she'd got over it.

'I don't want to eat it,' Peter said.

'The way I look at it, we can get our meal over with, then we can concentrate on getting ourselves settled in in the chalet.'

'It's a lot of money just to get something over with.'

'Only money, ducks.' He wasn't at all put out. Perhaps being hit had made him, too, feel that any little difficulties had sorted themselves out. Dad was looking a bit shifty. He glanced back towards her, then at Jack. She realised exactly what was going through his head. Rose and Jack were back to normal and he'd been left high and dry, clutching his bad-temper like so much unwanted baggage. So unfair, him being left the only one at outs with the family. He waved his hand as if to say well, that's all done with, then realised it was the one with the finger standing to attention like a toy soldier, and put it back in his lap pronto.

Serve the silly old goat right, putting his nose in where it's not wanted.

She got out of the car. The restaurant was one of those roadhouse type of places, a long low building with small trees in pots along the front of it. There were quite a few cars in the car park, some of them very smart ones.

The others got out of the car too, all except Peter. She could see his small red face through the window, for all the world a miniature version of his grandad. He was bawling his head off.

'What on earth's the matter, Peter?' she asked.

Jack bent in through the door and hoiked him out. His little arms were flailing, and one of them caught Jack a blow on the cheek, more by accident than design. Jack must be feeling in the wars this afternoon, poor man.

'Hey-up,' he said, 'what's to do here then?'

Peter was crying too hard to reply.

'That fish wasn't yesterday, anyway,' Donald said, 'it was this morning.'

'Thank you very much, Donald,' Rose said.

Peter's crying had turned into those hiccuping sobs toddlers are prone to do. He rubbed his eyes where the tears were stinging him. She put her hands on his puffy cheeks and wiped the wetness off with her thumbs.

'What is it, little man?' she asked him.

'I don't like eating fishes,' he said. He shook his head to make great big noes, nearly wriggling out of Jack's arms with the size of the movements. 'I don't like eating them.'

'They would probably give you an octopus to eat instead,' Donald said, 'if you asked for one.'

Peter spoke in a harsh confidential whisper, looking at her big-eyed: 'I don't like octy pusses as well. Octy pusses what I don't like.'

'I don't know what's got into you, Donald,' she said, 'but you're not too old for a smack.'

'Same as me,' Jack said. 'I'm not too old for one neither.'

'No, but,' she said, feeling her face go red in turn, 'the little chap's getting himself all in a lather.'

'What it is, is fear of fooderies. You see it a lot in my

line. Grown men bursting into tears at the sight of a café.'
He gave her an innocent look over Peter's anxious little
head. 'Grown women too.'

'Or some snails,' Donald told Peter. 'You like eating
them.'

The lady came out of the dark. The café was big and there
was a door at the back of it. People were eating all over the
café. While they were eating they were roaring. It was dark
in the door. All the fishes were in the door. They killed
the fishes in there. The lady brought Peter a plate. It had
a sausage on it. And it had beans. It had an octy puss on it
as well, what made Peter cry.

Mummy said whatever's the. Peter said he didn't like
them. He didn't like eating octy pusses. Donald said snails.
Grandad was looking. He blew his whiskers to look.
Mummy said egg, silly. She said, I told them not an egg.
You had an egg this morning. Grandad said egg-bound.
Peter said I thought it was an octy puss. Donald said. Peter
said I don't like snails now. I liked them and then. Now I
don't like them any more. I don't like octy pusses too. You
like eggs, mummy said. I don't like eggs too, Peter told her.
I don't like eggs any more, now I don't. Leave the blinking
egg, daddy said. Leave it on the side of the plate, that
blinking egg. A lot of mither that blinking egg.

Mum said talk about the terrible twos. Donald said, 'Mum,
he's three, or haven't you noticed.'

'Thank you, Mr Clever-Clogs. I do know how to count.'

'Well, you said twos.'

'It's just a saying. You can still have the terrible twos
when you're three. Look at you.'

'What about me?'

'You've still got them, and you're thirteen.'

'Very funny, Mum.'

'I don't know what's possessed you, the last couple of
days. I've never known you be so full of cheek.'

'It's just the journey,' dad said, 'that's what's got him so worked up. Peter, I mean.'

'To tell the truth,' grandad said, 'I thought I was going to have a choking fit again, like I did this morning on that bit of bacon. I could feel a tickle at the back of my throat. Whether it was a fishbone, I couldn't say.'

'Dad,' mum told him, 'there wasn't a bone in that plaice. You couldn't have had a better served piece of fish.'

'You've changed your tune,' dad said.

'I believe in giving credit where it's due, that's all. It went down like swallowing an oyster.'

'I don't like –' Peter said, and stopped.

'He was going to say he doesn't like octopuses,' Donald said, 'and then he noticed you said oyster. He doesn't know whether he likes oysters or not.'

'Nor do I, for that matter,' mum said. 'It's just something to say.'

'I don't like them,' Peter said, 'I don't like oyster pussies too. I liked snails once but I don't like them any more as well.'

'Tell you what you do like,' dad told him, 'you like ice cream for pudding.'

'Yes, I like that, what I like.'

'I thought you did. It's apple tart and custard, or ice cream.'

'I want ice cream.'

'What flavour do you want?' Donald asked. 'Do you want –?'

'Please stop stirring the pot, Donald,' mum said.

'I want ice cream favour, the favour I –'

'I think I'll have ice cream and all,' grandad said, 'it might relax my throat.'

Peter screwed his face up, and spoke in a funny grunting sort of voice, as if he was threatening somebody: 'I'll have ice cream. It might relax my froak too.'

'Tell her I'll have the tart,' dad told mum.

'Tell who?'

274

'The girl.'

'Why not tell her yourself?'

'I'm just off to see a man about a dog.'

'I want to see a man about a dog as well,' Peter said.

'Stay where you are, Peter. Honestly, Jack, can't you just wait two ticks? I'll never catch her eye. I never catch their eyes.'

'Not enough experience of eating out, that's your trouble.'

'Whose fault's that?'

'It's you who's wanting to save up for a house.' As soon as dad said that he went bright red. Donald watched the words go across the table and hit mum, so she went bright red too. Dad said: 'Your dad'll flag her down, won't you, Dad?' He looked down at grandad's sticking-out finger, then back across at mum. He gave a sneaky little smile, like you do in class, too fast for the teacher to see. She looked where he'd been looking and then smiled back, through her red face, and they both went back to normal again. Dad got up and went off across the room to where it said Gents.

'Don't you like it?' mum asked.

'What?' Donald said. 'Don't like what?'

'Your tea, silly.'

'I'm eating it, aren't I?'

'That's what I mean. We've all finished, long ago. You seem to be making such a meal of it.'

'Well, sorr-*y*. I thought it *was* a meal.'

'It wasn't bad, that white sauce on the plaice,' grandad said. 'I liked the slices of egg in it. Makes a change from just boiled.'

'They *were* boiled,' Donald said.

'The fish, I mean. I've had enough of plain boiled fish with no folderols to last a lifetime. Come to think, it *did* last a lifetime.'

'Donald,' mum said, 'you're getting so sharp you'll cut yourself one of these days.'

'Life blimmin time of boiled fish. Just lying there dead on your plate.'

'I cutted myself once,' Peter said. He rolled his eyes to try to make it sound more important.

Donald didn't say anything more but concentrated on finishing what was left of his grub. When he was on the last mouthful, mum said, 'I'll tell you something about yourself I expect you don't know, Donald.'

'What?'

'You chew every bite you eat exactly seventeen times. I've been counting them. I think I noticed it before I noticed I had.'

'I thought that's what your teeth were for. To give stuff a good chew.'

'What my teef are for,' Peter said. 'My teef are for biting with.' Instead of biting he showed his teeth like a dog does when it's growling, which screwed his nose up into a crinkly little red ball. It reminded Donald of something he'd seen before. Suddenly he remembered what it was: his mother's nipple, when she used to breast-feed Peter in the old days. The memory made sweat suddenly come on his forehead.

'Have you noticed how Peter boasts all the time?' he asked.

'It's not really necessary,' mum said, 'when you're eating food as soft as fish and boiled potatoes. Different with chewy things.'

'I always boast all the time, I do,' Peter said.

'Next time I'll remember to swallow stuff whole,' Donald said. 'Anyway I want to go to the toilet.'

'If you do that, my lad, you'll choke like me,' grandad said. 'Not that I swallowed stuff whole. What I think is the bore of your throat gets narrower over the years, same way water pipes fur up.'

'No need to take the hump,' mum told Donald.

He went off to the toilet quickly, before Peter said he'd taken the hump too.

When Donald got to the Gents a funny thing happened.

276

Dad was standing by the things where you pee, talking to a bloke. They had their backs turned and didn't see him come in. The man said about a good little business he had, making something to do with gramophones.

Dad said, 'I've got a nice little business, and all.'

'What line you in?' the man asked.

'Garage trade. Car repair.'

Donald thought it must be a slip of the tongue, but the other man said something about cars, and dad said yes, yes, and laughed. Donald didn't have his pee after all, just went straight back to the table. He wondered if he'd heard wrong, if dad had said café instead, not garage. But you couldn't get away from them talking about cars.

'Did you see your dad there?' mum asked.

'He's just coming.'

To Donald's relief nothing was said to dad about him going to the bog as well. When dad finally came back all mum said was, 'We thought you must have flushed yourself away.'

'Good as,' dad said. 'Where's me pud then?'

Chapter Twelve

Ruth didn't have time to take Gyp on a proper walk, just once round the block. He got one on him when he realised they weren't going along the footpath into the copse, and took it upon himself to refuse to move his legs.

He stood there with them completely rigid, like the legs of a tiny table. She tried to talk him round but he wasn't having any. In the end she just pulled him along as he was.

His eyes nearly popped out of his head with the strain on his throat, and she didn't like to think about the state of his paws. Could do with those little wheel things she couldn't remember the name of, that you have on furniture. All she could think of was castor-oil. Could do with castor-oil, for that matter, or some sort of oil, to help him along. Mrs McMahon would give her eye teeth to have the use of *her* legs, she told him, and you've got four perfectly good ones which you won't use for love nor money. Come to think of it, they'd be a bit small for Mrs McMahon, she suddenly thought, and couldn't stop herself from bursting into laughter, right there on the street. It caught her so much by surprise that she did a tiny wee in her knickers. Only a drop but it made her think thank goodness you *have* knickers.

A man going past in a white linen jacket and straw hat, not a boater or anything, just a normal kind of hat only straw, gave her a straight look. Perhaps he didn't believe a woman should laugh on the street, like not smoking a cigarette. He looked as if he was just off to play bowls.

It was surprising how heavy Gyp was to pull along, with

no co-operation at all. By the time she got back home her shoulder and whole arm ached.

She hadn't been back five minutes when the postman knocked. He stepped back a step when she opened the door and she wondered if her house smelled, like their house did when she was a child. She couldn't stop herself sniffing, to check, then she gave a cough, as if she had a little cold. Nothing. Of course if it was *your* house you'd be the last to know. But there was no reason why it should. She didn't know what the reason had been when she was little. Maybe her mum didn't put out the rubbish often enough. In her heart of hearts she'd always thought it was because her dad was like he was.

To her surprise the postman burst into song. It was 'Oh what a beautiful morning.' He sort of puffed up when he sang, a bit like Mario Lanza. His neck went all red and his eyes were almost as popped out as Gyp's had been.

Her first reaction was: thank goodness. That's why he'd stepped back, to give himself room to puff out. Her next thought was: it's my wedding day, and the postman's singing to me. She felt a tear form in each eye. I'm springing leaks all over the place, that's the trouble, she thought. He didn't have such a good voice as Mario Lanza, which was the only drawback.

When he finished the verse he took out his hanky and dabbed his forehead with it. Ruth sniffed, to make it look as though her eyes were just watery with her cold.

'Give myself a heart attack,' the postman said.

'It was very nice.'

'Can't stop myself, lovely weather like this.'

'I thought you was just doing it on my behalf.'

'I was, dear lady, I was.' He did a bit of a bow. He was quite plump even though he'd gone down a bit after the singing, and didn't bend in the middle all that well, especially with his heavy bag of letters hanging down.

'Cause it's –' She still couldn't say my wedding day, she didn't know why. The idea of it made her feel embarrassed, almost ashamed. 'My birthday,' she said.

'Well, many happy returns.'

'Funny part of it is, that's my favourite song.'

'Then you're welcome to it. I hope this is a nice present,' he said, giving her a packet and a letter in a brown envelope. He went off down the path.

It was just her Great Universal Stores catalogue and a letter about the rates. What did she expect? The only people who knew about her getting married today were Gerald and Mrs McMahon. Mrs McMahon had given her her present already, and a nice one it was, even if they did have a bit of a row after. A present well-earned, you could call it. Gerald wasn't the type to send a card. Much as he could do to get out of bed in the morning. But with any luck he'd turn up at the registry office. He meant well. Ten to one he'd buy her a box of chocolates. That's what he understood by a present. It would have been nice to get a card from Jack, but what he said about making a cake was the same thing, it was his wedding too, so it would be like as if he was sending *himself* a card, if he'd sent a card.

She still half expected a post-office van to come round, and deliver her cake. Funny how you can half expect something when you know it can't happen. You can't send a cake in a parcel, for one thing, even two parcels, because it's so fragile. All the decorative bits would break off. Sometimes wedding cakes have a bride and groom on the top, little doll type of things, and those would be certain to snap off because you could never pack them up properly, which would be bad luck for definite, worse than a mirror. Another reason: cakes were jolly heavy, especially ones with a top cake and a bottom cake to them. There was all that fruit, which weighed a ton, being that was why people usually only ate a little slice, because it was so rich it filled you up before you knew it. Last thing you'd want to do was cart the cake from her house to the Griffin pub for the reception. Best bet, have it delivered direct to the pub in the first place, save a journey. How delivered, she didn't know, being the packing problem. Maybe they have a baker's van, to take it direct. They must be making cakes all the time and having to take them places. Or Jack could fetch it along on the back seat of his car.

Suddenly she had a thought which stopped her in her tracks, just going in her bathroom to run her bath. Cake, with an up part and a down, all that heavy fruit, marzipan, icing sugar, the rest of it, there's a terrific quantity there to get your teeth into, and only a handful of people to eat it.

She felt a little panic for a moment. Whatever would they do with all the rest? Wouldn't it look bad to have a lot of it left over? She remembered a do they'd had once in the Swan for one of their regular customers, Tommy Fenton, on his eightieth birthday. They'd done it at lunchtime because he'd stopped coming in in the evenings, said beer at night made him have to keep getting out of bed, with him being old these days. It was funny how he said about being old, he said it like something that would pass off in the course of time, just a bit of trouble he was going through, like when you have a cold, more or less. He'd been a worker in a cotton-mill. She could remember what his job was called: doffer. No idea what the word meant, of course. He'd tried to explain it once upon a time, but it could have been French as far as she was concerned. It was funny how you could remember a word that was not a scrap of use to you and you didn't even know what it meant, and forget loads of the ones you use every day.

She turned on the taps. All they'd provided for Tommy's birthday was a load of sandwiches, nothing much to write home about, cheese ones, ham, and some other ones she couldn't remember now. And a little cake, a sponge one, owing to the heaviness of fruit. It had eight candles, one for each ten years. Tommy was as pleased as punch. It made him feel important, as if he was king of the pub for the day. But hardly anybody was eating save Tommy himself. His mates always came in in the evening, like Tommy had used to do before he was old. Still, if he wasn't old, he wouldn't have been given the cake in the first place.

What Tommy did, he scoffed sandwich after sandwich, just to make the plate go down.

Gerald told her after, he knew someone once in his younger days who won the pools, and what he did was go out with a friend and buy twenty portions of fish and chips from the fish and chip shop, just because he wanted to buy lots of something. Wanted a treat. They ate as many as they could get down, then dropped the rest in a ditch.

She didn't make the bath too warm, with it being a hot day already. She wanted it to be refreshing. They gave Tommy's sandwiches to anyone who came in the pub that lunch, just to get them looking eaten. Even so there were still a lot left. They told him they would give them to his pals that night, but by then they'd become a bit sad and curling, so they chucked them away.

But cake's different. Tommy's cake had gone at lunch, that wasn't the trouble, with it being light, and people having a sweet tooth on the whole. Hers was a different kettle of fish, being a heavy kind of one. Sometimes wedding cakes were practically black, inside. But she could still take a leaf out of his book, and give pieces of hers to people in the Griffin, well-wishers you might call them. Also with wedding cake you can send slices in little boxes through the post to people. She could send one to her sister Janice. That would give her a surprise.

Guess what I'm washing? she suddenly asked herself. She realised she'd given herself a good old soaping between the legs, and was now doing likewise with her bosoms. One of those times when you're glad no one's looking at you. She blushed as she thought about it. One thing I've got to remember to do, she thought, I've got to watch how I walk. She'd caught sight of herself not long ago in a big shop window, and realised that she walked leaning forwards from her bottom. When you do that it makes you look as if you are just about to rush off somewhere, any second. Also, it makes your bottom waggle, which can be seen by those coming along behind. Behind my behind, she said out loud. She said it again in a funny voice, very high: behind my behind.

The other problem with walking leaning forward is that it makes you look a bit potty. What she had to do was keep telling herself: shoulders back.

Trust Jack still to be somewhere else even on holiday. True, Rose could see him, more or less, or at least his arm coming out of the water in a tiny loop. He was so far out to sea she could no longer be sure whether she was actually seeing him or just imagining it, making him up out of the movement of the waves and the light on the surface of the water.

She had to beat down the panic that kept rising in her stomach. Being out that far seemed to be asking for trouble, as if the deep water there was bound to suck you down. The sort of swimming she did she was frightened of getting out of her depth. She needed to know the bottom was there to put her feet on. She only had to do a stroke or two too many, or be pulled out a little bit by some wave, and she seemed to forget how to swim altogether.

She'd gone for a dip yesterday afternoon and during it, on a couple of occasions, had found herself floundering about, struggling for survival, while two yards away people were calmly throwing a ball to each other, or even being soppy. There was a young couple who kept on kissing in the sea. She wouldn't like to do that personally, too like kissing a pickled egg. It was only sheer embarrassment that had stopped her from crying out for help. It would look so silly being rescued from a tiddly bit of sea like that. With people so near you wouldn't need to bawl your lungs out, you'd say help, help, just in an ordinary voice, excuse me, but I seem to be drowning. The fact of the matter was that you could drown in a puddle or a garden pond, if you tried hard enough, but being a grown-up you should confine your drowning to deeper water if you wanted to keep your dignity. The trouble was, that was what Jack was doing.

Talking of dignity, the thought had struck her that when he was swimming he didn't have a limp. It had been painful to watch him walk down the beach in his bathing trunks, with one leg bowed outwards from knee to ankle so it looked like one of those elaborate furniture legs from times gone by. People had looked up at him from their family groups on the sand, as if they could tell somehow before they'd even set eyes on him, as though he must cast a different shadow from everybody else. That alone would make you swim, and swim.

It didn't help that the people who were staying in the next chalet to theirs had had experience of a drowning tragedy.

The woman had introduced herself as Mrs Green, just as if she was on surname terms with her own self, which meant she introduced herself back as Mrs Willis, as if she was too. 'I'm Mrs Willis,' she said, thinking: when I get to know myself better I'll call myself Rose. Thinking about that had made her remember that day when Vera told her to call her Vera, and one thing had led to another. Not that there was any danger of doing anything silly with Mrs Green, who was a little woman with a mouselike face, rather fierce. In Rose's experience mice themselves were rather fierce, the way they seemed to scurry right at you.

Mrs Green's neighbours, back at their home north of Birmingham, in a midlands village somewhere, were a bit of a nuisance, apparently, always making a noise. The husband would rig his wireless up outside while working on his car, that sort, and every year they made a fearful hoo-ha about going on their holidays. They always set out in the early hours. 'Like children waiting for Santa Claus,'

Mrs Green said, for some reason, which made Rose think of the way Jack had changed her watch and alarm clock to make sure they got off first thing.

It gave her a pang that she'd been so angry about it, and also about spending money in that restaurant. It had been a nice enough meal and got their holiday away to a proper start. While they were eating their pudding, background music had been turned on, much to the children's amazement. 'Why have they got music playing?' Donald asked, and dad said, 'So as you can't hear the noise people make while they're eating,' which had made Jack laugh his socks off, but it was true in a way.

Any rate, to compound it all, these neighbours of Mrs Green's used to warm up their car for about half an hour before they set out, it was part of the ritual. They'd be coming and going as if they were moving house, not just going away to a caravan for a couple of weeks. On this particular occasion, which apparently was last year, they did all the usual business before setting off. 'We were glad to see them go,' Mrs Green said, 'or hear them go, I suppose I should say, being the middle of the night.'

The neighbours arrived at their destination in Devon around lunchtime. The woman was busy unpacking. The teenage boys went down to the beach, and within a couple of minutes one of them was dead, drowned. He'd seen someone he thought was in difficulties and gone out after her, and that was the end of him. All that fuss setting off, and they hadn't even emptied their cases before tragedy struck. The woman had said to Mrs Green, 'I never want to go on holiday again, so long as I live,' and then she said 'Isn't it awful, I feel sorry for myself because I never want to go on holiday again. I think, all those years ahead, and no holiday.' Mrs Green said, 'I kept thinking to myself, I wouldn't have minded their blessed car making a racket half the night if their lad could be alive again.'

'Funny thing,' Rose had said, 'I knew a woman once, who lost her boy.'

'Drowned?'

'No. He died of inflammation of the brain.'

Mrs Green had given her a puzzled look, as much as to ask what she was driving at. She wasn't quite sure herself. It was that woman thinking about no more holidays, reminding her of how Vera had talked.

She'd opened her mouth to say something in explanation and then stopped herself in the nick of time. Goodness knows what would have come out. What could have possessed her?

It wasn't as if, as if she even liked Mrs Green very much. Not her type. Little mouse face pointing about, bright little eyes. As she thought about that on the beach, she felt herself go hot around her own eyes, not that it mattered all that much, since she was pretty well hot all over. Not my type, she thought, well for goodness sake, of course she's not my type, she's a girl. Mrs Green wasn't a girl of course, she was a grown woman, late thirties like herself, but Rose didn't mean girl like that, she meant *girl* girl.

As it was, Mrs Green had let her off the hook. Mrs Green's mind had gone back to her bereaved neighbour. 'What she really said,' she'd told Rose, 'when she said about never going on holiday again, was, as long as we both shall live. Never on holiday again, as long as we both shall live. Wasn't that a funny way to say it?'

To Rose's surprise dad looked up from his paper and said, 'That Mrs Green in the chalet next door seems a nice little woman.' It was funny how somebody else could catch what you were thinking about.

'Do you think so? I didn't take to her a great deal myself. Something about her set my teeth on edge.'

'I can't see why.'

'There isn't a why. She just did, that's all. Poky type of face. Poke, poke.' She sharpened her nose and tightened her mouth to show him that mouse appearance.

'Delicate looking person, I would have said.'

He would. Scraggy female, as far as may be from mum's

286

generous build, no wonder she appealed to dad.

'She was telling me about her neighbours losing a son at the seaside. Drowned.'

'Another reason for staying at home,' he said. He had a funny way of shaking his head just a tiny bit, almost like a tremor, when he was feeling self-righteous. He settled back in the deckchair which he insisted on renting for a bob a day, and shook out his newspaper again. 'Says here about a young Irish feller, building worker, staying with a landlady in our neck of the woods, Manchester, went out with her for a day trip to Blackpool.' He stopped and gave Rose a long look over his spectacles, as if she ought to be able to guess the rest.

'Oh yes,' she said, 'and I suppose he did something that got him hanged by Mr Pierrepoint.'

'What he did was go for a swim.' He found his place again with his thumb. 'Then lie sunbathing for the rest of the day. Then he had to be sent home to his digs from work the day after, with sunburn. Spent the next couple of weeks in bed, with just trips out to buy himself aspirins. Killed himself by swallowing a whole bottleful. The coroner states he left behind a note with the heading "suicide". His back was burned raw and the suffering had got too much.' Dad looked up again, not at her but at the blue blue sky, and shook his head, a proper shake this time. 'Silly apeth ought to have gone to the doctor's and had himself treated.'

Rose realised straight away why the poor Irishman hadn't. His pain wasn't from an illness or an accident, it was something he'd brought on himself, so he didn't feel entitled. She felt a sob rise inside her at his despair. I'm a silly apeth too, she thought, sitting here feeling sad about people that other people keep telling me about. What it was, she was full to the brim with sadness about Vera, exactly as if the two of them had had a long relationship with each other that had now come to an end, instead of just a brief period when they'd been close; so full of emotion that she had to find an excuse for letting some of it out so that she wouldn't burst into tears, or just burst. She thought of those words of Mrs Green's neighbour: as long as we both shall live. That was exactly how she felt about Vera catching that dream bus of hers to Newcastle upon Tyne.

'Talk about holidays,' dad said.

'I don't know about that,' she said, 'but I don't like Jack being so far out.'

Dad looked quickly out to sea, but not long enough to pick out Jack. You could only see him if you knew he was there, in any case, him being practically on the horizon. How far away is the horizon? she wondered.

'He'll manage,' dad said. 'Seventeen-year-old Canadian girl swam the Channel the other day. She nearly got disqualified when her coach ran into the sea to hoik her out. The crowd all shouted "Don't touch her, don't touch her", so she was left to crawl ashore.'

'Just because some girl in the paper swam the Channel doesn't mean Jack can. Mind you, he won't be far off, the way he's going.' She looked over at Peter who was sitting on his haunches smacking a sandcastle flat with the face of his spade. 'Talking of sunburn, I think I'll give Peter another go with the Nurona cream.'

She called Peter over and did his back. It was one of the things she didn't like much, rubbing cream into a warm back, especially when she came across grains of sand. While she was doing that, Donald came over. He didn't seem to be with them much, on the whole. Yesterday he'd discovered a family with a couple of girls in it sitting nearby, one of his own age, plain as a pikestaff, and one, French of all things, who was a bit older and was staying with the family to improve her English.

The French one was good-looking in a well-rounded fashion. It would turn to fat later, but Donald couldn't be expected to foresee that. He had just arrived at the age. Rose had watched him looking at the girl, eyes fixed on her bosom. How you could stay surprised by the hour was beyond her. She all but told him to stick his tongue back in, but remembered that such words could have a bad effect in later life. Donald had insisted they come back to the same spot on the beach today so he could resume his gawping. Didn't say that, of course, talked about the view and whatnot. View of what? that was the question. One bit of beach looked precious like another as far as she was concerned, but he'd led them to the exact spot, probably drawn here by a ghostly bust, like with radar in the war, and sure enough the family with the girls were also sitting in the exact location they'd had yesterday. Rose felt secretly proud to see her son old enough to begin to make a fool of himself.

'Can I have an ice cream, Mum?' Donald asked.

She looked over. Yes, the girls were eating ice creams. Not palsy-walsy enough to buy Donald one while they were at it.

'All right,' she said. 'Get one for Peter too. What about you, Dad?'

'Not unless you want my ears to fall off,' dad answered unexpectedly.

She looked at Donald. One thing Donald had learned to do was raise one eyebrow, which he did now. She suddenly felt a pang that he wasn't learning French at school. It would be so nice if he could talk to that French girl, la de da, in her own language, instead of waiting while she got out her bits of English. Put him on a par. Perhaps dad was right to worry about the education he was getting, old know-all. 'What do you mean,' she asked him, 'your ears?'

'When I eat ice cream the coldness goes up my cheek-bones and into my ears. It used to give me toothache, in the old days, when I had my own teeth.'

'But you had ice cream only the other day, in that restaurant we went to,' she said.

'That was my mistake.'

Donald took her money and got to his feet, showering Peter's creamy back with sand.

'Oh, Donald!' she said. Peter didn't notice, too busy grubbing after something on the beach.

'You've got toothache of the ears, Grandad!' Donald said, and scampered off to the ice cream kiosk.

'I haven't got anything, as long as I don't eat bally ice cream,' dad replied, though Donald was well out of earshot already. That wasn't true, anyway, he'd always got something: when it wasn't toothache of the ears it was his throat furring up, or he'd clutch at his chest, refusing to go to bed for fear he'd die in the night. He could do with Mr Pierrepoint to come along and put him out of his misery.

For some reason remembering how silly he could be cheered her up no end. What a stroke of luck, the sun shining every day, the sky so blue. Just down the beach the waves were breaking, and little children were hopping over the foam. Peter had found enough horrible things lurking in the sand to keep him happy. Donald was sweet on his first girl. Dad could be grumpy to his heart's content. Jack was able to swim for miles and get out of his system whatever it was he needed to get out of it.

Of course he wouldn't drown. He wasn't the drowning type.

Once he'd been on a train and it had stopped in the middle of nowhere, like trains do. Out of the window was a muddy field and a bit of a wood. What he thought was: I'd never have seen this place in my life if the train hadn't stopped here. Maybe no train had ever stopped in this exact spot before and none ever would again. But you could only get to the exact spot *by* train.

He got the same kind of funny feeling swimming out this far. Just tiny creepy-crawly people on the beach. You could see a broad section of coastline, cliffs stretching away and tailing off, the pier to one side, a big ferry-boat parked alongside it, and in the other direction the end bit of the Isle of Wight in the distance, blue like a dark cloud, except there weren't any clouds.

God knew how deep the water was here. It was like swimming on top of the Empire State Building. He imagined level after level of fish as the water darkened, like folk going about their business on different floors of a skyscraper, none of them with a clue what people below or above were up to. And at the bottom in the pitch-black, maybe a sunken galleon, pile of skeletons, doubloons and all the rest of it.

Out this far the waves didn't seem to be making for the shore or going anywhere at all, except up and down. He didn't feel in any danger. The sea felt so thick it was almost rubbery and the sun shone warm on his head and shoulders.

His mind kept reverting to North Africa, probably because a job lot of water was much the same as a job lot of sand, a big amount of nothing. Even less after the bombing raid, which flattened their little makeshift conning tower and left most of the airfield buggered, runways covered in craters like some fat kind of acne.

Jack had been in a ditch for the duration of the raid, along with Codge and some others. Codge said it'd been dug to take overspill from the latrines but it seemed dry enough while they crouched down in it. I'll take the credit for any shit in here, Jack told him, got enough on tap. When the fireworks stopped and they were all set to work, tidying up as the squadron leader put it in his little speech, no Tommo.

Sergeant did the rounds looking for him. 'Where might *Mr* Tomlinson be, when he's at home?' he kept asking. Mister was his way of saying there'll be hell to pay, like when a judge puts on a black hat.

Tommo's done a bunk, the rumour went round. Nobody stopped to ask: where can he have done a bunk *to*? It was just as if they'd forgotten straight away what sort of a bloke Tomlinson was. He's like the rest of us, Jack told Codge, too scared to be a fucking coward.

Then a lieutenant came round to ask about him, when

last seen et cetera. It was the same lieutenant who'd come into their tent that time, and seemed a bit sweet on Codge, of all people in the Second World War to feel a bit sweet on.

As he swam on, Jack suddenly thought of something Rose had said once about her mum dying when only fifty-eight, in the late 1930s. 'Perhaps it's all for the best. She wouldn't have thought much of the war.' He'd thought at the time: Rose makes it sound like somebody not being bothered to go to the pictures.

This time the lieutenant was businesslike, wanting to know what state of mind Tomlinson had been in.

'Scared stiff, if he had any sense,' Jack said, and then could have bitten his tongue.

'When did you last –' the lieutenant asked.

'He didn't go AWOL,' Codge said.

'We don't know what he did,' the lieutenant said.

'Yes we do,' Codge said. 'We know he didn't go AWOL.' He got nearer the lieutenant and grew about a foot, a way he had when he was losing his rag. He was big enough to be going on with, without doing that. Jack had a sudden horrible thought that he was about to bring up the Veronica episode again.

'Thing about Tomlinson,' Jack said quickly, 'he's a homesick type of a chap.' It was the first point about Tommo's character that sprang to mind.

'All the more reason,' the lieutenant said.

'Hang on a minute. Wait your hurry, is all I'm saying. He's not going to get home by buggering off into the night. *This* is his only way home, staying here. Hiding to nothing, otherwise.'

'We share a tent with Tomlinson,' Codge said. 'He did not go AWOL. People need to think twice before they accuse someone.'

'I've not accused anyone.'

'He won't have done anything daft,' Jack said.

'Let's hope not,' the lieutenant said, which made Codge

jerk forwards a bit but the lieutenant scuttled off pronto.

'We don't need a pansy like that putting the bad word on Tommo,' Codge said.

'He was only doing his job, and it's not going to help if you get yourself up on a charge. We cut it a bit fine, the way we talked to him, in any case.'

'He calls Tommo a deserter, and I'll cut *him* a bit fine.'

'Tomlinson'll turn up. Then we'll see.'

He did and they did, but not for another day. He turned up nearly a hundred yards outside the camp altogether, at the base of a low ridge. But he hadn't gone AWOL. He must have taken the full force of one of the explosions, and flown there. His head was missing, and they never did find it.

Jack began to swim back towards the shore. Funnily enough, despite getting so aerated with the lieutenant on the subject of Tomlinson being missing, Codge made a sort of joke about him being found. 'He always said he was going to have his teeth taken out,' he said, 'but I didn't expect him to have his whole fucking head removed.' He didn't laugh, though. None of them did.

She got off the bus in Stockport centre. The registry office was across opposite, halfway up the hill. First off there was a road, down which you could see the railway viaduct with its big loops. The brickwork looked pink in the hot sunshine. On cloudy days you could see it was all dirty and smoke-blackened. Trust the sun to make everything look clean, Ruth thought to herself, good old sun, shining on my wedding day. On ordinary days the sun just shines or doesn't shine, nothing to do with you. On your wedding day, it seems like as if it's *your* sun, just for the time being. Specially when the postman sings 'Oh what a beautiful morning' to you.

Where the road to the viaduct met the main road was a pub called the Hatters. Could have had the reception there, she thought, almost next door, it would have been nice and convenient. All you'd need do was tell the guests we're popping next door now, ladies and gents. But probably Jack was pals with the landlord of the Griffin, and thought they'd be more at home there.

Then there were a couple of shops going up the hill, then the registry office.

There were six or seven steps going up to the doors, which for some stupid reason made Ruth's heart suddenly thump. What's wrong with a few steps, for goodness sake? Some words came into her head: ascending the throne, which was what they said at the coronation. I'm not going to become the flipping queen, she thought to herself, I'm only going to get married. Better watch my bottom, though. If I do my leaning forward trick going up the stairs I'll be all bottom from down below. Not that anyone would see, except shoppers passing by.

Then she noticed there was somebody standing on the top step of the steps, and that somebody was Gerald! Funny how you can look at people for a moment before you recognise them, and see them as if they're not them at all, just anyone, see them as they really are.

Gerald was tall and getting rather stout. He was too big for his suit. His jacket button was pulling at its buttonhole so it looked like a weeping eye. His trousers didn't quite reach his feet, which was strange because he couldn't have grown upwards since he last wore them. His tummy must be using up a lot of the material, and his bottom. But that couldn't be right, tummy and bottom wouldn't be using up *leg* material, now she thought about it, the legs were a different part of the trousers altogether. Trousers weren't like a skirt, they had more or less a bag part to put the man's tummy and bottom in. Also his private parts. Maybe it was Gerald's privates that had got too big. It's being my wedding day which has given me such thoughts, she told herself, and now it's about time I got more sensible. Then underneath the bag part, the legs, like two tubes going down. What it must really be was the tops of Gerald's *real* legs having grown thick, and so stopping the *trouser* legs from dropping down all the way. You'd need to grab them by the turn-ups and give them a good tug.

What it was, he must not have worn that suit for a long time. He must have got it out of the wardrobe just for her.

The idea of him doing that bucked her up no end. His plumpness was like a way of showing how long it had been since something as important as her wedding day had come along and made him wear that suit, like making an announcement in a very loud voice.

She suddenly wondered if he'd have to make a speech. If Jack would have to too. And her. No, the bride didn't have to make a speech. Did she? Maybe she thanked the bridesmaids. She could put her mind at rest in that case: no bridesmaids.

Anyway, Jack had said it would just be an informal do for a few friends, so nobody would need to bother their heads about speeches.

She hurried across the road and up the hill to the registry office. Gerald didn't notice her coming.

'Hello, Gerald,' she said.

'Oh,' he said, turning to her. 'I was wondering if I'd come the wrong day.'

'No, it's the right day all right. Shall we go in?' She suddenly felt all confident, seeing him standing there like a big lummock, popping out of his clothes. With men, you sometimes felt you had to grab them by the hand and tow them along, like mums taking their kiddies to school. She pushed through the doors.

There was a foyer type of place inside, with a carpet down. It looked as if it could do with a hoovering, then she saw the bits on it were confetti from an earlier wedding. There was a little table to one side, with a lady sitting at it. She must be like the person they have at the doctor's or the dentist's, Ruth couldn't remember the name offhand, the one who wrote you down in the book. Funny to be a wedding one of those.

'Hello,' Ruth said.

'*Good* morning. What can I do for you?'

The way she'd said the *good* was too polite by half, and knocked the confidence straight out of Ruth again. For two pins she'd say what she'd said to the postman, that it was her birthday. Of course that wouldn't do here.

She was just going to speak when Gerald did instead.

'She's gerrin married, what you think?' he said. He had a way of talking rather rough when he was flustered. Just as well he hadn't to make a speech, when all was said and done.

'I don't think so,' said the lady. 'Not this morning, anyhow.'

'You what?'

'There's no more weddings arranged till this afternoon. Perhaps yours is then. Is your name Mr Harrap?'

'No, it isn't. But it's not me, anyway. It's her.'

'I'm afraid it has to be the both of you, to be a proper wedding.'

'No,' Ruth said, 'it's me getting married to someone else, not this gentleman. Who I'm getting married to is, Mr Jack Willis.'

'I see. I have no Mr Jack Willis here. What's your name?'

'My maiden name's Pedley,' she said, 'Ruth Pedley.' Suddenly she felt as if a great ball of tears had formed inside her head, right out of the blue. It was like as if her head had turned into a bowl of water, like the bowl her goldfish had used to live in. She thought to herself: if the wedding lady looks up, she'll see the water behind my eyes. What caused it was mortification at saying maiden name. Pedley wasn't her maiden name, it was her name. You only had a maiden name when you were remembering your old name after you were married. It was such a stupid mistake to make, made you look as if you were boasting about being married when you weren't.

'Maiden name Pedley,' the lady said.

'Just name Pedley. Name of Pedley.'

'I thought you said Pedley.'

'I did, yes, Pedley.'

'Anyway, whatever it is, it isn't down here. Look for yourself.'

She turned the book round and shoved it towards them over the desk. Ruth and Gerald both looked down at it, not that she could read a word, with her eyes full of water.

'Tell you what,' said the lady in a nicer voice, 'maybe you got the wrong week. It's been known.' She pulled the book back over and began riffling through the pages. 'No,' she said, 'not a dicky-bird. Oh, hold on a minute. There's a Pearson. Did you say Pearson?'

'Pedley.' I'm getting sick of saying the blooming word, Ruth thought.

'Yes, Pedley. Anyway, that Pearson was a Mister.'

'You must have forgot to put it in,' Gerald said.

'I beg your pardon?'

'Forgot to write. It. Down.' He pointed down at the book with his finger. Crumbs, Ruth thought, even his finger's got fat. Funny how you don't notice.

'In this line of work, there is no such thing as forgot,' the wedding lady said.

Gerald turned away and looked towards the door in disgust. The wedding lady stared at her book. Ruth just looked at the table. Then the lady asked: 'When did you come in?'

Ruth looked up at her. 'What do you mean, when did I come in? I came in five minutes ago.'

'She came in not five minutes since,' Gerald said bad-temperedly.

'I mean, to arrange it. To arrange the wedding.'

'Oh, I didn't arrange it. Jack arranged it. Mr Willis.'

'You both have to arrange it,' the lady said.

The cornets didn't have round ice cream on the top but the tube kind, like a big section of solid toothpaste, with greaseproof type of paper wrapped round the outside.

Donald carried them back to where they were sitting and gave Peter his. Peter straight away tried to pull the paper off, and instead managed to jerk the ice-cream bit out of the cornet and drop it in the sand. He started bawling as fast as water coming out of a tap when you turn it on. One second completely normal, jigging about trying to get the paper off, next crying as if he'd been crying for a week, with his eyes all red and his nose scrunched into a red ball again.

'Oh for goodness sake,' mum said. 'What did you think you were doing, giving it him with the paper still on?'

'I knew it would be my fault,' Donald said. 'He drops his ice cream on the ground and it's my fault, even though I'm standing about a hundred yards away.'

Peter did a sort of hiccup with his breath being so squeezed, then carried on crying full-blast again. He shook his cornet. Maybe he was mad with it for letting the ice cream drop out, or maybe he just wanted to make sure everybody could see it was empty. It looked like one of those olden days type of torches that you carry round castles, that have flames coming out of the top.

'Well, you didn't ought to have been standing a hundred yards away. You ought to have been giving him a hand. Poor Peter.' Mum tried to pull Peter over but he shook her off. He wanted to wag his cornet about a bit more. The other thing the cornet was like, when you looked into it, was your eye socket when your eyeball had been whipped out, like Donald was going to have done to him once, before he got rheumatism in the blood in the nick of time.

'You want to try taking the paper off of somebody else's ice cream while you're holding your own in your hand,' he said. 'It's flipping impossible.'

'I must say, I don't like the way you talk to me these days, Donald.'

Peter squatted down over his ice cream. Some tears dropped out of his eyes and landed right on it. You could hear them make a little ticking sound as they hit the paper.

'He can have mine, anyhow,' Donald said. He looked over at where the girls were. As you might expect they were just finishing their ice creams. They would be doing something else any moment.

'You can buy yourself another one,' mum said, reaching over to her handbag.

'I don't want another one.'

'Hold your horses any road up,' grandad said. 'No need to give up on this one yet.' He picked the ice cream out of the sand. 'Give us the cornet then,' he said to Peter. Peter passed it over, and grandad stuck the ice cream back in. 'Look, the paper has protected most of it,' he said, peeling the paper off. Underneath the paper the ice cream was still clean but part of the top was covered with sand, like as if it had been sprinkled with grey hundreds and thousands.

'That's Donald's ice cream,' Peter said.

'All I have to do,' grandad said, 'is lick it clean.'

'What about your ears falling off?' Donald asked.

Peter let out a horrible high-pitched shrieking noise. His face, which had just got back to normal, went completely covered with fright. 'Ears fallen off,' he said. He tried to pull the ice cream out of grandad's hand.

'Steady on, young feller, you'll have it on the floor again if you're not careful. My ears will be right as rain. The sand'll have warmed the ice cream up.' He gave it a big lick. You could see the sand all over his tongue before it went back into his mouth.

'Oh, Grandad,' Donald said.

'That's Donald's ice cream, that one is,' Peter said.

'It's yours, pardon me,' Donald said. When you were young you could eat stuff that other people had licked. People were always chewing up your food for you. But you couldn't do it when you were older. You would keep imagining you were tasting the lick, even though it was invisible.

'He gave his me, Mummy!' Peter yelled.

'Oh, for heaven's sake,' mum said.

'I don't want any bloody blinking ice cream. I'm sick of bloody ice cream.' Donald shoved his cornet into Peter's hand.

'I'll have the rest of this one in that case,' grandad said. He licked a bit that didn't have sand on this time. Donald saw his white smeary tongue shoot behind his moustache. Next in the queue, Peter's tongue came out, to take a gob of his own ice cream, or Donald's as it really was.

'I think your father will have something to say about that "bloody" nonsense, Donald my son, when he comes out of the water,' mum said.

Donald walked off, over towards where the girls were. He could feel himself walking all cocky for mum's benefit, even though he didn't want to, the way Emb used to walk before he got broken.

'Don't must your ears fall off, bofe of them, Granpa,' Peter said. He sounded happy as pie now he had a big fat new cornet in his paw.

Here they found the unfortunate girl, seated, or rather couched like a hare – her head-gear dishevelled; her night-clothes torn and dabbled with blood, – her eyes glazed, and her features convulsed into a wild paroxysm of insanity. When she saw herself discovered, she gibbered, made mouths, and pointed at them with her bloody fingers, with the frantic gestures of an exulting demoniac.

Got herself into a fine old state, in other words, just because the bloke she was getting married to wasn't really her cup of tea. There again, people do fly off the handle. Ernie thought about that case where Mrs Lloyd did away with her neighbour Mrs Aldridge, and then got reprieved from the gallows the week before Ruth Ellis copped it. Just couldn't take any more of Mrs A's son piddling in the back garden, or whatever he did do, along with that unpleasantness about the chops.

A while ago little Peter was whacking a sandcastle with his spade, and a picture of Mrs Lloyd doing likewise to Mrs

300

Aldridge's head came into Ernie's mind. He was glad when Peter's attention got diverted by the prospect of an ice cream, even though that proved to be a proper carry-on in its own way. Peter was still at it now, with help from Rose. Even managed to get a trickle of ice cream going down the small of his back. Ernie's own cornet had long since been disposed of, went past his ears with no bother at all, though now it was stowed he was beginning to get the first sensations of heartburn.

He looked up from *The Bride of Lammermoor*. His own fingers were a bit sticky, which took away the pleasure of turning the pages. Donald had gone off to a family nearby, to moon over a couple of girls they had there, a little English one, pretty as a picture, and her tubby French friend with thighs like a horse. Donald was sitting a little to one side, playing five-stones with some pebbles, and talking to the girls whenever they let him get a word in.

Suddenly the girls stood up, dusted themselves off, and began to run down towards the water. Even from where he was sitting Ernie could see their feet fluffing up the sand as they went. Donald cottoned on a bit late, got to his feet uncertainly, and began to follow, running slowly, as much as to say I've got other things on my mind than running about after a pair of females. Then just as they were about halfway to the water the girls stopped in their tracks, turned round, and began to run up the beach again. They came past Donald on the near side, leaving him marooned. He came to a halt and stopped where he was for the time being, toeing the sand as if lost in thought. Meanwhile the girls went straight past their own family and trotted right up to Rose.

'Hello,' said the English one.

' 'Allo,' the French.

'Hello,' said Rose.

Being a couple of yards further up the beach Ernie didn't feel called upon to say anything. Peter didn't either, but what he did do, to Ernie's surprise, was puff out his tummy till it was round as a ball, like the way a bird puffs out its chest. Bit of a rum way to say hello.

The English one said her name was Christine, and the French one Françoise. Christine was a tiny little thing with a sweet face, the sort of eyes that crinkled, and wavy hair. Ernie didn't take to the French lass, no offence. Bit the same sort of build as my Dorothy, he suddenly thought.

'And here's little Peter,' said Christine.

' 'Allo, Pete,' said Françoise.

Peter abruptly deflated his stomach and turned his back on them.

'Be nice, darling,' Rose said.

'We asked Donald what his name was,' Christine told her.

'Ah, that explains it,' Rose replied, patting her head as if it had been a big puzzle how they knew Peter was called Peter.

The girls wanted to take him down to the water with them. 'Would you like that, Peter?' Rose asked.

Peter rubbed one leg against another, grasshopper fashion, then walked backwards towards the girls, humming to himself.

'He's rather shy,' Rose explained.

The three of them went off towards the sea, Peter holding hands with the girls but still facing Rose and Ernie, so he walked backwards the whole way.

Donald was still to one side, halfway down the beach, looking at a loss. Girls, Ernie thought to himself, there's a boy their age would give his eye-teeth to have a splash about with them, and who do they pick on but his three-year-old brother. He looked down towards Donald. Donald's face was sad and wan. His hair seemed to have been bleached by the sun, or maybe it was just the light shining through it. He only looked like a little mite himself.

All of a sudden a spike of pain shot through Ernie's head, from one ear to the other, as if the ice cream had decided to make its presence felt at last.

302

* * *

Peter wanted to go with the ladies but he didn't want to go with them too much because one of the ladies said pit. She said allo pit. Pit wasn't his name and allo wasn't hello's name. Every time she said words she always said not its name but another one's name. She was the big lady. The other one, which was not the big lady, said it the right way.

Peter was looking at grandad. He walked to the sea looking at grandad because he ate the ice cream. When you walk to the sea when your legs are the wrong way round for walking there, the beach goes up and up. Each little bit of walk you do, more up. The same beach as before but now it is in a more up place. Mummy and grandad sitting the same but now they are sitting more up. Mummy sitting on a towel, grandad on a deckchair. Donald was standing the same kicking the beach but he was more up as well.

'If you turn round you can see the sea,' the lady not the big one said.

'It's tickling my feet,' Peter told her. He turned round. There was a man swimming in the sea. When you swim in the sea you walk along with your arms. The man came in to the shore. Then he stood up and came out of the sea. The sea kept falling off of him.

The man was dad. Dad said time for grub.

Ice cream or no ice cream dad did one of his mimes about food. He had an invisible fork in one hand and an invisible knife in the other. His stiff finger poked out of the knife hand like when some posh lady pokes out her little finger while drinking a cuppa.

Rose pictured Vera drinking tea like that in Newcastle upon Tyne, out of a little bone-china cup with violets on it. Making a new start: she could be posh again. Nothing like losing your son in tragic circumstances for making you less posh. Not to do with money because Vera'd never seemed short of a bob or two, just a matter of not wanting to be doing with all that for the time being. One minute trying to get Victor to win the Stockport Borough fancy dress competition, the next standing at his graveside. The bit of nonsense she, Rose, had had with her that time proved the point. You don't get up to those sort of shenanigans if you're busy trying to prove to all and sundry that you're the bee's knees. But now, married to her company representative it would be back to fancy dress again. Vera dressed up as Mrs Wife. Aren't we all, Rose thought.

Dad stabbed an invisible bit of meat with an invisible fork, cut it vigorously with his invisible knife, then looked across at Rose to make sure she'd seen. That's who Donald gets his ability to raise his eyebrow from, she realised. But dad could raise it all he liked, they couldn't go until –

Right at that moment along came Jack, shedding water. When you see men in bathing trunks they tend to look like frogs, especially when they have a bit of a square build like Jack did. The water gives a glossy finish. But still alive, that was the important thing. And little Peter dancing about at the end of Jack's arm, he looked like a froglet also, all bendy legs and arms.

The two girls had sloped off back to their own party. Donald was still standing halfway down the beach like a spare leg, brooding on the injustice of it all no doubt: his three-year-old brother being a bigger success with the ladies than himself. You could almost see a private cloud hanging over his head. He always had to find something to be miserable about these days.

Enjoy the sunshine, she felt like saying to him, at least you're not dead and buried like poor Victor.

'I want my dinner, after all that,' Jack told her.

'Chops,' she replied. She didn't like picnics on the beach because of sand getting everywhere. That's what we've got a chalet for, she'd told Jack, somewhere to go back to. The first couple of days they'd been down here, Bournemouth had been packed, it being the bank holiday weekend and

304

lovely weather. Dad had read out of the paper about it. The whelk-sellers were doing a roaring trade, it said, though she hadn't set eyes on a single whelk-seller since arriving. 'I wouldn't know what a whelk looked like if it came up and hit me,' she'd told dad. It also said that people had slept in their cars and on the beach, which made her glad of their own little house, albeit wooden. Somewhere to go back to.

The other good thing about having a midday dinner was it gave you less to worry about in the evening. And breaking up the day made it not so boring being on the beach. She liked coming back in the afternoon and the light being different, the tide too, a bit, not that there was a lot of tide in Bournemouth.

'That's the ticket,' dad said.

'What you want to do with that stiff finger of yours,' Jack said to him, 'shove it in the sand like a tent peg. It'll anchor you if a gust of wind catches the deckchair.'

Dad chuntered to himself. Jack began towelling. Rose called Donald over and he came very slowly, like one of those deep-sea divers with weights on his boots.

The worst thing, thought Ruth, will be Mrs McMahon not saying I told you. 'I'll say to her, there he was, gone,' and she'll be nice as nice. That will be what makes me blart. Old droopy-drawers being nice to me and giving me a hug. Jack called her droopy-drawers sometimes. Or the old trout. That was in the old days more, when they'd been together the first time. I don't want to be comforted by someone who hasn't even got the use of her legs, was what Ruth thought. It made her blush a bit to think it.

Gerald didn't say I told you, but that wasn't so bad. He just said, better be gerrin back to the pub. You better, she said. If we'd had the wedding he wouldn't be getting back to the pub, he'd be coming with us to the reception thingummyjig. Blimmin cheek, she thought for a second, then realised that was silly. He didn't know what to say or do, so the only choice was hop it.

That was the word she'd been trying to remember, to call the wedding lady: receptionist. Funny how it comes back to you when you're thinking about something else.

Gerald took a few steps down the street and suddenly stopped dead, just as if he'd walked into a glass wall. He turned round. 'You want me to knock his block off for him, you just say the word,' he said. He looked at her with that look on his face, not sure if he'd said the right thing.

'Thanks, Gerald,' she said, 'you're a gentleman.'

He gave her a bit of a smile, quite timid-looking, and carried on his way.

Her legs ached as if she had been walking a lot, which she hadn't. She didn't even have on very high heels, being that Jack wasn't a tall bloke. What she wanted to do more than anything was get home and put her feet up for a while.

When she was small she had a little box she kept stuff in. She had a bottle of perfume, just from Woolworths, violet flavour, a hanky with a lacy edge and an R embroidered on it, and a funny little blue glass animal with very spindly legs. The box was a little wicker type of one, lined with silk, or material that looked like silk. She liked to open the box and inspect her things, but the best part was closing it again and sliding it away under her bed. Thinking of the treasures all sitting cosily in the darkness. That's what she could do with now, getting in a box herself and being slid safely under a big big bed.

Having a lie-down with the curtains drawn will do, she told herself.

But first off there was something she had to see about: go to the Griffin pub and check on her cake. She didn't expect anybody to turn up for the reception, because they'd have been at the registry office first if Jack had invited them, but what if the cake shop had sent her cake along, top storey and bottom storey, with all the doodahs on it, little bride and groom on the top, and there it was, plonked on the bar, with no one having a clue where it had come from or what to do with it? Eat it, she'd have to tell them, eat the blooming thing. The cake's on me. It wasn't really, of course, because she hadn't had to pay for it.

The idea crossed her mind that maybe it could be sent back. She tried to remember if wedding cakes had the names of the people being wed on them or if it was just general. To who it may concern. Probably it depended. If it didn't have Ruth and Jack but just Congratulations perhaps it would do for somebody else. It would have cost a bomb; maybe she could get the money back, or some of it anyway. It would be Jack's by rights but serve him bally right.

You could say a cake's a cake, but there was a world of difference between eating a wedding cake because it was somebody's wedding, and eating a cake that was going spare because no wedding. You might just as well eat a pile of sultanas and almonds and glacé cherries in that case.

But the most important thing was to not let it go to waste. If it did have Ruth on it and had to be eaten even without a wedding that was better than it just hanging around with nobody knowing what to do with it, people making jokes, it ending up in the bin.

Blow it, she said to herself, I'll get a taxi. She deserved a treat.

She went down to the Co-op where there was usually a couple lying in wait. She got in the first one and remembered right away why she didn't like using them, apart from how much money they cost, of course. It was like sitting in a little room, all by yourself, with somebody with their earhole to the door, which was the driver sitting in his compartment at the front. You felt lonely and on show both at the same time. Another thing was it made her tummy feel funny when the meter ticked over.

'Yes, duck?' the driver said. He didn't move his head to talk one inch. The only way you could tell it was him talking was his ears shaking a tiny bit as he said each word.

'I want to go to the Griffin pub on Didsbury Road,' she said.

'That's my girl,' the ears told her. He didn't move his head when he started driving either, it just stayed there, stiff as stiff. He could have been a statue, at least his head and shoulders, what they called a bust even though it wasn't a bust, like the bust of Queen Victoria in the first pub she ever worked in, nasty old face-ache. With Gerald people were either face-aches or honey bunches.

I pray I have enough in my purse, which was her next thought. She often prayed for things you shouldn't pray for, like having enough money in your purse or not missing the bus, instead of to heal the sick, which meant that her prayers had got very diluted. Which was probably why horrible things happen to me, she realised. She didn't dare look in her purse till she had nearly got to the Griffin, but when she did she had enough for the fare, and more. One prayer answered, my luck must be in. What I should have done, I should have prayed not to be let down on my wedding day. Too late, me all over.

There was a bit of a breeze on this part of Didsbury Road, quite refreshing being how hot the sun was, but in danger of lifting her hat. It was a little cloche one, nothing swanky, the sort of hat you might wear even if you weren't supposed to be getting married today, which was why she'd chosen it, to look smart but not draw attention. She clapped her hand on it to make sure a gust didn't send it flying.

The pub was quite a nice old-style building, with dimply bay windows. She went to the door and pushed it open. Inside, dark, with a smell of beer. There were a couple of men standing by the polished bar. They didn't turn to see who it was. Of course her cake wouldn't be here, she realised. Funny how you can understand something when you see for yourself. An ordinary dinnertime pub, no cake here for love nor money.

She stepped a pace or two inside, just to make sure, and looked around her as though her look was saying, not you, not you, like you do when you're looking for somebody you've said you'd meet in a place.

Chapter Thirteen

The chalets weren't much to write home about in themselves. From a certain point of view they weren't a lot different from those prefabs they kept putting up everywhere just after the war. But they were in a nice situation, surrounded by pine trees which gave off a spicy smell of resin in the heat of the day. Rose said about it to Jack, and he said it was just like the liquid they sprayed the café kitchen with, to keep the smell of cooking down, onions and cabbages especially.

Here and there you could catch a glimpse of the sea between the trees. What Rose liked best were the little paths they had, that went alongside the white cement roads and looped off to the individual chalets, with wooden edges and steps and a carpet of pine needles in between. You could walk on them barefoot if you should want.

What Rose was wearing were strappy sandals, also a white summer dress with a little floral pattern which had a nice way of swaying round her legs as she walked and making them feel cool. The sun was hot on her head and shoulders, though. When the shadow of a tree fell on her it felt so distinct you could swear it had weight. Dad kept telling her to wear a hat but she wasn't in a mood to take advice from him, and anyway she was only going as far as Mr and Mrs Green's chalet.

She tapped with her knuckle on the door. These places weren't designed for receiving visitors: no knockers. Knocked again, after a moment or two. A faint voice said hello, which she took to mean come in.

The front door of the chalets opened straight into their sitting-cum-dining-room. To Rose's surprise there was nobody there. The room was as neat as pie.

One of the bedroom doors opened. They led straight off the main room. The chalet was just the same as theirs except two bedrooms instead of three. Out came Mrs Green.

Her face was a bit pink, and her hair straggly. Her dress didn't seem settled on her properly. It was cream linen, straight up and down and squarish on the shoulder, rather old-fashioned looking. There was obviously nobody else about. What Rose thought was, she's been having a good cry, all by herself. She looked like a mouse again, but not a fierce one like before, just a bleary sad little mouse peeping out of its hole.

Rose wasn't one to be forward, but now she didn't feel she was being Rose at all, but somebody else. What this somebody else did was walk straight across the room, put a hand on each of Mrs Green's shoulders, and kiss her, not a long kiss but a definite one, full on the lips.

Then the somebody else took a step back, and said 'I'm sorry.' She was just going to add, about your boy, but stopped herself in the nick of time. The shock of that made her turn into Rose again. Perhaps dad was right: hot sunshine does jumble your brains. What she'd been thinking, or what this somebody else who had gone striding across the room and done the deed had been thinking, was that Mrs Green had lost her boy in tragic circumstances, and had been taking the chance of having a lonely little cry about him. But of course it wasn't her boy at all, it had been the lady-next-*door*'s boy.

Luckily Mrs Green didn't respond at all, not for nor against. Certainly she gave no sign of being shocked. Her lips had had a cool rubbery feel, like the tyres of Donald's old dinky toys, not that Rose had ever kissed them, of course, but she seemed to know what they'd kiss like.

I'm sorry for the kiss. That's what Mrs Green would think she'd meant.

'The others are down at the beach,' Mrs Green said, in a quiet voice. 'I was just having myself a little nap.'

Rose opened her mouth. For a moment she was going to argue. She was going to say, no you weren't, you were crying. Then she realised that was silly. Mrs Green had nothing to cry for. Her boy hadn't died. She didn't even have a boy. She only had a girl, ten years old or thereabouts, too young for Donald to be soppy about. The pinkness of Mrs Green's face: caused by sleep. The tousled hair, sleep. Bleary eyes, the same. The dress not quite settled on her, likewise.

'I was wondering if you knew where Mr Sumner is?' Rose asked.

'Mr Sumner?' Mrs Green didn't even seem to know *who* he was.

'You know. The owner of this place. The manager, whatever he calls himself.'

'Oh, Mr *Sum*ner.'

Who do you think I said? Rose thought to herself.

'I'm sorry, I'm still half-asleep,' Mrs Green said.

Perhaps that explained it. With luck Mrs Green had been too sleepy even to notice she was being kissed. Like Peter sometimes, when she went in to make sure he was tucked in all right. Thinking along those lines suddenly made Rose want to kiss her again. She felt quite wobbly, like you do when you're high up on the edge of a cliff and you half want to throw yourself over and be done with it, and half want to step back to safety.

'It's just that we've done a stupid thing,' Rose told her. 'I say we, but it was my father in point of fact. He's gone and seized up the gas meter.'

'How do you mean, seized it up?' Mrs Green furrowed up her forehead, which made her face look cross and reminded Rose she hadn't really taken to her. It was dad who thought she was the bee's knees.

'My dad's always been a bit cockeyed,' Rose said.

'Is that so?' Mrs Green asked it as if cockeyed was a recognised form of illness or handicap. Perhaps it was, considering you have to live your whole life without anything ever being properly straight or level, and your nearest and dearest do too.

'I was just putting on some chops for lunch and the gas ran out. I asked dad to put a bob in the meter and he managed to get it stuck in the slot. It won't come out and it won't go in, try as we might. My Jack had a pair of pliers from the car but it wouldn't budge.'

'You can do your chops over here, and welcome,' Mrs Green said.

'We had salad instead, thanks all the same. Chops tonight, all being well.'

'What he said, when we moved in, Mr Sumner, I think he said he'd be in his office every day between three and four. That little kiosk place, by the main gate.'

'Is that what he said? Jack went over there and couldn't find him. We forgot he told about when he could be found there.'

'Yes, three to four, I'm sure that was it. All right otherwise?'

'Oh yes, we're having a lovely holiday. Are you?'

Mrs Green looked up into Rose's face with those sharp little eyes of hers. She has eyes the way some people have teeth, Rose suddenly thought. Or some animals. No, I don't like her at all. Mrs Green's mouth bent a little, not much, like a stick in water. She had noticed the kiss, of course she had. And now she's grinning at me. Suddenly Rose thought of Vera and to her horror a sob shot out of her mouth. She patted her chest and shook her head a little as if recovering from a hiccup. Vera hadn't looked down on her because of a kiss and a bit of nonsense, the opposite. She had probably thought it was she, Rose, who had gone all snooty after the event. I could have kissed her whenever I liked, Rose thought, and instead I gave her the cold shoulder so she had to fall in love with a perfect gent instead and go off on that bus to Newcastle for evermore.

'Oh yes,' Mrs Green said. 'My word, you have picked up a good tan since you got here.'

That's because I'm blushing so much, Rose thought to herself. But the funny thing was, as she walked along the pine-needle path to her own chalet, her heart thumped at the memory of kissing Mrs Green, and she knew she'd do it again, given half the chance.

It had somehow become *Jack*'s blinking fault, which was a bit rich given dad had wedged the shilling piece in the meter in the first place. How he'd managed to get it so jammed it wouldn't budge a fraction of an inch for love nor money was a mystery. He must have superhuman strength, but only when doing something that didn't ought to be done in the first place.

All Jack had done for his part was try and extract it with a pair of pliers, but to no avail. True, it may have done more harm than good, causing the coin to get slightly bent and therefore more uncooperative than ever, but he couldn't be being blamed for that since the others didn't know. Also he'd used a spanner from the workbox in his car to try to hammer the shilling further in, which may have compounded the problem, but there again that was when Rose had gone off to the woman next door to try to find out how they could get hold of the camp bloke so, as they say, what the eye doesn't see, don't grieve, but grieve she bloody well did.

He'd spent best part of an hour in all trying to get the blasted coin to go in or come out; you got so you wanted nothing more in the world than to be able to twist the lever thing and watch the meter swallow its bob, like trying to get a pill down someone who's lying on their deathbed, so by the time Mr Sumner finally came round Jack wasn't as patient as he might have been and threatened to knock his block off for him, and it was that that had really got on Rose's wick.

Mr Sumner had stood there shaking his head and the meter had stood there in turn, like a naughty schoolboy poking his tongue out.

'This is one for the gas company,' Mr Sumner had said.

'We can't wait till Christmas,' Jack told him. 'All you need is a sodding Mole wrench.'

'Against the law, tampering with a meter.' Mr Sumner did a kind of fish look with his face and nodded it in Jack's direction, so to say, I'll leave you to take the high jump for that one, matey. Then he sucked in his breath and shook his head again, at the horrible prospect of touching one of the gas company's sacred meters. 'More than my job's worth.'

'For heaven's sake, Jack, no need to use bad language,' Rose said.

Jack looked round exaggeratedly, to see who he might have damaged with the word sod. Donald had gone off to try his luck with a pretty little French poppet on the beach, as much chance as an asbestos mouse, what with that English girl acting as bodyguard to make sure the other one didn't get more than her share of fun and games. Peter was squatting in the corner, talking to a spider. Dad was buried in his Walter Scott book, pretending all this was nothing to do with him.

'What I would say your job's worth, is keeping these chalets ticking over for the sake of people who've paid good money to have their holidays in them.'

'No need to come that tone of voice with me, thank you very much.'

It was then that matters went from bad to worse, culminating in Jack making a threat. Mr Sumner just spoke to Rose after that. He told her he'd try to get something done tomorrow.

'Fat chance,' Jack said, after he'd gone. 'More likely the middle of next week.'

'We're lucky we weren't thrown out on our ear, the way you behaved.'

'If nothing comes of it tomorrow, I shall be demanding another chalet.'

'What's the point of demanding, when you know you can't have? The place is fully booked, he told us so when we got here.'

'He'll have to do *some*thing, that's what I say.'

And then, suddenly, the rest of the day went out the window. Rose looked at him with utter contempt on her face, and said, 'You make me sick, you do,' and before he knew what he was doing he'd walked out the door.

Bloke told him a story in the war. Was at training camp, transit camp, some kind of camp. Waiting to be sent off somewhere, like usual. It was New Year. Jack had a notion that it was in Edinburgh for some reason, maybe because of the New Year part, big do in Scotland. They had a Hogmanay at the café one year, not a proper function, just the place being taken over by some of Ken's pals, private party. Stan had bought the haggises in from a tripe and cowheel stall in the covered market which got hold of them for him at less than the cost of making them yourself, so he said.

Anyway, there was this pair of blokes, out on the town, New Year's Eve, Edinburgh, got themselves pie-eyed. Ended up messing around in some park somewhere. There's this little wall. The other bloke goes waltzing up, and sort of skips over, the way you do when you're not quite sure you'll get over a wall clean, so you touch your foot down on the top of it on the way past, do it on purpose to save doing it by accident, stop you going arse over tit. Like a plane bouncing as it comes into land.

Then he disappeared, as if the ground had swallowed him up.

The friend bloke looks over, and sees that it's a railway

cutting. The jumping bloke is eventually fished out the bottom with a broken back.

You could feel how it must have felt.

Bit of beer inside you, not such a bad world after all. Hop up on the wall. Just a split second to discover there's nothing over on the other side, a lot of night-time but no ground. Hold your horses, what's this then? No time to stop your momentum.

Then falling down and down. Those were horses that couldn't be held.

It was Tomlinson who'd told him that story. The friend bloke a friend of Tommo. One thing you could say, at least the other bloke, the jumping one, was out of the war. Probably alive to this day, which was better luck than Tomlinson had.

Stride out of the chalet all in a lather and before you can bring yourself to a halt you've hopped in the car and driven to the centre of Bournemouth. Even as he went through the door Jack had a sort of notion at the back of his mind that he was taking what Rose said too much to heart. Later on he had a half-memory of getting a glimpse of her expression on his way out, and her being taken aback that he'd got himself so aerated. She probably wasn't that mad at him personally, just cheesed off about the chops and that. It was dad who'd got the bob jammed, not him. You didn't need to assume it was always you in the doghouse. His nerves were on edge today, that was the problem about it.

But the funny part was even when you knew you didn't need to have taken off like a rocket the deed was still done. That's why he'd remembered the story about the bloke who'd jumped the wall. You reach a point of no return. Well, not no return in this case, but after an exit like that you'd seem a bit of a clown if you came straight back. Give it an hour or two, any road.

He suddenly thought: it's just like being given a pass out in the forces. I've got a bit of time to myself. You can't say fairer than that.

*　*　*

When Donald got back to the beach in the sad afternoon sunshine, they weren't there any more. It was like when you were young, and playing a game in the road, it didn't matter how good a one it was, how many others playing it with you, you only had to go in for tea and when you came back it would be all over. Some of the same children might still be there but they would be doing something else and when you reminded them, they'd look at you as if they had no idea what you were on about. Sometimes even going to the toilet would be enough.

That was why he didn't like going back to the chalet for dinner. But yesterday and the day before it had been all right, Christine and Françoise had still been lying there sunbathing when they arrived back.

He wondered for a minute if this time he'd come to the wrong bit of beach, because even Christine's mum and dad weren't there either.

No; where he was was just the correct amount of distance from the pier, and when he inspected it he could even see some of the footprints and bum marks in the sand, and what was left of a sandcastle that Peter had mashed up with his spade. There was a man over to one side lying on a towel, asleep with sunglasses on, in exactly the same position as he had been this morning. Funny thing about him was he didn't get sunburned. He was quite pale and there was no suntan cream by him at all. Anyway, when Donald turned round he saw that grandad's deckchair was still in its place, with his newspaper on it to show it was taken. He always booked it for all day. Donald hadn't noticed it at first when he'd gone past because another family were sitting more or less where they'd all been in the morning, which was just a bit down the beach but still near the chair, so grandad could look down on them and be Lord Muck, which was what mum told him he was.

Now there was a fat woman in a blue dress by where

318

mum had been. Sitting on a rug on the sand made her triangular so she looked like a blue mountain with a boulder on the top of it, which was her head. Her husband was sitting by her, a very thin bloke with little points on his shoulders where his arms pushed up into them. Seeing him and his wife side by side made Donald think about spiders again. They'd done them at school last term in science, and Mr Whitlow had told about the female eating the male after mating. 'So think yourselves lucky, lads, that you're not spiders,' he'd told the class. Harty did his big insincere laugh he did whenever a teacher made a joke, whether it wasn't funny or was, a sort of waa waa waa noise, flapping his hand away from his mouth like people in band shows do with their trumpets sometimes, so it looked as if he was yawning at the same time. A lot of the girls rolled their eyes upwards in that way you do to say bo-oring but Emb laughed so much he nearly wet himself, probably did, being Emb. That lesson on spiders had been before.

While they were waiting for the camp man to come about the gas meter Peter had found a spider in the chalet, and Donald told him about the male spiders getting eaten. When you told Peter things he didn't know already he didn't say Oh or anything. He didn't even look at you. He sort of looked to one side and repeated it to himself in a whispery voice as if it was times tables or something that he had to learn by heart. He whispered more breathing in than he did breathing out, which made the words sound back to front, and sometimes he sort of sighed or shivered while he did it, like when grandad said a goose walked over my grave.

Donald wondered where his family would sit, when they came back. The beach was pretty full by now. Still it could be anywhere if Christine's family weren't here, for all he would care. He could sit anywhere too but he wanted to stay standing so he could try to see Françoise.

She wasn't among all the thousands of people on the

beach though, he could tell. It was funny how people on the beach, no matter how white or brown or pink they were, looked black in the distance, like shadows of themselves. But Françoise would shine or twinkle or something, or just glow. Maybe she would just be her own colour when everybody else was dark. He would have been able to tell it was her no matter how far she was.

He felt a kind of panic at how much he needed to hear her voice again. He tried to remember what it sounded like while he carried on standing near where they'd all sat only this morning, though that already felt like the old days, some place they'd all been together at in another life, so long ago that it made you want to weep remembering it. Sometimes he would have a very horrible thought. It would come into his mind how he'd been dead for years and years, so long he was completely used to it and had forgotten he'd ever been anything else. And then suddenly he'd hear or see something that came from earth, and the memory of how it all was in the olden days would come pouring back. It made him feel homesick for his own life.

He felt the same now, except it was just Françoise he'd lost, but that was enough. He couldn't remember what she looked like, even though he'd last seen her a few hours ago, but he knew he'd recognise her anywhere. He couldn't remember what her voice sounded like, whether it was high or low even, but he could remember exactly what it was like to hear her speak. The funny part was he could remember Christine in complete detail. She talked in a London voice, and couldn't stop jumping about all the time, like a monkey. She had a salty smell about her, not from the sea, more like the smell of nostrils. When she laughed it was nearly a scream.

Standing on the beach like this made him feel people must be looking at him. Nearly everybody else, as far as the eye could see, was sitting down, except for a few people who were playing ball. He decided to walk down to the water and stand in it for a while. People would think he was paddling.

He went out up to his knees. He had his bathers on under his shorts anyway, if he wanted to go in properly, though he hadn't brought a towel with him. He'd been in too much of a hurry to get out of the chalet to think of it. When they went back for their dinner it was just like being put into prison. They seemed to be there for ever. First mum started to cook the chops, then the cooker went out, then grandad got the shilling stuck, then dad banging away trying to get it to drop down, a little bead of sweat hanging from the tip of his chin and shaking while he worked but never dropping off, then them having salad instead, then dad going off to try and find the camp man and not finding him, then mum going off to ask the people next door where the camp man was, and then waiting for the time when the camp man would turn up in his office.

The waiting had made Donald go into a very slow panic. The day was going on and on, the sunshine was getting later and more yellow, Christine's family might decide to clear off and do something else. Donald had been back in the chalet for so long he could hardly remember being on the beach at all, it seemed like a dream.

Donald had begun to hate the wooden smell of the chalet. Grandad was sat in his chair reading out bits of his book, mum kept telling him, Donald, off for getting too big for his boots, Peter was in the corner staring at his spider, dad kept on kneeling at the gas meter to swear at the shilling. Donald felt he'd been sent to hell and could never find his way out again.

Then he remembered he was old enough to go off to the beach by himself.

Mum tried to stop him, but he reminded her he'd been to the Lake District with the Scouts last Easter, and went out the door before she had time to argue any more. But it had been a fat lot of use because he was too late anyway, they'd gone.

As he stood with the sea pushing and pulling his legs, Donald kept trying to remember the sound of Françoise's voice. He'd never heard anyone talking with a French accent before, at least not that he could remember, and yet he felt as if he'd heard it all his life, it seemed the proper way to speak, for girls to speak anyhow. It sounded exactly the way girls were. Christine might have been a boy, as far as speaking was concerned. French was the way the girl part of a girl should sound.

Donald suddenly remembered one word that Françoise said with such vividness it was almost as if she was saying it right now, in his ear. The word was orrible. She kept saying zis is orrible or zat is orrible. The way she said it gave Donald a trembly feeling in the pit of his stomach.

Donald looked out at the sea, and then he saw her.

She was in the back of one of those boats you pedal along. There were two people doing the pedalling. One of them was Christine. Her wheel seemed to be splashing a lot, and her sharp knees kept going up high over the side of the boat. Now he could see her he could hear her faint squeals of laughter, a bit like the cries of the gulls. The other person pedalling was a boy. He was much bigger than Christine and a stronger pedaller, so the boat was going round in circles. Françoise was behind the two of them, leaning over the side, trailing a hand in the water.

Perhaps the boy fancied Christine? Françoise didn't seem to be taking any notice of him. No, no boy could be interested in Christine. It would be like a girl being interested in Emb. Where had he come from? There was no sign of a boy this morning. He seemed to have sprung from nowhere, like an illness.

I knew this was going to happen, Donald thought. He had too, that's why he was so fed up at his family all going doolally and losing the will to live just because grandad had managed to get a bob stuck in the meter. Trust grandad. He couldn't just put the money in like everybody else and live happily ever after.

'Thank you very much, Grandad,' Donald said out loud. There was a very small girl in the water right by him, wearing one of those bumpy-looking bathing costumes, made of special crinkly material that was a horrible pink colour, with lots of frills and bows and things on it. Because she was quite fat she looked like a little beetle or bug of some kind. She must have thought he was talking to her because she turned round to look at him and just at that moment a wave came along and knocked her flat.

Serve her bloody right, Donald thought, and moved along to one side so he didn't have to rescue her. The water was only about two inches deep in any case. Perhaps Françoise doesn't like that bloke in the boat even if he likes *her*, he thought.

He tried to imagine how it had happened. The bloke liked Françoise, she didn't like him, but Christine liked him. Christine was the sort of girl who liked everybody. So the bloke tries to get Françoise to go out in a pedal boat with him, Françoise says no, Christine says yes, and they end up all three of them going. Françoise sits in the back, leaves the two of them to get on with it. She trails her hand in the water out of boredom.

The beetly little girl scrambled out of the water and ran bawling up the beach. Donald pictured Françoise getting back to dry land, cocking her head towards the boat bloke, telling Donald: 'I sink ees orrible.'

Orrible, Donald said to himself, trying to make it sound convincing. Blast it, he said, feeling tears come into his eyes, and turned and walked away from the water's edge.

Jack went into a little café just off the front and had a poached egg on toast. It was only just gone four but he was hungry already. Salad was fair enough when you were geared to it, but when you were expecting a proper midday dinner with chops and spuds and the rest it seemed like something and nothing. What they said in a book he'd bought years ago, about setting up in the restaurant trade:

the customer needs something to bite on.

The other thing which he believed was the three square meals a day formula being out of date. We are moving into the age of the snack, eating on demand, any time of the day or night. These milk bars and coffee bars where the young people went nowadays was the way to do it. If Rose's dad had been the sort of bloke to invest a few quid when it was most needed, he, Jack, would have been able to buy into the Station Café, and it could have been cashing in on that trade by now, instead of doing tea dances and evening dinners for the old fogies. The mark-up on a club sandwich and milk shake, plus speed of turnover, could keep your business hopping. It beat waiting all evening to take your profit from a plate of schnitzel into a cocked hat.

Serve the future, not feed the past, could have been his motto. Funny how he'd never been able to think up a good one for the garage. His mind always seemed to run on catering lines, even though he was able to make good money in the motor trade.

When he came out he walked up to the front. There was a bit of a park area at the top of the cliff, with a floral clock in it showing a couple of fuchsias to five. He didn't feel ready to go back yet, it would look as if he had his tail between his legs. The fact that he'd probably overreacted in walking out in the first place made him want to stay away longer, to prove his point somehow. In any case, the family would be still on the beach. Then there'd be the palaver of getting some grub together with the meter still buggered, which would probably lead to another row all over again.

At the same time, he felt a bit high and dry, being here all by himself. Late afternoon on a hot day when you didn't have anything in particular to do and anyone in particular to be with, could give you the heebie-jeebies, get you feeling sorry for yourself. At times like this you could do with pubs being open.

He sat on a bench for a while, watching people going

324

down to the beach in the lift jobby, halfway between a lift and a railway. Everybody was with somebody. Little kid with a bucket turned round to look at him, the way kids do, not a blink, then got yanked on his way by his dad. Boy and girl tootled past, arm in arm. One thing you could say, the human race was not going to die out. All on my lonesome, he thought to himself.

The sun was shining in his eyes, giving him a headache. He remembered going to Llandudno once upon a time, sensible type of beach, facing north so you could look at the water without a lot of dazzle. Funny thing was, people all sat the wrong way round with their backs to the sea, so they could carry on glaring at the sun.

'Go to the pictures.' He said it out loud, being as the idea had struck him out of the blue. A Teddy boy was walking by along the prom right in front of him, as luck would have it, his comb out to flip his duck's arse back in place where the sea breeze was blowing it sideways. Must have thought he was being spoken to because he stopped in his tracks and looked round. He was still holding his comb horizontal just in front of his forehead, all ready for use.

'Not you, sonny Jim,' Jack told him.

The lad opened his gob to say something back but couldn't think what, so shut it again. Face full of acne and bum fluff, reminded Jack of that lad of Eddie's a few years ago, what his name was he couldn't remember, doing call-up now, Eddie had said.

Peter was his name, that was a thing. It hadn't come into his head even for a second when they decided to christen Peter Peter. Probably would have put him off his stroke if it had.

Jack remembered the way his own Peter mixed Teddy boys up with teddy bears, and laughed out loud, which was too much for the youth, who went off at a high-speed walk, more a sort of speedy hobble, with his drainpipe legs flashing like spokes beneath his long jacket.

* * *

It was a glum do sitting on the beach in the late afternoon
while Jack was away throwing a tantrum somewhere, and
Donald wasn't much better, moping about without a word
to say to anyone, playing his five-stones. Those blessed
girls nowhere to be seen, that was the long and short of it
in his case. Consider yourself lucky, my lad, Ernie felt like
saying to him. Men and women been put on this planet to
get up each other's nose. Think of Sylvie, left high and dry
by that Popeye chap, also the poor so-and-sos in *The Bride
of Lammermoor*.

The bride, Lucy Ashton, having lost her marbles at
getting married to the wrong fellow and taken a few whacks
at him in revenge, gibbered for a time, then passed away.
The groom recovered from his wounds and shortly after
left the country for good, having vowed never to tell
anybody what had really taken place. The bride's brother,
Colonel Ashton, challenged the rejected suitor, by name
Ravenswood, to a duel on the links to the east of Wolf's-
hope. Whether it was golf-links wasn't spelled out, but
Ernie didn't know of any other kind. It seemed a bit rum
to have golf mixed up with duelling and wolves, but that
was Scotland for you.

Folk began to drift away from the beach with the onset
of evening, and the sun wasn't that high above the sea as
Ernie got towards the end of the book. While Colonel
Ashton waited for Ravenswood to arrive for their duel it
was the other way on: *the sun had now risen, and shewed its
broad disk above the eastern sea, so that he could easily discern
the horseman who rode towards him with speed which argued
impatience equal to his own.*

*At once the figure became invisible, as if it had melted into the
air.*

Our Jack, very similar. Rose just said something to him,
Ernie hadn't picked up what, but it wasn't likely to be
anything to make a fuss about, Rose being Rose, and Jack
was out the door and gone before you could say Jack

Robinson. That's what his name should have been, Jack Robinson. Before you knew it, somewhere else.

Ernie looked up and saw distant people flickering to and fro on the beach. Now the sun had got lower they cast shadows, which made them harder to pick out. You could lose them as easy as pie, like young Donald had lost his two young ladies.

He rubbed his eyes as if he had witnessed an apparition, and then hastened to the spot, near which he was met by Caleb Balderston, who came from the opposite direction. No trace whatever of horse and rider could be discerned; it only appeared, that the late winds and high tides had greatly extended the usual bounds of the quicksand, and that the unfortunate horseman, as appeared from the hoof-tracks, had not attended to keep on the firm sands on the foot of the rock, but had taken the shortest and most dangerous course.

One only vestige of his fate appeared. A large sable feather had been detached from his hat, and the rippling waves of the rising tide wafted it to Caleb's feet.

Ernie shut the book and leaned back in his chair, maybe a bit too hastily, as suddenly his head began to swim. Talk about quicksand: he felt he was falling down and down. He remembered that nasty remark Jack had made about using his stiff finger as a tent peg. Yes, he must have been in a mood even then, looking for a chance to stir the pot. Ernie getting that shilling stuck was a heaven-sent opportunity, leaving Jack free to moan and groan and act up as if they were all liable to starve without the use of the cooker for a day or so. Frightened little Peter to death: he just stood in the corner for half an hour staring at the wall. Little tykes like him could sense the temperature rising in a household faster than any thermometer.

But the funny thing was that now Ernie took Jack's advice, and poked his sticking-out finger as far as it could go into the sand. Straight away it made him feel more settled and secure. Lets me get my bearings, he thought to himself.

'You all right, Dad?' Rose asked.

'Just had a little giddy spell,' he told her. 'OK now.'

'We ought to be getting back, get some food into you all.'

'What I'll do,' he told her, 'I'll just nip down to the water and wash my feet, so as I can put my sandals on.'

Why he said that, well, he knew why. He'd thought to himself, perhaps I'm not well enough to climb up that what-you-call-it, that chine, and then all the way to our chalet. So what I'll do, I'll just trot down to the water's edge for a bit of a try-out, see what I'm capable of. If I don't peg out, maybe I'll manage it all the way home.

But of course it was so much nonsense, just gave him that much further to walk in all. He could have brushed his feet and just slipped his sandals on, no bother.

Still, having said it, better do it.

He picked up his sandals, socks and a towel, also took Peter's hand, to give him a trip to the water. Poor little fellow, he'd been looking a bit perplexed, perhaps wondering what had become of his old man. Having said that, he often looked a mite perplexed in any case.

He put his jobbins just out of the water's reach and had a paddle, still holding hands with Peter. Peter didn't say anything, just poked out his belly above his little bathing trunks, like he had this morning to greet those girls. Maybe it was his way of greeting the sea.

When they arrived back up the beach, Rose had got their things together. She had even sent Donald to take back the deckchair.

'I've got a couple of tins of red salmon and some bread and butter,' she said. 'That'll tide us over for the time being.'

Maybe it did, and maybe it didn't. Ernie had trouble forcing it down, that was the truth of it. He wasn't keen on fish at the best of times, and his throat took it into its head to go narrow again, so it felt more like as if he was swallowing pebbles than salmon sandwiches. There was a lardy cake for afters, though, which went down no trouble, probably due to the larger fat content in it giving his throat a bit of lubrication.

Jack went to the early evening showing of a war film, *Cockleshell Heroes*, which was about frogmen planting limpet mines. They did the raid by canoe, to keep their approach silent and avoid radar. It was the ending that struck home to Jack, the survivors walking along this road thinking about everything that had happened and bubbles popping up by their heads with the faces of their dead comrades in, sad music playing.

It was gone half seven when he came out of the cinema, the street half in darkness from the evening shadows. Could go home now. No, he thought, I've been gone this long, I'll be gone a bit longer. There was a pub just a bit up from the pictures, a small one, the size of a shop. It was called the Queen's Arms. In he went.

As he'd hoped, it wasn't one of those tourist traps, just a homely place with a shiny mahogany bar and Britannia tables, a few blokes in shirtsleeves with pints, local-looking types.

He ordered himself a pint and drank half straight down. He hadn't realised how thirsty he was until he tasted it. The sun must suck the juices out of you, day after day.

He could feel it give him a lift as soon as he put the glass down. It was going to be one of those nights when it has an effect on you. Nothing like a spot of unhappiness at home for making you feel your drink.

He was on his second when who should walk in but somebody he knew. Who, was a good question. Jack thought to himself, I'm acquainted with you, I can remember us talking together, but where and when, don't ask. He bent over his glass to avoid catching his eye for a moment, but to no avail.

'What d'you know,' the bloke said. 'I last clapped eyes on you in that bog just west of Winchester.'

'Probably see you in the one here, in a moment or two,' Jack told him. 'I'll need to go, any road.'

'Shush, you'll have folks talking.' The bloke gave him a big wink. 'I'll get you another one in, while you bugger off to the dunny.'

He was called Ronnie, Ronnie Stokes, came from Birmingham where he had a factory. It made turntables for gramophones, also similar things for toolmaking, anything with a spin on, as he said. It was the gearing that was the important bit, some system he'd invented himself. He'd told Jack all about it in the toilet of that restaurant they'd stopped at on the way down, and he told him all about it again now. He had funny drooping ears with the lobes hanging low like a pair of pink earrings, and just a fringe of hair round his head, but he made up for it with a fat handlebar type of moustache.

'The men at the works call me Jimmy Edwards when my back is turned,' he told Jack, 'but it doesn't bother me. They've got to call me something. The main advantage of it, is it's very attractive to women.'

'Is it?'

'Well known. Bigger the moustache, the bigger the you know what. It's a way of announcing it to the general public.'

'Ah, so that's your trick.'

'*You* don't need one, of course.'

'Beg your pardon?'

'Moustache, you dope. You got something better altogether.'

'What's that?'

'A limp. Nothing makes women get themselves more hot and bothered than seeing a bloke with a limp.'

'Is that so?'

'Not that they cut any ice in here, moustache *or* limp. Not a woman to be had for love nor money. I left my missus at the hotel we're at. The Grand or something of the sort. Maybe the Splendid. She got herself roped in for

330

bridge, so I saw my chance. But this is a blokes' establishment. What we might do, get ourselves tanked up here, then go somewhere else, try and net a couple of popsies.'

Jack had a hot sensation in his chest at Ronnie's mention of his limp. Why did he have to bring that up? It was something and nothing in any case. Most people never even noticed it. Ronnie was one of those funny so-and-sos, went crashing through the undergrowth like a tank, yet picked up every little thing that was going on around him. Oh, sod it. Jack was tired of losing his rag at everybody. He bought them another pint each.

'It was a war wound,' he said.

'What was?'

'My limp.'

'That so?'

Jack shook his head regretfully, to show he didn't want to go on about it any more. He never did. He'd never talked about it to anybody. What to say? He'd just told Rose he got injured trying to rescue a pilot who'd come into land with his plane on fire, which was true enough. Standing on the wing, peering into the cockpit. The little blackened bloke sitting in his seat staring forwards with just his eye sockets. Jack trying to stop the puke rising in his throat. Him standing on the wing, the frizzled bloke sitting in his seat, what to do? It was just like staring at that gas meter with the bob stuck in it this afternoon, nothing about to happen.

Then the pilot had moved.

Just like a clock, tick tock, the way the minute hand is still as still, then jumps to the next place on the dial. One moment sitting upright, next a few degrees to one side.

Sometimes one little thing can knock you sideways, and that's just what it was: one little thing, getting knocked sideways. Before Jack knew it he was falling off the wing.

The wing was sloping sharply, it was precarious anyway. When the pilot moved Jack must have jumped back and lost his footing, next thing he was tumbling through the air, just like that bloke in Edinburgh Tommo told about, thinking Christ, what did I want to go and do that for? all it was was the pilot just settling a bit, like clinker does in the grate.

A dead man jumps in his seat, you jump in turn, and before you know it you're living a different life from the one you'd have led otherwise, like a train that's jumped the tracks.

'One of those things,' Jack said.

'Bad luck.'

'If that hadn't happened, something else would have. Maybe better, maybe worse, who's to tell? Could have got myself killed if I'd stayed out in North Africa. It would have panned out different, one way or another.'

'I suppose.'

'Nuff said.'

'Nuff said,' Ronnie said.

Funny thing was he limped like all buggery going up the road to the chalet site. He tried to remember something comical a farmer told him once, when he did some holiday work for him before the war, about cows standing on a hill, with short left legs to keep them level. Couldn't remember how it went but that was the meat of it. Going up a hill, put your shortened leg out first, no problem. But when it's the turn of the full-length one, up you bob like a cork in water. Never noticed it as a rule. It was all in the mind, like as not. Limping in the mind.

The road seemed to climb for ever. What the time was, God alone knew. He tried to look at his watch but all he got was a luminous green blur. Him and Ronnie never did get out to net any popsies, so Ronnie's moustache wasn't put to the test, nor Jack's limp for that matter. Too busy jawing and downing pints. Also it got quite convivial in the pub as the night wore on. Bit of a singsong developed.

'You bin gifted with a nice baritone,' Ronnie told him.

'Shame they haven't got a piano in here,' Jack said. 'I could have done with a bit of a go on it.'

'You play, do you?'

'Just like Winifred Atwell, 'cept I'm white.'

'White and a feller.'

' 'Cept I'm white and a feller. Apart from that we could be twins. My piano, you wouldn't believe. Old lady whose it was lugged the blessed thing clean over the Alps.'

'Get away. What she do that for?'

'She was Austrian. War coming on. She was a refugee. The piano was a refugee as well. Play it to this day.'

'It survived its ordeal unscathed.'

'Completely unscathed. Needed a bit of tuning, obviously.'

'What would worry me, taking a piano over the Alps, the danger it would run completely out of control on a downward incline.' Ronnie shook his head and lowered his eyebrows, glaring at his pint of beer. 'Once started, never to be stopped,' he said.

'She was only a shrimp of a woman. Knee-high to a grasshopper, like my mum used to say. Became a friend of the family. In fact her and her hubby left me my business.'

'She had a hubby, did she?'

'Oh yes, she had a hubby, all right. He was a banker back in Austria.'

'He probably helped her manhandle the piano then.'

'I suppose he did. I never thought about it. He had to become a baker in Stockport, that's all he could get.'

'From banker to baker,' Ronnie said, 'what he did, he lost his n.'

'I suppose he did. I think he must have lost a lot more than his n, coming over all the way from Austria. But he worked like buggery, put his money away. He bought himself a garage as an investment. He could see a good buy when he saw one. Then he dropped dead, just like that. Left me the business. They didn't have children of their own. Nobody else to leave it to.'

333

'You owe them your work and entertainment, when you think about it.'

'You what?'

'Go to work in their garage, go home, play their piano.'

'I suppose that's what it boils down to,' Jack said. 'I owe them a lot.'

'Telling me you do,' Ronnie had agreed. 'By the way, on the subject of owing, time for another pint.'

The walk back was never-ending. Why didn't I take the car? Jack wondered. Bloody hell, he thought, I did. Parked it down the front somewhere. Oh well, it would do until tomorrow. Probably have wrapped it round a passing tree if he *had* driven it back.

Finally he got to the gateway. There was a whacking great tree each side of it, each one a darker black than the rest of the night. Like the flipping guards at Buckingham Palace, Jack thought.

He walked past the kiosk effort where Mr Sumner the manager had his office, sort of shook his head at it as he went past. Blow it, he thought after, it's your fist you're supposed to shake, but he couldn't be bothered to turn back and have another go.

All the lights were out in all the chalets. I'm a dirty old stop-out, he thought to himself. All the chalets looked alike. They were alike, come to think. Like peas in a blimmin pod.

The one he thought was his didn't look quite right. Then he realised; it was because their car wasn't parked beside it. Of course it wasn't, it had gone off on a holiday of its own, down by Bournemouth front.

He put the key in the lock. It didn't turn. It was one of those keys you have to think round its corner, or it doesn't go. Done enough of this sort of caper today, he thought, remembering trying to get the gas meter twister twisted, with the bob still stuck in its groove.

Then it turned.

He felt for the light switch and switched it on. It made

334

him blink. All quiet on the western front, he thought. They'd all gone to bed, of course. He looked round the empty room. Just standing still seemed to cause a clatter. Dead to the world, I hope, he said to himself. He realised he was starving. Nothing like a few pints of beer to give you a good appetite.

An idea came into his mind: those chops. What I'm going to do is, eat those blessed chops.

When he was lying in bed that night Donald thought to himself: I bet that boy goes to grammar school. He didn't know why he thought that, but he did. There were probably boys with teeth that white in secondary modern, but Donald couldn't think of any, not the type that flashed in the sun.

Donald had watched him get out of the pedal boat, stepping into the waves. Prolly only fifteen.

Only. Fifteen was enough.

The boy put his hand out to help Françoise. Christine sort of fell out backwards, all by herself. That's when Donald saw the boy's teeth, laughing at her. Françoise laughed too, with her little teeth like pearls. Even her mouth looked French. It didn't look like anybody else's mouth when they laughed, as though you could laugh in the French language as well as speak it.

While she was laughing she saw Donald watching them, and looked up towards him, not looking at him straight, more sidelong. She waved her hand at him a little bit, the way girls do, as if they're wiping something with a cloth. Then she looked back at the boy again.

She was waving me goodbye, Donald thought to himself.

The boatman pulled the boat to the shore. Christine was wagging her legs from under the water. The boy and Françoise took one ankle each and pulled her out of the sea, and the three of them flopped on the sand together. Donald didn't go near. Françoise didn't look over towards him again. After a little while they got up and walked off.

335

The boy was big and fair-haired, like somebody who would be an officer in the army some day, or maybe a pilot in the air force. Even with just his bathers on he looked posher than boys at secondary modern.

Another idea about him being at grammar was he looked as if he spoke French. That was why him and Françoise could laugh together in that way they had, because he could speak a bit of French the same way as she could speak a bit of English, which made him more her equal. One thing Donald didn't like about trying to get friendly with girls, you felt you had to pass a test of some kind to qualify to have a girlfriend, a sort of girlfriend eleven-plus. Girls seemed to be up on high, more important than boys, and you had to show you'd earned one, as if they were made of solid gold or something.

Peter made a whimpering noise in his fold-up bed on the other side of the bedroom. He must be having a dream. Donald lay still, waiting for him to settle. Peter smacked his lips and then started breathing easily again. Donald remembered Norman. They'd had an argument the other day, just before they came on their holidays. That was about the eleven-plus too. Norman wanted Donald to go on a bike ride with him. Norman had got a racing bike, to Donald's surprise. You didn't think of Norman as somebody who wanted to whizz about. With his square face and his smile and his bow tie he looked like a person that would want to go along more slowly. Donald had told him that, and Norman smiled as usual. He said, 'What I want to do is get myself a sports car. A racing bike is stage one.' It was as if you could start off with a racing bike, then put manure on it or something, and the next thing you knew it would have turned into a fully-grown sports car. Donald imagined Norman's sports car as a bright yellow one like Noddy's in the stories he read to Peter sometimes, with Norman tooting as he drove along.

But when Norman said about going for a ride Donald didn't want to go. He had just walked home from school with Emb. Emb had hardly spoken a word. That made him, Donald, feel fed up, but he didn't want to talk about it with Norman, he didn't know why. It was almost as if what had happened to Emb, whatever it was, was something that had happened to him, Donald, as well, and he didn't want to describe it any more than Emb did, as if silence was catching. Another thing was, his own bike had a puncture.

Well, mend it, then, Norman said, you're supposed to be good at that kind of thing. Since when? Donald asked him. That was probably when the eleven-plus started to come into the argument, though nobody had said the words. Since ever, Norman said, born like it, I suppose. Nobody's born being able to mend a puncture, Donald told him. Not for a month or two, Norman said, you just wave your arms about at first. Big joke, Donald said. Anyway I don't want to go. You never want to do anything, Norman said. You go around with that bloody Emb idiot, you never want to do anything with me. You know what I think? I think you're jealous of me for passing the eleven-plus and going to grammar school. That's what I think.

What made Donald angry after was that when Norman said those words he couldn't speak. Lying in bed now, in the chalet, he still did not know what he could have said. It was the same as when he saw the bloke with the white teeth and Françoise. The only words that would come into his head were some his mother said sometimes, when she was fed up of doing housework and stuff: sometimes I think the world's passing me by.

Donald woke up in the middle of the night wanting a drink of water. There was light coming through the cracks round his bedroom door, and noises from the main room of the chalet. Also a funny smell, which he'd smelled lots of times before but couldn't remember the name of. It was a smell he liked and didn't like at the same time.

He got out of bed and tiptoed to the bedroom door. He

could hear Peter breathing softly. He put his hand on the door handle and slowly turned it. The light made him blink.

Dad was there. He had a plate of meat on the table, the chops they had been going to have for dinner.

'Hello, Dad,' Donald whispered. Dad looked up towards him, put a finger over his lips, and shook his head. His face looked very red. Donald stepped over to the sink, got himself a cup from the draining-board, and filled it with water. He was just raising it to his lips when dad said something, so he turned to hear better.

Dad was holding a bottle of something blue. He said, 'Left it to me, lock, stock and barrel. She was like a mother to me.' His face started to go scrunched-up like Peter's did when he was going to bawl. Sometimes you could see Peter have a quick look round, to see if it was a good moment for doing it.

Suddenly Donald realised what it was he could smell, the blue stuff in the bottle, meths. Dad had got out the little Primus they used for picnics and put it on the table. What a brilliant idea, why didn't we think of it before? Donald thought. But it was a funny time to have your dinner now. And dad looked strange, wild-eyed and wobbly. He waved the bottle about almost as if he was going to take a swig from it.

He'd been strange all this holiday, bad-tempered, going off on his own. This morning he'd swum far out to sea for hours and hours. Donald remembered seeing him in the toilet at that restaurant they stopped at on their way down, when he was talking to that other man, pretending he owned a garage. Perhaps he was going funny in the head. Certainly he looked to be being clumsy, the way he was waggling that bottle. He was twisting the top off of it, muttering to himself as he did so, and swaying from side to side.

'Dad,' Donald said. 'You didn't ought to be doing that this time of night. It's late. We're all in bed.'

Dad took the cap off the bottle and lowered it very carefully to the top of an invisible table that was about six inches higher than the real one. He was looking at what he was doing that hard his near eye seemed to bulge out of its socket so its white shone white just with the sheer force of looking. It looked like the swollen eye a Sherlock Holmes has when he looks through a magnifying glass in a cartoon.

The cap dropped to the real table-top, and rolled off on to the floor. Dad grunted with surprise and jerked his head back. He raised his hand holding the bottle up to his face to scratch his cheek and lolloped some of the meths down his front.

Donald realised: he's drunk. 'It's too late, Dad,' he said. He whispered it, so as not to wake the others, but as loudly as he could.

Dad leaned down towards him. He pointed a finger at him. The bad part was, it was a finger from the hand that was holding the bottle. 'Eat when you want to eat,' he said. Then he said: 'Tick blinking tock.' He made his finger go from one side to the other like a windscreen wiper, which jerked the bottle again, and sloshed meths on to the table.

Oh God, Donald thought to himself, and turned to run for help. He forgot he was holding a cup of water himself and felt it run down his legs as he ran. He was just going to open his mum's bedroom door when he thought to himself, what am I going to tell her? Dad's drunk? After all the trouble they'd had today it would be the last straw.

I can't tell on him, he thought. You mustn't ever tell.

Yes he could, he had to, for all their sakes. He rushed to the next door, grandad's. See if grandad can do the trick, he thought. He opened the door into the dark room. Just in front of him, grandad was snoring peacefully.

By the time Ernie went to bed what he'd got was heartburn. That's what he called it, any road. It felt like a prong boring into the middle of his chest. But of course when you lay there thinking about it, other nasty feelings joined in, and you didn't know whether you were imagining them or whether you were getting worse. His heart felt fluttery, as if it kept missing a beat, and then he began to get shooting sensations in his arms and legs. Blow this for a game of soldiers, he thought to himself as he lay there in the dark, go on at this rate and I'll be surprised if I last till morning.

He remembered that bit in the book about the feather from Ravenswood's hat being washed to the feet of his manservant, Caleb Doodah. Wasn't possible to die in that posh fashion nowadays. Not the same thing at all, passing on and leaving nothing for people to remember you by, save maybe a hanky with a knot in each corner, spinning on the tide.

Then there was Donald's timid voice in the room: 'Grandad?' Next thing, the light was on, and Ernie was sitting up, trying to see through the dazzle.

Donald was standing in the middle of the room. He looked very young in his pyjamas, with his hair all over the place. Suddenly Ernie realised the lad's legs were wet, and his heart missed yet another beat. Bit of a trick, stringing together what heartbeats I've got left, he thought. 'What's up, son?' he asked Donald.

'Dad's got drunk, Grandad. He's trying to cook himself those chops. But he's pouring meths all over the place.'

'Why'd you not tell me, lad?' Ernie cried, and shot off the bed and past Donald towards the door.

'I did!' Donald shrieked out behind him.

In the main room the table was already flaming softly, the plate of chops just visible in the middle of it. Jack was looking down at what was happening in amazement. Ernie suddenly felt completely calm. What came into his head were some words said by Meg Merrilees, in *Guy Mannering*, which he'd read years ago: '*We'll see if the red cock crows before morning.*' Mannering had asked what she meant. '*Fire-raising,*' *Dominie told him.*

Then, as Ernie stood watching, the flames leapt up Jack's shirt-front.

Peter got off of his bed. He walked through the dark to Donald's bed. He said Donald.

Donald wasn't here now. Everybody kept on being not here now.

Peter walked over to the door where there was a thin light shining. He put his hand up. He could feel a round ball. He turned the ball. The door opened.

In the room there was Donald and there was grandad. And there was daddy.

In front of daddy an octy puss was on the table. It was a bright yellow one. It was waving its paws at him.

Then it jumped up on daddy. It wanted to eat him all up.

It wasn't an octy puss at all, it was a big shiny spider.

When Rose rushed in the rest of the family were already there, even little Peter who was sucking his thumb and had eyes as big as saucers.

Dad was tearing off Jack's burning shirt. Donald had got the bottle of meths. He ran to the front door, and put it outside. Dad shoved Jack's shirt on the floor, and stamped on it. Rose herself filled the washing-up bowl with water and chucked it over the table. The room filled with smoke and the horrible smell of cooked plastic.

The skin on the top part of Jack's chest was red, and some blisters were forming, but it didn't look too serious.

'All right, troops,' Rose said. 'Nip back to your rooms and get your dressing-gowns and slippers, then we'd better step outside.'

When they got outside she had another shock: the car was gone. For a second she thought it must have been in the fire as well, got itself burnt to nothing, but then she realised she was being silly.

'Where's it got to?' she asked Jack.

'I left it in Bournemouth. I'd had a bit to drink. Thought I'd better not drive,' Jack said.

She gave him a long look. 'It's my holiday and all,' he said.

'Some holiday,' she told him. She shook her head. 'You are a one, aren't you,' she said more softly. She wished she hadn't given him what for, earlier on. She hadn't even felt particularly angry at him. Everything had just got on top of her for a moment. 'Talk about Jack the lad.'

She sent Donald off to tell the Greens what had happened. Soon as maybe, Mrs Green came back with him. Mr had gone off to phone for an ambulance. And the fire brigade.

'Didn't Donald tell you we put the fire out?' Rose asked her.

'Better to be safe than sorry.'

Mr Green came along shortly after, with Mr Sumner. Mr Sumner looked as if he was about to say something, then caught Jack's eye and thought better of it. He shook his tousled head glumly instead. You could tell he was wondering why on earth he'd rented them the chalet in the first place.

In a few minutes the fire engine had arrived. It looked huge, parked beside their chalet, pulsing in the dark, like a big red monster about to eat the whole building.

'I'm sorry,' Rose told the chief fireman. 'We put the fire out.'

'Tch tch,' he said, 'do me out of a job, you will, missus.'

'It was my boy who saved us all, didn't you, Donald?'

Donald didn't say anything, just stood there with that shame-faced look heroes usually seem to have.

'And my dad,' she added. She looked towards him in turn. He seemed strangely different in the light from the fire engine, much younger. Then she realised his moustache had gone black, with the soot or the scorching, and she burst out laughing.

Mrs Green gave her arm a squeeze. 'You'll be all right, love,' she said. 'Shock,' she told the fireman.

The ambulance arrived a couple of minutes later.

'You all right, mate?' the driver asked Jack.

'I'll do,' Jack said.

'Better get you looked at down the hospital, in any event.'

'The rest of you can come back to our chalet,' Mrs Green said. 'It's only two bedrooms but we can squeeze. The kids can all be together. Your father can have the sofa in the living-room. Our Dennis won't mind kipping on the floor for one night, will you, dear?'

She lowered her voice slightly. 'And you can come in with me, Mrs Willis.'

'Oh, call me Rose,' Rose said.

'Rose. I'm Barbara.'

'It's very nice of you, Barbara, but I think I better go down to the hospital with Jack.'

'Oh well,' Barbara said, 'don't you worry about the rest of your gang. I'll make sure they're all right.'

'That's very very kind of you,' Rose said. She suddenly wanted to cry.

'Don't mention it,' said Barbara. She gave her a quick kiss on the cheek. 'You look after that hubby of yours, and we'll see you in the morning.'